MARCHING ON

BY

JAMES BOYD

AUTHOR OF
"DRUMS"

C

NEW YORK
CHARLES SCRIBNER'S SONS
1927

Printed in the United States of America

First Printing,   May, 1927
Second Printing, May, 1927
Third Printing,   May, 1927
Fourth Printing, May, 1927
Fifth Printing,   June, 1927

TO THE MEMORY OF
THE ENLISTED MEN
OF THE
CONFEDERATE AND UNION ARMIES

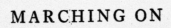

MARCHING ON

CHAPTER I

Sitting sidewise on the mule, young James Fraser swung his tired, heavy legs. Behind him through evening shadows and sombre trees he saw the bright green cotton patch, and in its corner, cocked up, the handles of the unhitched plough; ahead rose a wisp of smoke from the kitchen chimney. But only the cotton patch and the wisp of smoke relieved the vast and mournful scene; all else was dark pine forest and darker cypress swamp, draped in vines and Spanish moss, a shadowy underworld, lost to the sun, a world of sorrowful twilight, remote, unreal and lifeless except for one bird that flitted past, a furtive wanderer among the silences and grave, foreboding shades.

The sky above, seen through a pattern of branches, was deep blue, soft and brooding; westward its crimson sharpened the outlines of the trees, and this same radiance, faintly reflected in the east, appeared, a delicate aurora, above the Cape Fear country where the big plantations flanked the river. James Fraser had seen the region twice and now his thoughts followed the light in the sky and rested for a moment on the remembered rice-fields and great houses.

Like the radiant horizon, the Cape Fear plantations formed merely a narrow strip of splendor which followed the rich land by the river from Wilmington down to the sea. Outside it, lay nothing but hushed expanse of swamp and forest, untenanted except by some few hard-worked farmers like his father and some few men without a heritage who, sheltered in its depths, made shift by theft and begging to eke a living from the planters' bounty. Outcasts and scavengers, 'crackers,' they dwelt a race apart, despised by planters and by slaves and despising both.

But he himself, as riding along he watched the fading light above the Cape Fear, felt no such hostility. To him those great plantations seemed a fairyland, lovely, unsubstantial, unreal, and too far removed from his own life to be the objects of anything save vague admiration and shining, fragmentary dreams.

The chimney smoke was nearer now. The daubed stick chimney and the cypress shingles appeared. With flopping ears, the mule quickened his stride, the traces clinked. A row of bright quilts on the picket fence, a slender, overarching well-sweep, a cedar bush against the cabin's siding, and James Fraser was home. Sliding down into the sand, he pulled the collar over the mule's gravely presented head and turned him into the shed beside the woolly cow.

Back on the cabin porch he washed his hands most carefully, then held them in the last rays of the sun to dry and looked at them. They were still too big for him, he knew, and, with their cracks and callouses on the square palms and long square-ended fingers, they were too old also; at least, they seemed older than his loose-jointed body and smooth blunt face with its trace of color that marked him from the clay-faced natives. That trace of color was his mother's pride. She looked on it as the surviving evidence of the family's former high estate and fretted herself lest it should vanish among the region's agues, bilious fevers, and pickles, hog, and hominy.

His hands were dry. And still he looked at them. They were a good pair of hands for work. But, my lord, they were big for a fellow only nineteen. Too big. His mother said they were enough to scare a body; it was a pity, she said, that they couldn't have stayed slim and pretty. He himself didn't care about the looks; but he knew that he couldn't fiddle now as good as when he was a youngster and his hands were small and nimble. Other folks did not notice. They counted him as good a fiddler as any around there. He noticed though; so did his mother. But his father said that for a farmer there was no such thing as too big hands.

He combed his thick brown hair and wiped his feet on the rice sack lying in front of the kitchen door. His mother, a tall, broken-bodied woman, raised up from the stove and looked at him with eyes as black and keen as a squirrel's.

"You look nice," she said.

"Well," he muttered bashfully, "I aim to."

A smile touched her crooked, humorous mouth, then faded as she turned back to the stove. "I wish your pa would brush his hair. He don't, only on Sunday. By Sadday night he looks like one of these crackers back in the woods."

James Fraser sat down uncomfortably and brushed a dusty knee.

"Pa works hard," he ventured.

"I know," she admitted quickly, "and he always has.

I'll allow him that." She looked out over the scrubby fields and frowned. "But where's it getting us?"

To a question so broad, so searching, he could conceive no reply. Not that his mother expected one. She meant merely to show that his father did not prosper according to his deserts. But why that should be was a problem beyond him. He sat silent. His mother, however, was a great one for sticking to an idea. She went on.

"It looks to me like a man that works like him ought to be successful more. It ain't his fault, I know, but look at those rice-planters on the river. They just lay round in their houses all day and the money comes a-rolling in."

He roused himself. This was more familiar ground, besides there seemed to be some implication against his father.

"They've got the best land," he said stoutly, "and anyhow it takes niggers to make rice."

"Well, we had good land on the old place back of Halifax," she answered, "but it was just the same. The big planters with their niggers made all the money."

"Pa never was much of a hand to work niggers, I expect," he admitted, "and anyhow niggers is so high now that a man can't hardly afford to get him some."

"That's it," she burst out vehemently, "if a man's got no niggers, he cain't get them, and if he has them he keeps a-getting more and more and keeps a-branching out."

James Fraser curled his hands together and studied the problem.

"They say if a man is reliable he can get niggers on a note," he ventured.

"And so he can, but if the niggers die or the crop fails, you lose niggers and the land beside. And then," she concluded, "you're no better than a nigger yourself—or one of these crackers in the woods."

"But, Ma——"

"Hush your talk," she said, "here comes your pa."

Outside, his father's small, stooped figure trudged along under a heavy maul. With a tilt of his shoulder, he swung it to the ground and straightened up. His face, not much distinguished save for the gray mustaches and goatee, was now, as James Fraser could see, lighted by slow-mounting anger. He strode straight into the kitchen and sat down heavily.

"You're late," said Mrs. Fraser not unkindly.

His father wiped his face on his colorless sleeve.

"I've been getting out fence-rails."

"I thought I heard you quit an hour back."

"I did, but coming home I heard somebody in our swamp. It was one of those rice niggers from the Prevost plantation setting traps." His tired face flushed anew. "I told him if I catched him there again, I'd give him this maul where it would cure him."

"You ought to have carried him back to Colonel Prevost to be whipped," Mrs. Fraser said.

"What good would that do?" he answered. "It would take me half a day and then the Colonel wouldn't whip him."

As though baffled by the complexities of the conversation, Mr. Fraser shook his head wearily. Then his faded blue eyes seemed to struggle back to something more immediate and concrete and to harden as they did so. "I wish to God"—his face was that of a puzzled, angry dog—"I wish to God I'd busted that yellow rice-hand with my maul."

CHAPTER II

THE road which led from the Fraser's place to the Prevost plantation was the merest pair of cart-tracks, between which the sparse gray wire-grass had been slightly trampled down. Beneath the canopy of pine and cypress the world was hushed, hot, breathless, and the rare openings in locked branches showed only a brazen sun and a misty-blue oppressive sky. James Fraser saw the mule's ears droop; he felt the huck shirt sticking to his back and seemed to feel the wooden stirrups sticking to his brogans. Glancing down the mule's shoulder he noticed that the beast's brown lather had flecked the wool coat belonging to his father which hung from the saddle-bow. He untied the thong and carried the coat then on his arm. It had been loaned him for the occasion and if he brought it back sweat-marked, there might be a considerable fuss. He almost wished that he had left it home. It was a good wool coat, but though too large for his father, it was too small for him. However, he had no coat of his own, and this old coat, as he remarked to himself, had got no coat naturally beat to death. Inside the pocket was a black square-tie which his mother had told him he must surely put on before he got in sight of the Prevost lodge-gate. Otherwise, he gathered, the Colonel's niggers might take him for a cracker. At any rate, her last words had been for him not to let any niggers fling their sass at him. A lit-

9

tle uneasy, he gazed down at the ground. He'd never been around niggers much and he didn't know how a man could stop them from flinging their sass. They'd say things to each other when a plain man came along that you couldn't hardly find a handle to, and then laugh amongst themselves.

But when it came to the white folks, it was different. He wasn't scared of any white folks, no matter how high-toned they were. Not the men, anyhow. Why should he be? Hadn't his Uncle John, that time he came to visit, told him about the Frasers in the Revolution? Just because a man's family had had a spell of bad luck was no reason for him to hang his head.

Still, as the mule's short steps drew nearer the plantation, he felt his slight assurance ooze. For the letter which he carried from his father to Colonel Prevost was not calculated to make the Colonel feel extra friendly toward him. Its contents had been so thoroughly discussed the night before when it was being written that now he could repeat them almost by heart—could almost, in fact, see on the blue-lined paper his father's remarkably neat handwriting as it begged to advise Colonel Prevost that one of his negroes had several times been trapping on Mr. Fraser's place, and mentioned that once Mr. Fraser had lost a turkey. It then took occasion to address the Colonel in the hopes that the Colonel would see to it that the trouble was put a stop to and begged to remain the Colonel's obedient servant. There was nothing out of the way in the letter, —nothing that one honest man could not say to another,—but still to send it to such a dignitary as the

Colonel was reputed to be seemed somehow over-daring, somehow risky, almost an invitation to disaster. He wished that his father had himself gone to see the Colonel, and the thought passed through his mind that maybe his father would not have been so bold about that. He was mighty glad that a sentence proposed by his mother had been rejected, a sentence which announced that thereafter Mr. Fraser was prepared to shoot every Prevost negro that showed his head.

He had been on the Prevost domain an hour or so and now was crossing the last branch before the lodge-gate would appear. Dismounting on the farther side, he washed his face, put on his tie and coat and tried to smooth the wrinkles out of his tight mustard-colored trousers. He wished that he could see himself in the slow-flowing amber water. He must really look pretty good. But leaning over the edge, the most that he could make out was the clean white shirt and black square-tie; and, of course, his plain blunt face. He made a twist of broom grass, brushed the sweat off the mule, and mounted again.

Now through the trees he could see the broad flat fields stretching away and, just at hand, beneath the biggest live-oak in the world, the Colonel's gate-house, a cabin perched on four round cypress blocks. The rusty iron gates were folded back against the serpentine brick wall which wound away through trees to right and left toward cypress swamps. In the shadow of the oak a black, old lodge-keeper continued dozing as James Fraser rode by.

"That negro," James reflected, "must have about the

easiest job in all creation." For tradition held it to be
the Colonel's boast that his lodge-gates had never been
closed in forty years except on the day the Old Colonel
had died. James reckoned that the negro had nothing
to do in all his life except stand up and pull off his hat
when the quality came by. As for himself, if the negro
had so much as noticed him, he must have closed his
eyes right quickly again.

High corn covered the fields on either side. He heard
the measured thud of hoes and saw above the stalks the
bobbing heads of negroes. Around a turn in the road
an overseer in white linen sat a black and shining horse
and watched the work-gang. He gave James Fraser a
hard look, jerked out a "howdy," and shifted his gaze
back to the negroes again.

Through the heat-waves, shimmering above the sand,
James could make out farm-buildings, a high unpainted
barn, the peaked roof of a pounding mill. The big house
must be near and he was glad, for, crossing the merciless
little plain, he had begun to break out in a sweat again,
and now could not make up his mind whether to use his
clean handkerchief or save it. But not especially glad
either. Try as he would, he could not subdue his qualms
at facing such folks as the Colonel. He brought back to
his mind the half-remembered visit of his Uncle John,
when he himself was a small boy. He recalled the touch
of ancient, faded dignity which, in spite of evident shab-
biness and futility, hung about his uncle's figure; he recalled his uncle's tales of the Frasers' patriotic services
and former glory. Uncle John had talked big, no doubt;
to hear him you would think the Frasers had owned the

whole of North Carolina, but did not the reported ruins of slave quarters on the old Fraser place near Anson's, where Uncle John lived, show that there was something to what he said? Enough anyhow to prove that he himself was a somebody. Let him remember that. A flock of sheep, gasping beside the fence, sprang up at his approach, ran off, and turned all together to stare at him with stupid, hostile eyes.

A bridge across a black ditch—a feeling of removal, of impending stateliness and shade, and he was in a grove of live-oaks and could catch the first faint intimation of the river breeze. Shyly it fingered its way through the veils of Spanish moss and through the ponderous shadows of the great, oppressive trees. No other sign of life penetrated this primeval world unless it might be the faint, sad echo of the field-hands' chant which came and went, the merest longing sigh.

A lightening of the shadows showed that the house was near. James Fraser mopped his face carefully with the corner of his handkerchief and, passing by a brick smokehouse and a log kitchen, drew up without elation at the tall, unpainted gable end of the Colonel's home. He tied the mule to a ring set in a wooden horse-block, then hesitated. The mule looked mighty small and shabby beside that house. It was a question whether to use the back door, opening on a covered way between the house and kitchen, or to go boldly round to the double gallery at the front. A black face was peering suspiciously at him from the depths of the kitchen and waiting, he felt, on his decision. That determined him. He walked around to the front and along the gallery.

He sounded the knocker on a wide-panelled door. The brass reverberation echoed, stern and majestic, inside the lofty hall. With assumed indifference he turned to gaze between two great myrtle bushes out over the small box garden on the terrace, over the rice-fields far below, toward the broad, distant river and the wooded slopes on the other shore. The flat green of the flooded rice-fields where squat black figures lumbered heavily and the flat blue of the river wavered in the heat. But here, where the breeze moved through the gallery, it was cool enough; he wished that there was such a spot for his father and him after a summer day's work. They needed it a heap more than a planter who had nothing to do but make himself easy.

At the creaking of the door-hinges he turned and faced a barefooted yellow negro boy who smiled ingratiatingly, then made a faint grimace at James Fraser's severe stare.

"I want to see the Colonel."

The negro shut the door in James' face. Inside the house he could be heard hallooing, "Orlando, Orlando! Hoo-oo-oo! Whey you?"

A young girl's voice, quiet but clear and softly ringing, said, "Hush!"

James Fraser heard the negro's long mumbled explanation, "Yas, miss. White boy knock at de do' . . . See de Colonel . . . Yas, miss." But through it all the sound of the unseen girl's voice seemed to vibrate, to prolong itself, and in the silences to swell until it filled ever so delicately the uttermost dark recesses of the tall house.

The feet of the negro pattered toward the door again. It opened and James Fraser, peering beyond the boy into the hallway's shadowy depths, only half heard him say, "Miss Stewart say set down on de po'ch. De Colonel he come back directly." Still James Fraser stood there though now aware that the hall, save for an eagle-crested mirror and a dark, stern portrait, was empty. The negro fiddled with the door-knob. James came to himself, turned, and sat down on a willow chair.

Below him the rice-hands splashed slowly through the watery fields. A lumber schooner with bright yellow deck-load dropped down the river. Near at hand in a gleaming yaupon tree a hawk sat watching for prey with silent, hooded intensity. But though he dimly saw these things, his ear was listening for another echo of the voice within the house, the voice so different from the harsh blunt speech of cracker women, or even from his mother's rugged tongue; so different, indeed, from anything which he had ever heard that it had seemed just now to shower down on him light silver echoes from another world.

Footsteps on the sandy path aroused him. A small, neat, elderly gentleman in straw hat, blue short-skirted coat, and white cassimere trousers, strapped beneath his pumps, stepped gracefully between the two crêpe myrtles and came up on the porch. James Fraser rose.

"Good evening . . ." the gentleman said, and then hesitated as though seeking the appropriate form of address, while his bright blue eyes gave James Fraser a glance of inquiry touched with quiet appraisement as

well; "my boy," he finally added and took off his hat,
perhaps as a salutation, although he immediately fell to
fanning himself with it, while with his other hand he
undid the silver coat-buttons and loosed his stock.

James Fraser took off his black wool hat and clutched
it. "Good evening," he murmured. "Are you Colonel
Prevost?"

A slight shadow of distress passed over the Colonel's
pale, fine features.

"I am," he answered, "though the name is pro-
nounced 'Prevo.'"

"Yes, seh." James paused awkwardly. Was he expected to say the Colonel's name again the right way
or to call him "Colonel"—or what?

The Colonel smiled in faint but not unkind amusement.

"You wish to see me, I suppose. Sit down."

But James Fraser, standing desperately abashed before the Colonel, still had wit enough to know that to
take a seat might somehow put him in the power of this
man. He continued to stand stiff and awkward while
the Colonel, his graceful gesture toward the willow chair
half finished, showed some impatience.

"I can't tarry," James at last managed to say. "I
brought a letter." He fumbled in his pocket and thrust
the envelope at the Colonel. The Colonel received it
with the least inclination of his small gray head, placed
his straw hat under his elbow, and read the contents
slowly. A trace of color mounted to his pale cheeks.

"The infernal scoundrel!" he cried, and slapped the
letter against his palm. James Fraser clenched his

hands to his sides and caught his breath; there was no man living, of however high estate, who could call his father that. The Colonel was speaking again.

"The infernal scoundrel! I'll have him whipped, sir,—thirty lashes! and will you convey my apologies to your father—or would you prefer a letter to that effect?"

The anger, flowing out of James Fraser, left him so foolish that once more he could only stand there like a lump. This time, however, the Colonel ignored him; he seized a dogwood walking-stick that he had laid aside and pounded sharply on the porch floor. The negro boy appeared.

"Send a boy to tell the overseer I wish to speak to him this evening," the Colonel said, "and tell Orlando to bring two juleps out here on the porch."

He turned to James. "And now, my young friend, you surely must sit down and refresh yourself."

Well, thought James, everything seemed to be all right now; there might be no harm in that. He bowed as well as he was able and sat down in the willow chair. But he did not lean back.

The Colonel, on the other hand, leaned back comfortably, crossed his knees and proceeded to talk with facility and ease. He made polite inquiries for James' father and mother, discussed the crops, the weather, the state of the roads, merely pausing for James' belated and monosyllabic responses.

"Have you ever seen rice-fields before? No?"

The Colonel told how the fields lay below the river's high-water mark so that they could be flooded, how the gates and trunks and ditches worked.

"Yes, they are far below us." He pointed between the myrtle-trees. "That flight of wooden stairs leads down to them. There are sixty steps, each eight inches high. Now how many feet is that?"

"Fo'ty," James muttered shyly and subsided.

"Correct. This wooded knoll is forty feet above the level. Toward the north it slopes down to the river. You can see the cedars and the iron fence of the family burying-ground." The Colonel smiled. "That is one spot on the place that my negroes never bother. In fact, at a burying we have trouble to get them to row the boats."

James did not speak, but the Colonel was satisfied by his look of wonder.

"We always bury here by boat, and at night. The party goes down the steps and then is rowed up the main trunk to the burying-ground. What with the silence and the whippoorwills and the torchlight among the cedar-trees and on the big deep tombs, the negroes are mighty uneasy." The Colonel smiled again. "And yet in their hearts they like it." He went on to tell of their superstitions about the burying-ground.

But James Fraser hardly followed him. He was not interested in negroes. His thoughts hung back and dwelt on the burial itself. "My lord," he said to himself, "these folks don't even bury themselves like anybody else. And they are mighty proud of it, too."

The Colonel had passed on to other matters. He must mind his manners, pay attention to the thread of talk. He put his mind on it and, staring at the myrtle-trees, he tried to keep pace with the easy rapid flow, tried to be ready in advance when it should be his turn to speak. It was hard. The Colonel's fluent rambling, in such puzzling contrast to the long silences and sparse, well-pondered phrases of the country people, left him struggling far behind.

"You are looking at our myrtles," the Colonel said. "I suppose they are the largest and oldest you have ever seen. They were set out by Mark Prevost in seventeen twenty. 'King' Prevost, they called him; he had the original grant from the Lords Proprietors. Seventeen twenty." The Colonel paused impressively.

"Yes, seh," said James.

The sound of the front door slowly opening came to him as a relief. His thoughts flashed back to the soft, ringing voice. He looked up hopefully. A fat, severe negro in a frayed livery coat closed the door carefully behind him, while with easy skill he balanced in his left hand a little silver tray on which two tall glasses, sea-green, thick-frosted, mint-crowned, flourished delicately. With one brief, comprehensive glance at James, the negro presented the tray to Colonel Prevost.

"Every year," the Colonel went on, "in accordance with the terms of the original grant we make seven cuttings from those trees and send them over to England to the heirs of the Lords Proprietors."

"Yes, seh," said James.

Holding the thin, cool glass between his palms, he contemplated with admiration the marvel of ice in summer. The Colonel was raising his glass. James Fraser thrust his nose gingerly into the cool, graceful foliage and drank. The taste was cold, then sweet, then subtly thrilling. He drank again, and then once more until the thrill, still lingering on his tongue, spread through his veins and seemed to cluster around his heart and raise him to a state of strange content and dignity. A little more and he would be responding in kind to the Colonel's graceful flow. But limited as his life had been to topics such as crab grass and hog cholera, it was difficult to find a worthy subject. While he hesitated his mind glided back to the voice within the house. He leaned back, lay quiet, breathing lightly, and listened for it. Perhaps he heard it once or perhaps it once again was ringing in his brain.

The Colonel having finished his glass arose. "I expect my overseer will be coming in soon." He nodded gravely. "Present my apologies to your father."

James Fraser stood up and nodded gravely, too. "Yes, seh," he said. "I thank you."

Walking with him to the edge of the porch, the Colonel stopped and watched him mount the little mule. James Fraser gathered up the reins and raised as gracefully as he could his shapeless hat. As he turned away he stole a glance at the up-stairs windows. They were empty.

Before he reached home deep dark had fallen. As he rode on through the shadows and the sound of myriad frogs, the brilliant moments at the Colonel's seemed still to shed their radiance around him. He felt, it is true, relief at his escape from a manner of living so rarefied and grand and for his return safely and with credit to the life he knew. But though there might be no reason to attempt such lofty flights again, his visit had been an achievement to be proud of.

At the house supper had been kept for him. His father had gone to bed, his mother, her face between her hands, her sharp elbows thrust forward on the table, watched him eat in silence.

"Well, how did you make out?" she asked as he pushed back his plate.

"Oh, pretty good," he answered. "Pretty good. I gave the Colonel the letter."

"What did he say?"

"He said, 'The infernal scoundrel,' and I thought he meant Pa, but he meant the nigger. He said he'd have him to be whipped."

She brushed a wisp of hair away impatiently. "You didn't see him do it, though."

"No, but he was mighty obliging. He apologized to Pa and said he'd write a letter." James paused. "I told him not to trouble himself, though," he added with conscious satisfaction.

"You should have got the letter, son," his mother broke in. "Then we'd have had something to show for our pains. What else happened?"

"Well," he went on slowly, his spirits a little dashed, "then he asked me to set down on the porch and he had a nigger to bring a couple of juleps and we set there on the porch and talked. He was mighty polite and clever." His mother pressed her lips together. "And then I said farewell." His voice trailed off. Her disapproval, however, had passed on from him.

"That's a planter sure enough!" she cried. "He

thinks a few fair words and a julep is favor enough
for any poor man.   But he wrote no letter nor he
didn't ask you into his house."   She gave him a grim,
crooked smile.   "And I reckon he never took you by
the hand."   James Fraser did not answer.   "Did he
now?"

"No.   I don't recollect he did but it just didn't come
about that way.   I don't reckon he meant anything by
it."

"He don't mean anything," she caught him up
quickly, "except to keep his place and to see that we
keep ours."   She rose and snatched his plate from the
table.

"I don't know," he murmured wearily.   "He seemed
to be all right."

He heard the plate clatter from her hand; her arms
were around his head and pressing it fiercely to her flat
breasts.

"God knows," she cried out, "if you ain't the equal
of any boy alive!"

Lying that night on the pallet in his lean-to room, he
could not sleep.   He ought rightly to be tired.   It had
been a big day.   And coming home he had been tired,
sure enough.   But now, though not uneasy, he was
restless, full of vague stirrings.   He wanted—he did not
know what.   It must be something, because he felt a
sense of self-sufficiency, of power which waited to perform a deed.   He tried, but could not fasten on an
object.

Anyhow, he felt that he would like to play a tune or

two. He had not played so much of late. His hands
had grown so big and clumsy; his fingers overlapped the
strings and got in each other's way. It had put him
more or less out of the notion of playing. But now he
had the idea that he might be able to make pretty good
music. His body felt light and free and his hands felt
light and free, too.

He reached under his cot. At his touch a string gave
forth a soft, melodious hum. He sat up with the fiddle,
still reverberating, in his hand.

Quietly he opened the door and stepped out into the
starlight and the noise of frogs. Down by the woods a
sycamore root made a seat, used before. He squatted
and fell to tuning up, slowly, carefully. He planted the
butt of the fiddle beneath the angle in his chin, the
angle that always seemed so sharp compared to the
rest of his face. He took a good grip on the head and
sat holding his bow upright on his knee, figuring what
to play. Something to drown out the frogs. He
bounced the bow down on the strings and started
"Banjo Sam." He sawed away with quick, short
strokes; his brogans patted the sand. His fingers flew,
the fiddle sang, gained speed and power till it seemed
of its own motion to carry him along.

The frogs were forgotten, a thrill spread through him
as it had that afternoon when he drank the julep. The
tune ran on, smoother, faster, endlessly repeated. He
saw himself on the Colonel's porch,—he was not
abashed now, he was at his ease,—he would not mind
going back there,—he was a man of parts. By shot, he
would go back there, he would show them . . . and

then that ringing whisper. . . . He would go back
somehow . . . a man of parts. . . .

> "I was walkin' down the road,
> Met Miss Terrapin and Miss Toad,
> Terrapin she began to sing,
> Toad she cut a pigeon wing."

He stopped his playing with a sharp, high note. Its
echo hung about him, faded, transformed itself into a
whispered "Hush!" He tucked the fiddle under his
arm and strode back to the house as brisk as a mink.

CHAPTER III

BROAD, bare feet slapping on the kitchen porch made them look up from their breakfast. At the doorway, a grotesque silhouette against the morning light, stood Sam, the Scroggs' mindless boy. His thin hands hung, palms outward, below his turned-in elbows. His small head beneath the deplorable peaked hat was thrust forward in an attitude half curious, half deprecating.

"Howdy, neighbors," he piped, "Sal's dead."

"What!" cried Mrs. Fraser, "your sister Sal? Why, I saw her only just last week."

"Maybe so," Sam clicked his tongue. "But she's dead now." He stole into the room and stood before them writhing slowly.

"Sit down, Sam," said James' father, "and tell us what you are talking of." Sam slid into a chair, sat slouching, his long arms nearly to the floor. His pale blue eyes, seeking each of theirs in turn, betrayed a trace of puzzled wonder in disturbing contrast to his ever-smiling, rudimentary face.

"She died last night," he said. "I heard Ma fetch a holler and I knew what the trouble was but when I hollered, too, Pa frailed me. He said it was no time for monkey-shines, Pa said." He looked inquiringly into their faces as though solicitous for their approval. "Yas, neighbors. Sal died last night."

Mr. Fraser cast a farmer's eye out at the already brilliant, burning sun.

"It's hot. I expect the buryin' will be right soon." His face took on a certain helpless dignity. "I pity your ma—mightily."

Sam gave brisk nods. "Funeral to-night at six o'clock. They sent me to tell you all."

"We'll surely come," said Mrs. Fraser gravely. "I wonder," she added, "if your folks need me to he'p lay her out."

"She's done laid out," said Sam. "Poor Sal." He clicked his tongue again. His eyes, uncertain, mournful, were bent down at the kitchen table. Slowly they focused on a plate of rice cakes.

"Have a rice cake, Sam," said Mrs. Fraser. "You must be hungry."

Sam seized a rice cake. "Tired, too," he mumbled between the mouthfuls, "with all these goin's on." He thrust another rice cake in his mouth and stood up shifting from one foot to the other and gulping slowly. "Well, I must be travelling." His high voice took on a tone of some importance. "I've got to spread the news." Again his feet slapped on the floor-boards of the porch. "Yas, seh," he muttered to himself as he struck off with long uncertain strides across the sand, "I've got to spread the news."

James' father stood up and lit a corncob pipe. "Well, Ann," he said, "I reckon you'd best be fixed to leave by five." He turned to James. "You go to chopping weeds in that potato-patch," he said. "I notice it's been fretting your ma."

"Yes," said James, "but what are you going to do?"
"Oh," his father answered wearily, "I'm going back
to them rails."

It was well after six o'clock that evening when the
Frasers' covered cart, creaking softly through an opening in the ranks of dark, encrusted trunks, approached a
clearing, a field of stumps and scanty corn, and at its
edge, the sober group of mules and people and the one-
room shanty which stood for Sal Scroggs' funeral.

On the lean-to porch each pale, dark-clad man
came up in slow rotation and greeted James' father in
the manner of the countryside with a sidewise glance
and a swift, limp shake of the hand. Inside the cabin
where the women were, his mother was already lost in a
buzz of murmured "howdy's" and the recounted details
of Sal's death. Their harsh voices, somewhat raised,
were pregnant with relish and subdued excitement.

"A reg'lar dry ague," . . . "horehound tea and asa-
fetidy". . . . "Yes, ma'am, and a cabbage poultice
to boot." For a moment the men listened to the steady
flow. "She sure was took off sudden," they said
among themselves. "Looks like a good rain wouldn't
hurt the cotton none."

Their talk was pierced by the faint, sharp clink of
carriage harness. James turned his head to see a two-
horse family coach climb from the branch and trot
across the sandy field. The negro driver was about to
drive among the people right up to the door when
Colonel Prevost leaned out the carriage window and
called out: "That will do, Thad!" The Colonel stepped

out, walked to the group by the porch who had turned
to look at him. He bowed gravely; they made way
with a sort of surly deference and produced a keg for
him to sit on.

The Colonel thanked them but did not yet sit down.
He moved from group to group, kindly, impartial, over-
looking none, ready with a courteous, well-judged word
for each. They answered with respect but guardedly.

Mrs. Fraser, by now aware of the Colonel's presence,
had come out on the porch and planted herself beside
her husband. To her the Colonel bowed quite low;
he smiled into her black, unyielding eyes. Turning to
James, he held out his hand.

"It was a pleasure to make this young man's acquaintance."

While James was struggling for an adequate reply his
father cut in.

"I was mighty sorry, Colonel, to be obliged to send
that letter."

"Why so, seh? You placed me under an obligation.
I am happy to be informed when my negroes do anything amiss. Too often my neighbors will not let me
know and—" He checked himself but James knew well
enough that too often his neighbors took far different
means of righting their grievances.

"I'd have come myself," Mr. Fraser said, "but I'm
hard pushed getting out some rails."

"It would have been a pleasure to see you at Beaumont—but you sent a worthy substitute." The Colonel
ventured another glance at Mrs. Fraser. "Now about
rails—if you have any to spare——"

"Well, maybe I might by the time the crops are laid by. But I don't see how I can carry them to you."

Ben Scroggs, his eyes close set above his long, sharp nose, fumbled at his string tie.

"Well, neighbors," indecisive, he felt the stubble on his chin, "I reckon all the folks is about come."

Mrs. Fraser went back in the cabin; the Colonel dusted the top of the keg with his handerchief and sat down. Clustering on the porch, the men stared through the doorway into the windowless room whose flickering fire cast fantastic lights and shadows on the rough-hewn faces of the neighbor women, on the narrow, arched back of Sal Scroggs' mother and on the cheek-bones and the rodent mouth of Sal. Close packed along the benches the women sat rigid except for their hands' slow constant movement against the flies and gnats, and stolid save for the solemn gusto in their eyes.

"Friends," Ben Scroggs' voice was toneless, "we aimed to have a preacher but in this yer hot spell we didn't dast to wait. So I'll just ask Mister Roon to say a few words." He wiped the sweat from his face with his coat-sleeve.

Standing near James on the porch, a drooping, slope-shouldered old man gazed at the ground and stroked a beard a little too sparse and dingy quite to fulfil its patriarchal intent. He buttoned his black calico waist-coat in preparation, surveyed the company with eyes as mild and flat and shifty as a hare's.

"Brother Scroggs," he murmured, moving forward, "I reckon we'd best box the body befo' I start."

The women nearest the body stood up and grasping

three dishcloths that stretched beneath Sal's limp gray
dress raised her up deftly and lowered her into a shallow
pine coffin that stood beside her on the table. They sat
down and fell to fanning themselves again.

"And now, friends," Mr. Scroggs continued, "I
reckon we'll be pleased to hyer what Mr. Roon has got
to say."

"They's nothing I want to hear Old Man Roon say,"
a voice behind James whispered, "unless'n it's when he's
agoin' to pay the interest on his notes——"

"Hush your fuss, Will," a whisper answered. "He
kin talk good, the old man kin."

Meanwhile Mr. Roon was preening himself for public
discourse. He passed a hooked forefinger around the
neckband of his shirt, and in one practised motion
transferred his quid to a corner of his handkerchief.
Stretching out a dramatic talon toward the coffin, he
uttered a long, smothered groan. "Friends and neighbors! Thar she lays! A genuwine child of God!"

"Amen," the women said and rocked slightly. A
hound among their feet began a steady scratching and
two dirty babies, unrebuked, set up a howl. But Mr.
Roon was launched; smoothly, softly, easily he swung
into a recitation of poor Sal's hypothetical virtues. In
each brief lull, the women, tirelessly fanning, echoed
him. The men leaned motionless against the wall or
wandered off to chat and smoke and chew. James
Fraser braved his father's disapproving glance and took
a seat under a scrub-oak. It was within easy hearing, he
argued to himself, of Mr. Roon.

Far from embarrassed at the presence of the Colonel,

chief, as all knew, of those who had suffered imposture and pecuniary loss at his adroit hands, Mr. Roon now seized as it were upon the Colonel and incorporated him into his discourse. His voice took on soft persuasive eloquence, took on earnestness, intense and burning yet never failing in lofty, gentle forbearance. It was as though, convinced of his august mission, yet free from censoriousness or condescension, he would point the Colonel and all his other creditors to higher things.

"Friends, what do we see and behold on this mo'nful day? We see not only the lowly, but the high and mighty gathered toegether. And the high and mighty has no mo' power than the lowliest toe bring back this pore child. And so it will be on the day of jedgement."

The day of judgment was then described with no small, crude power. Self-hypnotized by his own sweep of rhythmic balanced phrases, Mr. Roon worked himself to a state of vague but irresistible potency. The women redoubled their cries, the men around the house stopped talking.

"And let us not fo'get that eveh person hyer, old and young, will some day reach the awful hour when they will be haled in jedgement befo' the great white throne." The voice ceased suddenly, low wailing rose, fell, quavered, died away.

Slowly a few men edged into the cabin, muttered, shuffled, came out bearing on their shoulders the pine box. The women followed and Sal's mother bowed forward on Mrs. Fraser's arm. The men fell in behind, except Ben Scroggs who, fumbling at his narrow mouth, led the way to the grave on the edge of the clearing.

He watched them lower the coffin and take up the shovels. As the first earth fell his weak, mean face wrinkled into a grimace, hideous yet desperate, tragic; he turned and pressed it against a tree.

The men relieved each other at the shovels. With satisfaction they shed their unaccustomed coats, rolled back their sleeves, waited anxiously for their turn as though, beside a chance to show good-will and sympathy, it held the welcome relief of familiar toil in this hour of formality, of inscrutable death and sorrow. It was for each at once his offering and his refuge.

When the turn came, each slid his knuckled left hand down the smooth-worn handle, balanced an instant with knees a little sprung, and then by virtue of some instinct of rough tact dipped up only the smallest shovelful, and swinging slowly, slipped it ever so softly into the grave.

The handle of the shovel was passed to James. He grasped it with a certain sober pride and having first paused to feel the heft, made a point of dropping the spadefuls so exactly side by side that they formed a smooth and level floor. He struck the point of the shovel in the ground and gave way to another, conscious that no one would likely show neater workmanship.

The grave was filled. The men took off their hats. The women followed Mr. Roon in a last "Amen."

They started to move back to the cabin. But Sal's mother, her thin back hunched beneath a burden, stood transfixed, her weary, gray eyes feeding on the mound of earth now gilded by the fast dropping sun, feeding with ravenous anguish and striving, it seemed, to pierce the clay, to penetrate the dark, mysterious abyss. They spoke to her. She only twined her hard blunt fingers. They urged her gently, strongly, took her by the elbows. She roused herself and, bursting out with petty, pitiful violence, worked her thin arms aimlessly against them. With low words of expostulation they closed in on her. Her hair came down and hung before her beaten face. Her struggles ceased. She put her head on Mrs. Fraser's shoulder and stumbled away.

Following behind that outworn, defenceless figure, James Fraser felt an unimaginably swift and dreadful clutch at his heart. The spirit within him fluttered. He raised his hands to his breast, he turned his head away as from a blow and gazed with dim eyes across the corn-field. At the edge of the forest, Sam, the mindless boy, was stealing slyly among the trees and peeping over his shoulder.

Back at the house they broke up into solemn groups and talked again of crops and of poor Sal's symptoms. Those who were leaving went into the cabin and gave Ben Scroggs and his wife the same single limp shake of the hand, the same veiled, sidewise glance. They climbed on mules or into carts and stole off through the forest.

The three of them drove home beneath the mild light of a crescent moon. James himself was busy with thoughts of rails for the Colonel; his father was silent; his mother, firm and practical as always, talked from time to time with the good sense and self-reliance she had shown during the afternoon. But as they climbed the little rise before their house she ceased abruptly. Conscious at last of the silence, James glanced at her. Her face was rigid, locked in struggle. As he looked two great, slow-dropping tears squeezed out from her crinkled eyes, tumbled down the furrows of her cheeks. With one distracted, ineffectual effort to cover her face with her shawl, she broke into terrible silent weeping. James stared at her, astounded. Then he knew. They were passing the vine-tangled mounds, the pine headboards where his small brother and sisters lay. What must he do? What must he do? But his father had shifted the reins to his other hand and put his blunt uncertain paw around his mother's shoulder.

CHAPTER IV

With unbelievable sluggishness the summer crept by. It was as if the hot, dead, humid air which caused man and all living things to breathe with slow laboriousness and stir reluctantly had laid its suffocation on time itself, until the days and hours almost ceased to move.

The mule, the cow, the hogs lay prone and panting, the birds hung motionless in the deepest shade, only the Frasers themselves resisted the oppressive doom. They roused themselves each morning against the summer heat, seeking by dint of will to free themselves from its coils, to gain, as it were, a little elbow room to fight their tireless enemies, the crab-grass and the flies. James Fraser spent weeks, months it seemed, stumbling through burning sand behind the dirting plough, then turning at the headland to stumble back again across a field so tiny as to be no more than a little breathless pocket in the forest.

His meals were eaten with the right hand while the other plied a turkey-wing against the hovering swarm of all small flying things. And these same swarms, still tireless and unappeased, strove all night long to enter his close hot lean-to room, stuff up each crack and cranny as he might. Naked and sweating, he would lie on his corn-shuck pallet and wish that he were like a regular cracker and could let them swarm and crawl with equanimity. But not being a cracker, he lay miserably

awake and listened as one by one the insects found
new apertures and buzzed infallibly toward him.

On those interminable unhappy nights he often, for
his solace, would think about the words regarding rails
which passed between his father and the Colonel at
Sal's funeral. His father at the time had dismissed the
Colonel's proposition, had answered, as he always answered, that it could not be done, that he had no
log-wagon. James himself had kept silent then but
he had done some figuring. And ever since his mind
had hung to the idea. Old Man Racker, the postmaster, had a pair of wheels; with them and their own
cart-wheels he could make a log-wagon. But how could
he get the wheels from Old Man Racker? He spent his
wakeful nights in figuring how, first, to tackle Old
Man Racker for his wheels; how to rig up the wagon;
what number of rails the mule could draw. The thing
became a fact. As drowsiness came on him, he could
see himself, everything in good fix, travelling the road
to Beaumont. And sometimes just before he went to
sleep, or maybe just a little after, he arrived, and driving through the gates, through the fields, and the grove
of live-oaks and of Spanish moss, pulled up before the
tall, unpainted house. The reins slack in his hands,
he sat there listening. Within, a girl's voice, soft but
ringing, whispered "Hush."

Early in September, just before the laying-by time,
came a letter to his father. It was put in James' hand
as he stood, on a Saturday night, in the slab shanty
which leaned against a sycamore where four trails met
and, serving as post-office and grocery for the neighbor-

hood, did a small business in salt, coffee, and sugar, and a large business in Monongahela whiskey.

While waiting to buy the family rations for the week, James was standing beyond the end of the plank bar and, as he always did, was studying a page of an old *Harper's Weekly* pasted on the wall between two joists. It was entitled "Entry of the Steam Locomotive, *General Andrew Jackson*, into the City of Wilmington, North Carolina, with the First Through Train of Cars from Weldon," and it depicted the General Jackson, scrolls of smoke belching from its funnel-shaped stack, its wide-spreading cowcatcher festooned with garlands, slowly steaming through a crowd of whiskered gentlemen who raised high hats sedately and of beautiful ladies in boleros and hoop-skirts who smiled in unison and waved their tiny handkerchiefs. Steam jetted from the General Jackson's cylinders and from the whistle over the boiler. The engine was wreathed not only with trivial flowers, but with the smoke and steam of power. Studying as he always did the details underlying this majestic effect, James felt new reverence for their practical perfection. He had figured the mechanism out for himself, he saw where the fire-box and flue must be, where the steam entered the cylinders and escaped through the valves, how the pistons and driving-rods worked. He knew that engine mighty near by heart, so far as he could make it out from the picture. There were lots of points, though, that a man would have to see an engine to really understand. He would give a heap to see one.

Along the bar drab-shirted figures hooked elbows,

talked sparingly but steadily under cover of hunched shoulders.

"Know that ba'r cub of Pogue's?"

A pause.

"Reckon. Pogue's got him chained to a stump."

"Well, Sadday night along come a fellow named Bullteel, from Bear Grass."

"Joe Bullteel? One-Eyed Joe, they name him. He got gouged couple years back at Petty Sessions."

Further reflection.

"That's him. But I always heard it that a fellow cut out his eye fighting with salmon-cans."

The point was argued. Details and figures were martialled with inexhaustible patience. General observations were interjected. "A can kin cut if a fellow knows the way to hold it." It was agreed that Joe had been cut fighting with cans at Petty Sessions. The tale resumed.

"Drunk, Joe was, and when he see Pogue's b'ar he wrops his arms around that cub's neck. 'B'ar!' he says, 'I'll rassle you fo' you hide.'"

The others waited, impassive.

"'You lay off that b'ar,' Pogue says, 'you liable to lose you ears.'

"'Well,' says One Eye, 'if he's a better b'ar than I am a man I've no complaint.'" The speaker finished his glass. He wiped his mouth in the crook of his arm. "And all this while the b'ar was preenin' hisself to start on Joe."

Slowly, with laborious exactitude the fight was re-counted.

"And Joe lay ther', his right y'ear was near about tore off. But all he did was laugh and laugh. 'Ain't he *severe*, though,' he says, 'the cute little son of a bitch. Look what he done to my y'ear.'"

Another round was served while the customers reflected without comment on the tale.

"Next week," a voice took up another topic, "I hyear the planters has they tournament."

"Wher' abouts?"

"The old field west of the Prevost place wher' the race-path used to be."

"What's the idea in these planters' tou'naments?"

"That's what I say. Now you take a goose-pullin' or a turkey shoot—the man that wins gets something."

"In a tou'nament he gets a wreath of posies. To give his gal."

This was considered.

"Posies is nice to give a gal. I don't say they ain't. But ain't that a picayune prize, though?"

In the lull which followed, Old Man Racker, the postmaster and storekeeper, turned slowly toward James, then struck by a thought, turned slowly back and fished three letters and a newspaper from the gourd that hung beside a shelf of patent medicines. He shuffled them slowly beneath the kerosene lamp, irresolute, yet with an air of profound and labored thought, as though on him lay the burden of deciding which it would be best to hand to James. He paused occasionally to scratch his brown, bald head with the corner of an envelope.

"Well, son," he said with infinite deliberation. "I reckon this yer's about it." He held out a letter.

"No, seh," said James, "that's for Sims."

"Sho," said Old Man Racker in a tone of disappointment. "You don't tell. Well, hyer's this blue one."
The blue one was addressed to James' father, sure
enough. The writing was his Uncle John's feeble, educated hand and the postmark was Weldon, near the old
Fraser place, but the date on the postmark was the
2d of August.

"Why," said James, "this letter's dated the 2d of
August."

"I reckon so," said Old Man Racker in cordial acquiescence. "It seems to me like that blue letter's been
laying here a month or mo'." He filled two small, thick
tumblers with whiskey and coasted them dexterously
toward two outstretched hands across the bar. "But
every Sadday you come in hyer it seems like that letter
naturally dodged out of my mind." He must have
caught some hint of foreboding in James' eye, for he
added in the manner of one who with commendable
impartiality merely states his grievance, "It's a funny
thing you didn't ax for it. Most folks that's expecting
a letter generally does."

James Fraser put the letter in his trousers' pocket.
Old Man Racker scooped flour, salt, and coffee into
paper bags and dropped the bags in James' sack. With
the sack over his shoulder, James passed behind the row
of figures in huck shirts and butternut trousers tilted
against the bar, and stepped out along the starlit,
sandy trail for home.

His father, as James had expected, was gravely angry at the letter's long delay. "It's not so bad that

Old Man Racker can't read," he observed to James' mother, "because his boys can. But he don't tend to his business. He's all taken up with selling liquor."

"Old Man Racker!" replied Mrs. Fraser. ". . . for a postmaster! You ought to write the government, Robert."

"Anyhow, I'll speak to him. He should make amends for this."

"Make him lend his pair of wheels, Pa," said James Fraser earnestly, "for our rail wagon."

"I declare," muttered Mr. Fraser as he opened the letter, "that might be an idea." He read the closely written sheets, then handed it to Mrs. Fraser. She ran through it quickly.

"Well, well." She gave a little sniff, half contemptuous, half pleased. "Shall I show this to the boy?" The letter was handed to James.

THE MANSION HOUSE
BLUE'S CROSSING
WAKE COUNTY

July 28th, 1859.

MY DEAR BROTHER:

I take my pen in hand to communicate to you my thoughts upon a subject which has long been occupying my mind. Although I bless God that I still continue to enjoy pretty tolerable health except for my regular complaint of the kidneys, I often reflect that my life in all human probability has run the best part of its course. I am therefore anxious while I still have my health for a visit here to our family place on the part of my nephew, James, who must by now be a fine, stout boy

and a credit to our race. It would be a fine pleasure
for me to meet again the youngest of our family, and I
believe it would be a fine thing for James, now that he
is nearly a man, to see the old-time place and hear about
his ancestors.

In these modern days I find that little attention is
paid to ancient tradition and honorable breeding.
Wealth is the only thing considered. Around us, as you
know, a new race of planters has sprung up. By the
rapid multiplying of their negroes and the high price of
cotton they have acquired wealth in a single generation,
and now assume condescending airs though God knows
what a research into their ancestry might not reveal.
Meanwhile, the old Colonial Revolutionary Families are
forgotten. Their glory is eclipsed by the seductive
brilliance of the dollar, and all that is noblest in our
history and legend is consigned to oblivion in the mad
scramble for negroes and cotton. And though some of
these planters are honorable gentlemen who can trace
their lineage to our earliest history, I do not hesitate
to say that many more are thorough scoundrels in
grain, who under ill-assumed, aristocratic airs are not
above selling their surplus slaves to the highest bidder
from the swamps of Louisiana, while some, to my
belief, are actually silent partners of the despicable
slave dealers themselves.

All this is hardly news to you, I reckon, but I seemed
to get started on the subject. What I set out to say
was that in this mercenary age would it not be well to
let your son have a glimpse of the old place from which
he sprang, sleep in the bed of old John Fraser, his Rev-

olutionary ancestor, and hear how he fought aboard the *Bon Homme Richard*, at the Cowpens, and in fact everywhere that opportunity offered. John Fraser, though shamefully neglected by history, was from the first the very soul of the Revolution in North Carolina. I hope, if I am spared, to write a book about him.

But to continue, would not such a visit give the boy a just pride in his inheritance, of more worth than material success which seems now to be so sought after, though not, I am glad to think, by you and me?

He could take the Wilmington and Weldon Railroad to Anson's and I would meet him there in the covered cart.

He will find the place not as well kept up as I could wish. The truth is I have not the means and have been obliged to sell off a piece of timber from time to time to keep going. This cleared land would make fine cotton if only I were fixed to get some negroes and hire an overseer. I figure I could have made five thousand dollars last year. But now the price of negroes is higher than ever.

Well, it is getting late and I must close. Please give my regards to your good lady and advise me at your earliest convenience.

Hoping this finds you as it leaves me,

Your affectionate brother,
John.

James Fraser was conscious that his father and mother looked at him, awaiting signs of his delight. He must speak.

"My land," he faltered, "that's mighty nice of Uncle John."

His father nodded solemn indorsement. But his mother's voice was insistent.

"Do you want to go, son?"

"I'd love mighty well to ride on those cars," James answered evasively.

His father embarked on ponderous reflections.

"Well," he said, "after the crops are laid by, I reckon he can go."

James Fraser did not speak. How could he hint at the fantastic thoughts flying through his mind? If he said he wanted to stay and go to the tournament they would think him as trivial and pleasure-loving as a nigger. And he could not further explain that he aimed to go in order to maybe catch a sight of a girl whom he had never seen, whose voice only he had heard, just once. Nothing could drag that explanation from him. It was just as well; they would put him down for crack-brained, sure enough.

"What ails you, son?" his mother asked. "You don't seem too well pleased."

"I was thinking about those rails for Colonel Prevost. If we could get Old Man Racker's wheels I could haul them."

"The Colonel's rails!" she cried. "I've heard of nothing but the Colonel's rails all summer! What's all the push about the Colonel's rails?"

James did not speak. He was uneasy at the idea of putting off the rail business. The Colonel might become impatient and decide to get out his own rails instead of waiting. In that case there would be no trips to Beaumont for him. And he was not especially eager to see Uncle John, vaguely remembered but on the whole an unknown quantity, or the old place either. He knew he was bound to be ill at ease.

Still James Fraser sat silent. The picture of the *General Andrew Jackson* in Old Man Racker's bar came back to him. If he went to Uncle John's he would see steam locomotives and ride on the cars.

Then he thought of the tournament. She was bound to be there like all the other planters' ladies. Anyhow he would take the chance and let the car ride go.

"I reckon I better stay and get fixed to haul those rails."

"Tend to business, eh?" his father grunted in satisfaction. His mother did not speak. She sat impassive, her black, squirrel-like eyes searching his face.

CHAPTER V

At the edge of the race-path field James Fraser halted. Beyond the stretch of tawny broom straw, an effect of lively elegance, of dignity and splendor was thrown into sharp relief against the ring of tall, dark pines. The weathered little grand stand was festooned with flags and bunting, crowded with gay shawls and parasols and flanked with twinkling equipages and saddle-horses who shook their crests beneath gay caparisons.

He looked in vain for the reassuring sober coats of country people. Planters' families only. The tournament belonged to them. He had not thought of that before; he had taken it for granted that all grades of people would be there, that he would mingle, inconspicuous, with others like himself. Even so he had not been altogether happy in his mind, not after a six-mile tramp with an uneasy conscience, a conscience which maintained inexorably against his sophistry that he had fooled his father and mother in order to get off for the day. He had, without, it is true, direct lies or at least without more than one, created the impression that he aimed to go to Beaumont to see the Colonel about the rails. Old Man Racker had loaned them his pair of wheels, so they were now able to make a wagon on which to haul rails to the Colonel's place. He had, however, had no notion of going to Beaumont. He wanted, for reasons of his own, to see the tournament. True, the

Colonel would most likely be at the tournament and
maybe he could see him. But that was not what he had
made his father believe.

Still it was done. The question was what to do now.
The carriage track in which he stood led straight across
the level field. If he followed it he would be exposed to
the gaze of the assembled gentry. He looked around for
a means of entrance less conspicuous. To the left, where
the encircling ring of pines came close, a wood-road led
off among the trees. That wood-road gave him comfort
and relief. If it had not been there he could, of course,
have made his way between the pines. But that would
have been unmistakably shame-faced and surreptitious.
This was, after all, a road and he could follow it without
discredit.

It brought him to the fringe of open ground behind
the grand stand, where, with chatter and well-relished
confusion, house slaves laid out their masters' picnics
on the grass, spread rugs by dint of endless consulta-
tion, argument, set out white plates and napkin-
covered platters, carried fat clinking hampers crowned
with bottle necks. They fell silent and exchanged
glances, swift, covert, supercilious, as James Fraser
passed.

The grand stand showed a line of beaver hats and
bonnets along the top. Animated, they swayed and
bobbed, and, as he looked, a gust of applause swept over
them. In the carriages on either end people, their
backs to him, stood up and waved, coat-buttons glinted,
hoop-skirts swung and caught the light.

He walked around the last carriage on the line and,

looking straight ahead, went up to the rail which fenced
the tournament ring.

Around its edge, where the last rider's dust still hung,
stood ten poles with arms like slender gallows. A
gentleman in a fringed crimson sash rode in, halted
beneath a pole and hung a ring on the cross-arm. He
continued thus around the circle. Meanwhile the little
crowd buzzed, chatted; outside the oval's farther end,
flashes of color and horses' tossing heads showed where
the contestants awaited their turn. The red-sashed
gentleman drew up before the grand stand, raised his
broad black hat. "The Black Knight!" he announced
with half-humorous sententiousness. Wheeling sharply
he cantered out the gate.

With a drum of hoofs a dark, slim figure galloped in.
His coat, his trousers, strapped beneath his pumps, were
black; he rode a black, high-headed, fretful horse; from
the brow-band black ribbons streamed behind. His
cheeks below his narrow, downy side-burns were white,
his shirt-ruffle showed white above his low-cut vest.
He was a proud young man.

Setting his lance he rode at the first ring, picked it
neatly off its pin. It spun down the shaft as he galloped
to the next, took it and, sitting erect and steady, held
straight on his course.

With five rings on his lance he came at his swift, even
pace to the pole where James was standing. His horse
swerved slightly, he missed the ring and the next two.

"Seven," a voice called from the stand as the Black
Knight finished. "Catlin, you're beaten."

The young man did not answer but he rode up to the

gentleman in the red sash and pointed furiously at
James. James felt a mounting flush, he was being
blamed, he guessed, for having frightened the Black
Knight's horse by standing at the rail. Even across the
ring James could feel the haughty exasperation in the
light-gray eyes. And though the older man shook his
head and promptly announced the next contestant, for
long after James could feel his neck prickling with
embarrassment.

Other riders made the circuit to the accompaniment
of cheers or light, good-natured ridicule. He regained
composure and was able to steal a covert glance at the
boxes ranged across the grand stand's front. In the
centre sat a tall, pale, golden-haired lady who must be
the queen. She wore a golden crown, and around her
sat other young ladies in smaller crowns. He studied
each. Some were mighty pretty and all were elegant
without a doubt. But instead of drawing pleasure from
the charming galaxy his disappointment and confusion
mounted. He had somehow imagined that he would be
able to pick out *her*, her whose voice he had heard inside
the house at Beaumont. She was surely here, for just
behind the Queen he saw the Colonel's fine-cut face,
his snowy stock, his straight slight shoulders of blue
broadcloth. Surely she must be here; and though she
was to him merely a voice, though he had formed no
picture in his mind of how she looked, he had thought
that once he saw her he would infallibly, instantly
know that it was she.

He persisted; he searched the seats behind the boxes
as closely as he dared, looking frequently away and

striving to seem casual, indifferent. He was on dangerous ground. These folks were not accustomed to having
a farmer boy inspect them at his leisure! But he could
not give up. He had planned, had schemed, had lied
for this occasion. Nothing like it would likely offer
again.

And he must make haste. Soon the gathering would
disperse, his opportunity have vanished. He searched
more earnestly, more hurriedly, more boldly; he even
edged along the rail straining to hear their voices and
perhaps to catch the note of hers. *That* he would be
sure of. But in the animated murmur all were blended
and though he thought at times that he did hear it,
it was more likely merely the familiar and elusive echo
in his ears.

And now the general hum of talk was drowned by
the conversation of the people in the long barouche
behind him. Dejected, he was hardly conscious of
their words—"rice cakes and a turkey basted with
butter and a dash of vinegar, just a dash . . . only
the best Madeira for the sauce, some people think
that anything will do. . . ." "I find nothing in the
Scriptures, ma'am, to suggest that one who puts green
Scuppernong in sauce is not in danger of hell-fire."
They laughed. "Doctor, I reckon you consider that a
sin against the church."

"What I like about the doctor's theology, ma'am, is
that a man can understand it. I know that my salvation is assured as long as I have old Aunt Flora for a
cook."

"Let's hope that she survives you, Mr. George."

"If not, it will be all the same. That old negress will raise such a fuss in heaven if I don't get in, too, that the angels won't be able to hear their own hallelujahs . . . not that Aunt Flora thinks I amount to much. But she won't be happy even in heaven without me to grumble at."

James Fraser was listening now, fascinated and scandalized. These folks mixed up salvation, liquor, parsons, and niggers in their talk—made a kind of joke of heaven, anyhow got fun out of talking about heaven— like it was any other place. No good would come of that.

They chattered on.

"You can get sewing-machines in Raleigh now . . . but I don't like them. They make me giddy. . . ." "Look at Cousin Sara's *challe de laine*. It was made on a machine and now, my dear, it's simply falling apart —after only five years."

"George, my boy, we are now definitely out of our depth. I can understand theology and Madeira but not sewing-machines and *challe de laine* . . ."

A burst of clapping. "Nine rings, madam. The best round so far."

"Charles Prevost took nine last year. A pity he's not here."

"A pity in more ways than one, Miss Milly . . . to think of sending him to Harvard College . . . a nest of abolitionists . . . at Chapel Hill he would have been among his own kind . . . or Princeton. Catlin Gregg says there are enough Southern gentlemen there to set a tone to the place.

"Princeton! A nest of Presbyterians!"

Another rider galloped past. The party in the barouche, oblivious, were in violent argument. "Don't
shout, Major."

"Damme, Madame, why not? Aren't the abolitionists making noise enough?"

A lady spoke. "But they are not gentlemen, sir."
The Major digested this thrust. The other man's voice
was calmer—in fact, dry.

"I envy the abolitionists, Cousin Milly. They can
practise their superior morality without its costing them
a cent. They can sow the wind and leave others to
reap the whirlwind. And believe me they mean to do
it. They will not rest until they have precipitated a
crisis."

"I quite agree, sir," the Major put in. "Theirs is the
mentality of the pyromaniac."

"I'm sure I don't know what that means," said
Cousin Milly. "But I don't know what the abolitionists mean, either. I'm sure no one could treat their
people better than we. Indeed, we spoil them. Did I
tell you what my Jimsie said to me last week. He came
in all excited and said, 'Mama, I want Daddy's pistol.'
'Good gracious, child,' I said, 'what do you want that
for?' 'That overseer's boy hit Drury,'—that's the little
negro we gave him—'and I'm a-going to shoot him.'"

"*Patris filius!*" the Major exclaimed in high approval. "His father—God bless his respected memory,
madam—would have done the very same. Ah, here
comes Fanshawe to announce the victor."

At the head of the cavalcade of knights the gentleman in the red sash pranced into the ring. He called out a long, fantastic name—Sir Something of Something—and taking a great wreath of roses from a negro servant's hand presented it to a shyly smiling youth in a jacket emblazoned with a coat of arms. The other riders, in line behind, each received a wreath of shining magnolia leaves. For an instant they kept their ranks, wreaths, flowers, ribbons, bright horses, swaying plumes making a brave array.

As they dismounted a flock of negro boys scurried up to lead away their horses. The knights filed into the stand. There was a murmur of applause. The winner's bashful voice was heard, "I crown you Queen of Love and Beauty." Another voice, a woman's, "Isn't she sweet? Isn't she *sweet?*" Laughter, the patter of hands. The new Queen, her maidens around her, was enthroned, saluted.

It seemed a curious performance, affected, dandified, and somehow stirring. These popinjays in costume making ornate addresses to their ladies with wreaths and flowery speeches! And all because they had ridden around a circle spearing little rings!

And yet James Fraser pictured himself, full gallop, in the circle—the rings clicked on his lance point, spun down to his hand. With the wreath of roses he mounted to the grand stand, bowed, presented it—to whom?

The crowd filed out of the grand stand, scattered among the picnics spread out on the grass. They called out invitations, pleasantries, gentlemen bent solicitously over ladies who hung upon their arms, ladies flounced out their flowered and festooned hoops and

sank down on cushions. To James Fraser, still standing by the rail, they seemed all to be sharers in some
intimate, gay secret. He shrank back behind the nearest vacant carriage.

Among the last to leave the stand, Colonel Prevost,
his small, slight figure remarkably dignified in its effect,
moved beside a group of older gentlemen. He responded courteously but his eye roved. James shrank further still. The Colonel saw him, left the others, but
not without a gesture of apology, and came toward the
rail.

"Well, my boy, I reckon you are looking for me."

James' hat was off. He nodded. "Yes, seh."

"And how are your father and mother?" The
Colonel's tone was one of practised cordiality. At
James' answer he inclined his head. "Indeed. I am
pleased to hear it." He fixed his bright blue eyes, his
eyes which underneath their liveliness and warmth
seemed to observe so much, to reveal so little, on
James' face. "I noticed you searching the stand."
James Fraser's breathing stopped. Like an animal he
stood motionless, frozen in the face of danger. What
might the Colonel not have guessed? But he was
speaking again, "And I presumed that you looked for
me."

"Yes, seh." James managed to make his whisper
prompt enough.

"Can I count on you for the rails? . . . Good. . . .
When? . . . Two dollars? A fair price. We will not
discuss it further." The Colonel nodded. "I must re-
join my party. Let me send you a glass of port by my

servant. No? Well then, I shall expect you to-morrow."

James Fraser moved along the rail, keeping well clear of the supper parties. He followed the Colonel with his eyes and among the group that welcomed him strove to make out which could be his daughter. But the faces of the ladies were not clearly seen, they were lost among a light confusion of fans, of Spanish shawls, of flowers.

In his room that night he felt under the bed for his fiddle, nursed it on his knees, dusted it off with a corner of the counterpane. He would have liked to go outside and play but his parents would think it mighty queer after he had said he was so sleepy. In that, again, he had not quite told the truth. That was the way of it. One pretense got a man balled up in a string of others. He had claimed he was sleepy as an excuse to get away before they should find out that he had not been to Beaumont. He had merely told them that he had seen the Colonel, that everything was fixed and he was to start next day. They had assumed that he had been to Beaumont. He was glad to leave them thinking so.

His thoughts wandered back to the tournament. It had been a fine show. But it had given him a queer feeling—to stand there right amongst those folks and yet know that, for all they were to him or he to them, he might be in the moon, or dead, just a ghost, belonging to another world, who, unseen, came to look at them. And then to think that she was somewhere there, and

that he did not know her. And that even though he
talked with her own father he could not ask him which
she was. Like a ghost he could watch but he had not
the right, the power to reach across the gulf, mysterious,
invisible, which separated him from them. But why
should he complain? Should he not have been able to
know her without asking?

Anyhow, what had given him the crazy notion that
she must be beautiful? A person could have a pretty
voice and still be mighty plain. There had been some
plain girls there. Maybe he had overlooked her.

Well, he'd start the job to-morrow. Most likely he
would find out before long what she was like.

He was getting sleepy, for a fact. He put the fiddle
back under the bed. The strings left his finger with a
reproachful and plaintive cry. To-morrow night he'd
play it.

CHAPTER VI

But the next night he did not play his fiddle.

Instead, he wandered over to the pasture fence beyond the barn and, crossing his arms on the top rail, thought over the events of the day. The stars and a crescent moon shed light enough to outline vaguely the scattered pines and the tall mass of cypresses along the branch; so vaguely, however, that the great solid trees seemed hardly more than a shadowy mist through which a man could push his way, leaving a wreck of black and silver fragments in his wake. He could almost see himself driving straight on, and powerfully, through the tinsel, unsubstantial scene. But what for, and whither? Why, toward the tall house at Beaumont without a doubt, and for—well, first let him go back and think from the beginning about the day.

He and his father had loaded the rail wagon, and incidentally, while he was mighty pleased that his father had gotten the wheels from Old Man Racker and gone ahead to fix up the wagon, he could not feel satisfied at its construction. The string piece between the axles ought to have been heavier and straighter grained. The way it was it couldn't last. He couldn't put in a new one though, not without hurting his father's feelings mightily. But maybe sometime he could get one out and have it ready.

To go back to the day. There would have been no

sense in wearing his father's coat on a job like that, but he did have on a clean blue-checked shirt and his brogans were greased, although by the time he got to the Colonel's lodge gate they were pretty dusty because he had to get off and walk up the grades. She had probably noticed how dusty they were; but if she had, she would understand. A girl like her would understand about that—would understand about everything. A girl like her—but hold on; he hadn't gotten there yet.

At the lodge gate the same old negro dozed beneath the live-oaks. In the fields beyond, the fodder had been pulled and the pea-vine hay stacked up in ricks around tall poles. From beyond the gin house came the long-drawn cries of negro hands and the smoke and rumble of a steam-engine threshing rice. The overseer was probably there, but he himself was doing business that day with no one but the Colonel; he drove on past the quarters and through the dark grove, till he halted by the horse-block at the gable end of the house. He had sat there for a moment on the wagon, half remembering his dreams and half expecting that he would again hear the ringing voice within. Of course, there was nothing, though he waited.

Then of a sudden, appearing, it seemed, miraculously from nowhere, a girl was standing before him, a bright and instantaneous vision of airy white sprigged muslin and two deep-gray, quiet eyes, warm, kind, yet humorously penetrating, that looked up into his. He had sat there speechless. This was the girl.

She spoke; she said "Good evening" with a little

lift of inquiry at the end, and her voice—*the* voice—ran through him like a flickering ray. That roused him, brought him to himself. And to his honor and credit he had been able to gather his wits together, swing to the ground, and take off his hat in the best style he knew how.

"Good evening, ma'am," he had said; his manner had been polite, respectful, yet sufficiently assured; and that, too, was well done. But then again, looking into those gray eyes, he had lost himself and stood there dumb. It had seemed then very queer that there should be a difficulty, for was not this the girl—the girl whose voice had reached him once before right there at Beaumont, and had so often since been ringing in his ears? What could be simpler than to tell her so? Or to burst out, "You were not at the tournament! I knew you couldn't be!" She would be bound to understand. But somehow he had not been so far gone in folly. What had stopped him he did not know; just his own born muteness he supposed. How often in the past he had cursed it and wrestled with it, but now he felt almost grateful, for this time it had done him a good turn, sure enough. A mighty good turn. If he had said a word of what was in his mind, she would have taken him for a natural born fool.

Yet, would she? Perhaps that impulse that was tugging at his heart was right. Perhaps truth and freedom had been in him at that moment just as they sometimes were, he felt, at a corn-shucking or barbecue when he had drunk more liquor than he needed. But at those times his mind, released and em-

boldened, had not turned to girls. It had turned to his
fiddle and made him believe in his soul that if the moment could only be prolonged he would be the greatest
fiddler that ever was. It had not turned to girls. Indeed, at such brief hours of emancipation it had turned
proudly away from such girls as there were, from the
country wenches who nudged and giggled, waiting for
some one to lead them to the woods. Though to be
honest, he sometimes thought of them when sober.

His thoughts checked shamefully. What in creation
was he doing thinking of country sluts right now? He
wasn't really thinking of them except, that is, of how
different they were. Yet a sure enough decent man
wouldn't think of them at all. One of those high-toned
planters' sons would probably be writing a poem about
her.

That was the trouble. He was of a different mould
from such as them and from her. He might be thrilled
by glimpses of their world but that did not make him
belong to it. If he had sense, he'd better stay away
and 'tend to his own business.

He paused again. Now what ailed him? He was
taking on as though he'd got deeply and dangerously
mixed up with the girl. Let him drop his foolishness
and look at the facts. He had merely said "howdy"
and asked where the Colonel was, and she had told him
where the Colonel was, and he had driven off. Those
were the facts and you couldn't get away from them,
and the more you looked at them the more ordinary
they became. Why, a man might do that to anybody—
say "howdy" and ask where somebody else was. He

might do it to an old woman, or another man, or a nigger.

The fact was that he didn't seem quite himself. He felt more or less nervous and played out, and that was the reason why a few civil words with a strange girl could fill him with so many notions. He probably wouldn't think anything of it in the morning.

He tried a scheme to prove to himself how fanciful his ideas had been, how commonplace and usual was all that had occurred. He pretended that he was telling about the events to his mother and father. At once, in the presence of their seasoned good sense everything shrank to its proper size—and that size was mighty small, about the same as seeing Sam Scroggs, drunk again, and much less than Uncle John's letter or poor Sal's funeral. The day's adventure, looked at so, made small news, for a fact. Small news. He raised his elbows off the fence to go back to the house.

As if that slight movement were enough to unsettle the precarious equilibrium of his spirit, something within him seemed to swell beyond all bearing, then burst into a thousand tinkling fragments which echoed her voice. The white-sprigged muslin floated between him and the silver of the moon . . . sprigged muslin, delicate and airy . . . and dark, soft gray eyes . . .

He was roused by the sound of chumping in the pasture. The little cow had grazed up near; its woolly coat catching the moonlight formed a faint halo above its figure. James Fraser, filled now with confidence and a large benevolent humor, looked at the halo and smiled.

It took a mighty pretty moon, he said to himself, to sanctify that worthless little cow.

Back at the house, his parents were in bed and he was glad. He slipped off his shirt and trousers and, sitting on the edge of his pallet, pulled out his fiddle very quietly. He did not dare to use his bow, but laying the fiddle on his lap, he bent over it, lightly fingering the strings. He dropped his head down lower to catch the faint melodious hum. By touching the strings with all the softness in the world, he could just sketch in a tune or two without awakening the others. That was important—not to disturb the others—not to disturb his mother—and not to be disturbed.

CHAPTER VII

THE hauling job went on so uneventfully that he began to think the hope, the thrill, the dangerous elation of that first moonlit night must have been part of some swift-passing, fanciful illusion. The moment when he had seen and talked to her became more distant; he saw it in its true perspective and realized that it was commonplace, lacking in all profound significance; at least it would be so regarded by all the world and by her, and it was just as well that he was coming to look at it in the same way. Casual and commonplace it had surely been. You could not make anything more of it than that.

As more days passed and he did not see her, there was a dimming of her image in his mind. The very image itself began to fade. At first he clung to it, strove to draw it back. Then his efforts ceased; he relinquished it with something like relief. It had been the cause of groundless and foolish exaltation. Its vanishing would leave him sensible once more, like other folks.

But though her image, ever and again resurging, struggling, as it sometimes seemed, like a living thing against extinction, did finally die away, her voice as he had heard it first, long before he saw her, as seeing her he had heard it again, continued at unpremeditated moments to ring with all its first soft clearness in his ears. By shot! he told himself grimly, if that was to go on, he might as well have had the image, too, instead of only a fleeting mist pierced by two gray eyes.

Each day he made a trip to Beaumont with a load of rails, sometimes two. On arrival he hunted up the overseer, who sent two negroes down to the pasture along the northern branch and there he waited while the negroes stood the rails in cone-shaped stacks around the pine-trees. To reach the spot—a stretch of wire grass and black sodden bottom-land among the scattered pines which marked the stream—he did not have to pass by the mansion but he did pass behind its grove of live-oaks and in doing so he always tried to penetrate their close, protecting shade. He would naturally be interested, he told himself, in seeing what would be going on in such a place as Beaumont. Once, among the trees, he caught a flash of white which, for the moment, excited him powerfully, though it was indistinguishable and, as he told himself soon after, might have been a negro woman's turban or a piece of washing on a line.

While the negroes unloaded the rails he took a few ears of corn out of a sack and threw them on the ground in front of the mule and then, withdrawing, sat down and ate some cold rations which he carried wrapped up in a newspaper. He did not speak to the negroes nor they to him though the pair of them was usually the same. One, called Logan, was a regular Guinea nigger with a little peaked head sunk down between enormous shoulders. His hide was thick and so black that had it not been for the light gray of his palms and the pinkness of his tongue, you would have thought the scoundrel was black all through. He was hard to understand, talking as he did the Gullah language of the Sea Islands from which he came. Taking him all in all—his skin, his ape-like build, the inarticulate, thick sounds he made,—he was as near an animal as you could get. The other negro, Rav, was light tan, spare, and tall. His nose had a bridge to it, his nostrils, though wide-flaring, were thin and flexible, some trace of distinction managed to survive his tattered shirt and high-low trousers of brown slave cloth, and he bore himself with a certain faded elegance which suggested that though now condemned to serve as a field hand, he might for-merly have been a house servant. He assumed the di-rection of the other negro and with ironic condescension addressed the dull squat Logan as "Big Hoss." "Big Hoss," he would say, "lay you' han' on this rail." And Logan, without haste but without resentment, would grab hold of the end and raise it up against the pile.

From his distant seat beneath a tree, James could not help watching the two slaves with a curiosity which overcame distaste and uneasiness. What were these strange, suspicious animals like inside? They might have more thoughts in their heads than a man would suppose; and if they did, those thoughts were hostile. A mighty good thing they were in slavery; it was the only thing that kept them where they belonged. His slow, logical mind proceeded with the theme. But if that were so, it was the only thing that kept the white man where he belonged, too; that is to say, on top. But that meant that the white man couldn't stay on top without slavery to help him; but that could not be so because the white man was the bet-ter and, in the natural order, belonged to be on top.

A lot of the landless white men in the woods, though, didn't live any better themselves than negroes, maybe not as well; but that was because the negroes had white men to look after them and the white men in the woods had nobody. By this time he was lost in a maze. Well, anyhow, he concluded, he hated and despised niggers and would be glad if there was not a one in the world. But if they had to be around, they ought to be slaves, every one of them; you could tell that by the way the free niggers carried on. Only with slaves around it looked like there was mighty little chance for a plain man to get anywhere. He recalled a letter to his father from his Uncle Andrew in Illinois. His Uncle Andrew had got to be quite a prominent man, he supposed, since he had moved out there, anyhow he was an assistant district attorney. He had written to tell James' father about the powerful speeches that Stephen A. Douglas, the head of the great Democratic party, had been making throughout the State. The Little Giant had wiped up the ground with an Abolitionist lawyer who had tried to debate with him. Uncle Andrew had added that Douglas had made a monkey out of the Abolitionist though the fellow looked like an ape anyhow. Every Abolitionist, Uncle Andrew concluded, ought to be hung. But though he loved the old North State and believed in slavery, he was mighty glad to be living in Illinois, a place where negroes were scarce. He thought that an ordinary man had more chance there.

He had finished his snack of corn-bread and bacon and was idly looking over the old copy of the *Wilmington Journal* in which they had been wrapped.

That sheet of newspaper, rumpled and greasy though it was, held a glittering world. It told of ships and cargoes, of grave affairs, of dignitaries. The first half of the opening page described a ball tendered the Oak City Guards of Raleigh by the Wilmington Light Infantry and preceded by a banquet wherein the toasts, beginning: "The Old North State the home of Beauty, Courage, Honor, Industry, Virtue, and Independence," stretched clear down the column to: "Our Brothers in Arms, may they ever be as they now are, the Exemplars of Youth, the Defence of Innocence, and the Conquerors of the Fair." He turned the page. An editorial dealt with the presentation of an ormolu clock to Major Cassius Pettibone, "gallant, courtly, and elegantly accomplished, the perfect type of Cape Fear gentleman," on his retirement as Clerk of the Court. A notice beneath it read:

A CARD

The undersigned, the friends of Gen. Roscoe and Mr. Handly take pleasure in saying that the unfortunate and regrettable misunderstanding between these distinguished and gallant gentlemen has been perfectly adjusted with mutual and highly creditable expressions of satisfaction and esteem and without, it need scarcely be added, in any respect compromising the honor of either party.

               O. SHEAN.
           WILLIAM ST. G. MUDGE, JR.

Ormolu presentation clocks—duels narrowly averted; they lived in an elegant, elaborate world, a world refined and complicated beyond all comprehension, those gentlemen of Wilmington. He read on.

There were news dispatches from Russia and Paris and California, a poem by "Menander" about his sweetheart's grave 'neath the yews, and advertisements still more fascinating. "Chamber Sets . . . Tête à Têtes . . . Divans . . . Circassian Hair Dye (instantaneous) . . . Essence of Bay Leaves (highly perfumed) . . . Prof. de Groth's Electric Oil . . . Beulah Female Academy . . . Under care of Dr. Pillow and Lady . . . Eureka Male Institute . . . none but good and docile boys wanted . . . Bowie Knives . . . 4 tierces Schiedam Schnapps . . ."

The right-hand column was ablaze with capitals and exclamation points.

RELIABLE AND SPLENDID LOTTERY!!!

STATE OF DELAWARE

A JEWEL OF THE FIRST WATER COMES LADEN WITH JOYS FOR THE SONS OF TOIL AND LIKE

LOVE'S GUIDING STAR

LEADS THE WEARY PILGRIMS TO ELYSIUM!!

$31,000 $8,000 $4,000

FOR THE DIMINUTIVE SUM OF FOUR DOLLARS AND A HALF ALL EARTHLY ANXIETY CAN BE BROUGHT TO A FOCUS IN THIS

MIRROR OF GOLD!!!

HASTE THEN AND LET NOT THIS VISION OF

EASTERN SPLENDOR

FADE BEFORE YOU BUY A PACKAGE.
!! GRAND AND BEAUTIFUL SCHEME !!

He turned the sheet over in search of further grand and beautiful schemes. There were none, but scattered over the back among other advertisements were many little black silhouettes of negroes running along with packs on their backs, each accompanied by a heading, "Ran Away," or "Ran Away from the Subscriber" or "$50 Reward."

He dropped the paper on the ground. Niggers again. He wished they'd all run away where no one could find them.

He leaned his head back against the tree as though to rest his mind from its fruitless labor. What was the use anyhow of puzzling over the insoluble? Better tackle each day's work without a question as his father did, plodding contentedly enough through the succeeding seasons. His mother, it is true, did not accept life with such docility, but what did she gain thereby? She merely skirmished to her own discomfort and in vain against intangible grievances.

The soft, yet strong, contented murmur of the pines, the branches moving slowly overhead, the lights and shadows moving on the ground, lulled him, gave him a drowsy security, a sense that things were as they were, immemorial, unchanged, and unchangeable.

He gazed aloft, up through the idly swaying branches, through the gentle shimmer of the long pine leaves, up to the sky above. Cloudless, imperturbable, it arched him over with its benign, unfathomable blue. He lay under its protection, content to accept unquestioningly the stir of branches, the warmth of sand against his thighs and the tree-trunk slightly shifting between his shoulders.

Within him and around him all peace, all quiet surety, was shattered to atoms by a presence. He did not move. For a moment he wanted simply to sit there without stirring, without breath, simply to feel her permeate the world and him.

Then he looked down. To his surprise she did not have on the white sprigged muslin; he had always thought of her as wearing it. But now her dress was of a smooth light green, close fitting down to the waist and then held out with hoops. This change in her attire caused him to look at her anew—almost as a stranger— and to notice things about her that he had not seen before—all in a flash—but he had time after the first electric thrill to feel with some surprise and some relief that, looked at coolly, though beautiful enough for any one, she was not quite as beautiful as he had supposed. That is to say, her mouth was a little wider and its half smile a little curved up at one corner, and her nose, instead of being strictly classic, turned up a little toward the end. For the rest, the hair was darkly clustered on her brow; the deep, gray eyes were just the same; and when she spoke the words were not sounds, but light.

"Good afternoon," she said.

At the sound it was as though a great, sharp-salted, foaming wave broke over him; he struggled through it to his feet and perhaps he answered her. At any rate she smiled. And now the magic wave, receding, clutched at him, sought to draw him to her, to pull him to his knees. He stood his ground while it drained away, to leave him numb and tingling. An instant more and he would be himself again. But now another subtler spell came flooding; gently it crept around him, held him mute and wondering, gained a strange and grateful potency till it seemed to flow above and through him, to embrace and warm his spirit, to lift it, lift it till it floated free, slipped its moorings and stole away, on and upward, leaving his body far behind. Now it was gone, this spirit that was truly himself, gone soaringly aloft, now it was lost in the blue above.

She was speaking again. At least her voice made music. Its echo died away. Then her words penetrated to him and he was able by dint of reluctant will to grasp their meaning. As if this effort or the words themselves had burst the spell he felt his infinitely distant spirit falter, turn, descend. It was flowing back toward his body. But so slowly. Would it come in time to answer her? She had said, "You have brought a lot of rails." But that was long ago. She could not wait forever. She would turn away, would leave him. With a sudden thunder of winds and oceans in his ears his spirit came. Now he could speak.

"Yes, ma'am. But they's many more to come." Incredibly, his voice was firm and easy. There was in it not a trace or tremor of the surge against his temples. If it were steady now, he need have nothing more to fear, for the surge itself after the first unbearable crescendo was beginning slowly to ebb away. But it was unbelievable that she should not have noticed the storms, the tides, the potent, vast enchantments through which, in the brief moments since she first appeared, his hurrying spirit had passed. And yet she gave no sign. Her smile, her eyes, were merely friendly and lightly amused as though he were a chance acquaintance, not a man who in the last three minutes had, there before her, gone a journey far into the unknown and then come back from regions whence, as he supposed, few had returned.

And in that journey, in that region of unplumbed and inscrutable blue, had he been alone? Or had she, perhaps, also been there? Had she by some uncanny triumph of deception managed to stand here, smile, talk calmly, easily, while in reality her spirit had departed and was wandering far? That, above all things, was what he should have known. Yet surely had she done so, he would have perceived it. No, he had gone alone, leaving her there unstirred, oblivious. But why should there be a richness in her voice, a richness not noticed before, an overflowing richness which seemed, as the spell just now had done, to spread out toward him, envelop him? For she was speaking again.

"I suppose it will take three weeks or so to haul the rest."

He was instantly alert and practical. He knew to a day—but before he spoke he said to himself, "Now why does she ask that?" If he would but chance a bold stroke he might turn the question to his advantage. He looked at her and smiled.

"I'd be suited if it took a year." Immediately his courage failed. She would think him forward, would walk away. But no, she did not seem to mind although she did not answer; she seemed rather not to have heard. Her eyes had left his and were glancing anxiously through the trees toward the grove of live-oaks.

"I must be going." Her voice was impersonal and

cool. Her eyes still fixed upon the grove, she moved off through the trees, the green gown shining on her slender rounded arms and swaying lightly down from her waist. He stood rooted, stupefied, while his spirit tugged and reached out after her. She turned and threw a swift and smiling half glance back at him and then was gone.

He continued to stare at the opening in the trees where she had last been seen until he became aware once more of the negroes, Rav and Logan. He glanced at them furtively. They piled the rails with studious attention.

CHAPTER VIII

THE only question now was, "What to do? How to do it?" Each successive morning lurching along on a load of rails for Beaumont, he figured, puzzled, wrestled with the problem until it seemed as though his mind was about to give out on him, as though one more effort would totally break him down, would turn his brains to mush and leave him as wandering and witless as Ben Scroggs' boy. Then he would ease up awhile and let his thoughts drift; but always they drifted toward the same beckoning shore, the shore beyond the dark dim waters of his bewilderment where the figure, shining, slim and softly rounded, in the green gown, was ever moving and just vanished among the trees. There was some solace in the sight but after awhile the impotent gazing wearied him, his mind came back to face the actual question, "What to do?" It was easy to say, "Go seek her out," but he knew that however much he might assure himself that he came of good stock and need feel ashamed before no man, in point of fact, he could not face the Colonel, not with such a notion in his head. And even if he could, he knew that to do so would be fatal, might mean that he would never see her again. The best thing to do was to wait and hope that she would once more come down to where the rails were being stacked.

If only something would happen,—anything. No,

not anything. That was a dangerous wish; he took it back. It would likely bring him bad luck to make a wish like that. Wish or no wish, anything might happen, though. She might go away, she might fall sick. For all he knew—his heart stopped, she might die. He smiled a little wearily to himself; that was a mighty fanciful idea. And yet his heart had stopped just the same.

Then, thus bedevilled until worn out, he turned angry. What ailed the girl anyhow? What did she think she was up to? Why had she come down there that day? To see the rails? He gave a short and mirthless laugh, then turned sombre. He wished to God he'd never heard of her.

But whether he dreamt of her or belittled her made no difference; daily he searched the grove at Beaumont for a sign; the grove of live-oaks and of Spanish moss remained inscrutable.

He longed for anything which might come along to distract his mind. Therefore, when one evening on the porch, his mother, who had of late been baffled and made somewhat timid by his cold aloofness, ventured to remark, "The Racker boys were here to-day. They left word for you that they's to be a fiddlers' contest at the school on Saturday," he answered, "That's fine," with a heartiness which he could feel surprised her. "That's fine," he repeated. "They's not been one since last February."

"You won that, too," she put in with quick pride. He did not answer. Yet he had won, he remembered of course. But he only did remember. Last February now seemed so long ago and he himself so different. No use to start thinking that way again. He roused himself.

"I reckon I better put in some licks on that fiddle," he said. He brought his fiddle out, dusted it off by the light of the doorway, and tuned it up. It sounded mighty listless; however, he cocked his chair back against the wall and struck up "The Arkansas Traveller." It was a surprise how badly he played,—no swing to the beat, no chime to the notes,—a chicken could squawk a better tune. He made an impatient shriek on the strings and stopped.

"I ain't going to win this time, I reckon."

Out of the dark came his mother's voice tinged with subdued reproachfulness. "You've practised none of late."

His father, reading the *Journal* inside the door, lifted his inexpressive face above the sheet. "A man can't play the fiddle cocked back in his chair," he remarked in a tone of well-considered disapproval. James looked up in exasperation. He felt these days as though his father were a stranger, and an irritating one. His mother, too, was a little strange, but his father more especially. Anyhow, what did the old man know of fiddling; James had heard him play. It had been a sorry show.

His father was speaking again, this time as if he knew everything in the world. "To play the fiddle a man has got to set square." James banged his feet down on the porch and with the fiddle underneath his arm walked far out among the trees.

But the tune came no better there and after awhile

even the idea in his mind of how it should be played was crowded out by a shame-faced picture of the way he had acted on the porch just now,—of his mother's distress, of his father's puzzled glance. His father was right. A man did have to set square to fiddle his best and anyhow, right or wrong, the old man had always done his best for him. He was a good man. And his mother,—well, he just ought not to be so ornery. He would not go back now till they had gone to bed, but he would not be so ornery any more. With the fiddle hanging silent between his knees he sat there till their bedroom light went out.

On Saturday night the schoolhouse near Racker's store was ablaze with lamps and candles borrowed from the neighborhood. The light streamed out the windows and shone in thin streaks between the logs of the side-walls to cast a fading glow among the trees where people drove up, hitched mules, formed small, low-spoken groups, or slipped away toward Old Man Racker's bar.

James Fraser took his fiddle from under the seat and followed his father and mother into the school building.

The benches were well filled with women and children who sat silent and motionless until the Frasers' footsteps sounded on the floor, then turned their heads slowly and slowly nodded to them in reserved and distant greeting.

"There's Jim Fraser," a small boy piped. "Hooray!" His mother checked him swiftly. She smiled and blushed. James tried to look unconscious but grinned a little. That small boy had made him feel a good deal more pleased to be there.

At the end of the room the teacher's desk had been pushed to one side of the platform and a row of chairs set out, on which now rested, wrapped in sacks or cloths or naked to the eye, half a dozen fiddles.

Three of the fiddlers stood in the corner by the platform. Big Tom MacGruder with the roan hair straggling down his neck propped a long arm against a log and towered over Esquire Wootten who had turned out in his black satin stock and steel-rimmed spectacles just like he did to try a case. The Squire blinked his little blue eyes up at Tom and nodded with suppressed earnestness. He was an earnest man, the Squire was, and an earnest fiddler, too, though he never won. As James came up the Squire's nods at Big Tom were shifted without interruption toward himself.

"How are you, James?" he said.

Big Tom swung around and dropped his hand on James' shoulder.

"Hi boy, how you comin' on?" He worked his sandy eyebrows in a grimace of friendliness.

Behind these two, leaning gracefully with folded arms against the wall, and ignoring their conversation, was Harry Horniblow, from Black Pocósin. His dark-brown tragic eyes stared at the floor, his narrow girlish chin hung down against his chest, the mouth half open as it always was, as though he were about to speak. But he never did speak except when drunk and then it was to break out in bursts of filth, uttered not with proper, hearty gusto, but with a harsh and desperate mockery. A puny, wild, uncomfortable fellow; but he could fiddle and would probably often win except that he put notions of his own into the old-time pieces and the judges did not like that.

"Howdy," he muttered without raising his eyes.

Big Tom had meanwhile got back to his topic.

"Why, dog my cats, if these Abolitionists ain't the meanest kind of scoun'rels." He stuck a huge fore-finger under the Squire's nose. "Suppose I tolled one of your shoats up into my hogpen and then wouldn't give him back." The Squire nodded. Big Tom had quite a following at his end of the county and must not be offended. "You'd say I was a thief, wouldn't you?"

"Well, yes, seh, I suppose I would," the Squire answered guardedly.

"Why, of course you would," Big Tom's voice bristled with impatience. "You'd say I'd enticed that shoat away and stole him. You'd say I was a thief and a low-down, pusillanimous cockroach to boot." The Squire hesitated to go so far, but Big Tom ignored him. "And that's just what the Yankee Abolitionists are doing,—enticing our niggers North and then won't give 'em back, and that's what makes me say what I say." Big Tom was having a good time. He owned no negroes himself and everything he possessed, including his fiddle, was mortgaged to the limit. But he liked a grievance, Big Tom did. His eyebrows bristled, his face was red, he shook his fist at the little Squire. "And on top of that they preach at us," he gave a great, short laugh of withering scorn. "Since when has a man that steals a mule been entitled to preach at a man who works one?"

The figurative transition from shoats to mules had left the Squire somewhat at sea.

"Of course, of course," he said nervously. Big Tom, who might have had a few drinks, was not placated.

"Of course, what?" he demanded suspiciously.

Luckily at this point the school-teacher came in. A low-set young fellow, about twenty-two, with a bull-pup face, he edged his way down the aisle grinning at all and calling them by name. His coat, worn shiny, stretched tight over his muscles and over his hands thrust into the pockets. Folks had thought he would be too young for the job but he had whipped all the big boys in school singly and together, and now kept good order. Hard-headed in more ways than one, and free from all conceit, he often said he didn't know much but would guarantee to impart what ignorance he had to all his pupils. He really did know a heap, however, and James remembered that when he boarded with them he would get up at four o'clock on a winter morning to study law books. Dougald Cameron, his name was, from up in Cumberland, and James liked him the most of anybody in the neighborhood. For that reason he merely grunted when Dougald came up to them.

"Hey Jim," the teacher said, "How you making out?" There was something square and steady in his voice as there was in the way he stood. "Squire, how are you, seh? Mr. Tom?" He turned back to James. "We weren't sure you'd be here. I'm glad you are."

"Yes," said James. "I'm here."

Big Tom, abolition wrongs still on his mind, swung
round.

"Teacher, what's the curse of this yere country?"
he demanded.

"Ignorance," said Dougald promptly.

"No, seh," said Tom, with violence. "The damn
Yankee Abolitionist. If you wasn't a teacher, you'd
know that."

Dougald grinned good-naturedly.

"Well, you can't get a man that knows everything
for three hundred dollars a year." While Tom was
seeking to adjust himself to this unexpected turn the
teacher went on. "I reckon we'd better start. These
folks have been here an hour or more."

"What about the other contestants?" said the Squire.

"They're down at the bar with the rest of the boys,
but I told Old Man Racker to roust 'em out. I expect
they're coming now."

And, indeed, with fragmentary songs and cheering
the patrons of Racker's bar were straggling up the hill.
They fell silent as they reached the door, entered with
sheepish grins, and stowed themselves away among the
crowd. All except the fiddlers; they came down the
aisle headed by Uncle Dunc, the neighborhood buffoon.
Red and reeking from Old Man Racker's bar, Uncle
Dunc blew out his walrus mustaches and slapped his
paunch.

"Heyo, folks!" he shouted. "Heyo! Eve'ybody
happy? How you all livin'?" He executed a little
step. The small boys whooped, the girls tittered, the
women looked askance. Behind him came Banjo Bill,

a dark, little pock-marked man, and the two rat-faced Racker twins who nudged each other and exchanged mean, mirthless smiles.

The fiddlers climbed up on the platform and taking their seats commenced a tremendous tuning up. The shuddering schoolhouse bulged with their vibrations until it seemed that one more note would burst it open and prostrate every man and woman there. Abruptly they ceased and sat back, gazing out over the people's heads, impassive and unconcerned. The schoolmaster climbed up and stood in front of them.

"I'll ask Mr. Racker and Mr. Roon to be the judges," he announced. "The prize will be two dollars for the best fiddler and a dollar for the next best." He turned to the contestants. "Why don't you gentlemen give them the 'Mississippi Sawyer' while I collect the money?"

Without an instant's hesitation the seven fiddles struck up the old jig tune at break-neck speed. Dougald Cameron stepped down among the crowd and was soon lost in intricate calculations with the heads of families.

When at last he came back on the platform they stopped their swiftly jogging music and became statues once more.

"I reckon we'd all like to hear Esquire Wootten first," said Dougald. "Esquire Wootten will play—" he bent an ear down toward the Squire, then straightened up—"'The Arkansas Traveller.'" He sat down on the platform's edge. The Squire rose, handed his bow and fiddle to James who sat next to him at the end of the row and moved his chair into the centre of the stage. At a serious nod James handed him back his fiddle. The Squire tucked it under his arm, spread out his short coat-tails carefully, and sat down. It took him a little time to adjust it under his chin against his high satin stock. He poised his bow and began a measured stamping with his foot. At the fourth beat he broke into the tune. Three times he played it through methodically, then standing up without emotion carried his chair back to the line.

"Now Mr. MacGruder will play—" said Dougald. "What tune, please?" he whispered. "'The Blockheaded Mule.'"

Big Tom hitched his chair forward, rubbed the red stubble on his chin with his bow, and tackled the tune with a vigor out of all proportion to his fiddle's faint squeaks. At the end he shot himself back into line defiantly with one great shove.

So it went on. The Racker twins played fast and badly, with a devil-may-care air and a meaning glance at the girls. Borrowing a fiddle, Banjo Bill played a tune in grim, perfunctory style as a mere accommodation. He was waiting his chance on the banjo underneath his chair.

"Uncle Dunc," Dougald grinned as he made the announcement, "will play, 'Sparrow in the Ash Box.'" The people rustled, nudged each other in anticipation. Hot and beaming, Uncle Dunc capered forward with his chair, bounced down on it and struck up the swift, jerky tune. He beat a tremendous rhythm with his feet, jerking his fat knees high in air. He called out figures while he played, "Fo'ward and back!... Swing you' partners!... Down the middle!" And at the end he shouted "Heyo folks!" and waved his fiddle round his head in large, expansive greeting. Encouraged by their silent grins, he planted his fiddle against his stomach and sawing away at a jig, performed a waddling, nimble-footed dance until a rip in his trouser-leg spread half-way up his ham. The people broke loose in one explosive shout and Uncle Dunc sat down well pleased and puffing mightily. James felt ashamed to see fiddling turned into such buffoonery. The old man ought to have more sense, and the people ought to have more sense, too. It looked like they preferred monkey-shines to music. They surely did; for now Harry Horni-blow was playing a piece that he'd got from God knows where or maybe made up himself, a kind of moaning, lonely piece played with a low, far-reaching cry that made James Fraser's hackles rise; but at the finish the people merely shifted awkwardly in their seats. He felt sorry for Harry, but he need not have. Indifferent, unperturbed, the sallow, girlish youth continued to finger the strings and stare into space as if he were alone and practising.

Now James' name was called; instinctively he gave a hitch to his chair. But immediately he knew that his heart was not in the business.

He was playing mechanically: "Money Musk" the piece was; he could hardly keep his mind on the tune; his thoughts and eyes wandered out over the people. That crowd of folks whose applause he had sought so keenly were now nothing to him. Even his father looking up at him critically but with firm confidence was little, somehow, to him now. Even his mother proudly expectant was less than she had been. Only one thing meant aught and there was no use to think about that. In fact, the idea of this contest was that it would take his mind off it. He smiled deep down inside himself. It hadn't worked that way.

When he finished he was conscious of a sort of void in the room; the people never applauded, it was not their way; but always before, he could feel their approval flowing out toward him. Now it was missing. He didn't mind though, except for his mother and for the small boy who had hollered out "Hooray! here's Jim!"

The contest moved along; each fiddler played again in turn and Banjo Bill got out his banjo by request and cut loose with "The Yaller Gal."

"I reckon we ought to give him fifty cents," said Dougald with enthusiasm. James nodded. He didn't care if they gave Bill all the money. He only wished he hadn't come himself,—in the last three years since he was fifteen he'd never been beat except by one stranger from Raleigh. And he wished, too, that his father and mother wouldn't keep looking at him.

There was a stir in the back of the room and a great craning of necks. A fine young man with a shiny walking-cane over the arm of his light plaid coat and an older man in mild side-whiskers and a beaver had entered and were making a way for some one.

James Fraser, as twice before, felt the air surcharged with tiny sparks and tinkling sounds. But why must she always change her dress? For now she had on a low-crowned hat with a plume along the side and her deep-purple gown ended in bracelets of fur around the wrists. He was just conscious of another proud, pale girl beside her. The blood was springing to his heart, to his cheeks, perhaps. He lowered his face.

At first he merely sat there scarcely breathing, floating, suspended on the bright and buoyant air, then as his thoughts took shape he wondered what had brought her here. The notion for a frolic, perhaps. Or had she come to hear him play? That was beyond all reason. Anyhow, she would hear him. He gripped the neck of his fiddle. Yes, she would hear him. When was his turn to come? How soon?

Again as he waited he felt the strangeness of this life. They two were now together, almost—were under one roof—in the same room. If life were real, he would walk down to her and take her hand. He could see himself doing so, and perhaps that picture was reality; perhaps this life, these walls, these stolid people were the dream. But hold on—not so fast—suppose he did so—did so even in his mind—how would she act? What would she say? Perhaps she would crimson, and start back, shocked, grieved, astounded. No! Let him not become so bold, even in his dreams.

But he could play and none take it amiss; that was what he was there for. He could play. Now, you Dougald, call my turn!

Then he was out in front, his knees spread wide, the fiddle well planted under his sharp chin. He hunched his shoulders in the tight coat, shot out the bony wrist of his bow hand, and grinned at all the folks. Two strong taps of his foot and he struck up "Leather Breeches"; not so fast at first but with a good, big, easy swing:

> "Mammy sent me off to school.
> Leather breeches and a lop-eared mule.
> I lit on a stump when the jinney shied
> But leather breeches saved my hide."

"Leather breeches—leather breeches—" He was swinging along now for sure. As he rounded into the chorus he gathered a little speed,—not too much—a man would hardly notice it, just enough to pick those folks up and carry them along.

A few of them began to tap softly on the floor, then more. Now for the chorus again—and make her roll! "Leather breeches—leather breeches—" the tapping grew to a steady stamping. They were with him now. "Leather breeches—leather breeches—" the schoolhouse rocked and trembled to their tramp. By shot! the whole round world was swinging to his fiddle. Once more he'd make it spin——

And now he'd quit. He shot the bow across the strings, jumped up and grinned at them. Seizing his chair, he took a long easy slide back to his place in line. They did not cheer him but they sat, rapt and eager, still tramping to the echo of his tune.

A few more pieces by the others and then the judges wagged their heads together. Dougald mounted the platform. "First prize to Mr. Tom MacGruder, second prize to Mr. James Fraser." The people rose in silence and began filing out the door. Dougald handed James a dollar in change.

"What ailed you the first round, Jim?"

"You started too late, son," his father said with grave disapproval. "A man's got to 'tend to his business when he fiddles." His mother merely looked at him unhappily. He avoided her eyes and though he knew they were following his he could not help a long searching glance toward the other end of the room. The elegant party from Beaumont had gone.

CHAPTER IX

NEXT day as, seated beneath a pine, he was finishing his meal at Beaumont, the Colonel's team, pulling a low-hung phaeton, came through the woods. The back seat was hidden by a fringed, white canopy, but on the front seat were the two young men who had been with her at the fiddlers' contest. James hastily stowed the remnants of his dinner behind a stump.

The younger man, wearing a broad Maracaibo straw hat and a linen suit, drove, and now that James looked at him, he guessed that he must be her brother, who was supposed to be away, attending a certain Harvard College in the North. Undoubtedly his fine-cut features and even his dark eyes somewhat resembled hers, but James liked him no better on that account. Indeed, he resented his presumption.

Sitting beside the college youth the other man, in a short reefer coat and a curious cap with ear-muffs tied up in a bow on top, stroked his side-whiskers and smoked a thin cigar. On the back seat underneath the canopy James could now see the proud, pale young lady of the previous evening and just make out beside her the corner of a green and shining skirt.

The phaeton pulled up and she, leaning forward across the proud young lady's knees to catch a glimpse of him, cried "How do you do?" and smiled. James Fraser took off his hat.

She jumped down from the phaeton and came toward him with her light swaying step. The whiskered stranger followed her. Her brother from the seat of the carriage turned and spoke to the proud young lady, who looked indifferently at James, smothered a yawn, and put up a small lace-bordered parasol.

James stepped forward to meet her until he was as close as he thought prudent; then he stopped and bowed, unable to think of anything to say. But she spoke quickly.

"That was surely a fine concert." She looked at her companion. "I don't suppose Mr. Higgins ever heard such playing before. He is from Boston."

Surely, James reflected, there must be something to say about Boston if a man only knew what it was. He felt a little bitter. These folks took him at an unfair advantage, ranging as they did so easily over such vast fields. These thoughts passed swiftly through his mind and vanished before the fundamental cordiality of the countryside.

"I hope you are enjoying your visit, seh," he said to Mr. Higgins.

For an instant Mr. Higgins seemed to be taken somewhat aback, then he responded heartily: "I should say so." But that seemed to be the limit of his resources. Again her skill was brought into play.

"You must have been surprised last night to see us all come in," she said to James.

"Well, yes, ma'am, I was, but I was well pleased though."

She laughed. He had never heard her laugh before. He cast down his eyes, lost for the moment in his thoughts. He had thought that he knew all her perfection but a man didn't know anything about her until he heard her laugh. There never was such music, such good nature, mirth, and charm. Now she was speaking again.

"My brother just came home from college. He broke down from over-work, he told Papa, and Mr. Higgins has come with him. . . ."

"To try," Mr. Higgins interposed, "to help him make up some of the ground he lost while he was over-working."

James eyed him with less respect. The fellow was only some kind of schoolmaster after all. He needn't to carry such a high head. Perhaps they made more of schoolmasters in Boston. The man's suit of clothes must have cost thirty dollars.

Mr. Higgins now addressed himself seriously to James. He knocked the ash off his cigar in preparation. James stepped on it to put out any chance spark among the pine-needles.

"It is very interesting," said Mr. Higgins, "to see the South after having read so much of it."

"Yes, seh," said James. "What all have you read?" he inquired politely.

"There is a great deal being written in the North," Mr. Higgins answered, "about the South. No doubt you have heard of the interest there in slavery?"

"Not much," James said. "Oh," he added casually, "I've heard that the abolitionists are stealing niggers." Again she laughed. Mr. Higgins stroked his whiskers.

"But surely," he said, "as a practical man you must have some opinion on the question of slavery."

James would have liked to make some profound observation, but he could merely say, "Well, the niggers are here and that's about all there is to it."

"But you do not esteem them highly," said Mr. Higgins with an air of discovery.

"Esteem?" James nearly grinned right in the stranger's face. But he only said, "Well, niggers is just niggers."

"But surely," Mr. Higgins was persistent, "they would develop into something better in a state of freedom."

That was too much. The man, beside being curious out of all reason, was a born fool.

"I'd like to see every free nigger shot," he answered briefly.

"Ah, indeed." Mr. Higgins' ruddy, complacent face first looked shocked, then glowed with conscious morality. "I suppose you slave owners all feel that way."

"We don't own any niggers," James answered shortly.

"But surely—" Mr. Higgins began.

"But we want to keep them in their place," James cut in with an air of finality and turned away to her. What ailed this Yankee, anyway, standing here asking nit-wit questions and leaving the lady out altogether?

"I hope your brother's health is better," he said.

"I'm sure it will be soon," she answered. "It was just a case of too many cigars and sherry cobblers, I'm afraid, and perhaps some faro mixed in."

It was delightful to hear her run on like this as if he

were a real friend instead of—instead of what? Not a stranger, that could not be possible. Yet what? While these thoughts passed through his head, Mr. Higgins' wandering eye had fallen on Logan and Rav who, having paused in their rail-piling to drink in the splendors of the party in the phaeton, now fell most assiduously to work again.

"By Jupiter!" he said, "there are two black boys now. I'd like to talk to them. Do you suppose they'd mind?" She gave him an amused and hopeless look.

"I reckon they can stand it." She started to call them over but Mr. Higgins was already on his way to the pile of rails.

"Well, what do you think of our Northern friend?" she asked.

"I expect he's a mighty clever gentleman," James answered evasively.

"Charles says that there are lots of them like that in Boston," she announced.

"Is that so?" He gave difficult but sincere credence to this information. He was about to add that Boston must be a mighty curious place, when she broke in.

"Let's listen to what he says." James nodded. There was intimacy in this.

"Well, my friends, you seem sufficiently contented," Mr. Higgins remarked; his voice was loud and jovial without sounding at ease. The negroes stopped work and stood, their eyes downcast, their hands hanging, half smiling in a deprecating manner. In his embarrassment Logan gripped the sand with his black toes, while the yellow negro, Rav, raised his eyes to the level of Mr. Higgins' waistcoat and licked his lips with his tongue.

"I said you seem sufficiently contented," said Mr. Higgins. The two stood as before, except that the smiles vanished and left them abject,—not that they did not aim to please this white man, but the crisply spoken syllables and the flatness of his intonation left them at sea as to whether the stranger intended greeting, question, or reproof. Mr. Higgins attributed their silence to profound and secret grief.

"I suppose your life, however, is hardly as easy as it seems." Rav, the thin yellow negro, did not reply. He knitted his brows in thought. He was beginning to have an inkling of the stranger's meaning. But Logan, the Guinea negro, though completely stunned by Mr. Higgins' speech and manner, spoke up promptly. It was necessary, he felt, that something should be done to placate this curious apparition. He therefore grinned widely with simulated merriment and thinly veiled anxiety, and muttered, "Yasso. Truth, too. Yasso. Ha!"

Mr. Higgins was somewhat disconcerted by the apparently insupportable delight with which Logan acknowledged a truth which one would think must be for him profoundly mournful. But he persisted.

"I suppose you would rather be free, eh?" He looked at each of them in turn. This time Rav understood but still he did not answer. He stole a glance at young Charles Prevost on the seat of the phaeton and at Charles' sister standing beside James Fraser. When he did speak it was with pleased self-importance but guardedly.

"Dat depen', suh, on de circumstance. Yes, suh, it depen' mightily. A heap of free niggers mighty bad off." Observing that Logan was straining to catch the meaning, Rav condescended to interpret for him. "White gent'man say, you want to be free?"

Logan's fixed grin vanished. He popped his eyes out in astonishment.

"Who? Me? Free? No." A look of triumphant cunning crossed his face as though he had detected a trap which had been skilfully set to catch him. "Whar rations come f'um den?"

"Ah, I see," said Mr. Higgins slowly in a tone pain-fully at variance with his words. He moved back to the phaeton.

"Extraordinary chaps, these black fellows, Charles."

Charles Prevost, who had been leaning down and talking to the young lady in the back of the phaeton, glanced up. His face, showing softly white beneath the shadow of his broad hat, had a look at once gallant and astute, but underlying these superficial aspects it held a boyishness, a sweetness, a fundamental and inde-structible innocence which, without effort, without knowledge of its power, or even of its own existence, would be able, James Fraser reluctantly admitted, to draw to itself the hearts of many men and women.

"I reckon they seem like that to you," he said to Mr. Higgins. "But then you seem so to them, too, I ex-pect." He smiled with a simple amusement which robbed his words of irony. The suggestion, however,

was enough to make Mr. Higgins moody. In the pause
Charles called to his sister, "Stewart, shall we go?"

James Fraser came to himself. During the time that
they had stood side by side, watching and listening, he
had grown to feel that the two of them were spectators
—that all the rest was a mere play which was being
enacted for their passing entertainment, or perhaps as
a trivial but sufficient pretext for them to be together.
But at this call for her he instantly knew to what fantastic lengths his thoughts had carried him. She belonged to the play and if there were a spectator, it was
himself alone. Or more likely, he reflected, she and
her party were the onlookers and he and the niggers
were the show. But this harsh, chill thought had
hardly taken form before it was blotted out by the
sense that she was leaving—going away—another moment and she would be gone.

Already she was moving toward the phaeton; catastrophe was imminent. He rallied to meet it, cast his
mind for some word to say, some word that would have
value and significance. Some word, above all, that
would bring her back.

"I loved mighty well to have you hear me play," he
said.

"You played so well," she answered. "The judges
must be crazy."

"That was the second time . . . you heard," he explained. His voice dropped to a whisper, toneless and
painfully labored. "I didn't play well till you came."
He felt utterly sick and strangled, like a dying man
trying to say a last word. And as if this final effort

had been too much for him, his furious heart stopped.
He walked beside her in a trance, a void, a consciousness after death, strangely and suddenly detached, impersonal, dissociated from the crisis which impended,
yet listening with supernatural acuteness for what she
would have to say. She did not speak. Raising his
eyes, he saw that they had reached the phaeton.

A little life flowed back in him, enough to let him
answer civilly when Charles Prevost reached a hand
down to him unaffectedly and said, "Hello, seh. I
don't reckon we're acquainted. You're the best fiddler
I ever did hear." And enough to make him before-
handed with Mr. Higgins in helping her into the phaeton.

Then his hat was off—the phaeton was moving away,
was flashing through the trees; it was gone, and he
had never seen her face.

But he must not stand forever staring after it.

As he turned away, his eye fell on her narrow footstep in the sand. That she had made. There she had
stood just now. Only a moment before. Now she was
gone. He locked his hands together. Deep within him
his heart, beating against its prison, cried out, "Come
back—come back!"

CHAPTER X

AFTER that, each day as he drove his load of rails to Beaumont, he said to himself, "If she don't come by, I'll go to look for her."

He could no longer argue to himself that he might have been caught up by a foolish dream, a passing fancy; and however beyond all reason it might seem, he no longer believed that he meant nothing to her. So far the thing was clear, was settled. But that only brought him up against the question as to what it all would lead to. He was on dangerous ground.

Yet he would not turn back. Perhaps he could not. At any rate, no thought was farther from his mind. Just what he should do he did not know. Could he not, he wondered, at least get himself a little fixed up so that when she came by where he was working he would make a better showing? Then she could see that he was different from the ordinary run of country fellows, that he had a little style to him. His mother was making him a couple of new shirts. So far so good. But a shirt wouldn't help much while he still wore those copperas breeches. He reflected.

At Old Man Racker's there was displayed among the litter of hand-saws, steel-traps, log-chains, brogans, overalls, and woodenware, a brown kersey suit which he had never noticed much till lately. But on the last few Saturday nights he had been looking at it covertly. It seemed to be about his size. And the last time of all he had heard Old Man Racker name its price. Nine dollars. That had set him thinking more than ever. Each birthday since he was born his father had put fifty cents aside for him, put it in a separate pocket of the horsehide wallet that held the family fortune. The sum had reached nine dollars and a half. Leaning back on the load of rails, he drummed his fingers on his big-boned knee. Yes, sir, that was surely something to think about.

As if the very notion of the suit were bringing him good fortune, that evening, driving home through the woods beyond the Colonel's lodge, he saw her coming toward him on a little chestnut horse. Her dark blue habit followed her figure to the waist, then flowed down over the horse's shining flank. Her broad felt hat shaded her face, its brim curled up around a drooping feather.

As she came nearer through long shadows and sun-light gleaming level on the needle-covered ground, he felt, in the midst of triumphant exaltation, a pang that he was not wearing the suit right now.

The chestnut's slim white pasterns twinkled against the sand. The mule pricked up his ears, the chestnut laid back his and sidled, flared his nostrils, breathed out disdain.

For an instant James Fraser was preoccupied in fig-uring what the etiquette of this unforeseen situation demanded. If she were afoot he ought to get down. But would it look out of the way, since she was on horseback? Yet if he stayed on the wagon's high seat he would tower above her and that did not seem right. Then he remembered that when he stopped he might set the brake between the hind wheels. He could get down to do that.

Standing bareheaded, with a hand on the wheel, he made out to smile. But now that she was close, had halted, now that her eyes, almost concealed beneath her hat, were on him, he felt a swift and unexpected thrust of sadness. Exquisite the moment surely was. Yet in that instant of unhappy insight he saw it only as an exquisite premonition of disaster.

But he must smile in answer to that slow, warm smile of hers. And speak as well.

"You're out late," he said.

"I'll be home long before you."

"Well," he observed, "I reckon you ought to be."

"I knew you'd say so," she eyed him with dissatisfaction, "but I don't see why. What makes the difference?"

"The difference is that you are pretty and a lady." She ignored the compliment. "I think that makes too much difference." She ran her gloved hand up the chestnut's mane. "I'd like to be a man."

"What makes you say such a thing?" His tone was scandalized.

"Well," she countered, "how would you like to be a woman?"

He looked straight at her and grinned. "I reckon I'd rather have things just like they are."

She laughed. "Then I reckon I'd better be getting home. It will be dark in half an hour."

"But it won't take more than ten minutes," he pointed out hastily.

She pretended gravity. "You've changed your tune too late. My feelings are hurt. No, I must be getting on," she added seriously. "My father and the others expected me an hour ago."

"Did you get lost?"

"Lost?" She was scornful. "I reckon I know this country as well as any old gray fox. No; I went up to see Linda, my old mammy. Her husband is burning tar above the Northern Branch. I go out there to talk to her because she has the rheumatism. Generally I come home the short way across the branch, but the water is up now since the rains and Golden"—she patted the chestnut's neck—"is such a fool about water. He either won't go near it or else he gets in and lies down like an alligator. To-night he wouldn't look at it. So I had to come back around. I wish," she concluded in disgust, "I'd had some one to holler at him from behind."

"If you come by when I'm there with rails," he put in quietly, "I could do that."

"Thank you," she said. "I reckon the stream will be down by next week." She took up the reins. "I must go. Good night."

He took his hand from the wheel and bowed. "You ought not to try that deep water by yourself."

The morning when he drove his load of rails to Beaumont seated aloft in the new brown suit from Old Man Racker's was a day of triumph. But it was a triumph,

he reflected as he jolted along, which had been won
at heavy cost. It had meant long, exhausting, and
on his part, never frank negotiations with his parents
for the possession of the nine dollars and a half. To
his father the idea of buying a suit of clothes before
he had stopped growing was incomprehensible, while
by his mother, James suspected, the idea was understood only too well. In the end they had decided that
he had always been a pretty good boy and a good
worker, and that by some principle of abstract and un-
palatable justice he was by now entitled to make a fool
of himself if he chose. They even reached the point of
agreeing that it might be better for him to spend the
money on a suit of clothes rather than for some possibly even more disreputable purpose later on.

His difficulties had not ended there. The trading
with Old Man Racker had taken place of necessity in
the presence of the Saturday night crowd, who had
contributed comment, advice, and even more unwel-
come speculations as to James' underlying purpose.
And though he had done his best to outstay them at
the store, they had with cordiality insisted on standing by him in a body to see the suit tried on. The final
struggle had occurred this morning. His father's stupefaction at his buying the suit was nothing to his
state of mind on learning that James proposed to wear
it to work. But here James' mother had intervened.
She had approved of the suit no more than his father,
but she knew, James guessed, that once bought this
was the logical result. He had stood his ground and
left home wearing his handsome clothes. But not

without glances from his parents which seemed to bid
him a sombre farewell on his departure for some lurk-
ing and discreditable catastrophe.

However, once well on his way, his spirits rose. He
had seen and chatted with her twice since the evening
he met her on her chestnut horse. The Northern Branch
had gone down and once a week she came by on her
way to see her old nurse. Wednesday it had been, both
times, and to-day was Wednesday again. And he was
wearing the new suit of nice brown kersey, which fitted
him as nothing had ever fitted him before.

But waiting that afternoon, he did not quite dare to
put his coat on. It would look too much like showing
off, especially since the day was warm. And anyhow
his new trousers and the shirt his mother had made
looked pretty good. The coat, neatly folded, lay beside a tree.

The hoof-beats on the sand were not those of the
chestnut horse. But he looked up eagerly. A sleek
piebald pony pulled a little wicker carriage like an
easy chair on wheels. He eyed the rig with something
like contempt. It was no good for anything—a flimsy
little toy. At the same time he felt a twinge of envious
admiration for folks with the means, the independence,
and the fantastic notion to ride around in anything so
useless. Did the ridiculous little trap belong to some
visiting planter's daughter or to her?

The cords in his neck went taut, his heart died down
to nothing, then started hammering at a small vein in
his forehead. Over the wicker dashboard he caught a
glimpse of white-sprigged muslin and the eyes of Stew-

art Prevost. Beside her peeped the face of a little negro
boy, shy but preternaturally observant.

"You're not riding the chestnut," he said.

She leaned forward on the seat. "Isn't it a shame!
He overreached. I think he did it shying at a turkey
buzzard. It got up right under his nose."

"That surely is too bad, ma'am. I'll tell you what,"
his tone was judicial, "you just cover that cut with
warm tar. It'll cure it up right away."

She nodded emphatically. "That's just exactly what
I did."

"You didn't do it yourself, though?" He looked at
her amazed. "A horse is liable to kick like fun against
warm tar."

She smiled. "That's exactly what he did, too. But
I was watching. And then I hollered at him and he
stopped."

He frowned. "Why didn't you let one of the niggers
do that?"

"They were scared," she answered simply. "Golden
has all the niggers scared." Her tone was proud.

"I wish I'd been around. I could have done it. Animals," he explained shyly, "will most generally let me
handle them."

"Well, he's all right now, I reckon." Her eye wandered over him. "Why, I declare, that looks like a
brand-new suit."

He flushed deeply. "I got it a little while back," he
mumbled, failing utterly in his effort to be casual. "It's
just a plain suit."

"It's a pretty color." She looked beyond him. "And
there's the coat!"

"Yes, ma'am. I laid it off. It's so warm."

She jumped down from the carriage. "Dansy, hold the pony."

The little negro went to the pony's head and attempted to raise it from the ground. The pony kept his short, stout neck obstinately bent and continued to graze, oblivious. On his next attempt Dansy discovered that his trousers, incredibly too large, were about to leave him. He gathered them spasmodically around himself and thereafter stood a respectful observer of the pony's foraging.

With a laugh at Dansy she moved to where the coat lay on the grass, and James Fraser, though filled with foreboding, must follow her.

"Put it on," she said. "Let me see how it looks."

His heart dropped like a plummet. "It looks all right," he muttered in a suffocated voice. "Just like the trousers."

"Put it on."

"It's nothing special," he pleaded. "Just a ordinary store suit."

"Let me see."

My Lord, he might as well give up! With a sigh he picked up the coat, put it on and stood before her grinning miserably.

"Now button it up."

God in the mountain! That, too. What if those niggers were to see him? He stole a glance down the branch. They were out of sight. With paralyzed fingers he fumbled at the buttons.

"You surely do look nice." Her glance was boldly

admiring, yet somewhat mocking too. His heart fluttered and quailed. Now she was walking around him in a circle. He heard her pause behind him and say judicially, "There's a little wrinkle at the back between the shoulders. It's because you stand so straight," she explained. Her fingers touched the wrinkle. A fire shot through him. He wanted to turn and seize her. Instead he mumbled, "There's some one coming," in a strangled tone and tore himself away.

She clapped her hands lightly together. "You surely do look nice!" she cried.

He fumbled once more at the buttons, took his coat off awkwardly and laid it on the ground. He had not the courage to look at her but he could feel veiled and mischievous amusement in her eyes.

Another horse was coming down the hill. My Lord, it must be the Colonel! But no, it was the black horse he had seen at the tournament and on it, still darkly dressed, was the pale Black Knight. He rode up looking straight at Stewart Prevost with light, sardonic eyes. His broad black hat came off in a sweeping arc.

"Good evening, Miss Stewart."

Though she looked straight back at him and smiled she seemed to flush.

"Good evening, Catlin. I didn't know you were coming over."

He cast a swift cold glance at James.

"I'm sure you didn't."

"You must stay for supper," she put in hastily, then paused an instant and looked down at the ground. That instant's pause decided James. He picked up his coat.

"Good evening, ma'am," he said, and started with long strides back to the pile of rails. Behind him he heard the Black Knight dismount to help her into the carriage. He heard the hoofs of the pony and of the black horse moving off together. But though she was riding away with Catlin Gregg he did not dwell on that. His thoughts travelled back to the figure he had cut just now; he built up the whole absurd picture,— himself standing, ill at ease, in the new coat, grinning like an ape, and she walking around him and laughing at him. And maybe too, he had been seen from the hill, been laughed at by Catlin Gregg. Maybe right now as those two rode between the trees he was a joke they shared.

He twisted his lips in a grimace of shame. He could be little more than a joke to her. For had he not waited long enough, given her all the chance his self-respect would allow, for her to introduce him? And what had she done. She had hesitated, looked away, let him stand deserted.

CHAPTER XI

NEXT day, to his surprise, while waiting in the pasture for Rav and Logan to unload the rails, he saw her white dress moving among the trees on the high ground above him. She did not come toward him but walked along the ridge. She stopped and looked down to where he sat. He tied the mule up to a tree and followed her.

As soon as he had come near she turned and it seemed to him that perhaps she flushed; at any rate she looked away, but by the time he was close enough to speak she was well poised again and even somewhat distant in her manner.

"You are not eating your luncheon?" she said with a cool smile.

"I saw you."

"But a man must eat." She gave him a sly look.

What was all this talk about eating? He hadn't come up here to talk about eating.

"I can eat any time," he answered briefly. "You are afoot to-day."

"My brother has the pony cart. He and Catlin and Lulu Gregg have taken Mr. Higgins on a picnic." James recalled without pleasure the existence of these others. "My father couldn't go, so I stayed home."

He wondered idly what ailed the Colonel.

"I hope the Colonel is well, ma'am." He made the inquiry as a matter of course, but, while he spoke the words, the surprising and despicable thought crept into his mind that if the Colonel were sick he would be comfortably out of the way.

"Oh, yes," she was saying, "he is quite well, thank you, but they have been having trouble with the pounding mill. Papa is afraid he won't get our rice to Wilmington in time for the next Liverpool boat."

She was being pleasant. Maybe she was trying to make up for the day before.

"Well, what seems to be the trouble?" he asked judicially.

She became animated. "I don't know. I wish I did, but you know they never will tell a woman anything." James nodded. She went on, "The negro engineer is sick and the overseer doesn't understand engines. Everything seems to be all right about the engine but they don't get any power. The October crop will be coming along right soon and half the September crop is still in the shocks." From where they stood they could see a line of negroes carrying yellow bundles of rice on their heads and another gang in the next field chopping with sickles at the yellow grain.

"I wish I knew about such things," she said.

"Well," he admitted, "steam-engines are mighty interesting things to study,—for a man, that is."

"Oh," she said, "do you know about steam-engines?"

James was about to admit that his study of engines had been limited to the *Harper's Weekly* picture in Old Man Racker's bar, but he thought better of it. For one thing there was no use to mention Old Man Racker's bar to her and then for all he knew, maybe he did know about engines; anyhow, there was no use denying it.

He decided to shift to safer ground. "Why don't he borrow an engineer from one of the other plantations?"

"Papa despises to ask for favors, and they are all so busy thrashing now."

"But anybody would be pleased to help the Colonel," he said heartily.

"Well, he did have Major Gregg's negro engineer come over. The Major's man fussed around but the engine don't seem to run any better for it."

"How's the Major's crop coming on?" he asked suspiciously.

"I don't know. I asked Lulu Gregg but she don't know a thing that goes on, on their plantation."

"Well, maybe the Major told his nigger to try to fix the engine," he observed acutely, "and maybe not. I reckon if the Major's crop is first to reach Wilmington it will fetch the biggest price."

An angry flush sprang to her cheeks. "Major Gregg is a gentleman," she said shortly, " and a friend of ours."

To this he did not reply. He had blundered head-on against a rule of planter etiquette. All the same, he reflected obstinately, it was not common sense to think that one man would help another to beat him to a market.

But now her flash of anger had passed. She looked at him kindly.

"I declare you're as jealous for our crop as if you'd helped to raise it," she said.

"I don't want any one to take advantage of the Colonel," he answered firmly.

"Well, you needn't to worry about Major Gregg," she said.

"I expect not," he answered. "But still," he went on doggedly, "the engine is not running right."

"I know," she sighed. "I wish I were a man."

"I'm glad you're not," he answered. "You said that once before."

She gave him a look of humorous archness, started to speak, checked herself, turned grave. "I'd like to be of some use," she said slowly.

"Well, I reckon there's plenty to do around the house, and with all the nigger women to look after," he answered.

"Oh yes," she said. "There's a-plenty. You know, I think that's what wore my poor mother out. She never got a rest, and she could do things a heap better and easier than I can. There's work enough," she reflected, "but it's always the same. You never get anywhere."

"Well, a man's work is always the same, too," he replied. "It changes with the seasons but it never gets any different."

"But a man is free," she said. "He can go where he likes, he can travel, he can go into politics."

To this he did not reply. It might be true enough of her world but had little to do with him.

"Well, I reckon you can travel," he suggested. "Don't you all go North in the summer?"

"We used to go to Saratoga," she admitted, "but we don't any more. The Yankees began asking our servants if they would like to be free. We go to the mountains now. But anyhow that's not travel." Her tone was disdainful. "Resorts are all the same. Nothing ever happens there. The ladies sit around and talk all day and the men play billiards and drink cobblers and make pretty speeches to the ladies."

He did not comment on this last remark but he pondered it with satisfaction. So pretty speeches then did not mean everything to her.

"I'd like to go around the world all by myself," she said.

"I expect most people would like to do something different from what they are doing," he observed.

"Yes," she answered. "What would you like?"

"Me? Oh, I don't know. I reckon I'd like to fiddle the best in the world. Or maybe I'd like to make steam locomotives and run them."

"Why don't you do it?" she urged.

"A man can't make a living fiddling."

"But the railroad. Couldn't you go out West where they are building them?"

Profound disappointment overwhelmed him. After all there was between them, she could casually urge that he should go away. It had, as he suspected, meant nothing, then, to her. A bitter thought struck at him. Perhaps she wanted him to go. It vanished swiftly but left him chilled.

"I reckon my dad could not make out without me," he answered dully.

"But you would make much more money in the end."

He turned on her, ironical and grim, "In the end that

would be fine! But what about now? It takes money
to go West."

"Yes," she said easily. "It would take some money.
But then you'd get it back."

Anger surged up, darkened his eyes. "You planters
don't know how people like us live." He looked away.

She was distressed. "I suppose money is scarce with
you. I'd never thought of that."

"I reckon you never did. Planters think that the
difference between themselves and us is that they have
family." He favored her with a derisive half-grin.
"But it's that they have money."

She colored brightly. "That is not a fair thing to
say." She paused, "I don't know much about money."
She looked up at him, hesitated, looked away. "But I
have some of my own and if you would like to go out
West, I could help——"

That should have melted him. He knew it in his
heart. Instead he rushed to meet the low suspicions
which crowded toward him. Why had she come to-day,
alone, on foot? To talk to him, without a doubt. And
he in his fatuous conceit had thought at first that it was
because she felt some eagerness to see him. But now
the truth was clear even to his blind eyes. Had not
Catlin Gregg taken in the situation at one cold glance?
Had not she hesitated, been confused? She had been
caught. The game was up. Now she must get rid of
him. That was why she came. And had she not been
clever—the way she had led him on to talk just now?
What means simpler than to pay his passage West?
Clever. She had made one mistake though. By her

offer she had placed him in the class of poor whites, landless, niggerless, prideless outcasts ever ready to accept the planters' dole or even to nibble surreptitiously around the edges of their abundance. By shot, she took him for a cracker! He turned his back.

"You reckon I'd take money from you?" His voice was tight and small. "You think I'm just like any cracker in the sticks—humbly glad to get a dollar from my betters. You think that outside your own selves and the other planters, folks are all poor trash, worthless, shiftless, hanging 'round hoping for a few cents or a basket of cold rations." He ought to stop. But he was going on. "Let me tell you. My folks may not have land and niggers but they know how to hold up their heads. We're not beholden to any one alive!"

In the pause which followed she did not speak. And he, lost in folly, must fill the silence with a final fling.

"Keep the money."

He raised his hat stiffly and walked away not looking behind but conscious that she gazed after him.

He had not gone many steps before remorse and self-contempt overwhelmed him. He wanted to turn, run back to her. But hard pride formed like a lump in his throat and stuck there. He would act as he pleased, nothing could stop him; and right or wrong, he would never hang his head before anybody. But the lump in his throat oppressed him, choked him, almost sickened him. He cast a shamed-faced, desperately anxious look behind. In her white-sprigged muslin she stood just as he had left her, as though struck motionless by the manner of his departure. At the sight, the lump in his throat, the hardness of his heart, the very fibre of his bones began to melt. He must go back to her. But she saw he was looking at her and, turning, walked quickly away through the trees.

His muscles tightened to run after her, no longer for the purpose of making it up with her or for any purpose save pursuit itself. He wanted to run,—to hunt her,— catch her.

The brief, wild instant passed leaving him cold and sullen. Walking on down the hill, he gave himself up to bitter, fatuous reasoning. The blame was hers; he had been willing to humble himself before her, something he had never done to any one before, but she would not wait for him. Well, let her go, then.

As he hitched up the mule his fingers were numb; he felt faint and ill with anger, with frustration and with a sense of his own fatuity. He had started up that hill to talk to her, confident and eager. Now things were all messed up and he was sick at heart. But did he not know why? Had he not acted like a baby and a fool? He jerked a strap tight. No, by God! a man had to show some proper pride and self-respect.

CHAPTER XII

But as the days passed and he did not see her again he drew less comfort from the conviction that he had played a manly, self-respecting part; the conviction still remained, though there were moments when he bitterly and darkly suspected it. And even at its strongest it ceased to fortify him against the mounting waves of desolation which swept over him. What did it matter how much the independent man he was? He was now alone, bereft.

For a time he lived to himself, apart, in suspicious, over-sensitive silence; but in the end he was drawn to his mother, from whom of late he had seemed estranged, as though she could protect him from ill fortune or perhaps from his own folly. And yet when the moment came, when sitting alone with her one evening on the porch, her rude but kind and anxious voice had reached him through the dark, hesitant, awkward, yearning toward him, "What ails you, son? You don't seem yourself of late. Is there aught on your mind?" his heart, despite its loneliness, had closed against her. For a moment he had longed, had fought to speak up. It was no use.

"Oh, I'm all right," he mumbled gruffly. He seemed to feel her worn hand, stretched out to touch him, hesitate, falter, fall to her side defeated.

And he too was defeated, as he felt, by this queer life of hostile circumstance without and a hostile, senseless nature of his own within. At times it was as though his spirit, meant to be free, struggled in vain against the bonds of fate; or again he thought that the bondage had been laid upon him by himself alone.

This last idea gained strength, took hold of him. He came to feel, between the periods of blank desolation, that within him lay the power to break the spell. Whether he pictured her as vanishing through the trees or as still standing, casting after him a wounded, inquiring glance, he felt that he must seek her out, that he had only to find her and all would be well. It was no use to reason, to argue, the matter was beyond all that. It was a question of strength, of blind daring and blinder faith which would somehow of itself dissolve all troubles and bring its own desire to pass.

Why, he told himself, growing bolder, he had puzzled over things without need, made them more difficult than they were. It was simple enough, he saw that now; and he saw simple and striking pictures of what he was to do. He was to go to her, stand before her, humbly as he ought but without abasement, and tell her that she was beautiful and good and that he had been a fool. He seized the vision, hugged it to him, dwelt on it till he could see every fold in her dress, every soft change of her gray eyes. It came to hold for him the certainty of fact, so much so that he drew real comfort from it and ease of mind. But he was no less eager to enact the scene, to set all doubts at rest. On the first clear moonlight night he would go.

On a Friday evening, striding through the shadows and the faint scattered silver of a crescent moon, he was on his way to Beaumont. The shadows were gently shifted by an evening breeze, the moon and stars seemed sharpened by the first hint of autumn in the air. He stepped along briskly, cool and vigorous, one arm swinging free, the other elbow pressing against the fiddle in its green flannel cloth. At every stride the bow inside the cloth ticked rhythmically against the fiddle's back; he wished he knew how many ticks would take him to Beaumont, so that he could count them.

It had only occurred to him to bring the fiddle at the last moment, but he was mighty glad he had thought of it. There was nothing else which he could bring her that she did not have; but he could play a few tunes: she would like that. And playing just for her, he would make good music. All the same he wished he had practised more of late.

He passed the slumbering lodge gate and the great live-oaks. The fences made a lattice pattern along the road, the fodder stacks loomed in the moonlight, he heard the nibbling of night-grazing sheep and down by the quarters a negro's endless, aimless song. Then the lights of the house—her house—peeped through the grove; he quickened his pace. Once he was among the trees the lights appeared to vanish. Not knowing their habits, he feared for a moment that they might have gone to bed like country folks as it was now near eight o'clock. He hurried faster until he saw that the house, screened till now by branches and Spanish moss, was actually ablaze in every room. To see it thus lit up filled him with immense relief and with admiration, also. This great, glowing hive called to his mind the sight he had once had of the night packet passing down the river, her many lighted ports and cabin windows forming one harmonious vision of airy and mysterious splendor.

Next, an uneasy question rose—perhaps all these lights betokened a festivity, an elegant gathering. His heart sank. For him that would be the worst of all. But maybe they lit their house that way every night. He wished he knew their customs better. At any rate there were no carriages before the door.

Stepping cautiously across the porch he could hear no unusual hum within. He let the knocker fall. Its echo died; he stood listening to the light, wooden whirr of the frogs in the rice fields below. The moonlight touched the level floor of mist which lay above them and near at hand it threw deep, soft shadows among the foliage of the two great myrtle trees which flanked the steps. The door was opened by the yellow negro boy. James took a half step forward and looked at the negro disapprovingly.

"I want to see Miss Prevost," he said.

The boy's mouth, set in an impudent grin, fell ajar; he stared at James with stupefaction, with stupefaction so profound and undisguised that it drove straight into James' heart, chilled it, shook its high confidence. His errand, seeming just now simple, natural, inevitable, was suddenly clouded with doubt, with the shadow of folly, of absurdity. His errand was grotesque, even this nigger knew that much. He gripped his hands tightly at his sides. But was it? He knew his own mind. Was he going to let a nigger stare him out of it?

"You hyear me?" his voice was hard and taut. "I want to see Miss Prevost."

The negro turned and fled.

The worst was over, he had stood his ground, put doubt to flight. Now when she came the rest would be easier. He would ask her to sit down on the porch and there in the shadows he would talk to her as he had planned. Maybe she would walk a little way among the trees with him, maybe she would take a seat on an old gnarly root and let him play a tune or two. If he could only play once—for her—alone—there would never be any trouble between them after that. He could see her now seated on the broad low root, her dress flowing gracefully down from her waist and spreading on the ground, the trunk against which she leaned shading her slim, strong body and seeming gravely to take it under its protection, the moonlight slipping through the branches to touch her hair, to touch her soft delightful arms.

The footsteps which broke in on his dream were not hers. Instead, the Colonel stood before him bending forward a little in his tight blue coat and peering, but with no effect of rudeness, to make out who he was.

"Why—" the Colonel swiftly checked astonishment. "Oh, young Fraser. Good evening." He paused. His keen blue eyes took in the fiddle under James' arm and instantly withdrew.

Mechanically James took off his hat. He must speak.

"Good evening, seh—" Now what? In a blinding instant he knew that he was doomed. A back-country boy in cow-hide brogans calling on the Colonel's daughter. He had gone mad. There was no hope for him now —or ever. Then the whirling chaos of his brain bore to the surface a shred of desperate courage. Let him go down fighting. There was nothing to lose.

"I came to see Miss Stewart," he murmured in a strange, far-off voice.

The Colonel's straight back stiffened imperceptibly, but his courteous expression did not change a hair's breadth.

"To see my daughter," he echoed in a grave, utterly impersonal tone.

"Yes, seh."

"Will you kindly wait here?" Without pausing for James' answer the Colonel faced about and walked slowly down the long hall, passing before the dark stern portrait, then turning into the room where she must be.

With the Colonel's departure some faint hope revived within him. The Colonel, he told himself, had at least gone to tell her—that much at least was gained—and she would surely come out. But then what would he say? How would he act? For he knew well enough that the Colonel would remain with her most punctiliously. He would not be able to say to her the things that he had come to tell her; and would he be able to say anything else, with the Colonel there, so polite and grim? It would be impossible; he almost wished she would not come. But no. The very thought of her just within the house made him forget all else and simply long to see her, face to face. For an instant he had the frantic notion of calling out her name. But that would never be forgiven, it would gain him nothing, even from her.

The Colonel was coming back again. His heart pounded in a tumult of eagerness to see her, of fear, of chill prostration at his dilemma.

The Colonel did not speak until he had stopped square in front of James.

"My daughter is engaged at present." The words were said in a slow, courtly tone but with unmistakable emphasis. James Fraser saw the full meaning of the speech, felt the full measure of the blow. But as if it were not enough, the Colonel went on with a quiet gravity which for an instant muffled the stinging force of his words: "If in the future she—she should be at leisure, she will be pleased to let you know."

James Fraser felt his soul shaken within him. It seemed to topple, to fall through unnumbered abysses of dark disaster, to lie prone and lifeless in some un-fathomable void.

And yet not wholly lifeless—now it struggled feebly, now it put forth some tiny, indestructible residue of strength and, rising up, whispered to him that he must hold himself erect, must bear himself with dignity be-fore the Colonel. Dignity. He seized on the word, he clung to it. Here was something that he must do—something that he must maintain—maintain blindly, unquestioningly, hopelessly, for its own sake. Dignity. He inclined his head gravely without haste, without humility, without confusion.

He tried his best to speak carefully and exactly though his tongue was thick and singularly awkward.

"Yes, seh, I reckon I understand. You need not to worry about that. Good night."

"Good night—" said the Colonel and hesitated, "—my boy. I am sorry."

To James' amazement the Colonel held out his hand. James Fraser was betrayed into starting back, into flushing darkly, but immediately he was steady once more.

"No, seh," he said. "Excuse me, but I don't shake hands where I'm not wanted." He turned and stepped carefully down between the myrtle trees and along the path to the driveway. As he passed around the end of the house he was conscious that the Colonel still stood in the doorway looking after him. He heard the door close. Instantly, at the sound, his courage, his firm high bearing left him. A shudder seized him. Like a man with the ague he was shaken with passion, with anger, with fierce despair. His head swam so that he had to lean against the horse-block, grip it with his hands. The fit passed, leaving him deathly cold; but now he could walk on.

As he raised himself to go he heard the sound of music in the house,—the shallow, heartless tinkle of a mandolin. He gripped his fiddle under his arm and started running.

CHAPTER XIII

FAR down the river the steamboat fluted. With her slender smokestack rising high between her hunched paddle boxes, she looked at a distance like a queer, unwieldy swan. A tuft of steam preceded another quavering whistle; shrouded in a heavy fulmination of fatwood smoke she waddled close in and after many thunderous churnings of her paddles and a bedlam of signals from her engine-room bell, succeeded in dealing the pier a shivering blow. Her gang-plank cracked down on the pier head, a negro deck-hand slid ashore and picked up James Fraser's carpet-bag. From the gilded pilot-house aloft a furry face leaned down and shouted, "Anybody else?" James shook his head and went aboard.

In the hold all was dark except for a small window where a boy with a blue cap cocked over one eye looked at James inquiringly. Irresolute, James stared back at him.

"Deck or saloon?" said the young boy briskly.

"How's that?"

"What class passage?"

"I reckon I want a cheap seat," said James slowly. The young man grinned and shoved a pasteboard across the counter. "Two bits. You go there." He pointed forward. James drew a quarter from his pocket and laid it down gingerly.

"I'm obliged," he said.

He made his way between windlasses, coiled hawsers, and big black iron cleats and, taking a good grip of the rail, peered cautiously over the side. Already the water slipped swiftly by. He wished to go up in the bows where the even scrolls of foam divided and reared up their heads, but fearing that this would make him conspicuous to the elegant passengers on the deck above, he contented himself with leaning on the railing and gazing at the receding shore line.

It would not be much further up the river, he knew, till he could see the rice fields, the terrace, and tall unpainted house at Beaumont. He would be able to see it but he did not want to. Not ever. Not so long as he lived. Turning away, he went to the other rail and stared at the distant yellow sandy bluffs crested with foliage, at the river's smooth blue floor, at the bubbles and flashes of foam which coasted past the vessel's side.

They must be passing Beaumont now. Resolutely he kept his eyes fixed on the water, streaked with curdling white and green, ridged with smooth furrows which spread wide, slid away forever.

A sudden fear seized him. What if the Colonel's signal flag were up? The boat would then put right in to the wharf. And when it got there, the Colonel himself might be waiting to come aboard. Or she. By shot! rather than catch a sight of them again he would drop swiftly over the side and swim away through those pale-green indifferent waves.

But the boat held straight on its course. The danger now was past. He dared to look around.

Both river banks stretched away, remote, monotonous and uninhabited. At times they passed a grassy island, or the tilted poles of a fish weir, but otherwise the scene remained unchanged. In this solemn monotone of sky and water and distant flanking woods, his mind, no longer distracted with novelty and the sense of dangerous adventure, could swing like the boat through vacancy. Only it swung back—not back to the night at Beaumont, to the tinkling mandolin, the sound of his own running feet—that he would not allow—at least not more than that; he hurried away from it, leaving the tall dark gables behind him as he had done before. He fastened firmly on the detailed preparations for his departure. The preparations, now that he came to think of it, had been made by his mother with surprising willingness. He had said, "I reckon I'd like to go away a spell," and looked askance, expecting a powerful fuss. She merely answered soberly, "Where do you aim to go to, son?"

He paused in his thoughts. Had she heard him pacing during all that sleepless, half-crazed night before? How much did she know? How much did she guess?

And even his father had said only, "Well, those rails are near about all hauled. I can handle the balance myself." His mother must have told his father something; he would never of himself have said that. But he had said it and gone on, "He can go to brother John's if he's a mind."

"I might," his mutter lacked conviction; he had no heart for Uncle John and tales of family grandeur. Family grandeur! "Or maybe," he suggested, "I could get a job in Wilmington. That way I could send some money home this winter. I could come back for spring planting."

"Whichever you do, you must write us a letter." His mother had shot him one swift, startling glance of tenderness, of helpless pleading, of fierce, wild passion. But her voice when she spoke again was firm. "I want you to agree to that, son."

"Yes, ma'am, I will."

With no further discussion they had fallen to work. That night he had greased his brogans with the heel of a tallow candle and, wrapping them in paper, packed them in his father's carpet valise, together with his shirts and socks, his new brown coat. His mother near the stove was filling an old salmon can with johnny-cake and smoked beef, and his father, having extracted his horse-hide wallet from a chink beneath the eaves, sat withdrawn in conference with it at the far end of the kitchen table. He combed at his gray goatee with two scarred fingers; his puzzled dog-like eyes peered into the depths of the wallet, mutely reproachful, as though they searched in vain for the nine dollars James had drawn for the suit. He reached his right hand in and fumbled with slow awkwardness, then laid three silver dollars upon the table.

"Now, here's three dollars, son," he strove to say the momentous words in a casual voice, "and the fifty cents of your own money."

"My land! yes, seh," said James.

"Only don't spend it on victuals," he cautioned and pointed to the salmon can. "You've rations aplenty for the trip."

"Let him spend it as he likes," his mother cut in. "He might want to buy a plate of ice-cream in Wilmington."

Mr. Fraser stared at her in stupefaction. "Ice-cream? Why, Ann, do you know what ice-cream costs? Ten cents a plate. I saw the advertisement in the *Journal*." He shook his head gravely. "Ten cents for a plate of nothing. Boy, you'd best stay clear of that Palmetto café."

"Let him do as he likes," his mother repeated. "But what he really needs," she added more reflectively, "is a new genteel wool hat."

"What's the matter with his old?" said Mr. Fraser.

"It's lost all shape."

"Well, it keeps out the weather. That would be throwing money away, to buy another hat. If he's buying clothes, let him buy him a good, stout pair of brogans." Mr. Fraser pointed to the shoes in the valise. "Those are near about wore out and I notice they pinch him some. Yes, sir," he added with immense conviction, "a man must have brogans for winter work."

"But where's the fun," asked Mrs. Fraser, "in buying a pair of brogans?"

To a question so beside the mark and so beyond his range Mr. Fraser attempted no reply. He pushed the silver dollars across the table and shut up the horse-hide wallet. Mrs. Fraser inspected them carefully, and taking a patch of calico from the kitchen shelf and a threaded needle from a lump of beeswax, sewed two of them inside the bosom of the checked shirt which James Fraser was to wear on the journey.

And then this morning—already it seemed long ago—he had stood on the porch in the green dawn and listened to his father's parting counsel. "Be civil, but don't take up with anybody, and don't take a drink from anybody neither. I put a little jug of corn in the valise, so you've no excuse."

"And don't get talking to any women," his mother chimed in. "Now, get you gone. You'll miss that boat."

That was the way it all had been. He could picture every line and word and movement. He would always carry them in his mind, would cling to them. Whenever he got lonely or dwelt on the scene that night at Beaumont he would bring his mind back to those last hours in his home, to his father and mother, those two well-worn familiar figures, now beautified by distance as they had already been beautified in his disaster, who, inarticulate, impotent to utter the thoughts that gnawed at them, pottered and fumbled with all care and earnestness, fixing him up to travel.

They passed other more magnificent plantations, some painted, some of brick, and each secluded among its sombre groves, withdrawn from the river and from its neighbors. But even Orton, tall, white, and colonnaded, finer no doubt than the Executive Mansion or even the Capitol at Washington City, failed to move him. They all belonged to a world not his, a world, rich, elegant and proud, which held no place for such as he.

And in what world was there a place? That was a problem he must try to solve. He could work as a hired

man, of course, either at Uncle John's or some other
farm or else back home when he felt able to face again
the scene of his catastrophe. But, as his mother once
said, where was it getting him? A man could not save
money on a laborer's wages. Why, a man could hardly
live on them. The fact was no farmer wanted a hired
man; he would rather buy a nigger whom he could treat
as he'd a mind. Besides, white hired men had a bad
name with the farmers, and in fact the most of them
did not amount to much. They were poor trash mostly,
barren of pride and ambition. They felt that their work
was really nigger work, slave work, their one idea was
to do as little of it as they could. They were free men,
so they said, and by rights should not have to do such
work at all.

No; without money, land, and niggers there was
nothing in the farming business. But what else was
there for a young fellow like himself? He could not become a lawyer or a doctor even if he wanted. That,
too, took money. Maybe he could be a storekeeper,
though he was mighty little drawn by the prospect of
handing dry-goods over a counter, of bowing and smiling to the ladies. And then, in a town, niggers might
come in to buy things.

He could think of no other job unless it might be
driving a stage-coach. But he reckoned they would
want older men for that, also he had heard the pay was
not so good now that the railroads were coming in. The
thought arrested him. Might there not be something
for him in the railroad business? He knew nothing
about it except the *Harper's Weekly* picture and the

accounts of wrecks in the *Journal*. But they must have some one to mend the wrecked cars and engines, get them back on the track and on days when there were no wrecks, keep them in fix to run.

A haze of smoke against the blue of the sky showed that the city was not far away. Beyond a reedy island the river narrowed and a multitude of roofs climbed up a hill above a cluster of shipmasts. In midstream two tugs butted shoulder to shoulder against the bow of a great packet-steamer and threw up flat, smooth swells of water with their screws. The packet swung around in the narrow channel, turned her paddles and sounded a long, deep warning. She shot past them, a vision of white and silver. Handsomely dressed passengers waved with calm good-nature from the rail.

Gliding by a long brick warehouse with many iron doors, and by a very broad paved street which led up a hill between gay painted shops, the boat sounded her engine-room bells, backed her paddles, and brought up against the piles of a roofed-in pier.

James Fraser passed again through the dark hold and gave up his ticket to the youth in the blue cap. He shuffled gingerly down the cleated gang-plank and paused on the dock to take his bearings.

Down another gang-plank aft the saloon passengers in their Guayaquil straw hats, their well-brushed beavers, their tassels, bustles, and crinolines, came ashore, to be greeted by their colored servants with exquisitely deferential grins, and driven stylishly away.

James picked up his valise and followed them.

Their carriages' light rattle was drowned in the rumble of drays on the bricks of the market street. Low-hung loads of bales and barrels rolled down the grade, fat, crested horses bore back on the breechings, sedately responsive to the whoops of negro draymen.

On each corner by the water front three groggeries were advantageously posted. Above them the shops began—first dusty windows filled with rope and marlin, on which hurricane lights, sea-boots and black sou'westerers were casually displayed. After the sea came food—dressed hogs on hooks outside wide doors and, within, herrings, Swiss cheeses and tubs of sauerkraut mingling their odors with that of the damp sawdust on the floor. A hardware store exhibited a kerosene-lamp or two and a vast array of bowie knives and derringers, and at the topmost corner two great jars of lambent fluid flanked a heap of Pectoral Compound and Hall's Elixir.

On this corner James Fraser paused to look around. There was fascination and splendor no doubt in these shop-windows. This first view of Wilmington ought to be for him a mighty big occasion. But it was not working out just so. All the way up the street he had tried to pretend to himself that he was having a big time. But now at the top, he knew it was no use, the pretense fell to pieces, he felt only empty, desolate, alone, a homeless outcast, peering at shop-windows, at people, all strangers, who drove past in carts and carriages, walked past in beavers, swallow-tails, greeting friends, passing good words among themselves, but all alike careless, oblivious of him. He had been exiled from his home, his narrow bed, his place at table, and from the

shining region of his dreams, to wander in a wilderness
of strange, indifferent faces.

He looked around as though he sought escape.
Ahead, the broad street, ascending now more gradually,
passed between further rows of shops, close-built and
rendered fanciful by curious wrought-iron balconies.
To his right a narrower street dipped down to a long
market-shed and a squalid gully, then rose up a wooded
knoll where handsome houses showed glimpses of their
square and solid elegance among the trees. To his left
this same street ran, unpaved and level, flanked by the
weighty business houses of the town. Brass plates beside their portals announced with dignified reserve that
banking, export, marine insurance, and other grave
affairs were here enthroned. And these solemn intima-
tions were further reinforced by the great stone lintels
and steel gratings of the first-floor windows.

Clearly no refuge for him lay there. Just what would
form a refuge he could not say. Nothing, he supposed,
short of his home—its weathered siding flaked with
moss, with shadows of the sycamores, bright counter-
panes hung out to air, the lazy drift of chimney smoke
up through the small, deep clearing in the forest.

Still he continued to stand and search for what he
knew he should not find; not it nor anything like it.
The solid avenue of commerce stretched away till
shrouded in a pall of smoke—smoke, heavy, black, and
curly, far different from the light blue spiral of which
just now he had been thinking.

As he looked, he heard, coming from within this pall,
the long, high whistle of a locomotive.

He picked up his carpet-bag and headed for it.

Oblivious, he passed by gentlemen in tight fawn-colored trousers and clerks with green baize bags. Inviting cross streets led on the one hand up a slope to neat houses set behind open-work brick walls among gardens of lilacs and magnolias, and on the other hand dropped sharply down a cobbled grade to ship-masts and the river; but these, too, he passed by.

Just before James reached the railroad-yard the street lost its magnificence and became abruptly a mere sandy road that divided a litter of riverside negro shacks from a paling fence. But he took no note of the street's decay, for above the fence at that precise and unforgettable moment an Olympian figure in blue overalls, feet astride and body canted forward, glided high aloft through space on the top of a shunted freight-car. The figure crouched down, turned an iron wheel and then, its flight arrested with a clash of couplings, descended from view. Peering through a crack between the boards, James saw the man swing casually to the ground and light a pipe. He hurried on to where the fence curved back to form an ill-kempt open space before the station, and doubling furtively around its end, he soon returned to where the dignitary smoked. Preoccupied in studying the other's brawny arms and sardonic smoke-grimed visage, James Fraser came up face to face with the railroad man. Abruptly he halted, stared at him in uncomfortable silence. Too late, he realized that he had neglected to prepare himself with a suitable opening remark. He could in his extremity think of nothing except the customary "Howdy" of

the country folks, a manner of address which he felt
to be inadequate and which was evidently so regarded
by this grim rider of machines, who blew out a cloud of
smoke, spat powerfully with an imperceptible movement of his lips and grunted, "What you want?"

"Why," said James with painful hesitation, "I just
thought I'd like to see these engines and cars."

The brakeman's brief stare at him was utterly detached and unresponsive. He turned away from James
and, squatting on his haunches, hung his big arms over
his knees and proceeded to smoke himself into a state of
profound abstraction. There was nothing for James to
do except to stare at the string of box-cars on the siding.

But he could not stand forever in a presence so august and uncommunicative. Reluctantly he picked up
his valise again. At that moment a big light-colored
negro appeared around the end of the car with a long-
nosed oil-can dangling from his hand. Coming slowly
along the track, he stopped at each car-wheel, lifted an
iron lid and oiled the journal-box. Between the journals
he let the nozzle of the can hang down so that the train
oil dripped beside him and on his naked foot. Watching
him vanish around the last car, James was startled by
the brakeman's voice, "Look at that Gode dam niggeh."
James looked at, or rather after, him obediently. The
brakeman's voice took on the bitterness of years. "Too
lazy to tip up the nozzle of his can."

"Niggers is that way," James hastened to agree.

"Nary a one of 'em worth that!" the brakeman
snapped his blackened fingers. "Why the company

buys 'em beats me. They betteh spend they money hiring white men."

"Yes, seh. I reckon it's white man's work, sure enough." His voice had the overheartiness of servility. Still he felt that their acquaintance was making headway.

But the brakeman subsided again. James stood mute. All was lost. No, by shot, he would not give up. He had an idea.

"Yes, seh," he said with studied sympathy, "I reckon a man gets mightily played out with this work, and dry, too, what with all this yer smoke." The brakeman deigned the merest grunt. "Yes, seh," James went on, "I reckon a drink of good liquor comes in mighty handy in this business."

At this remark the brakeman nodded curtly, as though assenting to a self-evident but abstract proposition. James gazed in detachment out across the freight-yards and murmured, "I got a jug of mighty good corn hyer myself."

"What?" said the brakeman.

"Yes, seh." James knelt down and opened the carpet valise. "You try it."

An hour later, James Fraser, his mind confused by the jargon of link motions, steam-domes, and eccentric blocks; his eyes still swimming with visions of locomotive engines, their long, slim boilers sweating, their funnel-shaped stacks breathing sparks, their cow-catchers outspreading grandly beneath their glittering brass work, was listening to the brakeman's parting counsel.

"Go see the shop boss in the mo'nin'. Tell him Bill says you all right. Bill," he thumped his grimy chest, "that's me!"

"I'm mightily obliged," said James. "I hope I get a job." He paused. "I surely do. If I don't, I reckon I'll have to go to stay at my Uncle John's. I've not got but two dollars and a half," his tone was diffident. "Do you reckon that would pay the fare to Anson's?"

The brakeman's glance was haughty. "Fare?" He seized the lapels of James' coat with solemn affection. "Fare my old breeches! You tell the conductor Bill says you all right." He inhaled deeply and turned grave. "And in them caws don't set neah the stove. That's wher' the passengehs gets burned up in a wreck. And if you feel her leave the track, get undeh the seat and stay ther' till she stops rollin', then kick the window out and watch out fo' jagged glass."

"Yes, seh," said James, dubiously. "Do they have many wrecks?"

"Wreckingest road in the Union." The brakeman eyed him proudly. "Why, my old breeches! I've seen dead passengehs piled up like cord wood." Still holding James' lapels he rocked himself slowly to and fro. "So long, brotheh," he said earnestly. "Take care you'se'f." He released his hold and tucking a red flag beneath his arm, disappeared, walking steadily but very wide, among the sheds and freight-cars of the yards.

BOOK II

CHAPTER XIV

THE high, dark cavern of the railroad shops was pierced by a dusky shaft of light. It slanted through the wide doors at the western end, and glinting on forge, on crane, on half dismantled box-cars, fell square against the locomotive engine on which James Fraser worked. Crouched down beside the cylinder, he tapped with a copper hammer on the cross-head, paused, peered, wiped his hands on a piece of waste, tapped again. The hammer blows re-echoed through the cavern and died away among the shadows of disabled cars and fragmentary engines.

Footsteps crunched on the cinders, the broad, square silhouette of Bill, the brakeman, showed against the light.

"You ready to quit?" he said. "Le's go get a drink."

James stood up stiffly and blinked his eyes at Bill. "I can't quit yet. I've got to shimm out this cross-head gip."

"Blame me, boy," said Bill in a voice of mingled awe and irritation, "if you ain't earnest!"

James shook his head in disclaimer. "They'll want this engine to-morrow." Bill was not impressed.

"Let 'em wait," he admonished grandly. "Let 'em wait."

"But they's got to be something ready to take out Number Two," said James.

Bill put on an expression of masterly acumen. "Why?" he said. "You tell me why?"

James tapped the piston-rod with his hammer. "If this engine ain't ready, Number Two can't go out."

Bill nodded his satisfaction as if this answer had delivered James into his hand.

"Well, if she can't go out, she can't go out."

"But, my Lord," said James, "they're liable to bounce me out of here if I don't 'tend to business."

Bill permitted himself a short derisive laugh.

"Bounce!" he said, "Bounce my old breeches! The company's lucky to get good men like me and you and they know it, too." He stuck an impressive forefinger at James' nose, "And if eveh the yard boss says pea turkey to me, right ther' he loses the best Gode dam brakeman in the Union."

To this proclamation, often heard before, James did not reply; he turned back to his work, fitted a shimm against the seating of the guide, marked it with a piece of blue chalk, fitted it again. He clamped the shimm in a bench vise and filed at it. The metal shrieked, fine silver flakes sprayed out and dusted the bench's greasy planks. Short of the blue chalk mark he stopped and blew the filings off the warm black file. Whistling soundlessly in sober contentment, he took the shimm back to the engine, fitted it, crouched, squinted, wiped it, made another mark.

"What ails you—" said Bill after a gloomy pause, "is that you naturally enjoy to work."

"I reckon so," said James absently, filing away on the shimm.

Bill walked off in disgust. "Anyhow," he called back from the doorway, "I'm going to Foretop's tonight." His voice was aggrieved, defiant.

'Foretop's.' The word thrust into James' consciousness and carried with it glimpses of thick tumblers filled with liquor, of rank cigars, and ribaldry, and of the strange faces of seamen from foreign lands.

"All right," he called after the retreating Bill, "I'll be ther'."

In a gully by the docks a pair of port and starboard lights, shining red and green on a greasy doorway, marked the widely known place of Foretop Smith—Foretop's Place, that was what they called it. The term was vague, but 'place' was as good a word as any for this greasy doorway and the reeking rooms and devious passageways which lay beyond. The door itself swung easily but it swung swiftly, too; there was no trouble about getting in but a man had to be quick about it—he couldn't hang around the front trying to make up his mind; and even if he could, Foretop would not allow it. He was as broadminded, he often said, as any man alive, but there were two things he wouldn't stand for: one of them was hanging around in front and the other was throwing knives. "If a man won't keep his knife in his hand to fight"—he had once remarked to James after an affair in which one of Foretop's negro bus boys had been unintentionally punctured by a flying bowie knife, "if a man won't keep his knife in his hand to fight," said Foretop, "he's got to do his fighting somewheres else. He ain't coming in here." He had

pulled reflectively at the tuft of red hair above his forehead from which he got his name, then dropped his red-
haired hands down on the table and stared at James, a
big, slow-moving, judicial bear. "That's a dago trick,"
he had added conclusively.

As James Fraser drew near the door he looked around
instinctively to see if he were observed. What difference
it made he could not have told; few people in Wilmington knew him even by sight. For a year and a half now
he had been buried in the shops, living in isolation, cut
off, except for occasional letters from home, from the
sort of life he had been raised to. Yet he could not help
feeling that the fact that he came from good folks must
be generally comprehended, and that respectable people,
seeing him slinking into Foretop's, would stand as
sorrowful witnesses to his fall—not that he had done
anything so very bad—he liked his liquor well enough—
too well, maybe—and he liked to mix with the battered
characters and strange, seafaring men who gathered at
Foretop's bar. Their colorful eccentricities, their
friendliness, fuddled though it might be, were in warm-
ing contrast to the frigid aloofness of respectable folks
in Wilmington. He pushed in the door.

A long, dark hall showed a dim stairway and on the
right three broad streaks of light, three doorways
representing the divisions into which Foretop most carefully separated his world. The first was the regular
bar, the second the back room, furnished with tables
and reserved for mates, captains, and other exclusive
persons. At the back, convenient to the ladies' entrance,
was the family room devoted to intercourse between
the sexes.

The bar whose brilliance now burst on James' winking eyes seemed at the first flash to consist of an infinitely long, colossal mirror and innumerable lights, endlessly reflected, which gleamed on ranks of bottles and of tumblers, on brasswork and nickelwork, and on many monumental copper spittoons. As his eyes grew accustomed to the brightness, the familiar antlers above the mirror took shape, then the two handsome oil paintings—one of the horse, Ben Morgan, trotting vigorously in a high-wheeled sulky, the other of a beautiful lady attired in a pair of butterfly wings, who gazed with justifiable admiration at her reflection in a pool. Concerning this last as a work of art, Foretop himself held convictions which caused him to ignore the practical comments of patrons who viewed with purely anatomical interest the lady's generous contours. Those contours invariably caught James' notice when first he entered the bar and often during a lull in the evening his glance would wander back to them. He respected Foretop's views on art; he regarded the vulgar commentators as guilty of sacrilege; at the same time he often wished that there were a lady like that around and that he could get to know her.

Below the mirror a line of patrons stretched along the bar. In seaman's caps and jumpers, in flat wideawakes, in flashy roundabouts and beaver plugs, they hunched their shoulders above the long mahogany, threw their heads back to drink or turned them sidewise in conversation, nose to nose.

Bill was not among them. Slipping in between a broad, tow-headed sailor and a man in tight checked coat and trousers James laid a dime down on the bar. The free negro barkeeper was all attention.

"A whiskey sour," said James. The negro bowed with more elaboration than James liked. It was as if he meant to indicate that, although a negro, he alone of all those present was conversant with high etiquette. But gazing into the mirror while the negro squeezed a lemon, James Fraser felt that he himself, in his dark brown coat and dark plaid bow-tie with fringed ends, stood out in that row of rough-clad or flashily bedizened individuals as some one out of the ordinary. Perhaps the negro had meant merely to indicate as much.

Enjoying this gratifying reflection, he consumed his whiskey sour in dignified reserve. The gentleman in the checked suit cast one swift, steely glance at him and then resumed his tale of three-card monte on the Charleston packet. The sailor lolled on the bar till the draw-strings at the back of his trousers seemed ready to burst. He scratched at the short yellow hair behind his ears till his cap fell over his eyes. Like a ship riding to her moorings, he swung his great bulk slowly from side to side and finally just as the whiskey sour was being drained brought up against James' elbow.

"Hey, you," said James severely, "You want a heap of room."

The swaying gradually subsided, a great stupid, moon face peered down at him. "'Scuse," said a low melodious voice. The big head made a slight but ponderous obeisance. "'Scuse. Har drink?" Won by the giant's clumsy, childlike courtesy, James grinned up at him.

"I reckon I don't mind." He thrust a hand out, "Fraser's my name, seh." His hand was enveloped.

"Karl Bjorkman," the sailor said. He reached the other hand across the bar and clamped the negro's elbow. "Drink—" he nodded toward James, "young fela."

"Whiskey sour," said James promptly. "Kummel," said Karl.

"Well, here's your hea'th, friend," said James when the yellow-green and the white drink stood before them on the bar.

The big Swede touched his glass to James', "Skol," he answered and threw back his head.

They continued to treat each other. The Swede had nothing further to say but from time to time he crinkled up his little blue eyes and beamed down on James as though between them lay some longstanding and ineffable secret. James, while touched by the other's affectionate fidelity and admiring his capacity to down the fiery kummel, kept looking around for Bill.

As the tally of whiskey sours mounted, his thoughts left Bill and drifted off to subjects far more abstract and grandiose. He thought of his work in the shop, how quickly he had learned it, how well he did it. It took a few drinks to give him an idea of his own worth and even so, maybe he didn't know it, maybe he was going to be a big man in the railroad some day, maybe the president. He saw himself in an office with a frosted door. And when the planters came in to try to get their cotton hauled, what would he tell them ? He caught a glimpse of his own grim, crooked smile in the mirror behind the

bar. He checked himself. "Kummel for **Karl**," he said
gravely, "and a whiskey sour."

His thoughts were off again. A year and a half in the
shops, and by shot! he knew more than any of them
except the boss,—making better money, too—sending
three dollars home every week and still had enough left
to enjoy himself. A good thing he'd left home—he'd
show 'em—go out west maybe when he'd learned the
game.

"Har drink?" said Karl.

And now a cool, refreshing numbness flowed down
over him and tingled in his hands. The shop, all practical affairs, even his own body were forgotten, ceased to
exist; nothing remained except a thousand twinkling
lights, his tingling hands, and the essential spirit which
was his true self—a spirit, fine and free, confident,
meritorious, a thing apart, self-sufficient, absolute, and
indefeasable, which swung triumphant through a glori-
ous, twinkling maze.

CHAPTER XV

Up through the vast and vaguely exhilarating region in which he hung, faint sounds ascended. At first he took them to be merely the touch of music proper to the constellated scene; but their reality grew manifest, became insistent; with a sense of satisfaction in his own acuteness he recognized the notes of an actual fiddle. Useless to attempt deception on a man like himself; he could tell a fiddle as far as he could hear one; one fragmentary squeak had been enough. A mighty unmelodious squeak, too. Indignation marshalled his floating faculties. He listened. Again the squeak, flat and whining, a squeak, in short, which in the nature of things should not be allowed. The matter must be attended to. It was necessary to see this fiddler.

He took a final grip on the edge of the bar and headed for the doorway at the rear, very proud to find that he was walking straight and steady. He passed through the room where Foretop's more select patrons sat in groups of two and three, and pushed aside a red, fringed portière beyond.

The family room was all festivity; a dozen girls and women in cheap gowns of brilliant silk whirled round in the embrace of gentlemen friends, nestled close, clutched, burst into high, unmeaning laughter. In a corner beside a nickel-plated stove a sour, pimpled young fiddler scraped away. James fixed on him an eye of grave disapprobation, but before he could advance, the crimson bulk of Foretop Smith was planted in front of him.

"Good evenin', Jimmy," his tone was friendly yet alert, his big arm stretched carelessly across the door frame.

"How you, Foretop," said James with dignity. "I came to hyear the fiddler. Used to fiddle myself some."

Foretop considered this statement, contracting his ruddy eyebrows in thought.

"This is a birthday party," he observed slowly. "Special music and all."

"Private party," James' manner was sedate almost to the point of hauteur. "All right, Foretop." Inclining his head in lofty acquiescence, he turned away. "Perfectly satisfact'y." The phrase, he felt, was well chosen.

"Hold on," said Foretop, his voice sank confidentially. "Fact is, every girl has got a gentleman friend to-night and when that's the case you know we don't like to let more in." He nodded sagely. "It makes trouble." His arm dropped; he seemed to expand to large and generous proportions. "But I know you, Jim. You're all right. Come in and hear the music."

Again James bowed. "Perfectly satisfact'y," he observed as he passed through the door.

He edged along the wall and sat down most abruptly in a green plush chair beside the fiddler. He listened with mounting exasperation to the halting, scratchy tune; he tried by nodding his head to spur the fiddler into the rhythm. The boy had no notion of the time— no notion either of how to make the fiddle ring.

Now he finished his tune. He wiped his snipy nose on the back of his hand and gave James an ill-favored glance. "A man can't play without he has some liquor," he observed.

Swiftly James took the fiddle from between his arms. "Give me the fiddle," he said. "I've had enough for two." A mean look came into the fiddler's narrow eyes; he started to speak.

"Whatever money comes in is yours," James murmured absently as he tuned the strings. The fiddler subsided.

A girl, her figure boldly outlined by her orange dress, caught sight of him. She tossed a curl back and smiled on him with heavy archness.

"Look, girls! here's little Willie in his roundabout." They crowded round him cackling. "Play us a piece from Sunday school." "Willie's the bully boy." "He's got on long pants, too." The gentlemen friends made a show of grinning at James with the supercilious good nature of cosmopolitans.

"You want me to play?" he demanded sternly.

"Why, sure, sweetie."

"Then hush your fuss."

Magnificently he turned his head away from them and dropped his chin. It felt sharp against the fiddle's shoulder, the strings as he fingered them in preparation pierced sharply through the numbness of his hands, through the mist in which he drifted, brought him to himself. He was able to play. Without a thought he raised the bow, he tapped twice on the floor, and struck up "Leather Breeches."

"Mammy sent me off to school,
　Leather breeches and a lop-eared mule,
　I lit on a stump when the jinney shied,
　But leather breeches saved my hide."

As with down-cast eyes he swung slowly, steadily through the tune, bright skirts, sea-boots, cracked patent-leather shoes, and cassimere pantaloons swam across the blurred circle of his vision on the floor. He did not want to watch them; only to play. The tune was taking shape, gaining power. He drew a deep refreshing breath and raised his head.

His gaze, unseeing, dwelt above the dancers, lost itself among the scrolled leaves of the paper on the wall beyond. Against the wall a brightly colored blot was swimming. It was a picture in a gilded frame. His eyes came to a focus.

In the lithograph a lady holding a little girl by the hand stood at the gate of a neat, white farmhouse and waved farewell to her fine, young farmer-husband who, with fowling piece, game bag, and retriever, departed down the road. As James Fraser, gazing, played on firmly, rhythmically, it seemed as though he, too, were journeying down that avenue between the trees; it seemed that the avenue itself led backward to his home; the laughter, scuffle, and scrape of the dancers grew faint—was left behind—the music of "Leather Breeches" grew stronger in his ears—now he was home among the pines and cypresses—now he was in the schoolhouse playing for the prize before the upturned faces of the folks—of his mother and father—of Old Man Roon and Dougald Cameron—of the little boy who had hollered out, "Hurrah! here's Jim."

Then something happened that he had thought would never happen again. In her dress of purple with the dark fur wristlets she came through the schoolhouse door and looked at him. A vise closed on his throat, a thin vein snapped against his temple. He must stop playing. No! No! He must go on.

Her eyes were on him. He played for her. He made the fiddle speak, call out her name. As though that cry had startled her she vanished in a mist. Once more his swimming eyes saw only the wallpaper's green scrolled leaves. The crisis was past. But he must be on his guard. He must not look at the gilt-framed picture which had led his thoughts so treacherously. He shut his eyes.

On the hill where they had stood together he was leaving her in anger. This time he would not look behind. But he did. She stood in the white sprigged muslin dress beneath the pine-trees, her hands clasped lightly before her, her lips half parted in wonder and distress, gazing after him. Gazing after him. He shot the bow across the strings and thrust the fiddle at the pimpled youth.

He heard the dancers stop with cries of disappointment; he heard the rattle of silver coins on the floor. "They're yours," he told the fiddler, and stumbled heavily away. The girl in orange clutched at him. "One more tune, just for me." He brushed her aside and steered back to the bar.

"Whiskey sour."

Big Karl's voice, soft, sympathetic, descended to him.

"You look for gurle?" James did not answer. "Not can find? Har drink."

He drained the glass in one long, breathless gulp. The whiskey hit him with a shock, sent his stunned mind spinning through infinity. Through gales and slanting mists he was riding, buoyed up by the gently swaying bar. It was a fine, stout bar; he clung to it, rode out the gusts on it, safe, triumphant. When now and again the room, intruding into the void in which he floated, would gather itself and sweep slantwise around him, he would grasp the rail and call out, "Whiskey sour."

The bar itself showed signs of slipping treacherously away; he would soon be cast adrift; no one could save him; a haunting thought drove at him through chaos; no one but her. What then? He soon would sink— sink into nothingness where not even she could follow him. He would elude her. Ha!

But instead of welcome catastrophe, the tumult ceased, the seas turned calm and cold, his mind turned calm and cold and marvellously clear. "Why sink to nothingness?" he said. What had he to fear? Who was she to plague him? What was she to him? She was a girl and girls were plentiful. Plentiful. Just now—in the dance-room—hadn't the one in orange, the bold, high-breasted figure, swayed invitingly before his eyes?

Another thought—to go off with a fine strapping wench would somehow be a masterly revenge. Yes, that would be a good joke on the planter's daughter. A damn good joke. And one thing sure, if he did that, she would forever cease to bother him. The fiddle still sounded from the back room. That orange girl would still be there.

He pushed in through the red portière. Immediately it seemed as though the girl in orange had been looking for him. The others still whirled round and clutched each other but she came up to him and with her hands on her hips and her head tilted back stood very close, gazing into his eyes with mocking inquiry. She breathed deep till her orange bodice stretched taut across the swelling contours underneath. A hot fit seized him— left him cold and shivering.

"You want to dance?"

He couldn't dance the way these town-folks did and anyhow that was not what he wanted.

"I can't," he mumbled gruffly, still staring at her bosom.

Her shallow, weary eyes gave him an appraising and not unsympathetic glance.

"I guess you're too far gone," she observed. "You hold your liquor good, though—for a kid," she added. They were standing against the wall, she holding his elbow with a firm proprietary grasp, a grasp which he first resented, then depended on to steady him, and at the last felt imparting hot strength to his veins.

"Where's your fellow?" he asked suspiciously.

Her eyes snapped. "I gave him the ta-ta, the lousy tin-horn gambler." She squeezed his arm. "Ain't you the bully boy for fiddling, though." This undiscriminating phrase called, he felt, for detailed explanation and disclaimer. He embarked on a labored exposition of how a man really ought to fiddle,—how he himself could really fiddle when he was in practice, how far his playing to-night had fallen short of that high standard, how far that standard itself fell short of a certain inexpressible fiddling which lay somewhere beyond. He felt that he must passionately defend this hypothetical fiddling from well-meaning but unenlightened persons, that the essential fiddler within him was bound by some high obligation to describe this fiddling to the girl in terms suited to her understanding. Such terms, though, were hard to find and as he fumbled for them they turned and fled away, and all terms whatever turned and fled after them. His voice trailed off.

"Sure," said the girl. "I used to study piano myself."

No use. For a moment he lay buried in deep frustration but immediately his self-pitying spirit was borne aloft on a tide of profoundly wise acceptance of all things as they were. Let him take this girl for what she was; she could not understand the things which floated in his mind but she herself was many things desirable. Let a man take from women what they could give him and not expect too much. Let him be easy-going in his mind and idly content, knowing that nothing, that no woman, mattered much. This girl's bright breasts were straining toward him. "Come on," he said.

Once in the dark hall he was proudly triumphant; this girl, he made no doubt, had waited for him—had waited on the chance that he might return. That was the kind of girl to have. A wave of tenderness, of self-compassion, of desire swept over him. He pictured her boldly outlined figure as he had seen it in the room just now. He stretched out his arms.

She threw her body against his—a body so hard and dead that it struck him over the heart like a treacherous blow. His heart stopped. He turned cold. Before he could move her lips were on his cheek—spongy, dead lips, clinging, trying to draw the life from him. He pushed at her desperately.

"What ails you?" her harsh voice cried.

"I—I've got to go," he mumbled.

"You—" the word was a lash. He fumbled in his pocket, emptied it at a clutch, and held the money out to her.

"Here, take this. It's all I've got."

Her breath hissed. She took the money, then drew back her hand. A shower of money flew past his face— a coin cut him across the lip; her high voice welled up in a stream of dreadful filth. He turned and stumbled down the hallway, groping for the door. He found it, plunged between the lights of red and green into the cool, deserted street. The door closed noiselessly behind him. A misty moon dozed overhead, a night breeze freighted with faint music of the frogs stole up from the river. From the dark hall beyond the door came high, hard, mocking laughter.

CHAPTER XVI

For a time he kept pretty quiet after that. In the evening, feeling dutiful and chastened, he stayed around the Torkers' where he boarded, helping Mrs. Torker with the dishes or earning Mr. Torker's gratitude by putting a washer in the kitchen-pump or a new gas mantle in the mohair-furnished parlor. Then he went outside and sat down on the flimsy, lilac-darkened porch and listened to Mr. Torker's views.

Those views embraced the known world, the future life, and baptism by immersion, and though James knew the most of them by heart, he liked to listen, half asleep, to the soft, soothing reiteration of Mr. Torker's voice and the acquiescent squeak of Mrs. Torker's rocking-chair. From Mr. Torker James gathered that no one could complain of the grocery business these days if it were not for credits and bad debts, that it was a wonder some people had the face to come in the store and charge another thing, and that these folks had better take heed in view of the fact that the present age was about to see the fulfilment of certain prophecies in the Book of Revelation, which, though specifically directed against the Yankee nation, might well involve the unregenerate debtors of Mr. Torker's store.

Mr. Torker was not alone in foreboding evil for the Yankee nation. There was a good deal of talk about the Yankees everywhere these days. Mr. Cassidy, in the house next door, had come back from Boston with a stock of dry-goods and a report that the people up there were worshipping John Brown in the churches like he was Jesus Christ. The Kansas murderer had tried to start a nigger insurrection in Virginia the summer before and had been naturally tried and hung. After the first excitement no one had paid much attention to him, least of all the niggers, but now it looked like the Yankees, who would supposedly be the first to want to forget about him, were bound to make him into a saint; in fact it looked like there might be something in what old man Torker said, and that the Yankees, having been beguiled by Satan, were hunting around for an Antichrist. It is true that Mr. Cassidy was somewhat noted as a liar but he had brought back Boston newspapers with the sermons printed in them.

"My Lord," James pondered idly to himself. "What ails those Yankees?"

That very question James heard called out of the dusk by Mr. Cassidy one evening as the light thump of Major Cassius Pettibone's malacca stick was passing by.

"Good evening, Major," Mr. Cassidy had said; then, "Major, what ails them Yankees?"

The thumping ceased. The thick, hearty voice of the Major called out, "Heyo, Cassidy. Come down here."

The Major leaned against the picket fence and fanned himself with his beaver hat.

"So you want to know about the Yankees, eh?" he said, in a tone which indicated pleasure, pride, and well-founded admiration for the questioner's good judgment in addressing him.

"I cain't make 'em out," said Cassidy.

The Major covered his shining head with his beaver.

"Well, seh," he remarked, raising his voice for the benefit of any chance bystanders, "during my fo'ty years in politics, where I hope I was happy enough not to disappoint the flattering confidence of my constituents, I observed the Yankees mighty close. And though now retired, I trust not without honor, certainly not without a gratifying token of esteem, I refer, seh, to the clock, which now adorns my parlor mantelpiece and, striking every hour, reminds me of my generous suppo'ters." This James recognized as the ormolu presentation clock which the Major never failed to introduce. "And though now retired," the Major reiterated, "I still feel it my duty to continue to do so."

Just what that duty was, James, having lost the Major's thread, could not be sure. Nor did the Major further explain, for at that moment two citizens crossed the street to listen. "Walter . . . Henry," said the Major cordially, "I am glad to see you gentlemen. We were just discussing the Yankees." He raised his voice again. "The Yankee, seh, can be explained in just one word and in only one." The pause which followed was of nicely calculated length. "Money. Money, by God, seh!"

"They're mighty close traders," said Mr. Cassidy ruefully.

From his breast pocket the Major extracted a huge white handkerchief.

"Gentlemen, who grew the cotton for this handkerchief?" He flourished it. "We did," he answered in a voice so grieved, so righteously indignant as to make

that very handkerchief seem the product of his auditor's
stern toil. "But do we get a fair return for our industry? No, seh. A bare pittance, seh. Just enough to
keep us going." The Major's voice sank to a confiden-
tial and suspicious whisper. "But this handkerchief
comes mighty high, gentlemen. You can get one in
England for half as much. There must be a big profit
somewhere." He raised his voice again. "There is.
And who makes it? The Yankee manufacturer. Well,
then, a sensible man would naturally ask, why don't
you get your handkerchiefs from England, where the
prices are fair? You know the answer: The tariff keeps
them out. And who makes the tariff? The Yankee
manufacturer." The Major replaced his handkerchief
and patted his vest significantly. "Right there's the
story, gentlemen. Whatever little money we make, directly we have to pay it out for Yankee goods. And on
top of that he treats his own help worse than the sorriest
niggers we have down here. And on top of that he
preaches abolition at us." The Major dealt the gate
post a flat-handed blow. "Do you want to know what
the Yankee's motto is? It's money for himself and
morality for everybody else."

The slow rattle of wheels approached. The town
garbage cart moved across a circle of light from a street
lamp; beside it walked Beau Bill, a little wiry, rat-faced
negro in a linen duster and leghorn hat.

"Beau Bill!" the Major called out.

"Yas, seh, Majo', hyar I is." His tone was one of
forced and anxious levity.

"You're late," said the Major with affected sternness.

Beau Bill's voice was troubled. "Yas, seh, I'se mightily behin' my time, an' da's a fact." He had taken off his hat and stood with his head tilted to one side in uneasy deference. He now made as if to put his hat on again and continue down the street.

"Hold on," said the Major. "How come you to be late?"

Beau Bill held his hat before him in resignation.

"It was like dis, Majo'. Dey was to be a ball at Henry Highpocket's las' night and on account of me making de roun's and knowing all de nigger gals like I does, Highpocket ask me would I be de manager of de ball." He craned his neck forward and swallowed. "And I say would dey get a per*mit* fo' de ball. And dey say dey would, and I say I would." Beau Bill beat a light, nervous tattoo on the top of his hat. "Well, bless gracious, ef 'bout de middle of de evening de patrol ain't come in and say 'Whar de per*mit?*' an' I say 'Highpocket got it.' An' Highpocket," he rotated his hat slowly between his hands, "Majo', dat Highpocket say he don't know nothing 'bout it and dat I is de manager of de ball, and de nigger gals what I invited dey all stan' by dat yaller Highpocket and de next news you know I's in de calaboose."

"Of cou'se," said the Major, "of cou'se. It's a mighty serious thing, Beau Bill, to hold a ball without a permit."

Beau Bill's indignation at the treachery of Highpocket and the gals had given him courage.

"Yas, seh, Majo', I reckon so. But it's a mighty se'ious thing to fling Beau Bill in de calaboose. Des' like I tol' de Jedge. 'Jedge,' I say in de cou't dis mo'n-in', 'Who own me?' Jedge he 'lows de inco'poration own me. 'Well,' I say, 'Jedge, if a man own a nigger and de nigger git in de calaboose, de man try to git him out so he kin go back to work. How den kin the in-co'poration shet up its own nigger, an' de onliest nigger dat it got?' And den I say, 'If you shet me up who tote de gobbage away?' Jedge he can't say who tote it. 'And mo' too,' I say, 'How about dem hogs dat gits de gobbage? How dey gwine to make out when Beau Bill don' carry 'em no gobbage? And what 'bout de old sows da's got little pigses? What dem little pigses gwine to think when dey mammies don' get no gob-bage?'" Beau Bill waved his hat up and down in slow, solemn incantation. "'Jedge,' I say, 'Is you gwine to visit my sins on dem pigs unto de third and fou'th gen-eration?'" He smote the mule's rump for emphasis. A cloud of dust flew up, the mule awoke and moved on to the next house. Beau Bill, now worked up to a fine pitch of righteous dignity, remained to receive the ironical applause of the group around the Major. "Yas, gem-mens, when de Jedge see I kin quote de scripture, chap-ter and verse, he tu'n me loose." With a triumphant bow he gathered his flapping duster around him and followed his cart into the shadows, where he still could be heard muttering of Highpocket and the girls and wrestling with an iron can.

During Beau Bill's recital James Fraser had come down to the fence in order to enjoy the negro's tribula-tions. The others now laughed once again and then broke up to wander down the shadowy street. The

Major alone seemed loath to leave the spot where he had analyzed the Yankees and displayed the humors of Beau Bill to such advantage. He peered around him and, catching sight of James, approached ponderously along the picket fence until he was close enough to envelop James in the faint and delicate aroma of snuff and of cherry brandy.

"Good evening, son," he said with conscious dignity and still more conscious heartiness. "Do I know you?"

"No, seh," said James. "I don't reckon so."

"Tell me your name," the Major said. His air of kindly authority indicated that as an office-holder for forty years, he did no more than exercise a benevolent right. "Tell me your name."

"James Fraser."

"A mighty good name, too." The Major cleared his throat. That point was settled. "What do you do?"

"I work in the railroad shops, fixing engines."

"That's a mighty fine thing to do, a mighty fine thing. I never meet a skilled mechanic but what I feel I ought to take off my hat to him." The Major said these words as though they conferred the final stamp of approval. "Yes, seh," he went on, "what we need is skilled mechanics, men who can build up our railroads and our factories and make us independent of the Yankees. You heard me speaking of the tariff just now." His words were an announcement rather than an inquiry. "Well, seh, when we develop our own manufactories that tariff which at present despoils us of our hard-won earnings will work directly in our favor and make us the most prosperous people the world has ever seen. And

when that day comes it is to our skilled mechanics that
we shall owe our prosperity." His handkerchief was
out again and flourishing. Just then, however, the
clock struck nine.

"Hello," said the Major, "nine o'clock. I must go
home and see that my niggers are safe indoors before the
patrol catches them." He nodded. "Good evening,
my boy, my hat is off to the skilled mechanics. What
name, please? . . . yes, yes, of cou'se."

The Major's cloudy bulk and the scent of snuff and
cherry brandy vanished up the street.

James walked back to the porch with a new idea of
his own dignity and broad, historical significance. He
had always thought that he had gone into the shops because he wanted to get away from home, because he
liked the work and because he saw a chance to make
money and maybe get somewhere. But there was evidently more to it. He saw now that he was one on whom
the leaders like Major Pettibone relied, to whom they
gave their respect as to a man who had gallantly and
boldly chosen a calling which would lead the South to
new wealth, new achievement.

As he climbed the steps Mrs. Torker's rocker ceased
its squeaking. He felt that she and her husband were
listening critically for what he should have to say on
his return from worldly intercourse. He decided to say
nothing and sat down on the porch in silence. The cur-
few bell was ringing. It ceased. A stray negro hurried
by toward the safety of his master's house. And still
James sat quiet. Mr. Torker could contain himself no
more.

"You were talking to old Cassius Pettibone," he said. In view of the impending Day of Judgment, Mr. Torker had long since discarded titles.

"Well," said James carefully. "He was talking to me."

"He's always full of gin and politics," said Mr. Torker without heat.

"And ain't he the man, though," Mrs. Torker added, "to make a nobody feel like a somebody."

James met this thrust. "I don't reckon I'm such a nobody," he answered stoutly.

Mr. Torker seized this opening with alacrity. "Every man is a nobody," he observed, "until and unless the Spirit of the Lord has laid hold upon him."

CHAPTER XVII

JAMES FRASER had never given much thought to the peculiarities of Yankees. The only one he had ever met —Mr. Higgins—he had dismissed with a casual if wondering appraisal. Mr. Higgins had been beyond all comprehension and embarrassingly queer, but harmlessly so; however, it now appeared that if you got enough Higginses together they were liable to do most anything. As the spring and summer passed the town began to vibrate to tales of Yankee imbecility,—not dangerous imbecility, because Yankees lacked the courage to be dangerous, but mighty exasperating just the same. Not content with worshipping John Brown they had carried their fanaticism into politics. Even the Yankee Democrats, always before good friends of the South, succumbed to the universal Yankee frenzy. They raised an antislavery fuss at the Charleston Convention and busted the convention up. Next the Black Republican party, newly organized, swept Yankeeland by storm and at a tremendous convention in Chicago, put up Lincoln, an abolitionist country lawyer, and a man named Hamlin who was known to have negro blood in his veins. All this James Fraser gleaned from listening to arguments on street corners and among the mechanics and yard-hands who ate their dinners out of tin pails together each day in the shadow of the railroad shops. The whole business amazed him, then stirred his sullen anger. He had never thought about the Yankees much, still less about the Union, but had reckoned both were good things in their own way. He knew that the folks where he was raised were pretty well satisfied with the Old North State and had no wish to mess with the Yankees or with the Union. On the other hand they had no idea that any one else had a right to mess with them. And now it seemed like these Yankees who had robbed the South of her money for years, and for years had starved their own workers to death, had suddenly started to fret themselves into a lather about slaves. Whether a man looked at it as a statesman, like Major Cassius Pettibone, or as an exponent of the Book of Revelation, like Mr. Torker, all agreed that there was no limit to Yankee foolishness.

Bill, the yard brakeman, having once seen something of the world as a passenger brakeman, assumed among the roundhouse group the rôle of an authority on Yankees.

"Talk to me about Yankees," Bill declaimed, ramming a sausage home with the heel of his hand, "Why, my old breeches! A Yankee will make money out of the Day of Judgment. I remember we were coming down from Rocky Mount one night and there was a Yankee travelling man that started to peddle patent medicine through the car. I told him it was against the rules and he sat down. Along about White Oak she left the rails and turned over. I crawled out from the baggage-car and all I could see was a cloud of dust and that Yankee on a stump hollering out, 'Ladies and gentlemen! Here you are! Electric Elixir for cuts, bruises, abrasions, and that sinking feeling!'"

less men watched the train's long stop imperturbably.
Then in a fury of bell ringing and of throaty whistles
the engine would start again, and if the road was pretty
straight, their speed would mount to five, to ten, to
fifteen miles an hour, till the rattling windows tried to
jump out of their frames and the kerosene-lamps overhead kicked up against the ceiling. To James Fraser,
clutching the edges of the red plush seat, these moments
of high velocity were dangerously intoxicating. He
felt that to a man who thus, enveloped in smoke and
an unsupportable, maddening din, annihilated space,
all things were possible. He felt that if he had a mind,
he could dive right out the window and, freed from
earthly trammels, soar away to join the startled turkey
buzzards. Not seriously, of course, but just enough to
give him a sense of vast emancipation.

Remembering Bill's solicitous advice, he had taken
a seat at the end of the car farthest from the stove.
There was small temptation to do otherwise, for the day
was hot and bright, despite which, however, the stove
was kept well stoked with pine knots, possibly for the
purpose of vaporizing the tobacco juice that by the
better class of travellers was invariably directed against
its glowing sides. There were other travellers less con-
siderate. It, therefore, gave satisfaction to James, who
had fortified himself with a small chew of Bully Boy, to
walk down the aisle from time to time and deposit the
surplus where it would redound to the credit of his
bringing up. On these visits to the stove he was able
to make covert inspection of his fellow passengers, to
note the hard-voiced Yankee merchant, who looked so

staid and sober among the gold seals and flowered plush
waistcoats of the up-country planters and the splendors
of the handsome matron who, with an entourage con-
sisting of a lace-swaddled baby, a little boy in a velvet
roundabout, two negro maids, and countless portman-
teaus and hat-boxes, had preempted the better half of
the car. She sat unmoved, her green mantua drawn
close about her, amid her party's unrelieved confusion.
The baby cried, a portmanteau burst open, the negresses
ate lumps of pork fat and licked their chops, the little
boy leaned out the window, and was hauled back with
a cinder in his eye and a face as black as a Christy min-
strel. It was all the same to the handsome matron.
Across from her an ancient lady, a mere withered heap
of ostrich plumes and jet, sat very rigid, vibrating every
bead in indignation at the aromatic snores of a gentleman in a sky-blue neckcloth obviously the worse for too
many convivial precautions against the journey. Her
mounting sense of outrage took concrete form when
Captain Joe, the conductor, stoop-shouldered, deprecating, gently officious, requested her fare. In a vibrant
voice she denied the obligation to pay for transporta-
tion under circumstances so abhorrent to a lady. With
all possible deference, and a bow cut short by a lurch of
the car, Captain Joe, while expressing the highest esteem
for Miss Miranda's private character and social position, begged to be excused from sharing her view.
Brushing aside his formal compliments she proposed,
for the benefit of the now attentive car, a series of
rhetorical questions which ended with the demand if
he thought she was going to pay good money to be

cooped up alongside of a drunken, snorting pine-rooter. She paused dramatically while every ostrich plume quivered a mute accusation at the unconscious gentleman in the blue neck-cloth. Captain Joe took off his hat and gazed at the large brass plate inscribed "Conductor" on the front of it as though he would draw reassurance from this tangible evidence of his official status. But the old lady turned her back on him. He put his cap on again dejectedly and came down the aisle.

"Miss Miranda is a mighty fine lady," he observed to two old planters in front of James, "but she always was set in her notions. I declare I don't know what to say to her," he added superfluously enough.

The planters nodded. One stroked the long gray hair on his neck.

"They ain't a thing a man can say when a lady gets set that way."

The other, somewhat younger and sharper featured, cocked his head judicially.

"It appears to me like she ought to pay her fare." He looked up at the conductor as though he had contributed the most helpful suggestion in the world.

"Yes. That's so," Captain Joe admitted. "Everybody ought." He seemed to feel that thus to state the principle in general terms somewhat reduced its disquieting application.

The younger old planter sharpened his features, he frowned.

"But she won't pay it. That's where the trouble is." Again he seemed to feel that he had done much to solve the difficulty.

His gray-haired friend roused himself.

"Won't some of her kin pay at the other end?"

The conductor was not hopeful.

"She's fought with all her kin."

The planters were dejected.

"A person makes a mighty big mistake to fight with their kin," said the younger. The older shook his gray head.

"That's too bad."

"It sho'ly is," Captain Joe agreed, "because she's a mighty fine lady. Only," he continued, "she's got this idea about paying fare. Another time it was because the roof of the car caught fire. I let it go then but the company people of Wilmington blamed me some for it."

At this point the Yankee who had been watching the conference with interest got up and joined them.

"What's the difficulty, gents, what's the difficulty?" he rapped out with a proprietary air.

Captain Joe hesitated, seeming to sense that the new-comer might not prove sympathetic. The sharp-faced planter inclined his head toward Miss Miranda.

"That lady don't appear to be inclined to pay her fare."

The Yankee rubbed his hands together briskly.

"Won't pay? Thunderation! She's got to pay. Passenger's a party to a contract."

The conductor was offended by the Yankee's assurance.

"But how you going to do if she won't pay?"

"How? Thunderation! Put her off next stop. Just a matter of business."

Captain Joe stared at this ruthless being in astonishment.

"How you going to put her off?"

It was the Yankee's turn to stare.

"How? How? Why, my soul, like anybody else."

The planters were now aroused. They conferred together in whispers, each keeping a hostile eye on the Northern man of business. They reached down into their pockets, passed silver dollars to the conductor.

"Take out whatever it is, Captain," said the elder, "and let the lady ride."

"Of course," the Yankee cut in, "if that old party's without funds, I'd be glad to come in myself."

The younger planter gave a short, dry laugh.

"Funds! Why if that lady owns one negro, she owns fifteen."

At this the Yankee subsided into dazed silence. Meanwhile the conductor was speaking.

"I declare, I surely do appreciate this, gentlemen," he said. "It relieves me from a mighty embarrassing situation. No one cain't say I don't try to be accommodating," he ventured. The planters nodded. "Why, on this very trip I am carrying a pair of cassimere pantaloons for Judge Sellers at Halifax, and the Judge is Miss Miranda's own second cousin. I reckon you gentlemen are acquainted with him. He's a man about my size and he got me to have the pantaloons made to my measure at Wilmington. Then I've got a possum dog for Kinney Bethune at Rockey Mount, and a spool of ribbon that my wife matched for the Jennings girls there. Their niece is fixing to marry a gentleman from

Virginia in October. At Sweet Gum I've got to find old man Denahay and tell him that his son-in-law's in jail again. Yes, suh, I try to be accommodating," he repeated, "but when it comes to collecting fares I feel like the company holds me mo' or less responsible."

The Yankee here capitulated. He turned away and went back to his seat, where for some time afterward he stared out the window in a state of deep dejection.

The conductor, wreathed in contentment, moved back to the rear car. The planters resumed their discourse.

"Cotton's up again, I see."

"So's nigger property. 'Pears like you can't have one without the other."

"And you can't get the niggers that you used to, neither. In Wilmington they are selling Virginia niggers as prime field-hands that would have been rated half-hands in my dad's time."

"You can get 'em if you know where to look. They say they's a good many coming into South Carolina."

"But they say a good many of those smuggled niggers dies. Anyhow, they can't talk English and besides, a man might get in trouble with the government."

"Sho! Not with a South Carolina jury. Why, they won't even convict the fellows that brings 'em in from Africa."

"Well, things are liable to be different after the election."

The older planter shook a melancholy head. "Election! I've seen a heap of elections in my time. Things are never any different."

"Maybe so. But it looks like something was bound to happen. If Breckenridge gets it, the government will let us alone. Law or no law, we'll get all the niggers we want."

"What good will that do? The more niggers the less they're worth. African niggers will break the market."

"But if niggers are cheap a poor man can get some and go to raising cotton and be prosperous."

The old planter was not impressed. "The more cotton the less it's worth." That was final; he looked out the window. "Anyhow," he added, "Breckenridge won't get it."

"Well, if Lincoln gets it those folks in South Carolina are going to bust loose. I spent a week in Charleston."

"Let them bust. They'll be no better off. What they need is less politics and more fertilizer."

"By God, seh," the other burst out, "you talk like a Yankee! Do you mean to say that if we all get in a fuss with the North you won't stick by your people?"

The older man remained unmoved.

"I expect I'll be ahead of you in mixing into the fracas. But not because I expect it to benefit the South—in fact it will likely ruin her—but because I consider Yankees sanctimonious, ill-bred, meddlesome, mean, and chicken-livered, and would be mighty glad of a chance to show my feelings."

Surprised at this turn, the other did not reply.

"I'm not fooled like most folks by talk of prosperity and Southern rights." The angular profile of his cheek flushed swiftly, "I just plumb hate the Yankees."

Toward noon the country changed. Quite a few pines still remained to show dark green among the hardwood trees which crowned low hills and sheltered swelling pasture land below. Houses were painted, rambling, ample, and roads were wavering streaks of vermilion clay. The rear door of the car was flung open and the conductor blew in on gusts of dust and down-pouring smoke, and fetching up alongside James, placed a hand on his shoulder.

"We're coming to yore station, son."

At the sound of the engine's lugubrious whistle Captain Joe hurried back to set the brakes. With shudders the train slowed down; stopped with a groan. James Fraser descended the steep car-steps and looked around. Except for a lean-to shelter with a bench beneath it and, beside the track, a padlocked tool-box, the scene consisted in one long, low, naked hill. There was no sign of the station-agent, or of any one. The conductor, standing by James' side, was much distressed. He seemed almost to regard it as a grave professional failure on his part, and to be considering how imperative was his obligation to hold the train until the agent should appear.

Meanwhile a negro threw the new switch-point off the baggage-car ahead.

"Maybe the agent stopped at the old Nayloe place till he heard the whistle," the conductor ventured. "If he don't come maybe he left the key of the tool-box there." He squinted up his mild gray eyes and scanned the hill. "Heyo," he exclaimed joyfully, " I reckon that's him now."

A little cloud of amber dust and a brown canvas top were moving slowly over the crest.

"Yes, seh," he said, "I reckon so. He drives a covered cart." The engineer blew a whistle of impatience. Captain Joe glanced toward the cab and vouchsafed a placating nod.

"Henry's fussing to get along to-day," he explained. "His wife's expecting a baby." He gave James a handshake, dignified and friendly, and waved a signal to the engineer.

"Well, then, son, I expect you're fixed."

Climbing aboard he pulled the signal cord. With a sharp whistle and a soul-shaking jerk the train started. A blur of faces at the windows shot by James and then the platform of the last car flinging from side to side and sucking little streams of dust behind it.

CHAPTER XVIII

THERE was small excitement on election day. Men went quietly to the polls, voted for Breckenridge, the Southern gentleman, and then sat round on steps and porches, spaded their backyard gardens or went down the river fishing. Not old enough to vote, and still unskilful in enjoying a city-dweller's leisure, James Fraser wandered rather disconsolately from group to group.

After Mrs. Torker's noonday meal of cold-slaw and salt mackerel, and after a couple of lukewarm drinks from a green bottle proffered by Bill, the brakeman, James wandered alone down to the water-side and sat down on the end of a deserted pier, feeling sleepy and somewhat bilious. Beneath his feet the oily water heaved gently and cast up varied blue and lavender reflections. The motion and the color were not agreeable. He half closed his eyes and leaned back against a hawser-worn pile. Across the stream lay nothing but the illimitable cypress swamp in which, save for the slender thread of the river and the slender thread of railroad, the city was marooned. The tall and countless cones of green stretched away as far as he could see, broken only by the ferry-house on the other bank and, upstream, by the rusty tin sides of a cotton-press whose mere wisp of smoke from the lofty stack showed that it slumbered through the holiday. Above the cotton-press two figures, huddled impassive in a boat, were fishing, and further up, the cypress swamp closed in on either hand until the river disappeared among them. It really was a mighty lonely place when you came to look at it. When first he came to Wilmington it had seemed the centre of the universe. Ten thousand people walking round the streets, building houses, running boats and engines, running banks and stores and factories, going to law, going to church, getting up schools and fire companies and balls. But now that he had got used to it he saw that it was just a little hill of ants lost in uncounted, silent miles of swamp. Looked at that way, it was lonelier than his own home. He'd be mighty glad when to-morrow came and he was back working in the shop. He'd half a mind to go up there now and just have a look around, but it wouldn't be the same with everything deserted; it might make him feel more lonesome than ever, and besides if it got out that he was up there on a holiday, the other boys might think he was queer. He leaned his head back against the pile resignedly. There was certainly nothing in the world like working on steam-locomotives. The thought came into his mind that if that time the Colonel's pounding mill had broken down he had known what he now knew about engines he could probably have fixed it the easiest thing in the world, and then things might have been different. But no, they would not. He could have built the Colonel an engine from the ground up and the Colonel would still have looked on him just the same, and so would she. What a man could do made no difference to people like that. What did, then? It was hard to say. You had to be the son of a friend of theirs, put it that way. And if you were, everything was all right, no matter what you did or couldn't do yourself. He had noticed some of these young sons of planters who came up to Wilmington for a spree. The most of them had no more sense than common and some of them a heap less; they had higher manners and acted like they were heavy coon dogs but when you came down to it what they said didn't mean much. Three of them had come into Foretop Smith's one night making a great show with their gold-headed canes and polished boots. The barkeeper had near bowed himself in two as he served them but when they had had a couple of drinks they giggled and babbled like children. Some of Foretop's simple patrons had been pleased, maybe because they were relieved to find that these young bucks were as big fools as anybody else. But he himself had itched to start a fracas with them and had begun manœuvring to that end when Foretop's paw, descending, had drawn him aside. Foretop, who had often stood on his bar unmoved while a dozen men from the ends of the earth bit and clawed and gouged each other on the floor, was now perturbed.

"It won't do to start a fuss, Jimmy. The police would close me up. That one in the brown satin waistcoat," he had added in simple explanation, "is a son of the biggest planter in New Hanover."

And then another time when he had been waiting his turn in the shop of Henry, the free negro barber, two heavy young swells had come in. The negro had dropped his customer and conferred with them in deferential whispers. James could not catch what they were

saying but he had a pretty good idea, for at the end that
smooth rascal, Henry, had inclined his head in melancholy acquiescence.

"Yes, indeed, seh. I know the one you mean. She's
gone back to New Orleans." No, sir, they weren't
much, these young planters, and that was a fact. It was
a fact that gave him some grim satisfaction but it was
also a fact which made no difference. They weren't
much—but they didn't have to be. He was in a cage.
And once you had a man in a cage it didn't take much to
keep him there.

A footstep sounded on the heavy planking of the
dock, a voice from home called, "Hi, Jim, I've been
looking for you." Dougald Cameron, the schoolmaster,
his square figure tugging at the seams of his worn kersey
suit, was coming toward him with the solemn sort of
half-grin which stood for the limit of cordiality amongst
the country folks. James sprang to his feet in one joyful bound, and then contained himself with more propriety.

"How you, Dougald?" he said gravely. "Where
you come from?"

"I took the holiday to come see Judge Seagrove about
the bar examinations." Dougald shifted a fat calf-skin
volume under his arm. "Then I hunted up your board-
ing-house."

"I'm glad you found me," said James earnestly.

"So am I," said Dougald. "Your folks will be
pleased."

He placed the law-book on the ground. "Coke upon
Littleton" the red label read. He gave two careful

pulls to the knees of his trousers and sat down upon it. James squatted against the pile.

"How's Ma?" he said.

"Finest in the world; and your Pa, too."

"That's good. That farm's a mighty big handful for Pa single-handed."

Dougald's eyes, young but tired and prematurely reflective, were crinkled by his friendly bantering smile.

"I reckon your wages help him more than you would."

"Cash money always comes in mighty handy for a farmer," James admitted. He wished that he had sent home more each week, then he would have gotten more satisfaction out of Dougald's remarks.

"I passed him this morning," Dougald went on, "on his way to Racker's store to vote."

"I reckon he voted for Breckenridge," James answered conversationally.

"I reckon so," said Dougald. "Everybody is." But he seemed to take no pleasure in the fact. James was puzzled. Who else was there to vote for except the Southern Democrat?

"I reckon you lost your vote by coming away," James said. "That's too bad."

"Yes," said Dougald speaking slowly. "I missed my vote." He picked up a big splinter from the dock and balanced it in his hand as though it represented a problem in his mind. "I've been reading a book." He spoke as if to himself.

"I expect so," said James amiably. "I don't reckon

you carry that thing around," he nodded at Coke upon Littleton, "just to sit on." He paused, then added, "How much do you reckon that book weighs?" It had occurred to him that he might be able to form some estimate of the size of the switch-engine fireman's Bible. But Dougald was lost in thought. His broad, short chin was drawn into his stock; above it his broad mouth made a straight grim line to where the clean-shaved, heavy stubble of his chops curved around it. His wool hat, neatly brushed, came off and was flung down on the dock, his stiff, black hair fell down and hung before the two low strong bulges above his eyebrows. After a time James said uneasily, "Dougald, what's on your mind?"

Dougald looked up, looked at him steadily. "See here, Jim," he said, "can I talk to you?"

"Why—why yes, why sure."

Dougald's look was grim. "I mean, can I really talk? Down there," he jerked his head down the river, "I can't."

"If you mean will I keep my mouth shut," James answered, "I will."

"Well, that helps some," said Dougald heavily, "but will you understand?" He raised up the splinter in his hand and looked at both ends carefully again as if it were the subject in his mind and he were thinking how to begin. "Well, this book," he said, "has given me new ideas."

"What, that law-book?"

"No, not this book," he paused painfully. "A book about slavery."

"My Lord, Dougald! You haven't been reading 'Uncle Tom's Cabin,' have you?"

Dougald gave a grunt of disgust. "Well, I've read it but that's the biggest fool book I ever did read. No, this was another book. I reckon you've never heard of it." He looked over his shoulder to make sure they were alone. "The Impending Crisis," it's called.

James' tone was still profoundly uneasy and disturbed. "Yes, I've heard of it. Why, Dougald, it's against the law to own that book."

"I don't own it," said Dougald, "but," he added more firmly, "I read it—twice. It's got sense."

"I thought it was an abolition book," said James incredulously.

"No, it's not that; it's something different. It was written by a man from this state." James waited. "He says," said Dougald in a low voice, "that slavery is what keeps the Southern poor man where he is and he proves it by figures."

"I reckon there are lots of poor folks in the South," said James, "but how does slavery keep 'em so?"

Dougald grasped the stick of wood firmly. "All the money in the South goes into slaves so there's none left for development. And all the slaves go into the hands of a few big planters." His face kindled. "Why, man, there's only five thousand people in the whole South that own more than fifty slaves apiece and there are five million that don't own any. Up North all a man has to do is to save up money enough to buy him a farm. He can hire hands to work it; down here he's got to buy the farm and the negroes too, and if the niggers turn out worthless, he's lost his money. He can't fire 'em like hired hands. And, anyhow, it don't pay to work just a few negroes; to show a profit you've got to work 'em in gangs. How can a poor man get a gang of negroes? And in any case, to make money off negroes you've got to raise negro crops, cotton and tobacco mostly, but you can't do that always on the same ground; you've got to clear new land and let the outworn fields lie idle. A poor man hasn't enough land to do that. Why, even big planters have been obliged to give up in the East here and carry their niggers out to new ground in Alabama and Mississippi and Texas. Negroes are worth more than land and the idea is to get the most crops out of the negro, not the most crops out of the land. That's a game the poor man can't play."

"I know the planters are on top," said James. How well he knew it! "And maybe that is the reason. It sounds mo' or less like sense to me. And it's as simple and plain as a, b, c." Frowning, he looked at Dougald through shrewdly crinkled eyes. "But if it's so plain and sensible, why don't mo' folks say the same? They's been slaves and poor folks long enough for people to figure it out."

"People are afraid," said Dougald. "This is not from the book. It's just my idea." He pointed the stick he held at James. "Maybe the planters think that slavery is right as a principle. I reckon they do." He twisted a corner of his mouth ironically. "But if so, they are mo' sensitive about it than they are about anything else that they consider right as a principle."

James nodded thoughtfully. The twist in Dougald's mouth widened to a grin.

"You can tell a planter that it is a mistake always to

keep his word or always to be courteous to a lady; you can even tell him that it is wrong to drink liquor or to race horses. He'll think you are a fool but otherwise he won't take it much amiss." Dougald tapped the stick on his knee. "But tell him that it is wrong to own slaves,——!"

James grinned. "He might not be too well pleased," he observed dryly.

"No," said Dougald. "They won't talk about it nor allow any one else to talk about it. In that regard planters are afraid."

"But they's only a few of them," said James.

"They make the laws, though," Dougald answered; "laws against abolition books and against freeing negroes and against teaching them to read. And the other folks are afraid in their way, too. They are afraid to see the negroes freed."

"You can't blame them for that," said James. "I can see how slavery hurts us, sure enough. But millions of free negroes would hurt us mo'."

Dougald seemed to commune with himself.

"That's a fact. You can't collect three million negroes and put them on ships and send them back to Africa, and you can't free three million negroes and turn them loose on the country. But it looks to me," he said firmly, "like we ought to let the new territories in the West to come in free, then there would be some place for our poor people to go."

"Yes, seh," James agreed, "that sounds like good sense."

"Well then," Dougald fixed his eyes on him inexor-

ably, "if a man believes that, how is he going to vote
for Breckenridge? Breckenridge wants all the slave
territory he can get."

Here was a dilemma. A decent man ought to vote for
Breckenridge; everybody knew that. He had nothing
to say.

"You don't know the answer," said Dougald, "and I
don't either. That's why I missed my vote." He stood
up, tucked the law-book under his arm, looked down at
James. "I've studied over this business more than
most," he said. "I've studied it the best I could;
and yet,—if the folks down the river knew I wouldn't
vote for Breckenridge, they would think they have the
right to call me a traitor. So I have to keep mighty
quiet." He reached a hand down to James, pulled him
up beside him and smiled. "This talk has made me
feel better though." Dougald pulled out a thick silver
watch from his waistcoat pocket. "I must be going,"
he said. "I'll miss that boat."

Their footsteps reechoed from deserted warehouses
as they walked in silence down the cobbled lane.

Under the pavilion on the steamboat-wharf the sharp-
faced young man who sold tickets aboard the boat sat
on a keg embracing one sharp knee. He smoked a cigar
and from time to time issued superfluous directions to
a tattered, gangling negro who was carrying kegs on
board. Then he went on board himself and disappeared
into his little ticket-office.

"I reckon I better be going, too," said Dougald.

He reappeared on deck and leaning over the boat's
railing continued to retail local gossip to James on the

dock below.   Old Man Roon was running for sheriff and was likely to be elected.

"Why, my Lord," said James. "He owes money to half the county."

"That's it," said Dougald. "All his creditors are voting for him. They think he might make enough money sheriffing to pay them back."

The court had given twenty lashes to a negro of Major Gregg's for teaching another negro to read. And Harry Horniblow had been sued by another woman for breach of promise. The jury had acquitted him on the grounds that everybody ought to know Harry by this time. "Oh," said Dougald with a look of uncommon sprightliness in his sober eye, "there was a lady inquiring for you the other day."

"A lady?"

"Yes, we had a school committee meeting at Colonel Prevost's. I happened to mention that I was coming up to Wilmington and just as I left, Miss Stewart came up to me while the others were talking to the Colonel and said, 'If you see James Fraser, remember me to him.'"

Chill numbness gripped James' heart, wrung it, spread treacherously through his veins; he felt weak and sick, doomed, desperately forlorn, cut off from life and all reality, even from Dougald who now was speaking again, telling more gossip from his home.

The steamboat whistle blew, a hawser slashed the water, the railing and Dougald leaning on it began to drift away. There still was time to leap for it, to seize it, clamber aboard.

Now it was out of reach. The crisis was past, he was

able to smile a stiff, inhuman smile, to wave in short jerks, mechanically. The boat swung in the stream. He turned and with downcast head and swift long strides hurried from the dock.

CHAPTER XIX

THE papers next day told how the Yankees had elected the Black Republican as President. Men spoke about it grimly. Let Lincoln himself say what he pleased about wishing the South well, it was an Abolition trick. No more than a threat as yet, but North Carolina was on guard. At the first sign of interference the Abolitionists would learn a thing or two.

It soon appeared, however, that the people in South Carolina were not disposed to wait until they were trampled on. Before Christmas they had withdrawn from the Union and set up for themselves. That was going a little strong maybe, some of the older men said, but after all they had a right to if they wanted to. It was their own affair.

Christmas itself was a dreary and uneasy day. James had wanted to go home and stay over New Year's but the shops just now were working overtime. The order had come that everything on wheels was to be put in shape, so he had only the day—a day of cold, clammy rain and streaks of sea-driven mist. The air seemed heavy with foreboding. Only the children shot off their firecrackers with accustomed gusto and the negroes by immemorial privilege paraded the streets that night in fantastic dress and costume, singing, dancing, and shouting "Christmas gif'!"

In the swift weeks that followed five more States left the Union, and meeting together at Montgomery formed a confederacy. As far as Wilmington and the Cape Fear were concerned that settled it. A thrill ran through the people. Here was a government of the South—a Southern Nation—springing into being, an Empire of their own, free from fetters, threats, and impositions of sanctimonious, greedy aliens, free to develop, to achieve dignity, prosperity, and glory according to the Southern genius. And it was all so simple: they had but to withdraw from the Union as was their privilege, to leave the government where they were now a meanly used, misunderstood minority, and join their strength to the new nation whose sympathy by birth, by breeding, by tradition, would be forever theirs. It was all so simple. How could any man hold back? They had the right and, anyhow, the Yankees wouldn't fight; a race of shopkeepers and bluenosed elders, they valued their skins as highly as their pocketbooks. Their government right now was paralyzed, distracted; their politicians, even their President, Old Buchanan, sought frantically to patch up some shabby compromise, to keep by trickery and trading what they could not keep by force. They would negotiate, palaver as long as there was hope, but they would not fight. A gentleman from Charleston, sent to encourage North Carolina, had stood up before five thousand people on the Court House steps. Hawk-eyed, pale and passionate, he had pulled a handkerchief from his tight broadcloth sleeve, a handkerchief far smaller and finer than Major Pettibone's. He had held it aloft, a fluttering wisp of cambric.

"My friends!" he had cried, "They won't fight! Bullies have ever been cowards since the world began.

They won't fight. With this handkerchief I'll guarantee
to wipe up every drop of blood that's spilled."

"You need not be alarmed," he had added loftily.
"You need not hesitate. There can be no doubt nor
danger in an issue between southern chivalry and
nothern traders." He clenched his hand aloft, then
pointed to the north, "Have not our representatives at
Washington for years challenged Yankee politicians to
make good their low slanders, to defend their vulgar
and cowardly abuse on the field of honor? How often
has such a challenge been accepted? And when our
representative, Mr. Brooks, had chastised a Yankee
senator who had insulted his family with all the vulgar
ingenuity of an educated gutter-snipe but who dared
not risk his skin to back his charges, what happened?
Was there a Yankee in the North who dared to raise a
hand in the whipped dog's defence? And then you remember Preston Brooks' triumphal progress through
the South. Why did we all accord him honor? Because he represented, typified the thousands of good
men in the South who stand ready to back their names
with their lives." His voice turned coldly derisive.
"And against these thousands not one man of that
calibre could be found in the whole pitiful Yankee
nation." Pitch by pitch he raised them to frenzy;
the crowd became a roaring, boiling sea of straining
eyes and mouths, of waving hats and sticks and banners,
so that when old Judge Seagrove, climbing painfully up
the steps, had waited, wonderfully gray and grim and
old, until the shouting ceased, and had then begun in
his dry, cracked voice, "North Carolina has never in

the past found it necessary to be shown her duty by emissaries from elsewhere. With all personal respect to our distinguished visitor, I therefore say that we should ask ourselves why is it necessary now?" he was checked by an angry murmur. He kept on manfully; through the growing tumult fragments of sentences still reached them. "No government has ever been designed with an implied provision for its own destruction. . . . What you propose is revolution and that, of course, is an inherent right. . . . But on what pretext will we go before the world?" Then some one shouted, "Hurrah for Southern rights!" A band struck up. They formed broad, lurching columns that stretched from curb to curb and marched away down Market Street. James Fraser, his arms linked with Bill and the switch-engine boy, looked backward as he tramped away. Judge Seagrove in his rusty black coat still stood on the Court House steps alone. His eyes strained after the retreating crowd as though he were never to see one of them again. Below him the gentleman from South Carolina, encircled by ribbons and leghorn hats, was being smothered under flowers.

The abolitionist Lincoln was inaugurated without incident though there had been sufficient talk of Southern plots to scare him into stealing into Washington City by night and secretly. Meanwhile the South Carolinians had mobilized and with their forces had ringed in Fort Sumter at the harbor's mouth at Charleston, had cut it off until it should capitulate, the flag come down and the last Yankee be driven from their soil.

There had been no clash as yet. The South Carolina troops, the Palmetto Guards, the Washington Light Infantry merely hemmed the lonely fortress in, covered it with their guns, lay watching it, silent, motionless, but ready. And as the Cape Fear, as the nation watched the two antagonists—on one side the flower, the gay charm, the dash and courage of the South, on the other the fort of square grim stone beneath the ancient flag, each lying so still, so dauntless, so intent, awaiting only one solitary gun—a hush fell on them and on all the world. The war-talk ebbed, the bombast ceased; in those foreboding, silent days men trod lightly even in their thoughts.

Then on a shining April morning newsboys were screaming through the streets, old men embraced each other, cried for joy, young men slapped backs, kissed girls, threw hats above the trees, negroes turned cartwheels, cackled frantically. Sumter had been attacked, had fallen! In gleaming pompons and pipe-clayed cross belts the Wilmington Light Infantry was coming down the street. The town fell in behind, around, before them. Ahead at the peak of the flag-pole before the City Hall hung a small, bright bundle, the new flag among the nations ready to break out to the breeze. The great, unwieldy phalanx lifted up their faces, drove onward toward it with a steady tramp and cheer. From every porch and balcony handkerchiefs waved and waved.

After that the end was swift and sudden. Lincoln had added the supreme touch to Yankee folly by calling on North Carolina for militia to put down what he termed rebellion in the Southern States. The governor's answer had been to seize Fort Caswell and the United States arsenal at Fayetteville and to call for thirty thousand volunteers. Already the Heavy Artillery company and the German Volunteers were drilling each night on the Light Infantry parade-ground before the eyes of all the girls in town. And these same girls began to look inquiringly at James Fraser and all young, able-bodied men still in civilian life who passed them on the street.

The Light Infantry had left the week before and were now in peaceful possession of Fort Caswell at the river's mouth. As their steamer, the rail a line of wildly waving shakoes, had left the dock James Fraser had wished in his soul that he were with them. But that would never have been possible. No man could join the Light Infantry unless the breeding of an old well-tested Wilmington family lay behind him. Soon they would be raising a company at home, he reflected, and that was where he belonged. But they had better be quick about it; if there were to be any fight at all, it would surely be over soon, and then how would he feel? If something didn't happen within a week he'd quit the job and go where he could get into the fuss. If only the Yankees would stand up long enough to give him just one crack at them. All of his past life seemed unbelievably dull and colorless beside this shining hour of action, glory, of bands and cheers and troops and waving handkerchiefs. Each morning on his way to work he bought a copy of the *Journal*, scanned it eagerly, he wrote home urgently for news. Before the answer came an item in the paper, al-

most lost among the blazonings of great events, told him
what he wanted:

THE CAPE FEAR RIFLES

"A number of gentlemen of the Cape Fear having
undertaken to arm and equip a company at their own
charges, a camp of instruction has been established at
Beaumont, the plantation of Colonel Prevost, and recruits are daily coming in."

He tore the item out of the paper and stuck it in his
pocket.

Down at the freight-yards, Bill the brakeman was
assisting very gingerly to place three sealed box-cars on
the siding by the freight sheds. Bill showed intense and
most unusual solicitude for those three cars. "Let her
come easy. Let her come easy," he intoned, standing
well clear of the rails. He waggled his hand emphatically to signal slow. As the switch-engine clanked away
he looked up with relief and treated himself to a chew.

"Bill," said James, "I'm going home. They're
getting up a company down there." He spoke casually
but he could not help expecting that Bill, the patriot,
would have for him a word of admiration and encouragement. Bill, however, merely shook his bullet head.

"You're wasting your time."

"What?"

"The Yankees ain't goin' to fight."

"Why, man, they're bound to fight!"

Bill pointed to the box-cars. "You know what's in
them cars?" he said. "Guns and ammunition from

New York. They ain't goin' to sell guns if they're goin' to fight."

"But they've got to fight," said James with some exasperation.

Bill's tone was lofty but soothing.

"You're a good boy, Jimmie, but Yankees won't fight. Why, I remember a Yankee comin' into Weldon fo', five years ago—" But James was in no mood for reminiscence. He walked stiffly away to find the boss and give in his time.

That evening the forward deck of the river steamer was packed with mysterious boxes which for size and shape might have been coffins except for the fact that two sentries in the uniform of the Wilmington Light Infantry, already considerably stained and dusty, stood guard over them. James was greatly tempted to engage these sentries in conversation with a view to learning what he could of military life. But except toward three young ladies on board they were excessively stiff and martial. In addition, each had a negro servant who made a great show of brushing his master's great-coat, fetching him food and drink from the first-class dining saloon and, in general, of establishing his own identity as the servant of a military hero.

The trip itself was interminable. The old boat throbbed and thrashed along, crossing from one green shore of pine woods, mottled with autumnal foliage, to the other, stopping at every landing-stage to give long-drawn, detailed, inconsequential news of public affairs.

As they dropped down the river he became conscious

that hourly the tall house of Beaumont was drawing nearer. Before, even though it had been named in the notice of the Cape Fear Rifles, he had given it small thought; the chance to enlist had taken full possession of his mind. Now he was soon to see the place which once he had hoped never to see again. As a matter of fact he had seen it several times since then on his visits home from Wilmington, and never without a pang. And this time it was still more difficult, because he faced the prospect of joining the company where it was camped on the plantation, of having perhaps to live for weeks on the very field where he had met defeat.

Still, he could face it, could face it so easily that it almost surprised and somewhat disappointed him. He was going to enlist; that decision seemed at once to have given him a dignifying purpose, an adventurous objective, a significance both noble and dashing which raised him above past sorrows, rendered him immune, superior to them.

This firm, unshakable poise was further strengthened by a roll of linoleum which lay beside his carpet-bag. He had bought it as a present for his mother just before he came on board. It had cost money, too. Four dollars. But he did not begrudge it. He knew how she had always wanted linoleum for the kitchen floor. No one else around home had it, in fact no one but themselves could boast a stove; all other families cooked on open fires. But that had made no difference to his mother, indeed her idea always was to be different from the other folks, her dread lest they themselves should sink till indistinguishable from crackers. She would be mighty pleased and he was mighty pleased right now—

coming home to enlist with a handsome present for his mother—he felt that he was a credit to himself, a man of merit and of glamour, above the reach of fate.

Thus when the high gray roofs of Beaumont showed among the trees he looked at them steadily and almost with equanimity. And if, against his will, an unhappy memory was about to thrust him through, it was checked by the flash of color on a tall staff which stirred against the sky. As he watched, it swung out on the April breeze, showed its fresh, shining pattern. His heart was quickened as with the thrill of drums and marching men. He wished that he knew how to give a salute, that he dared to raise a cheer. Instinctively he drew nearer to the sentries.

"The Colonel's got his flag up, I see," said one.

"Yes," the other answered, "I reckon he had that flag made ready on the day South Carolina went out." He shifted his rifle. "The Colonel," he added sententiously, "is a Southerner."

As they drew nearer James could make out figures on the Colonel's dock. One was in uniform; the light played on a sword-hilt by its side. As they came in shore the drab and clumsy silhouettes of the four others proved them to be negroes. The old boat butted against the piles, the officer came forward. It was Charles Prevost, very smart and slim.

"That's young Prevost," one sentry said.

"I know," the other answered. "He and I were rats together at V. M. I."

"He got his commission quick enough," the first resumed.

The other shrugged his shoulders elegantly. "He

can have it. I'd rather serve in the ranks of a company of gentlemen than command a company of crackers. Well, here he comes."

The two sentries stiffened to attention and gave an extra-military salute. Charles Prevost, smiling and blushing a little self-consciously, returned the salute with extra-military precision and jumped down on the deck.

"Why, hello, Carey," he said shaking the first sentry by the hand. "I'm mighty pleased to see you."

"This is Mr. Sherwood," said the first sentry.

Charles then shook hands with Carey's companion in arms.

"I have an order," he said "for four of your boxes of rifles." He produced a paper. "My negroes will carry them ashore."

"Oh, never mind," said Carey. "We'll do that."

"But surely, gentlemen—" Charles interposed.

But Carey had already shouted out, "Here, you boys," to the two body-servants. "Put four of these boxes ashore." The body-servants exhibited profound depression, not so much at the prospect of manual labor but because they felt that the deprivation of a single rifle would detract just so much from their masters' glory. So slowly and with such melancholy did they handle the first case that it took on more than ever the aspect of a coffin. The Prevost negroes, on the other hand, regarded the episode as a triumph for their family. They jumped down on the deck and wrestled for possession of the box. With some struggling and much recrimination the four cases of rifles were finally put ashore. Charles, shaking hands once again with the sentries, followed them. The engine-room bell signalled half speed ahead, the paddles began to turn. Standing on the dock, Charles cast his eye on James; his look of breezy general good-nature turned to one of recognition.

"Hello," he called out, "Isn't your name Fraser?"

"Yes, seh."

"Thought so. Coming home?"

"Yes, seh."

"You must join our Rifles. We need——"

"I aim to."

Charles laughed. "Good for you. I'll be on the lookout for you." He waved his hand farewell. The gesture was easy, cordial, almost affectionate, yet tinged with an indefinable and dignified propriety, spontaneous yet free from any hint of cheap camaraderie. All the way to the next landing where he was to leave the boat James considered within his mind how a young fellow got to be like that. Did a man learn how or was he born that way?

CHAPTER XX

James Fraser's home as he walked up from the branch, beneath the stars, looked mighty small, looked almost pitiful—this rude, unkempt little clearing scratched painfully from the heart of the immeasurable forest. There was something precarious about it, too. Unless his father or some other man of toil stayed there and kept scratching away, it would quickly vanish; the hog-pen of rails, the cow-pen of slabs, the flimsy house would tumble down, vines and creepers would cover the ruins, the trees would come in and close the tiny opening in their ranks. He had seen such abandoned places, many of them, where nothing remained but the marks of old furrows running through the woods, faint and touching memorials of laborious failure. His home was not the one immutable fact of the universe that he had used to think it as a small boy; on the contrary it represented an uncertain and unceasing struggle against the forest—a struggle in which the victory was mighty narrow. Yet as he looked at the patch of silver-gray fields and at the shadows of small, tumbled buildings, he knew that they had established for themselves a permanence in him far greater than in the days when he had thought them indestructible. As long as he lived, every rail and every shingle would be just so in his mind. He would be able to look at them and say to himself that he had had a mighty good home.

In the shadow of the porch his father and mother sat as though expecting him. His mother strode across the white sand and took hold of his sleeve.

"We reckoned you'd be along this evening," she said.

His father put down his newspaper, peered through his steel-rimmed spectacles and stood up, a sign, in him, of considerable excitement.

"Well, James," he said, "Well, well." He checked himself as though he had gone too far, then looked James over kindly but carefully and as if expecting to find marked changes for the worse.

"Yes," he said, "We reckoned you'd be along."

"How did you know?"

"Didn't you get my letter?" said his father stepping down from the porch slowly. He spoke as though he held James strictly responsible.

"No, seh," said James firmly.

"My land!" his mother cried, "I reckon that letter's still in Old Man Racker's store. The old man can't put his mind on anything but politics these days."

James sat his bag down on the porch. "Well," he said easily, "the old man never was much of a postmaster. How are you all?"

"All right." His mother's voice was mechanical. "Have you had your supper?"

"Yes, ma'am, on the boat."

"On the boat?" His father was grieved. "Why, they charge most anything for eating on the boat."

"I carried my rations with me," James explained.

His mother's tone was crestfallen, "I saved some beaten biscuit and a few things in case you'd come."

"Did you, sure enough? I could eat that fine. They don't have real good biscuit in Wilmington," he lied pleasantly.

Once in the kitchen, his father and mother noticed the roll of linoleum.

"What have you brought back?" his father said.

"Linoleum," he answered, "for the floor." He undid the strings and heavy wrapping-paper.

"Linoleum?" his mother cried. "Linoleum? Why where's your sense, son? You should have bought your-self some real good summer underwear." But her voice echoed incredulous delight. As the flowery pattern slowly unrolled itself she knelt down. She patted the smooth and brilliant surface. "My land!" she mur-mured. "Roses!" Her hand, thought James, looked mighty old and gnarly against that fresh and shining background. He was as well pleased as he could be that he had bought the linoleum for her. She looked up at him warmly and gave him her little crooked smile. "This surely will make a fine showing on the floor," she said.

His father now stooped down and turned a corner over. "It's got a good back," he announced with satis-faction. "That's the way you can tell good linoleum,— by the back."

"Yes, seh," said James. "That's what the man in the store said."

"It don't do to take everything those storekeepers say, though," his father cautioned him solemnly.

"No, seh," said James with some impatience, "but I could see for myself that he was right about this."

To this his father did not reply, but then he had a habit of never acknowledging when a point was well taken. With great care his mother smoothed down the curled edges of the linoleum.

"To-morrow," her voice was fresh and eager, "we'll have to lay it down."

"Yes," said James, "I've got some regular tacks in my valise."

While his mother crouched before the stove, made plates click and ring, his father, seated by the table, returned to his grievance, "That letter," he said, "told you what you wanted to know about getting up the company down here."

"I read about it in the paper," said James, "this morning."

"This morning?" His father was surprised into what might have been a grunt of admiration. Immediately he relapsed into cautious silence. "Well," he conceded at last, "you came right along.

"The company," he continued in a matter-of-fact tone, "is mighty near recruited up but I told young Charles Prevost to save a place for you."

"Yes," said James, "I saw him on the landing at Beaumont and told him the same."

His father, regarding that detail as closed, did not respond. He smoked and ruminated. "The company," he observed, "will be all right, I reckon, but the officers are too young. A man must have experience and judgment to be an officer."

"Who are the officers?" said James.

"Well, they are none of them elected yet but I

reckon Charles Prevost will be the captain. The Colonel's putting up most of the money."

"He ought to be a good captain."

"I reckon he would be," his father answered firmly, "ten years from now, but he's just a college boy and what training has he had except that he went through the Virginia Military Institute? A man ought to be trained in battle to be an officer."

"I reckon that's so," James answered. "But how are you going to train them in battle? They are mighty few battles."

Again his father did not answer. As a veteran of the Mexican War he was not pleased to have his military judgment questioned. He smoked in silence for many minutes and James did not venture further remark. At last his father thumped his pipe against the heel of his hand. "They are too young," he said.

His mother's voice, cheerful, strident, called. "Here's your supper."

While James tackled the biscuits and honey and the cold sweet potatoes his father sat opposite him and talked. His mother, seated nearer the stove, kept reaching hot biscuits from the oven. James did his best but soon he was obliged to shake his head in deprecation. He reached round to his coat which he had hung on the back of his chair, fished out a blue bandanna and wiped his mouth. "I'm through," he said.

His mother looked up grieved, almost exasperated. "Through?" she cried. "Why, you've not eat scarcely a thing. You'll lose your strength."

His father prepared for speech. He poised his pipe

in front of his mouth, wiped his gray goatee with the back of his hand. "He looks stout enough to me," he said.

"I've taken on weight," James acknowledged with quiet pride. "Muscle, too." Pulling back his blue-checked sleeve he closed his fist, made his forearm bulge. The muscle shot into a ridge which curved down from his elbow. But his fine, smooth skin was white from indoor work.

"Your skin's so pale," said his mother with quick concern. "It don't look like you could be healthy to have it like that." She looked at his arm and hand more closely. "Why, I declare," she said, "if you ain't dirty, son."

James pulled down his sleeve. "That's grease from the shop," he said. "It won't come off right away. I tried."

Iis mother was not appeased. "Lard will take it off," she said. Then seeing his discomfort, she added, "the most of it anyhow."

"A man can't work without getting dirty," his father observed sententiously. "The women never can understand that." He paused as though to recuperate from the effort of making so far-reaching an observation.

"But a man can get clean again," said Mrs. Fraser with emphasis. She shot a meaning glance at her husband. "Lots of them do."

"And as for being white and peaked," Mr. Fraser went on ignoring the issue, "a month's soldiering will make him brown enough." He paused again while his mind worked back to Mrs. Fraser's thrust. "Anyhow I always thought," his manner was laboriously pointed, "that you wanted the boy to look like a city fellow. City fellows are white." He leaned back, satisfied that he had delivered an adequate counter-stroke.

He enjoyed his triumph for some moments, then as if indirectly to hint at it, he said, "Yes, seh, a few months in the army will make a heap of difference in him."

"It made a heap of difference to my brother, Sam, sure enough," said Mrs. Fraser grimly.

Mr. Fraser gave her a look of concern. His uncle Sam, James Fraser recalled, in the same company as his father, had been killed at Buena Vista.

"I know Sam was mighty unlucky—mighty unlucky. He was a good soldier, too."

"It's the good soldiers that get killed," said Mrs. Fraser. James ventured a smile, then checked himself. His father evidently had no thought of applying the remark to his own survival.

"Not always," he said after due consideration. "A fellow in our regiment was kicked by a mule, trying to hide under a baggage wagon during a battle. I saw him afterward myself," he added conclusively, "skull popped wide open." He communed with himself, reconstructing the episode. "They gave him a military funeral though. The Colonel said as long as he was dead it wouldn't do no harm."

"Wouldn't do no harm?" his mother echoed. "What else could you give him?"

James grinned, but she ignored him. "Who ever heard such talk?" she added.

"It was a military funeral," said Mr. Fraser patiently.

Mrs. Fraser remained obstinately contentious. "But you have to bury the corpse just like any other funeral, don't you? And the man was dead, wasn't he?"

Mr. Fraser was perturbed but he remained patient. "In a military funeral," he said, "they fire salutes over the grave and the band plays. That's what the Colonel meant: would they fire salutes and all."

"Oh," said Mrs. Fraser, quelled at last by her husband's gentle stolidity. "I reckon he thought maybe it would please the man's folks."

"Yes," said Mr. Fraser simply. "He was a good colonel."

Having thus embarked on reminiscences of his military life, Mr. Fraser continued during the evening to call up incidents of the Mexican War. He had never talked so much. It seemed as though the prospect of James' enlistment, fanning slumbering fires within him, reilluminated pictures of that one colorful interlude in his gray life and established a new and altogether different, a manly, exclusive and secret fellowship between him and his son. James himself was aware of his own new status of equality, of the new right it gave him to free companionship with his father who, if not inherently superior, had always before remained somewhat aloof, officially the parent. There was established between them a comradeship in arms—a comradeship which no one, not even his mother, could wholly understand. Not even his mother? Perhaps she least of all. For as he sat there listening to his father's tales of action, delighting him with well-considered questions and comments, James seemed to feel that his mother, now busy with her sewing, had little sympathy with their talk. She said nothing but her silence was cold; and unhappy, also. Maintained unbroken, it chilled him in the end; it was disquieting to feel her sitting near at hand and yet withdrawn from him. A curious thought came to him. Could she be jealous of this new freedom, this man's talk between him and his father? Impossible. There was no pettiness in her. But what then? He did not know.

"Up he comes, hot foot," his father was saying, "'My God, Major,' he hollers, 'our own guns is shooting into us!'"

"'What of it, seh?' the Major says, 'ain't the enemy got their artillery to shoot into them?'"

James laughed.

"The Major," his father explained with care, "surely did despise artillery."

"Well," his father spoke with the sleepy contentment of one who has had his fill, "I reckon I'll turn in." He picked up his shoes from under the table; his knotty, bare feet tramped across the linoleum; from the dark bedroom James heard the click of a button as his father's trousers were flung across the footboard, then the rustle of a mattress and the creak of cords.

"You'll make a soldier, I expect," his father's voice was drowsy but confident. The flimsy bedroom door slammed shut.

For a long time his mother sat silent. Her broad, sharp shoulders were tilted forward, her sharp elbows rested on the table's edge, her eyes that could shine so black and keen were veiled, downcast, resting their gaze on her worn hands. James Fraser, feeling that his mother had been too much left out of their talk, had been estranged and wounded, sat ill at ease and silent, too.

At last she spoke. "When do you reckon you'll go to enlist, son?" Her tone surprised, alarmed him, wrung his heart. There was in it a touch of anxious humility such as she had never used toward him or any one; and below that, almost but not quite concealed, lay reserves of hopeless fortitude, such as were never till now suspected, and even now could only be guessed at, not grasped nor comprehended. Abashed and ill at ease, he felt that he stood, a lightly heartless child, before a depth of feeling beyond his shallow powers. He was silent; any word of his would only emphasize the gulf between them. The moment passed; his good sense came back to him, he rallied. She worried needlessly about him, magnified dangers, she always had.

"Don't feel bad, Ma," he said. "This fuss ain't going to amount to anything."

She kept her gaze fixed on her hands. "But why does everybody want to join the army, then?" she asked tonelessly.

"To show 'em we're ready," he answered. "When they see that they'll quit."

She did not seem to hear. "You couldn't wait for a while to see how things is coming out?" she said.

"I couldn't do that, Ma. All the young fellows are enlisting, and I've quit my job to come down here and join."

"I reckon you could get your job back," she said quietly. "A fine mechanic like you."

"But I've told Mr. Charles Prevost I'd join. The girls in Wilmington are going to make it hot for the fellows that don't enlist."

A little of her old irony came back to her. "I reckon so," she answered, "They've got no children." She fell silent, staring at her hands.

She roused herself, looked at him proudly, sadly. "You're bound to go, I know that."

"Yes, Ma," he said. "I'm bound to go."

There was an instant's breathless, penetrating hush. "How soon?"

He looked down at the floor. "To-morrow."

He heard her stand up, felt her pick up his hand which rested on the table and hold it lightly, firmly.

"I'll fetch some lard for these hands of yours," she said. "You can't go to Beaumont looking this way."

His fist closed for a second on her hard, blunt fingers.

"Yes, Ma," he muttered, "that'll be fine."

CHAPTER XXI

THE plantation of Beaumont had taken on the inappropriate and disreputable appearance of a county fair. Outside the Colonel's gate-house, planters' carriages, ox-carts, and riding-mules were tied promiscuously among the trees. Grave, leathery, country women and silent children picnicked together amid littered papers, while black-hatted men chewed and talked in motionless groups. Along the roadside the petty birds of prey maintained their roosts. A Jew sold calico and lucky stones from the tail of a yellow peddler's cart. A sign before a dingy tent read, "Daguerreotypes and Family Portraits." Beyond, a crowd around a shiny, silk hat struggled for turns at three-card monte and another crowd, well sprinkled with sunbonnets and lank-haired children, listened, stolidly intent, to a florid and pouchy gentleman who, mounted on a packing-case, proclaimed the merits of Electric Oil.

Inside the gate, the fields had been trampled down by drilling men, and even now a little squad of four recruits in homespun, awkward and sheepish, stumbled over the dusty furrows. A few young country girls looked on admiringly, spectators shouted encouragement or ironical comment. Across this field a cart track led to a row of tents and rough slab shelters which straggled through the woods. James' father slapped the reins on the mule's back.

"Yonder's the camp," he said.

His mother seated beside him in the cart remained

silent. As they approached James' heart turned swiftly, numbly cold. The camp, such as it was, lay on the very ridge above the swamp where he had quarrelled with Stewart Prevost, where he had walked away and left her. Already it had been desecrated till hardly recognizable. Trees had been felled to make a street of trampled sand. Newspapers, old clothes, broken boxes lay scattered between the makeshift tents and shelters where the men and boys from the countryside lounged, played cards, sat staring into vacancy or talked slowly and solemnly with their folks. A few had managed to give themselves a military air by thrusting dirks and pistols in their belts, but most of them were in their butter-nut and homespun. Their shy and enigmatic eyes had a look, not frightened, but ill at ease, caged, apprehensive. Now they saw the Frasers' cart.

"Heyo! Heyo!" the beery voice of Uncle Dunc was raised in greeting. "Here's Old Man Fraser, folks," he said, "and Jim."

Big Tom Magruder, wearing a cutlass strapped around his waist, came toward them; his roan hair hung down over his thick, red neck and over the checked brown collar of his shirt; he worked his sandy eyebrows and gave a wide-mouthed grin of recognition.

"Howdy, Mr. Bob," he said. "Hi, Jimmie! You come to look us over?"

Mr. Fraser stopped the mule. He looked down at Tom with quiet pride.

"He's come to enlist," he said.

Big Tom reached up and dropping his hand on James's knee shook it emphatically.

"Bully for you!" he said. "I thought you might be joining one of them swell city companies. We're plain and we're poor," he added impressively as though the fact conferred peculiar merit. "But we're a fighting crowd. Dog my cats, if we ain't!"

He was loud and hearty but his attitude was that James by going to Wilmington had somehow lost his birthright, become estranged, and that the virtues of home folks must be explained to him all over again. Mr. Roon, who had come up back of Tom, enveloped himself in his broadcloth coat and sought their faces with his shallow, shifty eye.

"They're God-fearing Christians and the Lord will never forsake them." Big Tom looked round in irritation. Mr. Roon had lowered the martial tenor of the conversation.

"All we ask is a fair showin'," Tom muttered bluntly.

But in truth as the cart moved once more down the road, the recruits appeared neither particularly aggressive nor virtuous; they seemed merely lonely country boys, distracted by the noise, the tumult, the excitement, and longing inarticulately for their accustomed solitude and slow, reposeful days. Only the Racker twins seemed quite at ease. They squatted on a blanket playing double solitaire, alert but casual, and stopping often to stare at passers-by with pale, lashless eyes, and to exchange rat-like smiles as though between them lay secret and inexhaustible resources of indecent humor.

In front of the last slab-shelter stood a hickory pole with the new flag hanging from it.

"This is headquarters," his father said.

Inside the shelter, wearing a gray uniform shell jacket, a red sash, and a sword, sat Catlin Gregg. He rested his weak, proud face on one slim hand and with the other fingered the downy sideburn before his ear. As the cart drove up, he picked up a long, thin cigar from the table and puffed at it industriously. Mr. Fraser drove the mule up to a tree, climbed down with deliberation, and hitched him, while James helped his mother to descend. His father led the way to the young officer; his mother and James followed in single file.

"Is this young Mr. Gregg?" his father asked.

The other waved his cigar in acknowledgment. "Lieutenant Gregg," he corrected lightly.

"My son here aims to enlist." His father's voice was grave and slow.

"Ah, capital, capital," said Mr. Gregg with perfunctory enthusiasm. He gave James an indifferent glance.

"Just the sort of fellow we want," he added condescendingly.

Mrs. Fraser broke her two hours' silence. She fixed her black, sharp eyes on the young gentleman. "You'll not get many like him," she said in a low, intense voice.

"No, ma'am, I dare say not. I dare say not," he agreed airily. He recollected himself. "Pray, ma'am, have this chair."

"I'll stand," said Mrs. Fraser. She kept her eyes fixed on Lieutenant Gregg while he opened a big ledger and wrote down James' name.

"Are you ready to join at once?"

"Yes, seh," said James. "I'm ready."

"You may go into this first tent here." He waved the cigar again.

The three of them filed out of the shelter. James and his father lifted a little leather-covered chest out of the back of the cart and carried it to the tent. His mother followed with the carpet-bag and a hamper. The tent itself was dim, breathlessly hot, and empty save for a bundle of bedding in one corner. They set down James' things and went back for his roll of blankets. Again inside the tent, they laid his blankets out neatly and placed his box and bag in careful array. His father and mother sat down on the box and he himself sat on the blankets at their feet.

"I tell you, Ann," his father said in a cautious whisper, "he's too young to be an officer, that young Gregg. A man has to have experience."

His mother, still smarting under young Mr. Gregg's patronage, was less restrained.

"No age in the world would give a boy like that good sense," she said, in a harsh, firm voice.

"Hush," said his father. "He might hear you; then he'd be down on James. It's a mighty bad thing," he reflected sombrely, "for a man to get an officer down on him."

"James should be an officer himself," said Mrs. Fraser. "He's got more sense."

Mr. Fraser looked scandalized but maintained his patience.

"Why, Ann, he's not been trained," he explained laboriously, "and the Greggs and the Prevosts are buying all the equipment for the company. Maybe he will be an officer some day." He proffered the notion merely as a consolation in her distress and without conviction.

"We'll all be home long before that," said James.

He tried to speak with heartiness, but his voice did not ring true. He had taken it for granted that his first hour in camp would find him lifted up with dashing courage, with a sense of romance, gay, adventurous, and with a devil-may-care and fitting self-esteem. But face to face with the camp's apparent tedium and dreariness, he hoped for the first time that the tour of duty would be short. Also for the first time he felt a premonition that more was involved in this military adventure than he had before supposed. Perhaps he had caught this feeling from the look in the eyes of the country boys.

Wishing that he were happier in his mind, that this moment of enlistment were as radiant as he had expected, James sat silent. His mother sat silent, too. His father, unusual with him, showed signs of restlessness; he pulled at his gray goatee; he fanned himself; he peered out through the flap of the tent.

"Well," he said at last, "I reckon I'll have a look round the camp. It will need a lot of fixing up before it amounts to anything."

Now that they were alone, his mother tried to rouse herself. She made her eyes meet his. "It looks like a nice place for a camp," she said conversationally.

"Yes," he answered.

"I hope they feed you right," she went on. "Anyhow, you've got your hamper and we'll be back next week."

"Yes," he said dully. "That's fine."

But rather than feeling cheered at the prospect of their return, he read in it a desolate significance. He would not see them till next week, then maybe till the week after, and then perhaps the company would be sent away and he would not see them at all. The tent was a suffocating trap in which he and his mother were ensnared; the very light which filtered through the canvas cloth had something about it unnatural, mournful, and foreboding. Yet for them to go outside would be to plunge into distracting superficial contacts with the crowd, to lose touch with each other. Many women would like at such a moment to display themselves, to gather for themselves some credit and distinction from their son's enlistment. She was too proud to seek such a petty triumph. Or perhaps it was now not a question of pride. Perhaps the prospect of losing him had turned her for the moment hostile against the world. At any rate she did not stir, but sat on the leather-covered chest looking now at him and now, whenever passing footsteps sounded, out the tent door with a grim and jealous glance as though she would repel whoever sought to enter. A man or two looked in, then hastily moved on. The tent grew hotter. Still she did not move, nor did she speak; she merely sat there upright on the chest, her square shoulders standing out beneath the ill-fitting, black silk waist, the big cameo tugging at the wisp of lace around her corded neck, the wrinkles of her white wool stockings peeping over the tops of her square-toed, lumpy shoes. Merely sat there, a gaunt, strong, battered figure of a woman, looking now at him, now at the door and always rolling her black string mittens in a ball between her palms and dropping them from hand to hand.

The spell was broken by the sound of an approaching fiddle, by laughter and ironic cheers. James Fraser looked out the tent door. The four recruits were marching back from drill and Uncle Dunc, alert as always to seize an occasion for comic display, had placed himself, fiddle in hand, at their head. He waddled briskly along playing a feeble and lugubrious march; a borrowed shako, much too small, nodded precariously on his head; the knot of a handkerchief which did duty for a stock had slid round jauntily under one ear; his old, green frock was buttoned so tight that the short skirts stood out behind, and swung perkily from side to side. He blew out his luxuriant mustaches and shouted:

"Right! Left! Hyer we come! The Royal Bear Grass Fusileers! Right! Left! Clear the track! The Sassafras Light Infantry!"

Behind him the four recruits, red-faced, and grinning with exquisite embarrassment, swung along with the clumsy stride of boys who had straddled furrows all their lives. At the right marched their drill-master, Dougald Cameron, a good-natured, easy grin on his bull-pup face, but otherwise martial and erect.

"Left wheel . . ." he called out. "Look out the way, Uncle Dunc. . . . Detachment halt. . . . Right dress. . . . Front. . . . Dismiss."

The four recruits faded swiftly from sight but Uncle Dunc, now the centre of all eyes, having thrust his bow in his galluses to simulate a sword, proceeded to perform the manual of arms with his fiddle.

"Shoulder, haw!" he shouted. "Ground, haw!" Then, "Load your firelocks!" He went through the motions of ramming and priming. "Aim!" He crouched and sighted in an attitude heroic and indomitable. "Fire!" He made a little pop with his G string. The crowd hurrahed.

"I declare," said Mrs. Fraser at James' elbow, "if he ain't the biggest old fool in the world. A man his age!" Beneath her indignation, however, lay reluctant but irrepressible amusement, with perhaps a touch of puzzled envy of one who was thus able to scatter shadows by his buffoonery.

Uncle Dunc had now drawn his bow from his galluses and, playing a quickstep, had embarked on an elaborate marching drill.

"To the rear, haw!" he cried. He whirled round till his coat-tails stood out stiff as shingles. "Sashay, haw!" He did a double shuffle, jumped up, clicked his heels together, waved the fiddle at the grinning circle. "Hi, boys," he shouted. "How you come on?" He wiped his blazing face on the tail of his coat. "Is they anybody," he inquired in more serious tones, "got a drink for the Sassafras Light Infantry?"

Dougald Cameron came over to them as the little crowd broke up. "How you, ma'am?" he said. "Jimmy, I hear you've joined."

"Dougald," said Mrs. Fraser in a relieved and friendly tone, "I'm mighty glad to see you. You take care this boy."

Dougald and James exchanged glances.

"I'll be all right," said James.

"He'll be all right," said Dougald.

"You take care him," repeated Mrs. Fraser firmly. "Ain't you an officer?"

"My Lord, no," said Dougald. "I'm just teaching them drill, what little of it I learned at school at Bingham's."

"Anyhow," said Mrs. Fraser, "you take care him."

Mr. Fraser joined them. He looked uneasily from James to his mother, then looked away. "Well," he said. "I expect we better be getting home, Ann."

"Yes," she said, "I reckon so." They all stood silent.

"I tell you what, Jim," said Dougald, "Why don't you ride with your folks out to the gate. You can be back for supper."

Without further remark they moved toward the cart. James climbed in after his father and mother. They drove down the company street, across the field, past the row of peddlers and gamblers beyond the Colonel's gate. At the edge of the forest Mr. Fraser pulled the mule down to the slowest walk; the old cart gently squeaked and swayed beneath the new, green leaves and the pine blossoms of pale lavender. Shadows and sunlit patches crept by on the ground below; the sounds of the encampment died away; the world was green and luminous and still. From time to time his father looked sidewise at them uneasily. But it was his mother who finally said, "Son, I reckon you better get down. They might not like you to come so far."

"That's right," agreed his father. "They like to have a man always around camp and ready for duty." He stopped the mule.

"So long, Pa. So long, Ma," said James brusquely. He gave them each the limp and formal handshake of the countryside, then let himself down over the wheel. His mother did not speak.

"We'll be back next week, son," his father said, and touched the mule up sharply.

James Fraser stood in the sun-flecked road and watched them out of sight, then he sat on a stump and looked down the road some more. He ought to have asked Dougald whether in the army a man had to be back for supper. He wished a man didn't; because just now he felt like he never wanted to eat again.

CHAPTER XXII

In their new gray uniforms they stood at parade-rest in the field. In front of them, the planters of the Cape Fear, their wives and daughters, were grouped around a bright silk standard. On either hand stretched a dark fringe of country folks and a darker fringe of negroes, who listened, solemn and heavily impressed, as the mustering officer from Raleigh, a little ramrod of a man in a tremendous red sash and tremendous white mustaches, droned through the Articles of War.

James Fraser, tightly buttoned in his jacket, did not dare turn his head, but he knew that the company must make a fine showing. During the past three weeks not only their uniforms had come, but also knapsacks, belts, cartridge boxes, and rifles for all. They now had something like the look of soldiers and were accordingly more cheerful. When first they put on the gray, brass-buttoned coats, the caps with patent-leather visors and thick gold letters C F R across the front, they had shrunk from each other shyly out of sight, but already they were drawing from those uniforms peculiar credit to themselves; they had begun to bear themselves more boldly, even with a rakish air.

"A man feels like a fool," Big Tom had said, "parading without a uniform. I reckon," he added, with a heavy grimace of humor, "that it comes too close to the chain-gang for some of the boys. But when a fellow's got a uniform on he feels like they was more sense to it."

Certainly James felt that there was sense to it as they stood, a brilliant line, displaying themselves for the admiration of the assembled countryside. He also felt increasingly that there was discomfort to it as well. Cautiously he tried to ease his creaking neck inside the collar. He wished he hadn't altered the buttons to make this coat fit quite so slick. Most of the boys had let theirs out and even then declined to button them except on special occasions, like the present. And that very afternoon when Dougald told Whitey Racker to button up his coat there had been a bitter and sarcastic mutter, "Won't the Yankees be scared though, when they hyear my buttons is all buttoned."

But James had wanted to make himself look like a soldier. He was number one in the front rank and everybody would see him when the company marched by. His father would be satisfied, his mother proud. Another thought, less welcome but insistent, had crept into his mind. He would be seen by Stewart Prevost. Right now she was standing beside the bright, new flag. He had seen her at once when they first came on the field. Against his will he had looked at her till afraid that she might notice. He would not look at her again. Nor did he need to. Every detail of her figure was vivid in his mind—the white, soft dress billowing light and airy from her waist, the wide, straw hat, its ribbon, brilliant blue, falling over the side, her slim hands in white, lace gloves loosely entwined before her.

No need to look again. For good or ill the picture would not fade. And was it for good, or ill? He did not know, he was not glad or sorry to have seen her. Or if he was, he was glad and sorry both. He had not wished to see her, not before now. And so far it had been no trouble to avoid her. She had stayed up at the house where, with other ladies of the neighborhood, she busied herself with shirts and socks for the company and with making the new silk flag. He had been relieved that there was no accidental meeting with her, relieved, too, that her nearness no longer caused his heart to flutter. He was a man, had grown wise; she now had no real power over him. She might call up old memories, but could do no more.

Still those old memories did persist and came to haunt him more than he had figured on. His heart might no longer be shaken by the thought of her, but it still could ache. He hoped, though without conviction, that when she saw him march past in his uniform hers would ache, too.

He recalled how she had made him try on his old, brown kersey coat when first he wore it. He had thought then that she was merely mocking him. But maybe part of her admiration had been real. If so, how much more would she think of this neat-fitting jacket with its twinkling buttons, this jacket, handsome in itself, and standing proudly as the emblem of a soldier of the South?

But most likely he was taking too much to himself. Most likely she had forgotten all about him. And nowadays there would be officers in red sashes. He craned his rigid neck. He'd better think of something else.

His eye wandered up and down the crowd, picked out familiar faces; Uncle Dunc, sobered for once, Mr. Roon, piously outraged that in the ceremony there was no part for him, Ben Scroggs' sallow jowls, distorted by his quid, the thick, pink tongue and bulging eyes of Logan, the Guinea nigger.

He looked straight ahead again to where his father and mother stood. Until he looked at them, those two familiar figures in their plain, dark clothes were lost in the sombre crowd. But once he picked them out, it seemed as if no one else was there but them. His father in his wool coat and a clean, frayed shirt was trying, as befitted a veteran of the Mexican War, to hold his stooped, old body in the position of a soldier. His shoulders could no longer straighten up, but he clamped his hands to his sides and drew his head back stiffly in an attitude ludicrous and pathetic.

His mother looked older, almost ancient, and utterly alone. She gazed fixedly across the parade-ground at James as though the few yards of trampled sand which lay between were infinity itself. Only when the mustering officer in his catalogue of offenses reached his periodic refrain, ". . . Death or such punishment as the court-martial may direct," did she shift her glance to give that small, portentous dignitary a startled look.

James himself could not attach importance to these Articles of War. He derived only mild amusement from the little ramrod's solemn monotone. As the list of offenses mounted he reflected that a man appeared to have more chance of being shot by a court-martial than by the enemy. He hated to have his mother look like that though. He glanced away from her.

Again his gaze swung back to Stewart Prevost. Her attitude was still the same. Her lips half parted, her dark eyes half shadowed, she listened with wondering patience to the mustering officer's voice. ". . . Death or such penalty as the court-martial may direct." It was as if this hard list of pains and penalties were more than she could give assent to, more than she could fathom. Puzzled, gently distressed, she seemed rather to accept them of necessity as the inscrutable decree of a power and wisdom far beyond her own.

But as he paused to read the meaning of her looks he was thrust through by another memory. It was so that she had looked, so that she had stood, on the day when he had walked away and left her. He tore his eyes from her. He must fix them elsewhere—anywhere. With concentration he stared at the two gold buttons at the back of Lieutenant Catlin Gregg's coat.

The mustering officer closed the little book from which he read. "Colonel Prevost," he announced, "will now present a standard to this company on behalf of the ladies of the Cape Fear."

"For God's sake make it short, Colonel," a voice behind James muttered. "My feet is burning up."

The Colonel stepped forward, removed his broad, straw hat, buttoned the top silver button of his blue frock. The sun glinted on his white, close-curling hair, on his stock, on his wide, white trousers and his patent-leather pumps. His figure, neat and radiant, seemed to shine with subdued and perfect elegance. Yes, he was sure enough, James grudgingly acknowledged to himself, the picture of a gentleman.

"Son," the Colonel's voice was kind but crisp, "let these men stand at ease; they must be tired."

"Yes, seh," said Charles and faced about. "At ease," he said.

A grunting sigh of relief went up from the ranks.

"My Lord! my neck. . . ." "Let's unbutton our coats. . . ." "You spit on my foot again, boy, I'll warm your pants."

"Hush your fuss," said Dougald Cameron's voice from behind the ranks, "The Colonel's talking." The murmurs subsided.

Though they could not wholly follow the Colonel's elegant flow they quickly gathered that they were fine men, patriots, defenders of the State and of southern womanhood. To this they gave their silent, serious assent.

Having touched on womanhood the Colonel went on to describe how the flag, which stood behind him, had been made by the ladies of the section. He bade them in the hour of battle remember the hands of those who had worked its stars and bars and, remembering, to fight for what every true man held most sacred in the world.

At the end the ladies came forward bearing the flag. Big Tom Magruder, who had been chosen as color-bearer, advanced with a soldier on either side of him. When he reached the group he took off his cap and bowed low.

"Ladies," he said in a loud voice, "we all certainly do appreciate this and that's a fact."

"Why, Tom, you're welcome. We were mighty glad

to do it," they murmured in reply. The little ramrod officer from Raleigh looked scandalized. Now Big Tom had the flag and marched back with it to the right of the line. As the flag passed James Fraser, its folds shining, rustling, swaying stiffly, he wondered what part of it had been made by her. A thought flashed through his mind. If Big Tom got shot, he would grab that flag and carry it.

CHAPTER XXIII

THE mustering and the presentation of colors stood for a long time as the high spot in their military career. Two months of tedium followed, broken only by rumors, each wilder than the first, and each more rapidly exploded. They received an issue of regular army tents, set them up proudly, struck them hastily, then set them up again in resigned disgust.

Early in July came sickening news. The Southern Army had met the Yankees at Manassas in Virginia and chased them clean back to Washington, captured whole regiments, captured generals, congressmen. They cheered as in duty bound but they almost cried with disappointment. The Yankees were whipped, the war was over and they had missed it, had never even left their home. Disconsolate, they settled back to wait for their discharge.

Standing before his tent, and looking across the fields, across a broad, black water-ditch, and over the tops of the dark live-oaks, James Fraser could see the many chimneys and high-pitched silvery roofs of Beaumont. But that was as near as he ever came to them. Always, when strolling off from camp, he walked the other way and sometimes, at night under his faded flowery quilt, he drew a meagre and fantastic satisfaction from the thought that right then he was nearer to her house than he had been all day.

The tent itself resounded unromantically to the

snores of Big Tom McGruder; beside him lay Dougald Cameron, a dark silent lump, and if there was a moon it sometimes slanted through the tent-flaps to the other corner where it lay on the pale, pinched face of Harry Horniblow, from Black Pocósin, which even in sleep seemed straining sightlessly.

Harry's face, thus showing in the moonlight, disturbed James Fraser, and by some far-fetched and unpleasing suggestion made him think of himself and of Stewart Prevost. The boy, or man, whichever he was, did not belong there; he had sneaked into the tent unbidden, just as he had sneaked into the company. Whether through stupidity, through indifference, or through an infallible instinct for the ironical, he had picked for his tentmates the three men in the company least congenial, and least pleased to see him. Certainly his welcome had been sufficiently brusque.

"God in the bushes, Horniblow," Big Tom had said, straddling menacingly above him. "How came you to enlist?"

Harry, lying on his blanket, in a pose effeminate and lazy, had been not the least abashed.

"Why not?" he had raised his melting, yet mocking eyes to Big Tom's bristles. "Ain't I tried all the women around here?"

Harry's face as it lay there in the moonlight, cautious, effeminate, secretive, sly, straining it seemed after something infinitely remote, maybe the moon itself, and etched with lines of weak and hopeless discontent, was not the face of one that James Fraser would choose for a friend. And yet it always set him thinking of his

own desires and of Stewart Prevost. But James liked
it no better for that. There was something befouling
and degrading in the power of this prematurely ageing
youth, of this filthy-mouthed mocker, this sinister and
tireless trapper of women, thus to intrude itself into
his dreams and quicken them. How or why it could do
so he did not know. Maybe, because Harry, he reflected bitterly, by mere chance and through no merit
of his own, possessed the secret, denied to him, of the
way to gain a woman's heart. Or again, maybe, because Harry, having gained a multitude of women,
seemed now no nearer happiness or satisfaction than he
himself in his failure to gain one. Either way, he hated
him and sometimes he would pull the tent-flap till the
face was blotted in shadow. But still it was there, still
he could see it in his mind and still it drove his thoughts
tumultuously toward her.

Most generally he fell asleep at last, to wander in a
region of elusive and uneasy dreams; at times, however,
he crawled from his blankets, fled from the haunting
presence and stole along the street of sleeping men out
to the spot above the swamp where he had left her when
they quarrelled long ago. By day the place was over-
run with people, was changed almost beyond recognition, trees felled, the grass tramped down, and littered
with casual refuse of the camp, the whole dejected
shabby scene a mockery of what it once had been. But
now, in the night, beneath the moon and stars, the picture, heart-stirring and heart-breaking, which it held
of her forlorn, of himself fatuous and stubborn, leaving
her, was recreated. He stood, an unhappy yet an irre-

sistibly thrilled and fascinated spectator of that old tragic scene. Right here, on this ground, beneath his feet was where the trouble had started. Everything had been all right till then. And it was all his fault. No, not all by a long shot. What difference whose the fault? He hunched a shoulder wearily. The trouble had come to pass and now things could never be the same.

And he, he was still her lover, he supposed. Yet if he saw her, however his heart might race and his spirit flutter, one eye would be always watching her for tricks. A fellow like Harry Horniblow worked things the other way. It was the girl who fluttered, and Harry who played the tricks. For a brutal moment, James Fraser wished malignantly for Harry's gift. He would make good use of it to teach her a lesson. He smiled to himself, then turned sombre. And if he did, what then? Would he be happier? He knew that he would not. Such a triumph was so fantastic that he could hardly picture it. But as far as he did so he was able dimly to guess that it would bring him only greater emptiness and misery.

He squatted on his heels. His arms hung over his knees, his fingers touched the sand. Right here, on this ground, he had walked away and left her. Walked away when he should have come back, been generous and kind. If, after that, she had let him be turned from her door, who was he to blame her?

But what was he to do? The time was short, or might be. They were sending lots of troops to Richmond and their own orders might come any day, and worse than that, in his watchings of the house, he had seen her from time to time, moving through the trees in company with a gray figure, in an officer's red sash. It might be her brother or some of the young bloods of the neighborhood who, now commissioned in various commands, stopped always on their trips up and down the river to take advantage of the Colonel's open house. But the figure was always the same, he was sure of that and he had a notion that it was young Catlin Gregg. A short pang of fear and anger thrust him to his feet. He strode swiftly to and fro like an animal behind the bars. Suddenly tired, he came to a stand with head hanging down. There was no more time for fooling; tired as he was, he must put his mind to work and figure out what to do. Anything might happen. Then it would be too late. That Catlin Gregg in his fuzzy sideburns—and she walking beside him through the grove of live-oaks, her dark eyes turned to his weak, conceited face, one rounded, shining arm swaying close to his—God in the mountain!

The next evening, not long after the last whistle of the daily steamboat had died away, the mail orderly came striding down from the Big House flapping his arms with excitement.

"Hi, you all," he intoned in a high key. "Come here, come here, you fellows."

They gathered around him.

"We're gwine to Richmond. We're gwine to move. Sure 'nough this time." They laughed at him.

"Stale fish!" they shouted, "Nigger news! Go fish fo' suckers, Ance."

Ance threw his head back like a turkey buzzard, his Adam's apple shot up in an indignant swallow. He licked tobacco juice from the corner of his mouth.

"All right, you slab-sided pine-rooters. The man that calls me a liar is gwine to go down on his knees to me by this time to-morrow." He glanced with theatrical aggressiveness around the circle.

"Maybe, Ance is telling the truth," drawled a voice well hidden in the crowd. "It's about the only way he could fool us." Ance wheeled around.

"Come out of that, you polecat, and show your face." He threw his mail-bag on the ground. "Let me catch the man that said that." He rolled up his sleeves. "Dog my cats, if I don't jump down you' throat and gallop the chitterlin's out of you."

The crowd made a rush for the mail-bag which they found empty, then closing in on Ance, who kicked and cursed most villainously, proceeded to pull it down over his head. In the midst of the struggle a lookout raised a cry of "Officers!" The crowd immediately dispersed. Ance also started running. His muffled curses buzzed inside the bag like bees in a stump. They ceased abruptly as he struck a tent-rope and shot out of sight.

A moment later the Racker boys were beating the Assembly on their drums. Then they all were standing in line, listening, somewhat awed, to Charles Prevost read orders about tents and baggage, about haversacks and forty rounds of ball cartridges.

"Sergeant, dismiss the company."

The men leaped high in air, gave shrill, long, quavering cries of exaltation.

"E-e-e-e-ya-ou-ou!" they screamed. "E-e-yi-yi-yi!" They sounded the thin and penetrating call of hunters in the woods.

But James Fraser, standing fixedly amid the bedlam, kept saying over and over to himself. "Off to Richmond at three o'clock to-morrow morning. Off to Richmond." Then "Stewart Prevost."

He hurried back to his tent. He knew that in his haversack Dougald Cameron kept letter-paper. He fumbled for it, found it and a pencil as well. He started to write.

"Dear Miss Stewart:—"

My Lord, his hands were dirty. He couldn't write to a lady with such dirty hands. No time to wash them now. He pulled out another sheet of paper and laid it under the fist that held the pencil.

"Dear Miss Stewart:" he read. What next? It was incredible that he could find no words to put on paper. Damn him for a fool, what ailed him? He'd better be quick about it. Some one would be coming along.

"Dear Miss Stewart," he read once more. Then wrote: "We are leaving before sun-up to-morrow as I reckon you know."

God, what a fool thing to say! Of course she knew. He bit at the pencil stub. "Come on, man, what are you made of anyhow? If you don't get somewhere in the next line" he told himself, "your goose is cooked. And so it ought to be. All right, here goes."

"I would love mighty well to see you before I leave. I will be on the north side of the branch all evening, opposite where I used to haul the rails to." By God, he had his nerve asking her to come out looking for him. "It is not very far from the house," he added, "and there is a foot-log across the branch in case you should be walking that way." But if she should not care to come, what then? See her he must. "Or if you would see me anywhere else," he went on, "I would go there, except that the Colonel does not wish me to go to the house. I hope you can do this please, as I want mightily to see you. Yours respectfully, James Fraser." He sealed the envelope and shoved the pencil and paper back in Dougald's knapsack.

As he had feared, Ance, the mail orderly, was in no favorable frame of mind to do a man a favor. The negotiation was maddeningly protracted.

"But I tell you, Ance," he lied with passionate earnestness, "they've got three of my shirts up there at the big house, and I'm obliged to get 'em before we move."

"Go fetch 'em yourself," said Ance. "I ain't no ladies' maid."

"Why, Lord A'mighty, Ance, you know we ain't allowed out of camp from now till we leave."

Ance's red-rimmed eye, far from melting, foreshadowed only savage exasperation.

"Hell's clinkers—!" he burst out.

"Look here, Ance," James cut in, trying to steady his tremulous and despairing voice, "I'll be fair with you, only don't tell the boys. Those shirts were made by a gal back in the sticks that thinks a heap of me."

Fear must have lent convincing pathos to his words,

or perhaps the sentimentalist in Ance was touched. His eye remained aloof, but his head, poised just now for cursing, drooped somewhat on his stringy neck.

"I'll tell you what," said James, "if you'll carry this note about my shirts I'll give you half a pound of Bully Boy and stand guard in your stead the next two times." Ance's eye did not relent but he stood up in the tent.

"Where is you' fool letter?" he said.

CHAPTER XXIV

In the intenser dark, along the branch, the frogs were rattling shrilly. The cypresses heaved up their bulk from the blackness and the endless iteration and standing clear, stretched light feathery branches across the stars. James Fraser lifted his face to the crusted trunks which rose up strong, quiet, self-contained, above the dark and the petty tumult. Immediately he dropped his eyes to the swamp again, to watch and listen.

Below him a line of foot-logs cut a slit across the branch and showed a narrow gleam of water. At the farther end, a shadowy pathway wound up to the house, the pathway down which she would come;—if she came. And if she did not? He tried to think what he would do. He'd cross those foot-logs, march up to the house and seek her out. He'd have it out with her in spite of all. Once and for good he was going to tell her how much he thought of her. After that she could do as she'd a mind about it, it was none of his business, he'd have done his part.

A sound like a footstep rustled near the branch. She was coming. His heart turned cold with nervous dread. It was nothing, however; only a rabbit or a coon. Like an animal released from a trap, his heart seemed to scamper frantically away. He turned mournfully sardonic. So he thought then of going up to the house and braving the Colonel;—when the very idea of her footsteps was enough to frighten him.

But when a moment later on the other bank, he saw her unmistakable, lovely silhouette, his heart, instead of fluttering nervously, gave one swift, joyful bound. He ran lightly along the foot-logs and stepping onto the other bank raised his eyes to hers.

The starlight touched her hair and shaded her face to a soft and misty oval in which he made out only her dark eyes and her strong, rich mouth.

"I'm mighty glad you came," he said. She reached out her hand. He took it, held it. It was cold. Yet from it, warmth and strength, peace, courage, and good cheer seemed flowing into him.

"I reckon we better go across," he said. "Sometimes the boys come down this side." He stepped out on the foot-logs, holding her hand behind him steadily. As they walked along the logs he thought that through her fingers he could sense the light and graceful swaying of her body. He would have been glad if the logs had stretched out till Judgment day.

They were on firm ground again. He turned to face her. Gently she drew her hand away but still she did not speak. He felt his courage waver. Maybe she just came down here as a kindness to him because he had asked her, because he was a soldier and was going away. Maybe she even felt sorry for him because the Colonel had been severe on him. Maybe——

But just then on the ridge across the swamp where the fire and lanterns of their camp swayed and twinkled, he heard the creak, the rattle of a loaded wagon. Their heavy baggage was starting for the dock. Before the sun rose the company would have gone. He would have gone. The wagons were groaning away across the fields. He saw a lantern swinging underneath a tailgate and glinting on the musket of a baggage guard. He looked back at her shadowy face, her mouth, her eyes, her slim, rounded arms and softly rising bosom. He would soon be gone. Still she did not speak. Continuing to stand there, silent before him, having come at his asking, suddenly, unbearably she touched and humbled him. His heart smote him till he wanted to cry aloud. His head dropped low, his hands locked tight together.

"I've been a fool," he said, then paused while she withdrew her eyes, cast them on the ground and seemed ever so slightly to shake her head. He unlocked his hands, drove a fist lightly into the other palm. "I can't think of anything but you."

"I didn't know that." Her voice was low and grave. They stood there motionless, fixed forever, it seemed.

"Nothing but you," he echoed. "That's what I wanted to say."

"I think that is a great honor," she said slowly.

"There's no honor." His voice was gruff. "I can't help it."

She gave a laugh, swift, uncontrollable but quickly mastered.

"I reckon I seem funny to you," he muttered.

"Oh no!" she cried out, "Not that! I wish more men were so sincere. Made-up compliments are what we get."

"I'm no complimenter." He spoke as though making a careful statement. "But I don't think of anything but you."

"I know you're not," she broke in quickly, "that was why I used to like to talk to you." She paused. "But then you went away."

"I wasn't wanted."

"Why do you say that?" She shook her head, gently reproachful. "I think you are too touchy."

"Touchy!" He almost laughed. "How often do you reckon I need to be shown the door?"

"But no one did that. Don't you remember? I only asked if you would accept a loan; or started to ask it." She looked away unhappily. "Perhaps that was a mistake. I was thinking only of the things you might do if you had a chance. But you did not take it so. Don't you remember? You walked away."

Didn't he remember? As if he ever could forget. But why did she dwell on that?

"I don't know what got into me then. I knew I was wrong all the time. That's why I came to Beaumont—that night. To tell you I was sorry."

"Came to Beaumont?"

"Yes, ma'am. And the Colonel said you—" his words were labored, "were not at leisure."

Her voice was exasperated, almost harsh. "What are we talking about?"

Was she playing a trick? He did not know, did not much care, nothing would turn him from her now.

"I reckon you know," he answered patiently. "You

were inside the house. I heard you playing the mandolin."

"I don't play the mandolin."

"I thought it must be you. That was what made me feel so bad."

Her eyebrows met in a bewildered frown. "It wasn't me; but I don't see why it should make you feel bad."

"When the Colonel sent me off it hurt me mightily——"

"Oh!" she cried, "I didn't know he had! I didn't. You must believe that."

"Yes, ma'am," he agreed mechanically—"and then when I was leaving I heard the mandolin, and I thought," he muttered lamely, "that you were maybe playing it as a joke on me because I'd brought my fiddle."

Her laugh was short, almost angry. "How could you? How could you be so—" She narrowed her eyes a little and looked at him.

"What do you think I am?" She glanced aside and laid her hand along her cheek in thought. "I understand, though," she murmured to herself. "I see how it must have been for you. My father has strict ideas." Her tone was firm. "But he should not have done that." Sadly she shook her head. "But how could you think that would be my idea of a joke."

"I said I had been a fool," he answered, "and I said it before I knew how things were."

"You see," he went on slowly, "I was just a plain fellow from the woods but I had some sense. I knew that to come to call on you with my old fiddle was a crazy thing to do, I knew it while I was waiting for the nigger to come to the door, and then when the Colonel gave me his message and I heard that mandolin I thought I knew that it was just the way the business was bound to turn out in the end. I thought that was bound to be the case because I knew that to come there was a crazy thing to do."

"Yes," she said again, slowly, "I think I see how things must have seemed to you. Why didn't I know you were there?" Her voice was taut and strained, striving he guessed to hide some depth of bitterness.

"I surely wish you had," he muttered.

"Now," she went on, seeming not to hear him, "we are like strangers."

"I tried to make out we were strangers," he answered, "ever since that night." His voice was suffocated. "I can't. I can't think of anything but you."

"I used to think about you, sometimes," she said, "and wonder why you had left. I used to enjoy our talks together. You seemed to have good sense. And no nonsense. It was different from the way most men talk."

"I just say what's in my mind." He tried to speak without pride.

"But I couldn't make out why you had gone away," she went on. "The quarrel we had over there," she nodded across the branch, "seemed like such a little reason."

"Well, now you know the reason," he reminded her. She gave him a puzzled, hopeless glance.

"Yes," she said, "I know the reason. I reckon you

think that ought to satisfy me." Her eyes flashed.
"But what is the reason? The reason is that you believed I had played a contemptible trick on you. A
vulgar and cruel trick, that is what you believed and
you think I should be pleased to hear it."

"Miss Stewart," he spoke painfully. "I said I was a
fool, I can't say more."

She would not look at him.

"When all this happened," he went on at last, "I
felt so bad that my sense seemed to leave me. I thought
that every one was against me. I wouldn't talk even
to my folks."

She was unappeased. "You took a long time to
change."

"I'm naturally slow to change," he said. "I reckon
the only thing quick I ever did was the time I heard
your voice in the house."

Now she looked at him again. "What time was
that?"

"Why, you know," he said patiently. Of course she
knew. She must know. "The first time ever I came to
Beaumont; with a letter for the Colonel."

"But I didn't see you then."

"I didn't see you neither, but I heard you say
'Hush' to the nigger."

"Well, what happened then?"

"Why, that's all." He was almost irritated at her
stupidity. "I just heard you say it, that's all."

She looked at him in faint amusement. "That wasn't
much to hear though, was it?"

"It was enough," he muttered doggedly.

For a long minute she was silent. "James," she said, "we must be friends again."

"Is that all?" he demanded bluntly. He thrust his hands in his pockets, took two strides away, then came back again to her. "I reckon it's all I could expect. But I'd hoped more. I surely had." He strode up and down. "I dread to go away," he murmured. "Some planter's son will win you while I'm gone."

"Not now," she answered. "I could not leave my Father for anyone. He is alone."

"There's Charles," he ventured.

She raised her hands quickly to her bosom. "Charles," her tone was breathless. "He's going with you."

"He'll come back directly."

She stood rigid. Her hands pressed tight against her bosom. "He won't come back," she whispered.

He moved a step closer to her. "Why, Miss Stewart," his voice was mild and kind. "The War's about over now." Still she did not move or seem to hear him. "By the time we get up there I reckon the Yankees will all be gone."

Now if she heard him it was as though from a great distance. Sadly she shook her head from side to side.

"And if we should get in a skirmish," he added earnestly, "we'll all be looking out for him. We ain't going to let anything happen to him. Everybody in the company feels that way."

Now she did hear him and smiled faintly. "I know, I know," she murmured. Her voice was tremulous, but warm. It trailed away.

"He won't come back," she whispered once again. "I know he won't."

"Why, Miss Stewart—" he protested.

But now she would not listen. "He won't!" she cried out shortly. Her voice sank to a low, distracted murmur. "I don't know what to do—just to stay here and see him go! I've been like a mother to him. He's been like a mother to me too, almost. He's brave, though, brave as a lion. He won't take care of himself. And full of fun—" She brought her eyes back to his face. "James Fraser," she said, "take care of Charles."

He took her two hands and held them quietly. "Miss Stewart, ma'am, I surely will."

As if this contact had brought her to herself, she gave him a startled glance. "I must go back," she said, "there is so much to be done." A note of pride came into her voice. "Over twenty of the men," she said, "have asked me to write letters home for them. They won't have anybody write for them but me."

"I must say good-bye," she said. There was something touching in the way she tried to make her words sound steady and insistent. He stood there silent, clinging to her hands.

He must not harass her now. "Good-bye," he said. "I'll do what I told you. I'll look out for him."

He led her across the foot-logs as before. Now she put more dependence on his hand. He steadied her firmly but his mind was busy elsewhere. She was writing letters. He had never thought about letters. They played little part in his life.

Now they were on the other bank. Still he held her

hand. "When we get up there," he said, "I would like mighty well to write you a letter to tell you how we are making out."

"I would like to hear," she said. "I will answer."

Then her hand was gone. Her shadowy figure was hurrying up the path. She did not turn her head or look behind, but long after her light and swiftly moving silhouette was lost from view, James Fraser stood transfixed among the mists and shadows, straining desperate eyes along the starlit path where she had gone.

CHAPTER XXV

THREE days later, grimy and tired, they rattled across a great, high railroad trestle toward a lofty city of innumerable brick houses, spires, and a tall, white, overtowering Capitol. Far down below them slid a yellow river, its banks crowded with tied-up shipping and the sheds and smoking stacks of ironworks and factories. Above the rattle of the cars they heard the ring of hammers, the rumble of drays and wagons on the cobble-stones, the toot of whistles and under all, an indefinable many-blended hum. Listening with uneasiness and awe, they knew it for the living pulse of the metropolis.

The reverent voice of Big Tom MacGruder, who had crowded half of his bulk out of the window, came floating back to them. "Boys, I can count seven saloons from here."

"How about spo'ting houses," said Whitey Racker with a knowing grin around the car.

"You better count them for yourself," said Tom.

Their wheels passed over the roofs of riverside warehouses and struck a deeper note as they reached firm ground. They clicked over switch points, tilted and groaned around a curve; the engine shrieked and showered cinders down, crashed through a dark, resounding train-shed and, with clanging bell, rolled out into the sunlit yard beyond.

As they stood, still hitching at their belts and knapsacks, lined up along the track, a distracted officer who clutched at his wobbling eyeglasses, at sheets of paper, pencils, note-books, scurried up to Charles, conferred in dramatic whispers, gesticulated feverishly, fluttered away.

"Who kicked up that reed-bird's nest?" said a dry voice from the ranks. They grinned with large good nature and a certain relief. They had met their first Richmond officer, and he wasn't much.

"We're going to march right down the main street," said Charles Prevost. "Right where every one can see us, so let's make a good showing. Every man keep step and look straight ahead. No talking, and don't spit so that any one can see you. Attention! Fours right. . . ! March!"

They stumbled and straggled over the rails and cross-ties. They coasted down a bank of cinders and plodded up an alleyway. The stiffness was beginning to shake out of them by the time they saw the wide, bright street of shops and tall hotels, alive with gay barouches, sulkies, tramcars, with plug hats, uniforms, and crinolines. They stepped out smartly, closed up, and dressed their ranks.

Bearing their new silk standard before them, Big Tom MacGruder swung his haunches with self-conscious majesty and the Racker boys struck up with their drums. By shot, those two worthless rats could beat a march! Their sticks whirred down on the drumhead, flew high in air, whirred down again. Behind him James Fraser heard the brogans of the company slapping the white dust of the street together. By that, and by a feel-

ing in his bones and up his spine, he knew that they were
marching to beat anything they had done before, like
regular soldiers, maybe better. These Richmond folks
would surely open their eyes. They would know that
the Cape Fear Rifles had come to town. He did not
turn his head, but he squinted out the corner of his
eye for a glance at the astonished citizens. But instead
of lining the curbstones in respectful admiration they
were going about their business. A couple of raga-
muffins ran beside the drums. A man or two called
"Where you boys from?" A lady reading the legend on
their standard cried, "Hurrah for North Carolina!"
But except for that, the crowd along the sidewalk flowed
to and fro, oblivious. Gentlemen raised beaver hats to
ladies, officers saluted them, and each other, stopped,
formed animated groups and—incredible!—continued
to chat together while the Cape Fear Rifles passed.

The other men also were beginning to feel that their
martial display made no impression. Their footsteps
lagged, they grunted, hitched the knapsacks on their
shoulders. They coughed, they cursed the dry November dust which hung about them.

"Ain't this a triumph!" muttered Ance, the mail
orderly, trudging beside James. "I reckon these folks
have been setting up all night fo' us." He rolled his
quid sardonically. Other voices muttered in the column. "Why don't we march at ease?" . . . "Plum
foolishness." . . . "Wher' do we camp?" . . . "I
wish I was a baggage guard."

By now they had passed through the thickly crowded
portion of the street and were toiling up a hill. Sensing

the impending disintegration of the company, Charles Prevost called out "At Ease!" With a concerted groan their muskets came down from their shoulders, their caps came off, they trudged along morosely. On their right the buildings ended, a sod-clad hill rose sharply to the tall white Capitol which they had seen from the bridge. Before it towered a lofty equestrian statue.

"That's the monument of Washington," Charles Prevost called back to them.

Ance threw the work of art a glance. "Is that a fact, Captain?" he answered politely. "Ain't the horse blowed up in his belly, though?"

"Maybe it's a mare," ventured number three with a grin of self-appreciation.

Number four was scornful. "That's the way they make statue horses," he said. "I seen one in Raleigh once." Silence fell again.

At the top of the hill, stately rows of residences, white marble steps and lintels stretched away. On the corner two girls stood chatting. Their small, round beaver hats nodded together; their netted hair hung low on their necks. At the sound of the company's footsteps they looked up, smoothed their satin boleros and the ruffles of their hooped skirts. Their eyes and cheeks were bright with mischief and good cheer. As the head of the company drew abreast of them they called out, "Soldiers, where do you all come from?"

"Brunswick County, North Carolina," the men called back, grinning with sheepish pleasure.

The smaller girl put her tiny muff before her face

and gave them a mouse-like glance. "Have they heard about the war down there?"

Big Tom MacGruder swung around and bristled genially. "Yes, ladies, we could hear you hollerin' mighty plain for help."

"Hurrah for North Carolina!" said the tall girl, waving her muff. She beamed on them delightedly. "Are there any more soldiers there like you?"

"They's heaps as brave," said a voice in the rear of the column, "but none as handsome." The silent country boys in the ranks grinned, blushed, and cocked their caps over their eyes.

The two girls, still waving, laughing, were left behind, but, long after, the company continued to step out more briskly.

As they marched on, the houses became smaller, then scarcer. They passed an open field or two. Negroes drove covered wagons loaded with supplies. Casual soldiers tramped by, eyeing the Cape Fear Rifles with silent curiosity. Then somewhere beyond the brown autumnal foliage of a wood, a military band was faintly pulsing. They passed the trees and a straggling line of hucksters' shanties and came with thrilling suddenness upon a white-rowed plain of countless tents, a plain which buzzed and hummed and rustled, a plain to whose swarming life there seemed no rest or end, except in the countless lazy spirals from the campfires which drifted idly up against the sky.

The importance of the Cape Fear Rifles was now diminished utterly. Accustomed for months to be the focus and the pride of all the folks in Brunswick County, they became merely a company of a regiment drawn from all over the State, from Allamance, Hoke, Chatham, Boone. There were broad-speaking, lumbering fishermen from Currituck, and hard-headed, hard-drinking Presbyterians from the turpentine woods of Cumberland and Moore. A company of lean and long-haired mountaineers from Mitchell, who clung tenaciously to their coonskin caps, disdaining to talk to low-landers, disdaining to drink the lowland water, squatted aloof and silent before their tents, their hawklike faces turned toward the horizon as though they hoped to catch a glimpse of the Unakas or hear the tinkle of the springs on Grandfather.

Outside the regiment were varied troops and uniforms beyond all counting. They came to know the drooping plumes and the shining thoroughbreds of the Black Horse Cavalry, the blue jackets of the Charleston Light Infantry, and the tall patent-leather shakoes and white cloth plastrons of the Washington Artillery from New Orleans. There were Texans in huge mustaches, fringed shirts, and broad wool hats and a Zouave regiment of small, dark, beady-eyed men who had come up from Mississippi, leaving a trail of wrecked saloons and outraged storekeepers in their wake. As to the other troops, from every State in the Confederacy, clad in every shade of gray, in stylish broadcloth of a light blue tinge, in the yellow green of homespun, copperas dyed, or in furry brownish butternut, it was beyond all power to count or name them.

Lost and lonely in this vast mustering, James Fraser

turned his thoughts back home. He dwelt, for his
solace, on the cabin, on his lean-to room, on the pines
and dogwood, the slow, brown streams and silent,
sandy roads; he even dwelt on the railroad shops in
Wilmington. But most of all he pictured the starlit
silhouette of Stewart Prevost and figured what he
should say when he wrote her. He bought a tablet of
writing-paper and a pencil from a sutler's wagon at a
price never heard of since the world began. It riled
him mightily to pay out fifty cents without a protest.
But he felt that to raise a fuss would be a small dis-
loyalty to her.

Working surreptitiously whenever he could steal a
moment from their unending drills, he used up half
the tablet in laborious failures, each one of which was
burned with equal secrecy. In the end, however, he had
it pretty good. At least it sounded about right as he
looked it over for the last time.

IN CAMP, RICHMOND.
November 28th, 1861.

DEAR MISS STEWART:

I said I would write to tell you how we all were making out. Everything has been fine so far. I will begin at
the beginning. We got to Richmond on the 19th inst. on
the cars. We marched right up the main street of the
city and every man marched like a regular. There is
an Alabama regiment camped next to us and you
should see them march. They look like a pack of pot-
lick dogs coming down the road. I reckon they are all
right but their officers are not like ours, besides they
are mighty bad to steal things if not watched. The men
in our company are mighty honest and good fellows as

"Ain't the Yankees got feet?" demanded Tom. "And let me tell you boys, they're goin' to use 'em too when we get after 'em."

"I reckon that's so," said Ance, unconvinced, "but it don't look to me like the mountains would be a good place to fight. It looks to me like if you chase the Yankees off one mountain maybe they would get on another."

"Man, it takes time to get on a mountain." Big Tom assumed the grave and patient air of a strategist. "And we ain't goin' to give 'em time. No, sir," he concluded, "they surely ought to send for us and I reckon they will."

To Big Tom's partial credit as a prophet, troops did begin to leave the camp for points unknown. Each day saw further rows of hard-packed, bare spots where tents had stood, and the raked-out embers of abandoned fires. Still the Cape Fear Rifles' turn did not come.

On a crisp November afternoon, James Fraser, detailed as the Colonel's orderly for the day, was sitting in his tightly buttoned and neatly brushed uniform, on a packing-case, outside the Colonel's tent. The Colonel, in the few weeks during which he had held command, had become a legendary figure. A well-to-do, plain farmer from Halifax, he had established himself in their esteem by the doggedness with which he fought and wrangled for their comfort and by a homely and unperturbed indifference to military etiquette that reached its climax in a ponderous hickory-stick which supported him on his tours of duty and even on parade, and had gotten him the name of Clubby Jordan.

As he sat on the packing-case, James Fraser could

hear Clubby inside the tent scuffling and grunting and cussing at his nigger in an absent-minded way. The negro answered with indignant and argumentative squawks; abruptly, he backed out of the tent, a little wiry ape, tugging behind him a large horsehair armchair which Clubby had brought with him from Halifax in order to fight the Yankees in some degree of comfort.

"How come I don't put de chair out?" he chattered back in the direction of the tent. "It might come on to rain, and den de chair git wet."

"Don't lie to me," Clubby's voice rumbled within the tent. "Ain't you an Old Sal nigger?"

Through the opening in the tent-flaps stepped a stoutly built old man in a loose alpaca coat. He rumpled his stiff, black, close-cropped hair and fixed James with a quick hazel eye. James sprang to attention.

"Old Sal never had a child," said Clubby, emphatically, "that couldn't tell the weather as good as ary tree-toad." He sat down in the armchair, pulled his copperas breeches over his broad, strong knees, waved an impatient flipper at James. "Set down, boy; set down." He threw back his head till hair showed at the opening in his checkered shirt. "'Simmon, wher's my pipe?" he shouted at the heavens. Shuffling out of the tent, the little negro produced a porcelain pipe and a box of sulphur matches from the tail of the shabby frock coat which he wore.

For some moments the Colonel busied himself with putting his pipe into operation. Then he leaned back, his thumbs in his rawhide galluses, and thrust out his

carpet slippers. These slippers at once engaged James
Fraser's eye. On a brilliant scarlet ground, one depicted a ruined tomb and a weeping willow and the
other a foxhound in full cry.

He was roused by the sound of the Colonel's voice.
"So, you're the orderly for the day, eh?" The tone
was humorous and quizzical as though the answer
involved a ridiculous admission on the part of James.

"Yes, seh, Colonel."

The Colonel grunted with the satisfaction of a man
who has scored a point. "Wher' you from?"

James told him. The Colonel grunted again. "Rice
country," he ruminated. "What's a prime field-hand
sell for down your way?"

"About a thousand dollars."

The Colonel pulled at his pipe. "Cheaper to raise
your own," he observed.

Taking his pipe from his mouth, Clubby then proceeded to cross-examine James on the agriculture of the
Cape Fear. So searching and minute were the Colonel's
questions that James was mightily relieved to see another orderly approaching with papers in his hand.
The new orderly clicked his heels and saluted with tremendous smartness.

"Orders for Colonel Jordan with the Commanding
General's compliments," he rapped out.

Clubby waved an aimless hand in greeting and took
the envelope. Turning sidewise in his chair the Colonel
explored the pocket of his coat extensively. He paused
to glance up at the orderly. "Set down, boy." The
orderly hesitated, then sat down stiffly on the edge of

the packing-case beside James Fraser. The Colonel brought up a pair of steel-rimmed spectacles bent hopelessly out of shape. "I reckon I must have lay on them," he observed resignedly, and proceeded to straighten them as best he could with his fingers. Now and again he tried the glasses on his nose and each time took a look at the orderly from Headquarters. "Wher' you from, boy?"

"From Headquarters, sir."

"You weren't born at Headquarters, were you?" said Clubby in a voice of simulated wonder.

The orderly turned pink. "I'm from Williamsburg, sir."

"Is that so? Well, well," said Clubby as though the news held deep significance. "How are the farmers making out down your way?"

"Very well, thank you, sir," said the orderly stiffly.

The Colonel had now got his glasses firmly fixed. "Don't thank me," he muttered as he opened the envelope. "I live clear down in North Carolina."

He bent forward and read the order carefully, following each word with his finger. He folded the paper, took off his glasses, dropped them and his pipe into his baggy pocket. Running his big thumbs slowly up and down his galluses, he gazed out over the tents of his regiment, just beginning to fade into the dusk.

"Tell the Old Man we'll be ready," he said to the orderly without a glance at him. The orderly saluted and was gone.

And still old Clubby stared into the gathering shadows of the camp and tugged at his rawhide galluses.

Then he stood up and buttoned his alpaca coat. "I'll
have some orders for you to tote around, son." His
voice was low and soft and kindly. A man might have
thought that he hated to give James the trouble. He
squinted up his little hazel eyes at James.

"If you've a gal in Richmond," he observed, "you'd
best kiss her good-bye to-night." James felt his face
turn crimson and feared that Clubby would note his
embarrassment. But the Colonel was already stump-
ing toward his tent and shouting, " 'Simmon, fetch out
that bagging and pack up this chair."

CHAPTER XXVI

THE country which they saw from the open doorway of the box-car was rich and fair. In fields of stubble and strong red clay, corn shocks stood higher than a man could reach. Pastures were dotted with fat and shining cattle. Farmhouses were of stone, their chimneys and outbuildings neatly whitewashed.

But the beauties of the Shenandoah Valley did not move them. They sat crowded in the box-car, which smelled villainously of hogs, of sheep dip, of fertilizer, and saltpetre, their thoughts fixed mournfully, bitterly, on their heavy baggage. Packed in cases, their over-coats, extra uniforms and shoes, coffee pots, frying-pans, camp kitchens, together with small and precious comforts, the private possessions of each man, had stood that morning a neat, imposing mound at the head of the company street ready for the wagon to take it to the cars, at the hour the regiment left Richmond. The hour approached, the company fell in and still no wagons came. Instead, a youthful aide from the General's headquarters walked by Charles Prevost on his way to the Colonel's tent.

"You'll be moving in five minutes," he called out airily.

"All right," said Charles, "but what about our heavy baggage?"

"Oh," with incredible casualness he threw the word back over his shoulder, "you're to leave that."

Charles hurried after him, came back despondent. It was true.

"Sergeant," he said, "break open those cases. Let the men take what they want."

So now they sat, oppressed by thoughts of their abandoned possessions, already, doubtless, the booty of those disreputable scoundrels from the Alabama regiment, and hardly less oppressed by the equipment which they had saved and carried with them. Crowded together, it seemed impossible to escape distressing contact with the multitude of pans and pots, of knives, shoes, hatchets and lanterns which they had managed to tote aboard the car. As the day went on, it was borne upon them that by some fatality they had, that morning, managed to save from their disaster only objects which were metallic and angular.

However, by sundown they would have arrived at the place where they were bound, Lexington or Lynchburg, or some such name. Then with their tents put up and ready for them as they had been at Richmond, their pots and kettles would come in handy.

But when the train did stop, just before dark, it was on a perfectly bare and uninhabited hill. Dazed and incredulous, they climbed down from the car.

"But where do we camp, Captain?"

The faintest shadow of a smile passed over Charles Prevost's face. "Right here." He grinned on them with affectionate encouragement. "Right here is where we start soldiering. Sergeant!"

"Yes, seh," Dougald Cameron grinned also.

"You see that woods, yonder? Detail five men and a Corporal to fetch fire-wood. There are plenty of axes. And there's bound to be water in that valley. Send five more men with pails and pots to get it. I'll show the balance of you how to make shelters with blankets. All you men fix bayonets."

While the wood and water details were gone, the rifles with bayonets fixed were thrust into the ground. Their blankets were snapped fast under the hammers and pegged down to form a small, half tent for each two men. Neatly aligned and spaced, their shelters made something of a showing and caused them to look down on other companies whose demoralization was more apparent. Not counting, that is, the men from Mitchell County. The mountaineers, without comment, had rolled up in their blankets and gone to sleep.

In half an hour they had drinking-water and a line of fires before the shelters in which they squatted, munching the biscuits from their haversacks with some contentment and self-esteem. There was still a blanket left for each two men and under this they crawled and, with their feet to the embers, made out to go to sleep.

James Fraser shared his blanket with Big Tom, who soon was snoring. But he himself felt wakeful and wonderfully alive. The night air and the loneliness seemed to turn him into an animal who should be prowling. He wanted to get out and sniff around. But it might get him into trouble. He slid out beyond the corner of the shelter and lay there looking all about him. A light breeze stirred along his cheek; above, the autumn stars snapped brightly. Back home those stars, a little mellowed by the milder air, looked down on her. Would she, he wondered, ever pause to think that they looked down on him? Pictures, familiar, shadowy, filled his mind. Drowsy, but bouyant, airy, he seemed to drift away toward lovely, vague, but well-remembered scenes with her.

The night chill roused him. With a shiver he sat up on his elbow, looked around. The field was strewn with shadowy, muffled forms, with spots of dying embers. On a little rise of ground one fire still was swaying, and in its light, their Colonel, Clubby Jordan, wrapped in a woolen tippet, and looking half a grandfather, half a tired child, dozed in his horsehair chair.

Next morning when he woke, feeling pretty stiff and blue, James Fraser noticed that the blanket shelter had come down and was wrapped voluminously around Big Tom's neck. Big Tom sat up and scratched his face.

"Hullo!" he said, "looks to me like I got the main part of this yere blanket."

"You got it all," said James.

"I laid a half over you," said Tom, "but I must have kind of got to reelin' it in, in my sleep." He battled his way out of the blanket folds and stood up. The other blanket shelters had also disappeared, only the line of rifles still stuck in the ground where the shelters had been. "The Captain's idea was all right," Tom observed, laconically, "providing a man likes to sleep with his blankets raised up off him instead of wrapped down around him."

The drums ceased beating, figures stirred on the ground, blinking eyes peered out, the voice of Dougald Cameron called "Raise up, you men! Raise up!"

His shouts were reinforced by a bellow from Clubby Jordan.

The Colonel had arrayed himself for campaigning by donning an officer's frock coat, somewhat too tight and a good deal too long, and by cramming his copperas breeches into a pair of yellow cowhide boots. These boots he whacked resoundingly with his hickory-stick.

"Now, boys, wake up, wake up!" He poked at a recumbent figure. "Come out of that, you 'possum!" The figure stirred. "I'm gwine to start this hyer war on time if it's the last act," Clubby muttered with determination. He stumped on into the next company. The men gazed after his sturdy back, the wrinkles of his ill-fitting coat stretched taut across it, and grinned with solid satisfaction.

They had hardly downed their coffee and biscuits before they were rolling their blankets, packing their knapsacks, and stowing or tying their pots and pans about themselves as best they could. Then they fell in, wheeled into column with the other companies, and trudged away across the field, feeling a little stiff and empty and a little strange. In front of them Clubby's wide-brimmed, wool hat bobbed up and down above a long gray horse, and behind the regiment Clubby's negro drove a farm wagon containing the officers' bedding and Clubby's chair. Across the field, they struck a ruddy clay road which wound down-hill, close-ridged with shoulders of gray-blue limestone. Below them stretched a bright green valley, flanked with the yellow, brown, and crimson of long, wooded hills. The scene beneath the sparkling, early sun was lovely, gay, and cheering. They whistled and chatted.

"Fat farming country" . . . "wish we had some of this pasture-land down home". . . . "We've got some just as good in Wake" . . . "don't these fellows live high, though; stone houses. . . ." "We got stone houses down in Wake" . . . "Two, maybe, and one's the jail."

As they struck the level, gaps came in their talk and laughter, grew longer when they started up a gentle but unending rise of ground. They reached the top in silence. Nothing was heard except the scuffling of their brogans in the dust and the clink and rattle of their manifold equipment. James Fraser saw a man in the company ahead pull a jack-knife from his pocket, open it with his teeth. An instant later, a folding lantern, new and shining, flew into the ditch beside the road.

Thereafter the day's march turned quickly into a blurred and painful haze,—a haze in which the beauties of the valley and the opulence of Shenandoah farmers were blotted out by the unchanging vision of swaying backs ahead and by the necessity, engrossing his mind, of remembering to put one burning foot before the other and at the same time to fight off the long harassment of his equipment which bit into his waist, his shoulders, and strove to bear him down. He had fragmentary glimpses of men falling out, sitting despairingly beside the road; of Clubby Jordan bouncing up and down the column on his curious horse, cursing and exhorting, piling men into the baggage wagon, pulling men out again, dismounting and hoisting three men on the gray. He was dimly conscious from the uproar that Clubby was pounding along somewhere in the rear and allowing no man to fall out without a bitter and insulting personal altercation. And ever and again, through this toilsome and interminable dream he heard the rattle and saw in the ditches the gleam of more abandoned camp equipment.

Then there were camp-fires and other soldiers sleeping in the angles of a rail fence. They were in a field, were told to fall out. He dropped down on the ground.

Big Tom MacGruder was pulling a blanket over him and shoving a cup of coffee underneath his nose. By shot! that coffee fairly nestled up against his spine. He felt much better now, but mighty sleepy. It was too bad he had thrown that axe and frying-pan away. No, maybe it was just as well, he was down to bedrock now.

Just before he dozed off he was conscious that a tall, strange officer was looking down at him. He heard him laugh and say: "For God's sake, Colonel, look at the junk this man is carrying."

CHAPTER XXVII

THE next day's march was different from the first; quite the opposite. The start was misery. They hobbled along the road beneath the unfeeling jeers of veteran regiments, they reached a wide, straight turnpike and fell in behind a marching column that seemed always to travel a little faster than they could walk and to throw clouds of disdainful dust back over them.

But after the noon halt, where they were served out cornbread and plenty of bacon from army wagons, and where, surreptitiously, they abandoned many extra blankets and pairs of shoes, they felt better. And when they hit the pike again they were able to look around them as they marched and take in what was going on. Girls and stout farmers' wives leaned over picket fences, waved or ran out to them with aprons full of russet apples. The infrequent negroes whom they met pulled off their hats in general obeisance and stared with popping eyes. At a stone-built, cross-road hamlet two young ladies dipped out cider from a hogshead and deftly caught the empty cups the men threw back to them.

In the middle of the afternoon, the column halted for a rest. Lying by the roadside, his back against a bank, his eyes fixed on a fat, sleek cloud seen through bronzed oak leaves overhead, James Fraser heard the sound of cheering drawing nearer. He sat up. The regiment ahead were on their feet, waving hats. A tall, dark-bearded officer on a little, rusty, sorrel horse was jogging awkwardly down the line. When he came to Clubby Jordan, who stood at the head of the regiment beside his long and sad-faced gray, he pulled up. In his old, wool hat and flapping, shabby private's coat the stranger looked like a gaunt, lean, circuit-riding preacher from the woods, one of these consecrated men; homely, earnest, mighty good, no doubt, but hopelessly inept, a man might hazard, unless he noticed, as James Fraser did, a certain bristling glint of iron in the beard and in the eyes behind the steel-rimmed spectacles.

Clubby Jordan, sensing that the stranger was, like himself, plain country folks, accorded him an easy "Howdy!" He looked again, saw gold stars on the collar and undertook a military salute, unfortunately frustrated by the bridle reins which hung over his arm. A gleam just touched the officer's stern, cadaverous face and was gone. He returned Clubby's abortive salute with surprising precision.

"Is this Colonel *Jurdan?*" He talked the hard, firm dialect of the mountaineers.

"Yes, sir," said Clubby, yanking the gray back from undue familiarity with the shaggy little sorrel. "Hold up, you horse! I reckon yo're Gineral Jackson."

James Fraser stood up, edged forward. My Lord! This preacher-looking fellow with his long legs swinging clumsily below his horse's belly, Stonewall Jackson! It couldn't be so. But if it was so, it was the biggest disappointment he'd had since he joined the army. My Lord! An old, back-country schoolmaster!

Now Clubby was pounding the macadam with his

stick. "These boys is plumb wore out! Not a damn thing to eat till noon to-day, sir!"

"That will be rectified at once, Colonel," said the other gravely. He paused imperceptibly. "But you should not swear." Clubby's mouth dropped open. But even while he stared in stupefaction, Stonewall Jackson closed his long legs against the sorrel and bobbed away. Colonel Jordan came to himself, attempted a dazed salute, and ended by scratching his stiff, black hair till his hat hung over one ear.

James Fraser used to figure afterward that the history of the next three weeks was written by and on his feet. Except for the question of rations, which now were plentiful, there was for him nothing much else to life but those two feet of his. He studied about them all the time, whether they would stand the punishment or give out on him. Every night he looked at them and figured what would be best to do, whether to prick the newest blister or just to grease it, whether to put on new socks or wash his old ones, or whether maybe, like some of the veterans, to tallow the inside of his shoes and not wear socks at all. Would linen bandages help to hold his feet together or make them swell? In the end his feet apparently figured it out for themselves. They thickened their soles and threw out broad, hard callouses wherever needed. He was all right now as long as he kept the same pair of shoes. And he was bound to keep them. There were stories in the papers about how so many soldiers carried Testaments and Bibles, and slept with them under their pillows, and that was no doubt a mighty good thing to do. But just now he was sleeping with his head right on those shoes, where no one could get them away from him. He reckoned the boys in the company were all right, mostly, but he heard some of them say that they weren't satisfied with the shoes they had.

While this education of his feet was going on, no man alive could have kept track of the places their regiment went to and came back from again. They had ranged up and down that valley and across it every way. They had marched at dawn, at dusk, by night, in rain, and mud. They had slept in hayricks, corn shocks, orchards, rocky caverns. If any Yankees were watching them, they must be dizzy.

But were any Yankees watching them? It seemed unlikely. They had started off stimulated by rumors of impending action; then had hurried back for a mythical battle somewhere else; next there were said to be Yankees gathering in the mountains and they took the road again. At first they had felt proud of themselves as they passed through a country town, had cheered and told the folks that they were off for a fight. The next time coming back they were more subdued, and the third time they would have given three days' rations to have marched around it.

So now when a cavalry trooper, having delivered orders to Clubby Jordan as he sat on the front porch of a brick farmhouse, pulled up before them, as they drank their morning coffee, to say, "Yankees coming down the valley! You boys gwine to ketch hell soon," they merely scoffed at him, weary and sophisticated.

"Ride on, Forager!" . . . "Sharpen your sword, you pig thief!" . . . "Dismount and grab a root!" This last was said in chorus and with pride, having just been learned from the veteran regiments and referring libellously to the cavalry's alleged tactics under fire.

That morning as they marched the call went up, "Here comes Old Jack." The General, his sorrel at a gallop, went past the column, jerking his head in absent-minded recognition of their cheers.

An hour later, to their immense surprise, they filed off through a pasture-field and lay down under a long, rail fence. Clubby Jordan got off his horse. "Put this horse in the barn, yonder," he said to his little negro, 'Simmon. The negro's alacrity made James Fraser think.

"My Lord!" he said to himself, "anyhow that nigger thinks they's goin' to be a fight." He peered between the rails. There was nothing in sight but another pasture field and, at its farther edge, a wooded hill. He pulled his head back and looked along the fence. The men of the regiment were peeping through the rails and murmuring to each other. A few cast anxious glances back at their officers.

Clubby's roar overwhelmed them. "Now, listen here, you boys! They's Yankees in yonder woods and if any man shoots wild, I'll tan his breeches as sure as I'm a Jordan. Now you all can load," he added casually.

James Fraser pulled a cartridge from his box, bit it, primed his pan, and rammed the cartridge home. He capped the nipple and thrust his rifle through an opening in the rails. A pleasant, exciting prickling seemed to spread out underneath his knapsack. He noticed with satisfaction that the opening he had picked was bigger than common on account of a crooked rail above it which gave a better chance to sight. He was not the least bit scared in the world, just pleased with himself and keen.

A curly ball of smoke jumped out of the woods and instantly he heard a flat metallic 'bang!' There must have been an order, for the other boys were firing. He fired too. There was nothing to shoot at but he took pleasure in the strong kick of the stock against his shoulder. Quickly he loaded again.

Now little puffs of smoke, and a rattling sound, were coming from the woods. Something hit with a dull whack against the rail; that made him pause; it must have been a bullet. He had never thought about bullets. Well, anyhow, the thing to do was keep on shooting. Only he wished there was something to shoot at instead of just the woods.

The noise and smoke were now tremendous, a fact which gave him comfort, then elated him so that he paid no heed when, from the tail of his eye, he saw a man crawl back from the fence with one leg dragging after him, and another roll over, grunting.

Then Clubby Jordan was astride the fence, hammering it with his hickory-stick and shouting,—was in the next field, trudging forward with his old wool hat waving above his head; and they were swarming over the top rails screaming "E-e-*a-a*-oo!"— Now they had overtaken Clubby. James heard him holler: "Hey, you, catch my stick and pull me along."

Scattering fire came from the fence along the woods. They quickened their pace, ran for it and clambered over with their muskets clubbed and ready. There was nothing but a hasty crackling in the underbrush and a few blue bodies lying among the leaves.

He ran on, up the hill, took a pot shot at a hurrying figure, then halted breathless on the crest and waited till the other boys came up. Below him, on a wood road, he could see the last of the bluecoats trotting out of sight. He fired after them and laughed. By shot! he was sure of one thing, now. Chasing Yankees was the most fun in the world.

CHAPTER XXVIII

But before there was a chance to chase the Yankees again, the first snow fell. Even Old Jack was obliged to admit that the marching business was played out at last. The army was broken up and scattered over the countryside to make out as best they could during the winter. Their own regiment was led by the usual well-mounted and casually cheerful aide through ankle-deep slush into a large bleak hickory wood and there told to make themselves at home. Below them a cold stream slipped between snow-capped stones and, beyond a white valley, etched with fences and bare trees, rose, sharp and clear, the Blue Ridge where the Yankees still hung on.

They bustled round, worked busily together like sagacious animals or ants; they chopped, they hauled, they built, they burrowed. Under the hickory-trees their lairs appeared in straggling rows; huts roofed with canvas or with boughs, dugouts, descending underground, chimneys of brick, of clay, of kegs and barrels.

Among them Clubby Jordan toiled, or at least followed their efforts with an anxious sympathy almost equally exhausting. And on occasion he could take an axe, and spreading his stout, short legs, nick a corner lock out of a log as slick as any man.

Charles Prevost, though no hand with an axe or other tools, was fertile in suggestions for their comfort, suggestions, however, which, like the blanket shelters on their first night in the field, while theoretically ingenious, invariably failed in practice. He recognized the fact with pleasing frankness and after that devoted himself to scouring the countryside in search of rations and comforts for the men. His winning personality produced results. Under his spell housewives surrendered treasured hens and turkeys, threw in pails of sausage meat to boot. The company lived high.

There were others who did not rely on a pleasing presence for success in accumulating useful trifles. The Racker twins soon had more quilts than any other men in the company and although each was accounted for by a circumstantial tale of the donor's generosity, the rest were unable to shake off the notion that the quilts had been acquired by means other than the charm of those two rat-faced young scoundrels' address.

The three men who joined with James Fraser in constructing the hut for their shelter were the same who had shared the tent at Beaumont: Dougald, Big Tom, and inevitably, Harry Horniblow. Harry had become an incongruous but accepted fixture in their society. They had begun by relishing the flattering if pitiable contrast which he provided to their own bluff manliness and vigor. The presence of the sallow, worn-out youth made them feel hard and hearty. And soon after, they realized that in addition to this advantage, Harry, though seeming puny and always on the point of exhaustion, never became exhausted. They were able to enjoy a feeling of physical superiority at his expense without additional labor. Also they grew to feel that from Harry's eccentricities they gained a certain bizarre distinction, gratefully pleasing in their so much more staid and legitimate lives.

When it came to building this hut for the winter, Harry justified their tolerance. The general plan, half dugout, half log hut, was Dougald Cameron's. The shingles for the roof were rived out by Big Tom. It was James Fraser who discovered in the ruins of an ancient farmhouse the tile flues for the chimney. But once the roof was on, Harry came to the front as a master of interior devices. The double-decked bunks which stood on each side of the hut were made by Harry, were corded by him as light and springy as any beds at home, and fitted with shuck mattresses as good as you could buy. It was all very well for Big Tom to say with an indecent grimace of his sandy eyebrows, that Harry ought to be a specialist on beds. Harry went on to fix up a table that came down from the ceiling on ropes, and two cupboards on each side of the fireplace. And though Big Tom, unrelenting, pointed out that Harry ought to be able to make a cupboard, as he had probably hidden in as many as any man in North Carolina, this was carrying disparagement too far. The trouble with Big Tom was that he had been the heavy coon dog when they were putting the roof on and he didn't like to see any one crowd him out.

But once their cabin was complete, and James Fraser, proud of his skill as a worker in metals, had hammered an iron bar into a crane for their pots and kettles, their cheerful zest had nothing left to work on. The duties of the camp were slight. The weather gave Clubby little chance to drill and anyway Clubby took small stock in drilling. He looked on it as a strange practice, harmless, for those to whom it afforded entertainment, but having no bearing on the business of putting up a fight. He would have liked to have had shooting at a target—plenty of it—but of all things in the Confederacy powder was the scarcest, so he was obliged merely to plod on his rounds from hut to hut, making sure that the rifles were clean. The bayonets, he paid no attention to; he was quite contented to see them used as pokers to stir up the fire or as spits for roasting meat.

In consequence there was little to do except an occasional orderly detail or turn at guard duty. On the other hand, James Fraser, at least, began to get a little tired of sitting all day in the smoky hut and spitting into the fire. He could not settle into impassivity like the others, most of whom seemed perfectly willing that the war should continue indefinitely on that basis. But he did not know how to break the spell which inactivity was casting over him. Dougald Cameron was all right. As First Sergeant he had his daily reports, his muster-rolls, and requisitions to make out—a hundred details which, seeming at first nonsensical, after a while gained value because of their use in killing time, and finally, in some mysterious manner, became profoundly important on their own account. And Harry Horniblow, either with leave from the Captain or without, was busily engaged in making an inventory, with notes for future reference, of all the maids and matrons of the countryside. It was for him a period of exhilaration. Not having yet made serious advances, he was able to imply, and perhaps himself to believe,—for although

precociously astute in all other matters, he was subject
to hallucinations regarding his invincibility—that a
boundless field lay open for his scandalous operations.
But James himself sank into apathy. He roused himself to write a dutiful letter to his mother, in which he
noted the food he had eaten for as far back as he could
remember, gave the names of the nine other company
commanders and the counties from which their companies came and made a list of those in the Cape Fear
Rifles whom his mother knew well, together with a
statement that all were in good health. He asked for a
pair of mittens and a layer cake, hoped that the war
would be over soon and that she and his father were
well. That letter was merely a duty. His mind was far
more agitated by the question whether to write again
to Stewart Prevost. He had not received an answer to
his letter and he did not suppose that he ought to write
her till he had. But on the other hand, maybe his
letter had gone astray; or her answer. Such a thing had
happened in a novel which he had read and again in a
play which he had once seen in Wilmington. In the first
instance, the lady had committed suicide, and in the
play—and this was more to the point—she had married
another man. What if that very prelude to tragedy
had occurred in his case? And yet he would not be
importunate.

Nevertheless the issue had to be fought out every
day, and though in the end he gained the victory, made
up his mind he would not write, it seemed at the cost of
all good spirits and vitality. He was beginning to sit in
his hut as listlessly as any of them. He did not yet

enjoy it, but it ceased to fret him. He would slouch on his bunk for hours, his mind a blank or idly ruminating on the food which he had eaten since he joined the army, the food that he would eat in days to come. The life was beginning to mould him to its pattern. He noted the change without much self-esteem, it is true, but without dissatisfaction. It made things easier. He saw that soon he would be as contented as the rest. Before that occurred, however, he would make one effort. He spoke to Dougald of a furlough home. The Sergeant shook his head.

"They aren't going to give many furloughs with the Yankees so close; there won't be near enough to go 'round. I can't put in your name ahead of the others, especially the married men. You see," he explained, "I'm supposed to be the Sergeant, and you're supposed to be a friend of mine. It wouldn't look right, James."

James nodded, but his thoughts were bitter. What was the sense of giving furloughs to married men? When a man was married, it was all settled. They ought to give a furlough to a fellow that was in love. He sank into apathy again. How long this state would last, no one could tell; probably till spring, till he could get greens to eat again.

But one day, looking from the doorway of his dugout, he saw, beneath the meagre winter sun, two bright, new-looking figures coming toward the hovels of the company. Their unsoiled uniforms, their shining buttons proclaimed them as recruits. But that was not what arrested him—recruits came drifting in each month to provide a brief, slight source of interest and condescending merriment. These figures, however, were reminiscent. As he watched them come nearer, self-conscious, awkward, sticking close together, he ran over the inhabitants of the Cape Fear country but without a clue. Then he made out the face of Bill, the brakeman, greatly changed by the forage cap and the uniform and by an uncertain air of blustering embarrassment. Beside him lurched the gangling young fireman of the switch-engine.

"Hey," James called out heartily, "when did you boys leave the roundhouse?"

Uneasy in their rôle of novices, the two affected not to hear him, came toward him, and, by swift glances which they attempted to make seem casual and indifferent, tried to make out who he was.

"What ails you, Bill?" said James, "Why don't you speak?"

They were now close and Bill, abandoning subterfuge, gave James an embarrassed stare. "Jim Fraser," he said, "I wouldn't know you. Doggone me, if you don't look like a smoked-out coon."

"And he's got a kind of a beard," said the fireman, anxious to relieve himself of responsibility.

James recollected that he had let a slight, tawny down grow on his chin and also that the smoke from the green wood fires in their cabins had dried out and blackened all their faces.

"Well I'll swear!" said James, "Come on in. Shake hands with Mr. MacGruder." He threw a chunk on the embers and sat down beside Tom MacGruder on the bunk opposite to them. "What brought you here?"

"What brought us here?" said Bill, indignantly. "Why Gode damn me, the war, man, the war!"

"Sure enough," James admitted, "but I mean, right here."

"We come to join the company," said Bill; "we knew you was in it."

"My Lord, that's fine," James answered, trying not to look too complimented. "I'm mighty glad."

"Yes," said Bill, "we reckoned you would be."

Big Tom cleared his throat in disapproval. "How's things down home?" he asked severely.

Bill rubbed his knees. "Finest in the world. This war's been the making of Wilmington. Lots of block-ade runners is comin' in and everybody's making money. There's folks come from all over the Confederacy to buy goods."

"This war's a mighty good thing for the South," said James Fraser, slowly, "I reckon."

"It sure is," said Bill. "I don't give a damn myse'f about the niggers one way or the other, but I like mightily to see the folks all prosperous."

"We all don't give a damn about prosperity," Big Tom gave Bill a disdainful glance, "but we like mightily to see the Yankees run."

The switch-engine fireman glanced around in order to estimate the advisability of venturing a remark. "I'd like mighty well to see 'em run too," he murmured shyly. "They're the meanest folks I ever heard tell of."

Bill jerked a thumb at him. "He's still got that eight-pound Bible on his mind," he explained.

"Well," said the fireman defensively, "there was

more to that Bible than just the weight, which was three pounds short."

"Is that so?" said James, encouragingly.

The fireman brightened. "Yes, seh," he coughed. "It was a illustrated Bible and in the front was a picture of the Garden of Eden. Yes, seh," he added after a moment. "Yes, seh."

He proceeded. "Well, a feller come to the house one day and when he saw that picture he laughed. He said he'd seen the same picture in a book about Mexico." He paused for his words to sink in.

Big Tom, however, was not impressed. "Well," he answered contentiously, "I reckon the Garden of Eden might have been in Mexico."

Bill sprang to the fireman's defence. "You mean to tell me that the Ark could have carried all those animals from Mexico clear over to wher' it had to set 'em down?"

Big Tom's face stiffened into an expression severe and oracular. "The Ark could do anything."

"Could it though!" said Bill. "Have you ever seen a picture of the Ark? She wasn't no sea boat."

"That's a fact," the fireman interposed in a hesitant manner. "They's a picture of her in the Bible. She looks more like a tobacco warehouse."

"There you are!" said Bill, triumphantly, "How's a tobacco warehouse goin' to cross the Atlantic Ocean?"

"I reckon the Lord can do anything He pleases," said Tom with an air of finality. Bill was unconvinced.

"If He'd wanted the Ark to take that trip, though, why wouldn't He have had Noah to build him a regular ocean packet? Then He needn't have had him on His mind."

It was Tom's turn to triumph. "How you gwine to get all them animals in a packet?"

The argument surged to and fro, simmered away, blazed up again. Big Tom leaned forward, and thrust a fist under Bill's nose. "I'm the color-bearer of this company," he shouted, "and if you think any raw recruit can come in here and sass me back about the Bible, just step outside!"

"Hold on, Tom," said James, "Bill's an old friend of mine. He don't know how things are in the army yet. Come on, Bill, we'll go find you a hut."

Bill followed silent, but bristling. "Just because a man carries a flag," he muttered, "that don't mean that he wrote the Bible."

"Not by a damn sight, it don't," the fireman echoed, growing bolder now that Tom was safely left behind.

"All the same," said James, "you boys had better pitch your tune a little lower if you aim to get on with this crowd. Where's your equipment?"

"Up at Headquarters," they answered in subdued tones.

As they walked up through the hickory woods Bill ventured another topic. "I wish I could write. I noticed they was mail come in on the wagon that carried us here."

James Fraser was off through the trees. "Great Day!" he called back to them, as they watched him in astonishment, "Why'n't you say that before?"

Across a lane, which ran along the top of the wood,

stood the fat stone house with two fat chimneys where
Clubby Jordan lived. James Fraser jumped over the
red puddles in the road, stepped across a narrow porch
and entered the mud-tracked hallway. To the left, an
open door showed Clubby's chair before the fireplace,
and through the right-hand doorway he saw the tables
stacked with army forms and with documents tied up
in bundles. At this table, a weazened pallid clerk, who
puffed away laboriously at a big cigar, was sorting
letters into piles. Elaborately, he affected to ignore
James as he stood before him. He inspected the ash of
his cigar; he hummed "The Officer's Funeral" in a high
tenor voice and went on sorting mail.

"Hey," said James, "you got a letter for Fraser,
Company C?"

With deliberation the clerk read the names on three
more letters and laid them on different piles. "We
don't give mail out here," he said.

James Fraser hardly heard him. Slowly he was reading the address on one of the letters the clerk had laid
down. Standing before the table, he spelled out, upside
down, the letters in a flowing hand.

"Mr. James Fraser, Cape Fear Rifles."

"Hyer's my letter," he cried out. The clerk showed
no sign of having heard him. James pointed, raised his
voice. "This one."

"We don't give out letters here."

"Man," said James, "I want to read my letter."

"The mail," said the clerk, "goes down to the companies. You know that."

"Well, I reckon it won't hurt you to let me have it."
James reached out his hand.

The clerk flourished his cigar, indignantly. "Don't you touch that letter. I'll have you in the guard-house, soldier."

"You won't have me in before I close up both yo're damn weasel eyes," said James. He leaned forward across the table.

The little clerk pushed back his chair in haste. "You touch me," he squeaked— "You——"

"Now, you boys," Clubby Jordan's voice sounded from the doorway. "Hush your fuss." The Colonel came between them and stood jiggling his big fists up and down inside the pockets of his alpaca coat. "George, give this boy his letter." He turned to James. "Take your letter, James." His fists stopped jiggling. "And if you come up here again to bullyrag my clerk, I'll warm you, son, I'll warm you!"

James Fraser saluted. "Yes, seh, Colonel," he said with alacrity and earnestness. "I certainly am obliged." He fled.

He hurried along the lane to where it entered an angle in the woods; he jumped over a ruined wall, landed in a little drift of snow on the northern side, and holding the letter tightly in his hand, walked through the trees till he felt he was alone. Then he squatted with his back against a tree and opened the envelope.

BEAUMONT, December 2nd, 1861.

DEAR JAMES FRASER:

Your letter, written from Richmond came only two days ago and I am answering it as soon as I can, though I suppose my letter may take as long to reach you. In fact it may be lost altogether as I hear that many letters to the soldiers are. It seems a pity that our Government cannot do better in this respect for I am sure that our brave men in the Army are glad to hear from home and surely they deserve everything that can be done for them. But my Father says that we should not complain because the Government is faced with many problems.

If I were Irish instead of French and English, I would say in this letter that you must let me know if you do not receive it, as I do not want you to think that I am neglectful of my correspondence. Indeed I think that to answer every soldier's letter should be the first duty, as it is the privilege of every Southern woman.

No doubt I have said enough on this score and you would rather hear the news of home. Your Father and Mother are well. I have not seen them lately but I get word of them in driving around the countryside to see how the families of the soldiers are making out. We carry rations and delicacies to some of the less fortunate ones and we have also formed a fund for their aid. It is beginning to be needed now that prices have gone up quite a little while the soldiers' pay of course remains the same.

None of this has any particular interest for you, I know. I write it only for you to tell the other men so that they can be assured that their families are well looked after while they are away fighting for our Country. And how gloriously they are fighting! A letter from Charles to my Father told how splendidly you all had met the Yankees and routed them. If only they could see the hopelessness of the struggle before it is too late,—too late for them, I mean, and perhaps too late for my brother, Charles. Do you remember my fears for him? I am sure you do. Perhaps I should not write like this, but my fears are still for him and I cannot bear to think that he might be needlessly sacrificed for a cause which is bound to win, which has won already, if only those deluded and blood-thirsty Yankees would face the truth.

I must close now to meet some ladies from the neighboring plantations who have come to scrape lint. If there is anything that I could do for you or send to you, I am eager to have you let me know. And now goodbye, I hope you are well and comfortable as I know you are brave and cheerful.

Yours sincerely,

STEWART PREVOST.

He laid the fine white sheet of paper on his knee and patted it. He looked across the dreary valley patched with snow, with frozen clay, with clumps of stark, bare trees, and shadowed by the cold blue hills beyond. He looked down at their huts, huddled among the slush and trampled mire, at the listless solitary sentinel dragging his caked feet slowly along his beat. He stroked the paper softly. The corners of his mouth trembled into a smile. Now he could last out the winter.

BOOK III

CHAPTER XXIX

THE winter wheat was barely peeping through thin
sheets of melting snow when they took to the roads
again. Again they had to toughen their feet to marching, this time on roads running with water or shoe-
mouth deep in rich, red mud. However, they were
stirring, thought James Fraser; thank God for that.
And all the world around them was stirring too. Plow
teams crawled across the fields, yearlings kinked their
tails and scampered. And best of all, along the streams
and water-courses they found young cress and brookside
greens to flavor their unchanging bacon. Then a belated winter night would seize and shake them as they
bivouacked in their flimsy blankets and they would
long for their smoke-filled, stinking huts again. At
last the sun turned mellow and a flock of blackbirds,
northward bound, bustled and quarrelled in the scarcely
budding maple-trees.

About the time that they were hardened to marching,
they were decreed by the perversity of their life to go
into camp in a valley hamlet opposite a gap between the
shoulders of the mountains. From this hamlet, a mere
sparse line of stone and wooden houses and a high,
white store and tavern along the road, they were supposed to watch the Yankees. And while they watched,
or at least watched for them, most of the troops that
had been with them vanished. Soon rumors, then
newspapers, came drifting back to tell how they and
the rest of the Confederate Army had saved Richmond

from McClellan and driven the Yankees back to their
boats again. The Cape Fear Rifles and Clubby Jordan's
Regiment had missed it. So far their military glory
rested on having, on one occasion, chased a few invisible
Yankees through a wood. Their regimental standard,
chosen by lot from the now discarded company flags,
bore no proudly mounting list of battle honors.

While they stayed there, watching for maybe non-
existent Yankees, and also watching their chance for
glory slipping away, Charles Prevost, though visibly
oppressed by disappointed hopes, continued faithfully
to scour the farms around in search of extra rations for
the company, and James Fraser was puzzled and disturbed in mind by being more or less singled out as the
one to accompany him. Why did the Captain so often
ask for him on these details? Did he know, or suspect
that there was something—whatever that something
might be called—between him and his sister? Was he
seeking to find out what sort of man James Fraser was—
or more likely, merely seeking a chance to say to him in
a kinder way, what his father, the Colonel, had already
said? At any rate James kept mighty quiet on these
foraging expeditions. So far as Charles Prevost was
concerned, he acted the part of a good soldier, nothing
more.

"They tell me there's a farmer's wife lives up against
the mountain," Charles said to James one day as they
tramped up a stony foothill road, "that's got the biggest
shoat in the Shenandoah Valley."

"Well," said James, "I reckon it would take a shoat
that size to feed the boys."

"She won't sell it though. That's how the foraging officer came to tell me about it.". They tramped along thus, sometimes in silence, sometimes exchanging fragmentary commonplaces. They reached high pastures, beyond which the mountain forests began, and paused for a moment to look back across the green and fragrant valley.

"James," said Charles, abruptly. "You ought to be an officer."

"Me?"

"You surely ought."

"Why, Captain, who gave you that idea?" He thought of Stewart. My Lord, he hoped she wasn't trying to mess in and get him promoted.

"I've been noticing you," said Charles.

"I don't reckon it would suit me."

"You wouldn't like responsibility?"

"Oh, I don't reckon I'd mind that." James paused. "But I expect I wouldn't get on with the other officers; I've small education."

"Why, man, that's just where you're strong. You can build a locomotive. There's some sense to an education like that. Look at me. I've been to Harvard College and I can't mend a two-tine fork."

He beamed on James, as if the spectacle of his own learned incompetence were the most refreshing in the world, then turned sober. "What good am I except to go around and pick up rations for the men? And any nigger could do that."

"You'd be good in a fight," said James bluntly.

"Who can tell? We've never been in a real fight, and

anyhow fighting's the littlest part of being an officer,
I'm beginning to learn that now."

"Fighting's the main thing in the end."

"Well, never mind," said Charles, a little impatient
at James' solid opposition. "Anyhow, I know you'd
get on with the other officers all right. This is no Virginia Regiment," he said firmly. "A man don't have to
be high-toned or have a college education to be welcome. Look at Captain Jennings! He ran a grocery
store in Hickory; and Bullteel was just a plain country
blacksmith; and then there's the Old Man himself."

James listened in amazement. The planter's son was
talking like a radical.

"No, sir," Charles went on, "we've got all kinds of
fellows for officers in this regiment, but they are most
all good, honest men, with sense and judgment. But
they're all kinds. I reckon that's why the regiment
don't get further. We're too plain for those plush-
collared staff officers at Headquarters."

"A man ought to be experienced to be an officer,"
said James, slowly. "He can't make mistakes."

"You would be all right," said Charles. "The Colonel
would be willing. He thinks you're all right. Up yonder
is the house where they have the shoat."

Turning to follow Charles, James flushed with pleasure. If the Colonel thought he was all right, it was
something to be proud of, as much praise, indeed, as
Clubby accorded any man. As for a commission, he
did not know, he had never thought of such a thing.
He wasn't afraid of being scared, he reckoned he would
be all right about that, but if they got in a battle, and

he made a mistake, and men were killed on account of it, that he could not bear. Then too, it would mean leaving Dougald and Tom, and Bill, the switchman. He paused at the thought of that.

But how would his getting a commission affect Stewart? Not Stewart herself, maybe, no, surely not, but certainly the Colonel. In the Colonel's mind an officer would be a mighty different proposition from a private. He was stopped by another thought. Did Charles Prevost know how things stood? Was this talk of a commission a good-hearted attempt to give him an even chance? An even chance with her? And an even chance against whom? It could be no one else but Catlin Gregg. James Fraser had a notion that Charles, underneath his flawless and universal courtesy, did not much like Lieutenant Gregg, in spite of the fact that he was another planter's son. And he had a notion too, that Gregg got letters from her often. His heart shivered within him. By shot! he'd better figure a long time about that commission before he turned it down.

A mountain cabin of squared logs showed beyond a turn and, behind it, in a pen of rails they could see the monumental back of a spotted shoat.

"There's our shoat," said Charles turning up a path between gnarled apple-trees.

At the sound of their feet on the porch, a flat, sparse-haired woman came to the door. "Howdy," she said, "what do you all want?"

Charles took off his cap and bowed. "How are you, Ma'am? I hope you're well?"

"If you're foragers," she answered, ignoring his

amenities, "we hain't nothing to sell." The wild, shy eyes of a little child peered out from behind her skirts.

"Well, there he is!" cried Charles, in a tone of cordial recognition. "He's the man I came to visit." He opened the cartridge box which hung behind the holster at his belt. "Yes, sir, he's the very man I brought something for." Pulling out a tiny paper-bag he shook a lump of brown sugar into his palm. The child's eyes widened, but still he hung back.

"What's this?" said Charles, "Don't want the sugar I've fetched him? Well, well, it looks as if I'd have to eat it myself." Shutting his eyes, smacking his lips, he made a great pretense of swallowing the sugar, then held out the lump again and laughed. The child reached out a tiny, hesitating hand.

"Say thanky," said the woman. Her voice was harsh, but she gave Charles a reluctant, black-toothed smile.

Ten minutes later, Charles Prevost sat on a split-bottomed chair before the embers and rode the youngster on his knee. "Yonder go the hounds!" he said, "Ow-*ou*—ow-*ou!* And here comes a great, big fence, he said. "Now horse, you jump."

Grinning in silent ecstasy, the boy sailed aloft till his shirt-tails stood out straight behind. "Hi, hi!" he crowed.

"Now, this shoat," said Charles, returning to the argument, "we'll pay good money for him."

"When the Yankees come by," the woman answered, "they paid gold."

"When we win the war," said Charles, "our money will be just as good as gold, and it's the good folks like you that raise hogs and corn and sell them to our soldiers, that are helping us to win."

"I'll be plain with you, Mister," said the woman, not unkindly, "we're poor, and Confidrit money don't go fur, hit looks like."

"Yes, Ma'am, I know, I know," answered Charles quickly, "we want to do the fair thing. We're bound to do it." The woman did not answer.

"Anyhow," said Charles, after a pause, "it won't do any harm to go and look at the shoat." He stood up and made a little motion as though to usher the woman out the door.

"I'll put on my brogans," she said, going toward the dishevelled bedstead at the end of the room. The youngster followed her but kept looking back at Charles.

"We'll wait outside," said Charles. "Go ahead, James." James Fraser picked up his rifle and stepped across the porch.

Instantly three rifle shots cracked out and a bullet slapped against the lintel of the door. He dropped to the ground. A mountain feud! My Lord, what a fool mistake! There was no more firing.

"By shot, Captain," he muttered, "that was close." He raised his head above the porch.

In the doorway, Charles Prevost crouched on hands and knees. His bright head hung slack between his forearms, and as James Fraser looked, he gave one dreadful, bloody cough and sank down on his face.

James Fraser felt his body freeze with fierce, sick despair. By God, who did that? He whirled around. In the road below the house three troopers in coats of

blue were peering at him through the apple-trees and
trying to load their carbines while they jerked at their
restive horses. "Yankees!" he called out.

The woman's hard-toned voice came back to him.
"Go after 'em!" She was kneeling beside Charles. "I'll
mind him." She gave a tug and thrust the butt of the
Captain's pistol toward James Fraser's hand.

He was running through the apple-trees; the troopers
were hurrying to load. One raised his carbine and fired.
Ahead of James, an apple leaf came floating down; he
ran faster. He must get close, make sure. Another Yankee raised his gun. A puff of smoke shot out of it.
James threw up his pistol and fired. With his carbine
still at his shoulder the Yankee went over backward off
his horse. James fired fast at the others as he ran. He
heard another shot and felt a razor-cut beneath his arm-
pit. A flying splinter stung him on the hand. A Yankee
fell on his horse's neck, hung feebly, dropped like a
bundle to the ground. The third man wheeled and
galloped. James Fraser emptied his pistol after him.
By shot, he missed him! He brought his rifle up and
fired at where the bobbing cross-belts met on the broad
blue back. He thought the man dropped the reins and
clutched the pommel but he couldn't tell. What God-
damned luck! If he only could be sure he'd got him.

The two blue bodies did not stir. As he ran back to
the cabin, the picture of them stood out in his mind.
Was one of them the man that shot the Captain! If he
only knew . . . he would raise his rifle butt above the
stiff dead face and smash . . . ! What was he saying?
He was losing his mind. Let him try to think. Maybe

the Captain was not so bad off after all. Chilled, blinded, sweating, he reached the porch. The face of the figure lying across the doorsill was covered with a blanket.

Far off he heard the woman's voice. "He never moved nor breathed." Dimly he saw her in the doorway. Inside, the little boy crouched, frozen like a frightened rabbit.

Now she stooped down as though to lift the blanket from his face.

James Fraser's soul seemed to burst out of him in agony. "God damn you!" he cried out. "Don't you lift that blanket!" He stopped in horror. He had cursed at her.

But she was not offended. She stood up. "He was a mighty pretty gentleman," she said slowly. "I reckon you thought a heap of him." James felt his face work. He nodded.

The woman waited, rubbing her knuckles awkwardly together. "You can have that shoat," she said at last, "for whatever you've a mind to give."

He could speak, now. "I'm much obliged. I'm mighty sorry I spoke so just now. Mighty sorry. I——"

"No harm is done," she answered, simply, "except what can't be mended."

CHAPTER XXX

JAMES FRASER never knew another moment's peace of mind until, a long month later, the regiment was on the march again. Only then, eating the dust which hung between the crooked fences, and pressing eastward toward what seemed at last a possibility of action, did he feel that he could somehow make out to get along, could maybe, if there was a chance of heavy fighting, focus his mind on that until the hour of battle and afterward come out of it, if he came out at all, with the sharp thoughts and bitter memories, which now oppressed him, a little dimmed. He felt that he had lived with those memories, or they with him, since time began. At least it seemed long ages that he had dwelt in the valley camp, alone and lightly shrouded by the unending summer haze, a haze which cut him off from the other men, half veiled their faces as it did the fields and mountains, and only revealed, in all their first unbearable intensity, pictures of the hour when Charles Prevost had died. And though from that moment he had known by heart each detail, and though each detail brought him only anguish and despair, he must forever be conning them over in his mind, must hug their sharpness to him in futile self-mutilation.

Even now, as he marched away from the tragic mountain, those memories still kept pace with him, kept pace with him whether he stared ahead at the long

strip of bobbing hats and swaying rifles or looked around
at the luscious August countryside.

He saw again the gleam of buttons on the Yankee
troopers' jackets; he felt the sting of flying bark against
his wrist; he heard a loose horse trot away distractedly,
and whinny.

Now he was hurrying back to the mountain cabin's
porch—he must have hurried, for the man in the four
ahead cursed him for treading on his heels,—was
hurrying back senselessly to find that which, inevitably,
and forever would be awaiting him.

The rest of that incredible day moved by in slow
procession—the solitary journey back to camp, stumbling, running along the stony road among the damps
and shadows—firelight on the face of Clubby Jordan,
whose hazel eyes gripped his as he blurted out his
story and fought with the twitching muscles around
his mouth to keep them steady—from the shadows he
heard the voice of Catlin Gregg, high-pitched and coldly
hostile, "So the Captain's dead, and you're back safe
in camp!"

Then came the single crumb of comfort. His grateful
memory dwelt on each firm, rough feature of Old
Clubby Jordan's face, as, eyes hard as agates and
mouth like an axe-edge, it turned on Catlin Gregg.
"Lieutenant, this yere's a good boy. I do not wish you
to speak so to him."

Of course they had sent troops to the mountain
cabin; they had found the dead Yankees and heard the
woman's tale; and thereafter neither Catlin Gregg nor
anyone else had raised a word against him. But he

could feel that the men's unspoken thoughts, charged
with frustrate and unreasoning resentment, involved
him somehow in the loss of their Captain. They could
not lose an officer so gallant, cheery, winning, without
deep-burning fury, and that fury was bound to find a
mark. Perhaps if they met the Yankees, they would
afterward feel less hardly toward him.

His friends were loyal; that much at least he could
fall back on. "Don't mind them, James," Dougald
Cameron would say. "They've been too long in camp."
Big Tom said nothing, but busied himself trying to pro-
voke outspoken comment on his friend with a view to
smashing the speaker's face.

Then Catlin Gregg was made the Captain, Dougald
Cameron left them to become Lieutenant, and James
Fraser felt that he would have to stand alone. And
he was just as glad. His friends were loyal but they
understood him no better than the others. They
thought his loneliness and silence had come from the
consciousness of the men's disapproval. He had to let
them think so, had to guard his tormenting secret
closely from them. He dared not, in their presence,
even think of Stewart Prevost. It would be easier
when they were gone.

But to his surprise Harry Horniblow now came to
his defense, assumed almost officially the rôle of cham-
pion. And more surprising still, he found in Harry
understanding, elusive and indefinable, but refreshing
beyond anything he had received from Tom MacGruder
and the rest. Seated with his foxy face between his
knees, Harry talked to James Fraser about the men,

their attitude, the ways of their dim minds, talked with a philosophic irony which braced and stimulated, which made a man hold up his head and grin at them with large, sardonic understanding. In addition, James gathered that any man that raised his voice against him within Harry's hearing was flayed alive by the nimble scorpions of Harry's tongue, flayed in a style of vitriolic mockery which shamed victims and onlookers into silence or maybe something like a change of mind.

All such troubles of loneliness and of misunderstanding by enemies and friends had been merely nothing, however, compared to the fiery ordeal of writing a letter to Stewart Prevost—a letter to tell her that her brother had been killed while with him whom she had asked to guard him. That letter, too, stood out with perfect sharpness in his mind, stood out word for word; and in his mind he must, to his anguish, read it, too, over and over again. "That is just how it happened," the last lines went. "They shot him before I had a chance to raise my hand. But I reckon that won't make any difference to you. I got two of the Yankees, and maybe I got the other as he was riding away, but that don't make any difference either. He was the best man and the best Captain there was anywhere at all and I would have been mighty well satisfied, Miss Stewart, if they had got me instead of him."

He could picture her right now wandering alone, in her white sprigged muslin dress, among the live-oaks of Beaumont, distracted, overwhelmed, crushed to earth by thoughts of her dead brother. As for himself, the most that he could hope for now was that her mind was

too preoccupied with sorrow to give a thought to him,
to heap on his name the reproach and bitterness which
alone it could feel.

The sun was sinking now, its long rays wove a pattern amongst the swaying rifles of the column. Ahead
he could see Clubby Jordan's horse turn off through a
locust-bordered lane. Each day from now on they
would make camp nearer the main Army of Northern
Virginia, nearer, he sensed, to action, to a great campaign. Perhaps he would be in battle, actual battle,
soon. He wondered with detached curiosity how many
nights he would see that old gray horse lead the regiment into bivouac. He didn't care if it were many, or
just a few.

That night, alongside Harry Horniblow, he lay curled
up against a prickly straw stack whose weather-beaten
top shone above them in the moonlight. Around them
other figures, dark moon-tinged lumps, lay in the
angles of the fence and under the locust-trees. In the
open field their stacked rifles stretched away, a line of
gleaming tripods. He could hear old Clubby's horse
blow through his nostrils and chump grass, he could
hear the sentinels tramping slowly and a low call:
"Corporal of the Guard!"

But though tired enough and comfortably fixed in
the loose straw, he could not sleep. Harry Horniblow,
too, though motionless, lay wide awake and turned his
pale, sharp, straining face up to the moon. He shifted
and gave James a keen sly look.

"Jim," he whispered, "you ever been in love?"

James Fraser did not answer. Was it the moon, he

pondered, or was it the close contact between his frame and the other's slim sensitive body which enabled Harry to read his thoughts? No matter. Since he read them it was no use denying it.

"I reckon I am," he said.

Harry nodded with the satisfaction of an expert. "I knew it ever since I saw you first at Beaumont." He looked at the moon, "I wish I could be," he said.

"You've had chances enough," answered James bluntly.

"Too many. That's my trouble." He pursed his thin mocking lips reflectively. "I've tried all the women," he said, "and they are all the same."

James Fraser pondered this observation. "I reckon they are," he spoke laboriously, "to a fellow that tries them all."

Harry shot him a swift, admiring grin. "Who told you that? You never found it out for yourse'f."

"I reckon I guessed it," James Fraser answered wearily. "It don't do me any good to know. I'm not born to run around with women." He paused. "And I'm not even born to get the one I want. I can't make 'em like me," he muttered enviously, "like you can."

"You're lucky. I'd change with you."

"You'd not be happy if you did." James Fraser's voice was grim.

"I'd be happier." Harry looked away and spoke as though he mused aloud. "I've run after women since I was a shirt-tailed boy, but I've never really loved a one, not like you do, and I never will. I think love is damn foolishness," he went on, "but I wish I could."

"Maybe you will, some day," said James, "I hope you have better luck than me. You're bound to. I know that. You don't know how a man feels," he added, "when he knows he can only love one and he makes a failure of that."

"You give up too easy." In Harry's voice were mingled envy and contempt. "Where's your grit?"

James did not answer. Harry spoke again.

"Her brother got killed when you were with him." James was half shocked and half relieved to hear his secret, so carefully cherished, so torturing, named with familiar ease.

"But that don't make no difference," said Harry. "Didn't you kill the Yankees? Up here the boys were hard on you, but back home they'll take you for a hero. There ain't a bit of sense to either," he added, with a broad, refreshing grin, "but that's the way things go. No, seh," he resumed reflectively, "that ain't your trouble. What you've got to look out for is Catlin Gregg."

"What do you know about Catlin Gregg?" The sullen resentment which James felt could not conceal a tinge of interest in his voice.

"He gets letters from her. I found that out from a fellow at Headquarters," answered Harry with cool assurance.

James turned on him. "What business have you got—" he whispered fiercely.

"It don't do any harm to find out how the land lays." Harry's voice was unperturbed. "You don't like me but you've treated me all right and I thought I might pick up some news that would come in handy."

James was silent.

"Catlin Gregg," Harry went on placidly, "gets letters, and of course his father is a friend of Colonel Prevost's, but still you have some chances." He paused as if to figure the exact odds. "In the first place," he said, "Gregg may get killed in battle."

"So may I," James answered shortly.

The boy's pale eyes glanced up at him impatiently. "Well, if you're killed, of course you ain't goin' to marry any one." He dropped them to the ground in thought. "The thing you ought to do," he said, "is to get a commission. Then her father would have to notice you. But you ain't goin' to get one while Gregg is Captain. If I was you," he counselled, "I'd wait to see what happens to Gregg and if he hangs on I'd get them to put me in another company."

In the pause which followed James Fraser came slowly to himself. He felt as though he had struggled to firm ground again from chill, befouling slime. "I wouldn't want anything to happen to Captain Gregg," he said. His voice was charged with earnestness and fierce, impotent anger against himself and Harry Horniblow.

Harry looked at him curiously, "Well," he said, "I hope you come out all right in the end. Yes, seh," said Harry, "I'd like to see you get what you want." He stared into the silver mist which stretched across the sky. "I never will."

Compunction seized on James. Harry was curious, different from anybody else, futile, and at the same time repellent, sinister. Yet Harry meant him well, had tried from his devious experience to help him.

"Maybe things will change for you, Harry," he said. "Lots of fellows run around and then they get in love and settle down."

"I never will," said Harry. "I'm finished." He laid a fist on the flat chest under his jacket. "There's nothing here, now. Maybe there never was. Maybe it's my fault, or maybe I was made that way. I've had my fling, and it was a fling, too, I'll tell you, boy. But now I'm sick to death of it." He paused. "If ever we get in battle, James, I'm goin' to get right out in front where the Yanks can see me." He gave a low, sardonic chuckle. "Won't the folks back home be surprised when they find out I'm a hero!"

CHAPTER XXXI

STILL they moved eastward. The country took on a pinched and worn look. Few crops were in the fields, few fences standing. Farmers' wives, weary and curt, had no supplies to sell. The men fell back again on meal and bacon. Each evening they made a little batter in their tin cups, twisted the batter around their ramrods, and held them to the blaze, then boiled a little coffee made of roasted barley. After that they rolled up, two and two, in their blankets and went to sleep.

On the march they had the lean, stripped look of veterans. Nothing of all their paraphernalia now remained except canteen and haversack and a single blanket hung over the shoulder. Thus equipped, they marched past wagon trains and parks of artillery with satisfaction, conscious of their severe and businesslike appearance.

Then they fell in with troops encamped along the road and recognized some they had served with in the Valley the fall before. They could not always place them, and once, passing a group of men they called out: "Ain't you all from the Eighth Virginia?"

A pause. "I reckon we *are* the Eighth Virginia, now."

My Lord, thought James in the long silence which followed, those boys have been doing mighty different soldiering from us.

That afternoon they saw the well-remembered iron beard, the spectacles, the broad wool hat, and sorrel

horse. Old Jack pulled up beside the Colonel and tried
to speak to him above their cheering. "When we goin'
to fight, General?" they called out in their exuberance.
He looked at them inscrutably and bobbed away down
the dusty road.

When were they going to fight? That was the question. They used to wander over at night to talk with
veterans of other regiments. As far as another fight
was concerned, the veterans, while showing none of
the agitation which some of the Cape Fear Rifles felt
in their inmost hearts, showed on the other hand a dis-
appointing absence of enthusiasm. They were indifferent, though patiently obliging enough to draw an occasional diagram in the dust with their bare toes, and to
mention unknown towns and rivers with casual familiarity. The upshot of it was, that if the army
marched south, it meant winter quarters, if it marched
north it meant a thrust at Washington or even Penn-
sylvania. And the arguments why General Lee should
do both, or either, as given by the veterans, were un-
answerable.

In the first light of a September morning, drums,
partly muffled by the mist, beat the long roll. Close by
they rapped insistently; further away, drums, hushed a
little by the morning haze, echoed and answered them;
and so on, into the uttermost distance, where the dusky
horizon seemed faintly murmuring with many unseen
drums.

Groping amongst each other, they fell in on the road
and stood listening to the sombre tramp of columns

and the rumble of artillery. At the first green streak
of dawn, they moved off, slapping their shoes on the
ground to warm themselves and shake off the early
morning chill.

They topped a rise right into the eye of the morning
sun. Its light slanted into the level valley below them
and showed a winding road alive with troops as far as
eye could see, and every lane close packed with canvas
hoods of wagon trains. James Fraser gazed at the
scene spread out below him with incredulous awe.

"This yere," remarked Ance, trudging beside him,
"appears to be a army."

A little before the sun was overhead, the broad road
which they travelled, emerging from a wood, was inter-
sected by another running north and south. Before
they knew it, they had turned the corner and were
marching north. A few men started to shout, "Hurrah!" but noticing that the veterans of the regiment
ahead, talking and whistling till now, had fallen silent,
they fell silent, too.

They marched on into that night; and when their
legs had turned to numb and aching logs, their tongues
to dust-encrusted lumps; when their shoulders creaked
and cried aloud beneath their bumping rifle-barrels and
their heads were light and empty as their bellies, the
order came, "Close up. . . . Close up." Too tired and
dazed to question a demand so out of reason they
stumbled forward faster, closed up their ranks and,
moving woodenly, their spirits tortured and driven by
the spell of their own staggering momentum, they
marched on into the next dim yellow day.

Stunned by their labors, they fell down and slept,
slept in a stupor, profound and deathlike, where nothing
could reach them save the dulled, ceaseless aching of
their bones and the ceaseless trembling of the earth
beneath the wheels of caissons and of guns.

Thereafter, as he moved his painful body, as he tried
to move his stumbling mind, James Fraser had a sense
that he and all of them were, to their own unhappiness
and misery, by some obscure compulsion, creeping inexorably away from the life they knew, creeping further
and further into a world remote, incredible, a world of
marching, a world which soon would lock them in its
forlorn and senseless spell, doom them to exile from their
past existence, to bondage in a region dim, bleak, gray;
wherein they only marched, marched the clock round,
marched beyond the count of days or miles, marched
until lost to man, to God, to their own consciousness.

And so it was. The mould, the pattern of life, broke
down. It could not contain their marching. And with
its breaking they struggled forward, without a look
behind, into the timeless void that waited for them, a
void where years and minutes were the same, where
thoughts, old dreams, food, mud, and weariness were all
alike unreal, a void where life, if a man could call it life,
held merely dim confused and fragmentary pictures
which whirled on aimlessly through space.

There were pictures of dead men lying tumbled by
the road, dead men that moved him no more than so
many logs. They were not real, he was not real himself. He might change places with one of them, he

thought in one of his grim flashes. None would know the difference. There were pictures of squadrons clinking past, slouching impudently in the saddles, eating stolen watermelons and spitting the seeds out viciously in answer to the trudging column's jeers. Once they lay, secretive, in a wood, and looked down on long lines of Yankee camp-fires. The night breeze brought to them the sound of singing, a deep full-throated chorus. James knew the tune and had heard the words from Yankee prisoners. As the sturdy chant, now loud now faint, came to him on the wind, he picked out words:

> ". . . body lies a-mouldering in the grave,
>   . . . lies . . . . . . grave,
>   . . . grave.
> His soul goes marching on.
> Glory, Glory, Hallelujah!
> .   .   .   .
>   . . . marching on."

He laughed silently to himself. The Yankees sat in camp and sang about marching on. But who was doing it? "Speak up, feet," he murmured, "tell those Yankees who's marchin' on."

Beside him Big Tom MacGruder gave a grunt of mirth.

"They'll find out soon enough."

"Gode bless my breeches," muttered Bill, the brakeman, "If I don't hope so. I'm walkin' on my ankle bones right now."

But though they passed off the Yankees' singing

lightly enough, that firm full-throated chant came back
to James to stir and trouble him. A man ought not to
pay so much attention to Yankee singing.

But what troubled him still more was a flash of a
girl's dress in a straggling country town. A white
sprigged muslin dress. His heart that had marched
with him until he thought that it must be beyond all
memories, all hopes, regrets, and fears, leaped high,
fell tumbling. Like a chained dog, he commented dryly,
that sees its master. For immediately he was himself
again,—that is, he was again the lean and dusty wolf-
man, ravenous in body and in spirit, into which his old
self had been changed. He was able to look at the white
sprigged muslin dress and see that the girl who wore
it was tow-headed and had stupid china eyes. Therefore there was no sense in getting excited about the
dress. A dress was nothing. So many yards of cotton
goods.

But after that the dress kept coming back to him and
though it, itself, was nothing as he had proved, the girl
who wore it was something, so much he must admit, and
in his thoughts that girl was Stewart Prevost. No
marching, however desperate and interminable, could
carry him away from her, no numbness of mind and
spirit could dull the sharpness of her image. He had
left, it seemed, all peaceful comforting thoughts behind,
nothing could keep pace with him except the tormenting
thought of her. And like a thrust at an old wound, that
thought no longer pierced him sharply, cleanly; rather
it bruised and sickened him to death. But there were
only certain moments when it had the power to assault

him. By day the marching column with its dust, its smell, and movement shielded him. At night he sank into depths beyond the reach of all things whatsoever. It was the hour before he slept that he feared, the hour when his racked body, rendered perverse by misery, hung back from sleep. But after a while his body learned that no recalcitrance could alter the decree: "Close up . . . move on." It ceased to struggle, sank obediently into torpor with a swiftness that defeated gathering thoughts of her.

In this torpor anything might happen to him or to the rest. It was a perfect similitude of death. There were stories of men who, lying thus after a battle, had had legs amputated by the doctors without awakening. There were stories of men who, falling into this torpor on the march, had continued, unobserved, to tramp down empty roads long after their regiment had gone into bivouac. And they themselves, lying stupefied by roadsides, had been ridden over by cavalry, trampled by infantry without awaking. They feared only the wheels of the heavy guns, and on that account they kept well clear of the middle of the road.

But one night it was raining, ditches both sides were filled with water, the road was a narrow unfrequented lane which, beneath the over-arching elms that bordered it, was not so wet as the sodden country round.

Two by two they rolled up in their filthy blankets, praying to go to sleep before the water in the lane soaked through.

Some one was kicking at him, striving to break through the sunken dome of sleep in which he lay.

Mechanically he struggled to his feet, ready to hear, "Fall in, . . . count fours." But these men were strangers who acted strangely. A moon was struggling through swift clouds. The men went down the lane kicking, pushing, rolling the sleeping forms aside. No sooner was their swift efficient bustle lost from hearing than the steady rumble of artillery came following behind. Far away it sounded like many little trains of cars. Nearer, the clumping of horses and the rattle of trails, of chains, of lynchpins shot the rumble through. The lead-team came abreast of him, two sad blaze faces, hanging near the ground, a figure hunched above their straining backs, motionless save for a gentle rocking. The swing-team followed, then the wheelers, then behind the row of dozing figures on the limber and the bumping rattling gun, a caisson team, heads drooping, caked feet wearily stumbling.

And so they passed, team after team of desolate, weary horses, compelled by the same fate that bound James Fraser to its wheel, to tread forever the endless path between the traces. Some groped their way, fumbling in a daze, some hung back from their collars, sullen from despair, indifferent to the black-snake whips which fell mechanically. Others, fearing the whips, made frantic scuttling haste; their bony heads tossed, showed white eyes and staring nostrils. But the most of them plodded dumbly, leaned their starved furry bodies against the collar and strove with shuffling legs to keep them there. Above them and on the chests and limbers nodded dark hunched figures, the attendant spirits of the sorrowful caravan, decreed by fate

to force these patient suffering horses on to their ap-
pointed doom.

Oppressed by the toiling horses and feeling on his
own pinched shoulders the drag of their mumbling load,
he groped in the mud for Tom MacGruder and the
blankets. He slid his hand between the caked and slimy
folds and, crawling in, nestled up against the big gaunt
frame, unhappy and lonesome in his mind.

Before dawn he heard in his slumber the grunting
salvos of the guns and, tossing once uneasily, saw
through half-closed eyes the heavens flickering to the
flashes. The picture, seen but an instant, merged into
his dreams. A moment later, so it seemed, they were
on the road again, were shuffling down a hill into the
sickly yellow forecast of another day. Its light, feebly
waxing brighter, touched the roofs of uncounted ranks
of warehouses, of uncounted strings of freight-cars.
Beside him Catlin Gregg twisted his caked lips into a
grin.

"This is the Yankee depot of supplies. Let every man
help himself."

Already gray-clad scarecrows were battering in the
doors. The Cape Fear Rifles, transformed in an instant
by the hope of food, gallantly charged beside them into
long, sweet-smelling caverns crammed with kegs and
barrels, with cases fantastically inscribed, "Tomatoes,"
"Preserved Peaches," "Swiss Cheese," "Smoked
Tongue," and "Coffee." They fought with other companies for the spoils. They skirmished with provost
guards for kegs of brandy, bottles of Rhenish wine.
They ate whole meals of caviar, emptied whole bottles

of French dressing and stretched out, gorged and boozy, to doze among the loot.

The provost guards were kicking at them. The sun was dropping down the sky. Dizzy, surfeited, they formed in column and climbed the hill whence they had come. As they toiled on in the dusk, in the dark, the heavens behind them were lit by the burning warehouses and rent by the long, unbroken detonations of ordnance supplies.

The marching roused them once again. They talked and laughed. They had raided the Main Base of the Yankee Army, left it a heap of cinders, gotten safely away. They had marched as men had never marched before. Now with full bellies they would move back to southern Virginia for the rest they had so richly earned.

At noon they halted and lay down in the angles of the fence along the road. In the usual ten minutes they would no doubt be moving on again. But the sun dipped down the sky and no orders came.

"It don't look right to me," said Bill, the brakeman, uneasily, rolling a Yankee caramel under his tongue. "Them Yankees is goin' to be plumb scandalized when they find we've burned up all they rations." The caramel, a visible lump, went down his throat. "It looks to me like we ought to get out of here."

Instead of getting out, they filed at dusk across a field toward the sound of distant musketry. James Fraser's lungs were tight, he felt of a sudden tinglingly alive and a little sick. But night fell. The firing ceased. Disappointed and relaxed, they stumbled on through a dark wood, halted at the edge and built their fires.

Other fires stretched away to right and left. By their light he could see the twisted branches of the trees and, below, a long, deep cut that looked as if a railroad once had run there. Maybe the railroad-tracks were just beyond, he thought, as he untied his blanket; maybe they were going home by train. He rolled himself up with a practised twist. That would be a nice way to travel for a change.

CHAPTER XXXII

Weeks after, marching on as ever, marching as they always had since time began, as they always would till Judgment Day, lost souls doomed to stumble through a never-ending hell of weariness, James Fraser shifted his dust-blinded eyes from the back of the man ahead and stared without hope about him.

Low hills, dark green, which flanked a flat, slow river, hemmed them in, and seemed to look down, unmoved, on their laborious and futile haste. Futile it surely was. All day they had shuffled forward to the officers' refrain, "Close up . . . Close up," and still those wooded hills were just the same. A man might think that he and all that ghastly, tattered column were caught in the treadmill of some tormenting dream. Only the trampled dust crept by, ever so slowly, under foot. For the rest, they might be frantic imbeciles marking time throughout the ages, veiled by the gritty haze of their unending shuffle, drugged with the stench of their own ravaged bodies.

Ahead, the column, a close-packed mass of broken hats, of old gray caps, of long-haired, weather-beaten heads, all bobbing beneath the swing of rifle barrels, stretched out of sight, out of all guessing. Behind, the patter of hurrying bare feet, the muffled slap of brogans, followed them as far as they could hear. There was nothing for a man to do except to shuffle forward without ceasing in order to keep pace with the bobbing caps, to keep clear of the ghostly footsteps treading on his heels. Nothing else to do. That was the one necessity of all existence. Whatever happened a man must march, must struggle on through mud, through ruts, through heat and cold, through drought and dizziness and fits of vomiting. A man must march. Must drag one numb and wooden foot before the other, must set his meagre shoulder against the gnawing of his rifle, his mind against the maddening slap of the haversack across his thigh. A man must march. In all the universe that was the only thing that mattered.

And so much did it matter, so wholly had its grim compulsion mastered him, that James Fraser need no longer concern himself with it. His body, his very bones had long since learned the inexorable decree. They had, after many pains and tortures, acquiesced and now could be counted on, without a thought from him, to move him forward as long as they could move at all. Twice of late he had gone to sleep while marching— like the fellows he used to hear about—and waked to find that his faithful, ravaged body still marched on. And when awake, as now, he could so to speak desert it, leave it to its misery, and wander among the scenes and fragmentary pictures that drifted through his mind.

Having looked at the mountains and seen that they did not change, he turned his thoughts loose, in hope that they would find something to feed on more satisfying than those forbidding hills. They flew at once to the last good food that he had eaten, long ago. He could see it as clearly as a painting on the wall, the big, thick slice of well-grained, ruddy ham with the smooth,

white fringe of fat along the edges, the fat itself edged
with a crust, brown, crumbling, sugary. On top of all
the dab of tawny mustard. By shot! that ham and mustard hung right there before him, moved him to the
depths of his pinched loins. His heart was almost
trembling, his dusty, sour mouth watered with desire.
Ham and mustard. He felt the firmness, the substance
of the meat, tasted its sweetness through the salt, and
the mustard's cheering bite. Ham and mustard. That
was the stuff a man could march on, fight on. And
hadn't he fought? He shifted his rifle and took a chew
of slippery-elm bark. If he hadn't fought there was no
such thing as fighting.

But that had been the day after the ham. The ham
had been taken from the Yankee storehouses. The
night he ate it they were camped in a wood above a
railroad cut. As he went to sleep he had thought that
maybe next day that railroad was to carry them back
home. That was what he had thought. He almost
laughed aloud. He was glad that no one had known his
guileless notion. It would have made a grim, relentless
jest for them. They would have called that next day
"the train ride" maybe, have likely called him "passenger" till the day of his death. A day which might
easily have come long before now.

But he was not grateful for past escape, or fearful of
future extinction; he was only weary. Still he could
think, could recall that day and many past events
more clearly than ever. Yet without emotion. They
were merely pictures to be looked at. Nothing was to
be thought or felt about them.

Though he could feel surprise no longer, he could re-member his surprise that morning, as looking across the railroad cut he had seen the long, blue, heavy-moving lines break from the distant woods below and creep up the meadow toward him. He had been startled. And yet it had not seemed real, did not seem real now. It had seemed queer, unearthly, strange, like an incredible and monstrous show. Behind him guns had begun to bump. Above him many shells were swishing. He and the others had gotten into the railroad cut and watched the meadows from the shelter of the further bank. The guns were grumbling. Among the blue lines, sprays of earth and white slow-curving smoke shot up like magic flowers bursting into bloom. Beneath the rain of flow-ers the blue lines melted away, flowed back in dots and streamers to the wood beyond the meadow. Nothing was left except thin veils of idle smoke and blue heaps inexplicably encumbering the ground.

All morning long the wide, blue lines had swayed up toward them and broken into fragments against the airy puffs of bursting shells. They came closer, close enough so that he and the rest had popped their rifles at them, adding a feeble crackle to the groaning of the guns.

Then a blue line had not turned back. It had come on in hurrying groups that stumbled forward clumsily, heads bowed against the blast of shells, of frantic rifle fire from the railroad cut. And though at the last they, too, had vanished, others followed. He had lain for ages, his breast pressed to the bank, ramming, firing, biting cartridges; he had cursed, had shrieked, had laughed—a dry blood-curdling cackle. Ramrods had jammed in red hot barrels, they had scrabbled for stones and hurled them at the ever climbing faces.

At last the faces climbed no more, the field in front of them was still as death, still as the mounds and strings of dark blue figures on the ground, still as the oddly tumbled heaps below his feet; the tumbled heaps of gray which gorged the bottom of the cut.

Before he had a chance to count or name those figures heaped behind him, far to the right the short, high Southern cheer cut through the trees. As far as eye could see, dingy lines, tipped by the sunset light, trundling long shadows ahead of them, swayed down the slope. He and the rest climbed out of the cut and, yelping from parched taut throats, tripping over the rigid lumps of blue, lumbered toward the dusk.

A man would think that day of victory would have been enough to last him for his life, enough to entitle him to ease and honor and plates of juicy meat. But it had only led to more relentless marching.

They marched further, faster every day. It was grotesque. Why did they do it? Why stand it? Their reward was that the wagon trains could not keep up. Horses foundered, faded away, even a yellow dog, a mascot who had joined them, broke down and must be carried. Without supplies, they shook the last dust of corn meal from their haversacks and thereafter lived as best they might by barter, begging, stealing, and twice, most sumptuously, on recent battle-fields, by scavenging among dead Yankees' knapsacks for bits of hardtack. Dead Yankees also yielded underclothes and socks and shoes and, for those who wanted them, money and rings and watches, provided of course the bodies were not already looted.

James Fraser himself took only hardtack and socks from them and he always cut the blood off the hardtack before he ate it. But many were not so particular. Once he had heard the Racker twins whispering together. A Yankee major was dying underneath an apple-tree. He had a big gold watch when first they saw him and they had figured how long he would likely last and had gotten back to him in good time. He was still alive. But the watch had gone. Their curses were low-pitched, filthy.

Yankee bodies could not always be found to supply rations. In fact they became scarce and so did all other sources of supply. In their hunger they pulled ears of half-ripe corn from the fields and ate them raw. That was a mistake. Diarrhœa followed, and cramps in their empty bellies. Foulness welled up within them, swirled around their brains. Seeping away, it drained them of strength and blood and courage, left them white-lipped, black-gummed, silver-skinned.

And still they marched beneath the morning stars, the noon-day sun, the dews of night. Their marching passed the bounds of credibility, the limits of human flesh; it became a vastly tortured fantasy performed by disembodied spirits. Nothing could change their fate— not even victory. Even death itself would be put to it to change them much from what they already were. And even after death no doubt they still would march on as now, would still, as now, fall down each evening in their tracks and lie there senseless, sweating with weakness and stinking to the heavens.

They could not quit. That was the curse that lay on them. Only a little while ago, sitting up stiffly in the dark, James Fraser watched the silhouette beside him tug with numb fingers at its shoes. It was Bill, the brakeman, and it seemed as though he could not move his hands. James reached down and tied the thongs.

"How you come on, Bill?"

"I started," Bill's dogged mutter answered, "and I'm bound to finish out." He turned his face. His eyes were black burnt pits. His cheek-bones shone sickly white beneath the stars. "But Gode damn me if I ever love another country!"

At the memory James started to chuckle weakly, but a dull gripe in his belly made him stop. He shifted his rifle to the left shoulder. With his right hand he held his pocket full of cartridges away from his body. They had long since discarded belts and cartridge boxes as so much extra weight. The only trouble was that a man got mighty weary of the heavy pocket flogging against his hip. He looked around. The mountains seemed a little lower. They ought to be; after all the marching he had done. They had come far that day, twenty-five miles he reckoned.

The night before he had huddled in his rags on a mountainside. At dawn the guns which had rumbled through his dreams were firing over him into a broad white lake of morning mist. From the mist, spires and roofs emerged, straight rows of houses and, last, a river curving around the crumbling town. Chimneys tilted and tumbled under the spatter of the guns, roofs burst into flames. In the streets little blue ants swarmed here and there distractedly.

No sooner had a horseman waving a white flag come out of the town than they were on the road again. They marched down through the streets where Yankee troops were stacking their surrendered arms. He had a chance to note them as he passed. They didn't look so bad. Maybe because they were fat, and for a long time he had seen only men who were thin. They were mostly just a lot of shamefaced boys who turned away from the passing column and looked down at the ground.

The column itself held straight on, did not pause even to gather in the spoils of war. And ever since, they had been toiling up the road beside the river.

A while back he had heard a man say, "What was that place wher' we caught all them Yankees this mo'nin'?"

For a time no one answered. James tried to think if he had heard the name. He couldn't remember. Anyhow, what difference did it make?

Now a voice was saying, "I tell you it *was* Harper's Ferry. Ain't I visited my aunt there in '44? And ain't this the Potomac River? And ain't that Maryland yonder on the other side?"

Harper's Ferry. He tried to think. Why, that was where the whole fuss started, where John Brown had been hung. If he'd known that, he'd have looked around more. As for the Potomac, which was always in the papers, it was here only a narrow stream, so small that, rounding a turn, he saw the column wading across it through the shallows. In a brief halt which followed, he and the others took off shoes and trousers and hung them on their rifles. Then their thin, white legs were pushing through the water, were fumbling on the bottom for a foothold. They lurched up the other bank and stopped a moment to put their trousers on again. A spire showed over the shoulder of a hill; the dust of the column headed toward it.

In the neat and peaceful little town through which they tramped citizens stared coldly, American flags hung over vineclad porches.

"My land!" cried a woman with contempt, "ain't they dirty!"

Beside James Fraser's shoulder Big Tom MacGruder, a hairy, flapping scarecrow, rallied to meet the thrust. "Lady," he took off his hat and bowed, "we always wear dirty clothes," his voice was sugary and mocking, "when we go to a Hog Killing."

By shot, thought James, the boys will remember Tom for that. He looked behind. No one spoke, but the men had turned to stare at the flushing citizens along the street and were showing their sorghum-blackened teeth in lean and wolflike grins.

That afternoon the marching stopped. Swinging off behind the other regiments through fields of trampled oats they halted in line behind a long, low, wooded crest. They had reached their journey's end. Without a word they dropped down on the sun-warmed grass and slept.

The wagons came up. They were given meal and

bacon which they toasted feverishly before their fires and ate half-cooked till they grew sick and dizzy. Then they lay down again. But now they could not sleep; they were restless, jumpy, and harassed. In whispers they talked together to ease their minds.

"I wish I was back in Wilmington," said Bill; "I'd go down to Foretop's and get me a whiskey sour to settle my stomach."

"I reckon we all wish something different," said James. "If you could have one wish, Ance, what would it be?"

Ance reflected. "Well, since it don't cost nothin', I wish I was back in Bear Grass with my gal."

Big Tom MacGruder grunted in disdain. "I wish we may be in Washington by Thursday."

"I reckon we all do that," said James. He nodded at the switch-engine fireman. "What do you wish?"

The youth twisted his starved body inside his jacket.

"Come on," said James, "take a chance."

"I wish," he muttered, in a suffocated voice, "that my bowels was in order."

"Damn me," said Bill in high approval, "if that ain't the best wish for all of us."

By the light of campfires, they could see the veterans of the regiment next theirs tearing up scraps of paper and handing them around. Bill, the ever curious, wandered over. When he came back he sat down without speaking and stared into the embers.

"What are they doing, Bill?" James asked.

Bill did not raise his eyes. "They're writin' their names on scraps of paper," he muttered uneasily, "an' pinnin' them to their coats. Each man puts his name on hisse'f in case—" his voice trailed off.

A gripe seized James. All they had done, had suffered was not enough. The gripe stole upward, clutched his lungs, closed, cold and merciless, about his heart. "My Lord," he whispered to himself, "it looks like a rough time, sure enough."

CHAPTER XXXIII

THEIR sleep, when at last they slept, was broken by the rumble of caissons on the road, by the clink of trace-chains and the creak of harness, by lanterns swinging in the field behind them and shovels clicking against shale. At last James Fraser seemed to sink into a deep, small, breathless cavern of unconsciousness. Then, almost immediately it seemed, the morning sun was shining in his face. He started up, his mind a blank, burdened by some dim and nameless dread. Resting on his elbow he stared stupidly at the oat field in their rear. In trampled patches stood line after line of guns in battery; beneath them lay the huddled forms of sleeping cannoneers. Now he remembered. This was the day of battle. That other battle had caught him off his guard. Before he knew it he had been in action and even then he could hardly believe that it was so.

But this time the warnings, the portents were clear. They clustered round like buzzards. Shadowed by their wings, helpless beneath their ominous gathering, his thoughts drew back from all impending terrors and fled away to Stewart Prevost, fled away for one perhaps final gaze. He saw her graceful, swaying image, smiling, half amused, half tender, as it used to smile, and as, since the day her brother had been shot beside him, it would not smile again. He had carried the image in his mind so long, had become so used to gazing at it, with

scarcely uttered hope, with weary and impotent desire,
that he had come to look on the image and on his longing
as for him the two unchanging features of the world. He
knew, though still incredulous, that the day which had
just dawned might mean the end of him and of them as
well. And still it seemed impossible that, if he were to
fall dead here in this field, in that same instant his dream
of her would vanish. The very lightness, the airy, soft
fragility of that dream should make it indestructible,
keep it, whatever happened to himself, beyond the
reach of bullets. But he knew it was not so. When he
was ended, the dream would end. After a thrust of
anguish he felt a sense of peace. Let the dream end—
he had cherished it too long, too much in vain. He had
grown weary. If he should go to-day, wherever dead
men went, it would be all right, most likely. The
dream would be ended, the struggle over and he would
find release.

A piece of the paper which the veterans used the
night before had drifted down not far from him. He
slipped out of the blanket and captured it. He laid the
paper on his canteen, fished out a stub of pencil from
among his cartridges and wrote:

DEAR MISS STEWART:
We are going to have a battle today and though I
hope everything will be all right, it may be that I will
not have any more chances to write to you. There is
nothing I have to say except that I have never loved
anybody but you and ever since that day I came to see
the Colonel at Beaumont, I have thought about you

most all the time. If I should be killed it will be all right, I reckon, only I wish it could have been me instead of your brother, Charles.

I am going to put this letter in my pocket so if you get it you will know that it was found on me, and that when I went into the battle I was thinking about you with love.

Your friend,

JAMES FRASER.

While he wrote the other men were stirring. In camp the sight of a soldier writing had provoked them to gibes, to humorous messages of endearment; now they glanced at him, glanced quickly away, tried not to disturb him.

Drinking his coffee he looked back over the rise of ground on which they lay. A pasture field sloped to a little stream where water maples, already turning scarlet, half veiled the gray roofs and white spires of the town they had passed through the night before. Ahead of them the pasture sloped up to a long, dark wood and a white church cupola which stood out sharp against the eastern sky.

Along those woods, with slow, quiet bustle, other regiments in gray were forming. Feeling curiously detached and numb, James Fraser threw the dregs of his coffee on the ground and fell in with the others. He stood at ease facing toward the wooded crest. With restless eyes he searched the landscape for the enemy. No sign appeared, but behind him he heard a stir among the guns. Looking back he saw before each gun a cannoneer leaning on his ramrod; other men trudged

up with round shot and bright red bags of powder.
The cannoneers spun their ramroads and rammed the
charges home.

Away to the left, with a dull bumping sound a gun
went off, then two more. He saw a curl of thin pale
smoke drift up above some locust trees. Before he could
figure what those guns might mean, the guns in the oat
field flashed yellow flames which dragged a curling ball
of smoke behind them and cracked the air to shivers in
his ears. The troops ahead tramped into the woods and
were lost in the nervous rattle of musketry.

Still they did not move; just stood in ranks along
the meadow—waiting. An officer galloped up the lane
to their right, stared at them, galloped away. Beating
his plowhorse into a canter, a farmer passed by in a
wagon; his long white whiskers streamed behind, his
eyes showed white with terror. A few small gray figures
straggled out of the wood that stood so dark against the
sky. Another little mannikin in a red sash ran up to
one, pointed his hand at it. A puff of smoke came out of
the hand. The other figure lay down.

"There's one deserter less," said Tom MacGruder.

Down the lane from the woods came an old man with
a knapsack. He carried his rifle in his right hand, his
left was clapped over his mouth. He swayed as he
walked. James could see the twitching of his fingers
above the tattered beard. Close by, where the lane
turned toward the village, a guard stopped him. He
levelled his bayonet at the old man's breast.

"Show blood," he said.

The old man took his hand down. Instead of a mouth
there was only a monstrous, dripping hole. The guard

raised his rifle. "Pass." The old man swayed on.
Just before he would have gotten out of sight he fell
down on his face. After hours, it seemed, two soldiers
wearing white armbands came out of the village, knelt
down beside him, stood up, crouched over him, rolled
him into the ditch.

Other wounded came down the lane, limping, slinking, reeling, marching stolidly, chattering crazily. The
guns in the oat field banged "one, two, three, four"
without ceasing. The battle in the wood widened to
right and left, swelled louder, died away.

Still they did not move. They lay down or squatted
in ranks and watched the wounded drift back to the
town, the gunners spin their ramrods, the cowed birds
flutter soundlessly in the bushes by the road.

They chewed tobacco, slippery elm, and blades of
grass. At noon they fished out bacon and hoe-cake
from their greasy haversacks and ate it where they sat.
Maybe it was the food which gave James Fraser peace
of mind, but after eating he began to think that perhaps
they would not get into the battle at all. He began to
fear that the letter in his pocket might turn out to have
been unnecessary. It might sound foolish, too. He
wanted to read it, but with all the men around he did
not dare.

There was a stir at the other end of the line. He could
sense a feeling running toward him that something was
afoot. Looking toward the lane he saw that one of those
cursed aides, so neat and shiny, was standing by Clubby
Jordan's long, gray horse and pointing toward the wood.

"Attention," the order passed from mouth to mouth.

"Fix bayonets." The dry metallic rattle ran along

the company. Old Clubby trotted up, thumping his legs mechanically against the gray. He rubbed his knuckles on his scrubby chin.

"Right up the hill, boys, and into the woods yonder. Come up, horse!" He whacked his hickory-stick against the horse's rump. A cloud of dust flew up. The gray laid back an ear and started crab-wise up the hill.

"Don't you fuss, Clubby," said a strong, harsh voice. "We'll be ther'."

Abruptly the oat field behind them seemed to heave and rumble with a salvo from the guns; with a swift rustling sound the shells passed overhead. At once from way off yonder and now above their heads, with high-pitched swishing, the Yankee shells passed by. He heard them thudding into the soft earth of the oat field which they had left. Then he heard a crash, and a ripping crackle. "My Lord," he thought, "they must have hit a gun. I'm glad we're gone."

In the dark wood all was silent. James walked on cautiously, looking straight ahead but conscious of pale arms and faces showing among the shadows on the ground. No use to bother about them now. A man had better 'tend to business.

At the further edge he saw the backs of scattered men in gray who crouched and watched in silence the fields beyond. As he passed on, one, a meagre shrivelled boy, lifted his powder-blackened face and gave him a glance from red and deep-sunk eyes, a glance detached, hostile, as though James were a stranger from some despised and distant world.

Before them down the slope, post-and-rail fences fol-

lowed a turnpike road. Old Clubby, buttoned to suffocation in his long frock coat, turned in the saddle stiffly,
looked back in irritation. His eye paused.

"Hey, you red-headed fellow! Pull down them rails
fo' me."

A gap was made. A whack— "Come up, horse!"
The old gray floundered over the rails. He snorted,
shied clumsily at a mound, all sprawling arms and legs,
which lay along the road, then shuffled into a cornfield
on the other side.

James Fraser's legs, as he threw them over the fence,
felt cold and far away. The corn was tattered and
trampled down. Not enough was left to cover the heaps
of gray and blue which wound between the rows.

Once in the field beneath the tall still tassels, he
stepped cautiously through the powdery loam, stepped
cautiously over crooked gray arms and twisted feet.
It was hot there in the narrow, faintly shaded lane.
Lonely too. He could hardly see the rest, only hear
them lightly rustling through the corn. In that
cramped low tunnel under the stalks the air was close,
was heavy with the odor of smoke, of sweat and blood.
He would be glad when they got out of there, got where
a man could see what he was doing and get a breath of
air.

"Guide centre! Guide centre!" the officers kept
calling. He heard the voice of Catlin Gregg, sounding
very severe, as if the boys had done something wrong.
Maybe Gregg was scared. Well, lots of folks were
scared. But there was no use to talk that way.

Abruptly he emerged into the light; blinking his hot,

dry eyes he saw with relief that the other men were coming out as well. Ahead a line of elderberries showed along a water-course and between two bushes Clubby was whacking his horse again to make him cross the stream. Three men ran forward and pushed against the big gray quarters while Clubby cursed them for their pains. "God's brimstone! Can't you puny weanlin's push? You push or I'll frail the everlasting gizzards out of you." The old horse teetered, slid down the bank and heaved out, grunting, on the other side.

The water smote James Fraser around the ankles as he waded through. He'd have given a heap to have kept dry shod. He had an idea that a man couldn't fight so good with wet feet.

They were in a stubble field on the other side and the officers again were calling "Guide centre! Close up! Close up!" Still they just walked along in line. He wished that they could charge and holler or shoot or something. But there was nothing to shoot at. A thought occurred to him. Maybe the Yankees would run away again. This time he would run after them until he got one. He would be all right if something happened, but he wished to God it would happen soon.

As he toiled up through the stubble field he warmed up a little and what with that and the sight of other long, gray lines and waving standards, surging slowly onward, by the time he reached the top he felt more like himself again.

And still there was nothing. Far off the guns worked steadily and shells were travelling overhead. Before them lay only a silent, motionless wood which dipped down into a ravine. They went straight into it. Now, by some instinct, they moved with caution, trod lightly. Not a sound was heard except the brush of branches across trouser legs, the light tap of twigs against canteens.

From the ravine, he could see daylight at the far edge of the woods. If they could get out into the open again he would feel easier in his mind. It was a mighty mean place here.

Above him he saw, standing motionless, a man in a blue coat, with a shining sword. For an instant he stared, then threw his rifle up. Before he could shoot, the world was overwhelmed, drowned out, by a roaring wave of musketry. He fired wildly through the roll of smoke which drifted down the hill. Around him men stumbled to their knees, crouched behind trees, stretched out flat on the ground and stared in stupefaction up the hill. He saw one start to run, heard Big Tom's voice, "Stop!" and the thud of a rifle butt against the coward's body. Standing behind a tree he glanced back. The man had dodged Tom and gotten clean away.

As he loaded his rifle he was conscious of Clubby Jordan squatting behind the dead body of the gray. He heard him holler, "Load your pieces, boys, we'll rush 'em next time." He heard a man sobbing "Ah— Ah—Ah," over and over again in a tearful, wondering voice. And just beyond him, in the oak leaves, Harry Horniblow lay on his back, his long, slim, fiddler's fingers stiffly curled, his meagre breast thrust upward in an arch of agony.

Now Clubby had his old wool hat on the end of his hickory-stick, now he was standing up, was trudging up the hill. The men hung back. Those trees and gnarled roots were mighty hard to leave. But Clubby's figure never paused nor turned to look behind. By shot, the old man was going there alone. They took long breaths, jumped out from hiding, and ran to catch him. They were closer to the summit this time. They could see bronzed, straining faces and blue caps just above the ground. They stopped to fire madly, then ran on. An answering volley met them like a wall. They pitched ahead, spun around, leapt high in air and fell down kicking. The woods were filled with their grotesque and dreadful posturings. They were stopped this time and no mistake. They made a snatch at the wounded and hurried down the hill.

Back in the ravine, James Fraser dropped to the ground the country boy he had been leading, and lay down close beside him. The sallow, stupid youth craned his head till he could see his legs.

"Will you look at that now?" he said with intense and reverent interest. "Will you look at that?" He gazed at the ooze of blood along his trousers as though it were a portentous and incredible phenomenon.

"Lie still," said James, "You ain't the only one."

He looked around to see what the rest were doing. They lay up and down the little ravine. Living and dead and wounded, indistinguishable, all hugged the friendly earth save where some fellow past all care of danger sat up to cough up blood or lying on his back swung his sharp knees unceasingly from side to side.

Crouching, Dougald Cameron stepped amongst them up the gully, matter of fact and serious. "Keep up a steady fire," he admonished. "We'll wear 'em down. We'll have somebody to look after these boys soon." He motioned toward the wounded with his pistol.

As James Fraser loaded his rifle, he got the idea from the sounds of scattered firing that the regiments on each side of them, veterans from Virginia, were also held up in the same ravine. This gave him boundless satisfaction. Their own crowd had not done so badly after all. Maybe in the end they would do as well as any one. But, my Lord, it was a mighty mean place! If there was just a chance to see what you were doing. Leaving the boy still staring at the bloodstains on his trousers, he crawled to the edge of the gully and found a spot where he could peep around a little hickory-tree. Once more the woods seemed empty. He shoved the rifle ahead of him, through the leaves, and waited, his eyes fixed on the crest above him. He saw the muzzle of a rifle moving slowly. He got ready. A blue cap showed behind it. He dropped his eye to the sight and fired. Two rifles beside him also spoke. Good, the boys were fighting back again. The distant rifle muzzle flopped down on the ground. Somebody must have hit him.

But as he lay there, watching intently, and firing from time to time, it was borne in on him that the Yankees would not give in too easily. They kept firing back, and every time they thought they reached a mark they shouted a heavy, deep-throated "Hurrah!" It was going to be a slow business. He was thirsty. He slid back into the ravine and took a pull at his canteen. The white face of Catlin Gregg turned toward him.

"Get out of here. This is for wounded men."

He crawled up to his tree again, his jaws locked tight with fury. But his anger sizzled, and for unnumbered hours afterward, it seemed, there was nothing to do except lie still and wait for a chance to shoot. His anger, his excitement, even his interest ebbed away. He grew dull and listless, indifferent to the firing. Tired of watching forever the wooded crest, he missed a chance or two to shoot and did not care. What was the use? They were getting nowhere.

The afternoon sun burned down on him through the branches. He was thirsty again. His lips were caked and his mouth tasted sour from biting the paper of the cartridges. But he would not slide back into the gully. He managed to draw his canteen up beside his face, uncorked it with his teeth and tilted it as best he could into the corner of his mouth. But he must have showed himself, for a couple of bullets flicked into the dead leaves beside him. He dropped the canteen, spilling water, and lay close behind his tree.

He had an uneasy sense that orders were travelling up the ravine. He heard the voices of Dougald Cameron and Catlin Gregg: "Load, and hold your fire."

"This time," said Dougald, "when we charge 'em, don't shoot till after their volley. Then fire and rush in at 'em."

Far to the left they heard the high-pitched Southern scream. They heard the sturdy "H-a-a-a-a" that Yankees gave. Both cheers were rolling down toward

them like a great ball of mingled sound which grew
and rumbled as it travelled. The regiment next to
theirs was up and running. Clubby Jordan was out in
front and Catlin Gregg, his face a white set mask,
walked past James' tree. "By God, he's scared!"
James thought. "But," he added in fairness, "he's
goin' on." He rose up with the others and followed. A
few were prodded and kicked from their hiding-places
by the sergeants. Some moved up the hill, walking
woodenly, jerking their knees like men in a trance.
But most of them, their comic, powder-blackened
mouths in pitiful contrast to their hunted eyes, stepped
swiftly, cunningly from tree to tree.

Clubby waved his stick and broke into a run. They
screeched and raced behind him.

As the Yankee volley smote them, James Fraser
found a tree. Around him some went down, others
stopped, turned to run. But their rifles still were
loaded. The thought held them. The wavering ceased.
They gripped their guns and dashed for the crest. A
line of Yankees, hurriedly loading, showed behind a
low stone wall. James Fraser halted, fired at an officer
who stood back of them. The Yankees rose up. Some
fired, some held their bayonets ready. They opened
their mouths and shouted. They seemed not men but
curious animals, dangerous and loathsome, who in
fear and anger hooted at him. He gripped his rifle,
screamed at them and ran.

An instantaneous shaft of flame—an engulfing roar—
trees, men, grass shredded by a rake of canister;
patches of clothing, branches, blood clots flew; the

ground was littered with flayed bodies blown from the cannon's path. He ran the faster.

Here was the wall and here the hooting mouths. He knocked a bayonet aside and jumped up on the stones. Frantically he thrust at the upturned faces. Faster! Faster! His swinging bayonet cleared a circle. They crowded just beyond and thrust back at him, swung at his legs. Their eyes stared into his, their blackened mouths gaped at him. They thrust their bayonets. He fenced against them desperately.

A voice of thunder cried "Surrender!" Then in low tones, but dreadfully distinct it said: "Shoot him." He snatched a look along the wall. There was no one on it now but him. He leaped back, turning in the air, tripped over a gray arm on the ground and ran. His stinging eyes were blind with sweat. His lungs and throat were seared and raw with gasping. But he must make his dead legs travel until he reached safe cover. The flat crack of a pistol sounded from the wall, it seemed as though a splash of icy water struck his ankle. Two steps more and his leg curled up beneath him like a wet leaf. Steadying himself with his rifle he hopped behind an oak trunk and sank down.

His heart was trying to beat out through his roaring ears. His chest was bound with iron, his fingers fluttered. At last a long, deep breath flowed into him. He stretched out, relaxed and drifted on its tide.

When he came to himself he was still behind the tree, but though the fire from the wall had broken out again and down in the hollow scattered rifles answered it, he had no longer any fear. He raised his head to take stock of things. Below him dead figures, looking

wonderfully flat and shrunken, lay among the leaves.
He edged an eye around the trunk and looked up the
slope. More figures lay before the wall and over a little
heap of them hung Clubby Jordan's cowhide boots.
He wondered why Clubby didn't pull his legs away.
That was no way to lie, with your feet hanging over a
couple of dead men. . . . Clubby was dead. Old
Clubby with his hickory-stick, his horse-hair chair.
The best Colonel anywhere at all. The heart within
him died. He was sick. He was through. He never
wanted to fight again. He did not want to march
again or bivouac without that sturdy, homely figure to
lead him on. Then he turned fierce. By shot! if he had
known of Clubby he would have stayed on that wall
and popped a skull or two before they got him. He
could not bear to look at the yellow boots which hung
there helpless. He drew his head behind the tree. He
shut his eyes.

Some one was looking at him. In a clump of sumac
bushes on his right lay a figure in an officer's red sash.
The face which, half hidden by the leaves, peered
fixedly at him, was the face of Catlin Gregg. Why in
the nation didn't he crawl to cover! Anyhow, why
didn't he say something if he wanted to, or else look
another way. "Are you all right?" James called in a
low, angry voice. Gregg did not answer, he merely
kept his eyes, helpless and inquiring, fixed on James
Fraser. He must be hurt bad. Maybe he couldn't
speak. Maybe he was dead. He felt immediate relief.
If Gregg was dead there was nothing to be done, he'd
stay right there, behind this oak. There would be no
question of venturing out there where stray bullets

were spitting through the trees and where the Yankees would open fire at sight of him.

Then the full significance burst on him. By shot, Gregg was dead and he was alive! Just what poor Harry Horniblow had talked about. He had never thought of that. Now Dougald would be Captain and maybe he could get somewhere. He had done as well as any of them to-day. And if he came home with a good record, and maybe a commission, what would her father say to that? Instantly he saw that if Gregg were dead it was mighty important for him to come out of this place alive.

But still Gregg kept looking at him. A bullet struck near his pale, disdainful face and it seemed as though he winced; ever so slightly perhaps, but there seemed to be a movement. James Fraser looked hastily away. Why had he kept watching? If he had not he would not have seen. He stared obstinately at the bark of the trunk in front of his face. But the eyes, he knew, were still fixed on him. He looked back again. "Can't you hyear me?" he shouted angrily. "Do you want help?" The eyes still looked at him.

Black fury seized him. Christ! Why couldn't the ninny speak! His lips drawn back with rage, he started crawling toward the sumac bushes. One thought was in his mind. If he found that pup was able to speak, Captain or not, he'd give him something to remember.

Now the Yankees saw him. Bullets whipped around him. Dragging his wounded ankle he scuffled awkwardly but fast.

Even with his hand on Catlin's arm he could not tell.

The arm was warm and limber but no sound came from the white, proud mouth. There was no time to lose. He pulled the arm across his shoulder and started back, dragging the body along beside him. He could only inch along. The Yankees would get him sure!

But no bullets came and as he reached the tree again he heard the Yankees call, "Hurrah for you, Johnny!" and give a cheer. Somehow that did not please him. They can afford to cheer, he reflected bitterly. They've not lost so many. He eased his burden to the ground and looked at it. There was no change. The eyes stared straight ahead. He put his hand on the wrist. Not a flicker. Even as he held it, he felt beneath his fingers the unmistakable chill and saw the gray-green leaden hue creep slowly to the face.

Through twilight and evening he lay there with the body. Night came. The firing died away, ceased utterly. With swift, incredulous horror he realized that his regiment had gone.

A silent figure crept among the trees, squatted by bodies, fumbled hurriedly. It was coming toward him. He lay quite still. He threw up his rifle. The figure squeaked and vanished.

A lantern was coming down the hill. It paused, moved on, threw wandering shadows among the dead. A ruddy, red-faced man in blue looked down at him, dropped on one knee. "Well, Johnny," he slipped a stout, white-banded arm under James Fraser's shoulders. "How about some brandy?"

CHAPTER XXXIV

RESTING his bandaged ankle against the brown plush seat in front, James Fraser looked through half-closed eyes at the other prisoners in the car. Old, broken hats nodded above the brown plush backs. A pasty face showed white above a straggling beard. An arm, thin, dirty, corded, hung across a seat. Two brittle, polelike legs stuck out into the aisle. Down the long car his eye found only misery, exhausted pallor, rags caked with mud, sodden with filth. No sign of health or hope or strength until it reached the sentry in his blue cape-coat who leaned on his rifle by the door. No use to look at him; he did not like it. Nor did he like to look at them. He kept his honest, ruddy face turned half aside and peered out the window of the car. James Fraser looked out too. The view was still the same. A black river rushed past over black stones. On the farther shore rose mountains, abrupt and stern.

A night and a day they had travelled in the train through the land of Yankees. A land, immense, coarse-voiced, alert, and powerful. A land of hard-built, rumbling cities, of prim and thrifty villages, neat fence rows and splendid, overflowing fields of corn. A land of satin boleros and deep-fringed merinos, of broad-cloth and shining stove-pipe hats. Of twanging speech, and eyes, not mean, but infinitely self-contented, shrewd, and knowing. A land, in a word, of strength, magnificence, vitality, and solid worth. But not the land he knew.

James Fraser still stared out the window. Let him take in all he could. Before the sun dropped down behind those iron mountains, he and the others would be in their prison. What it would be like he did not know. There would not be much to see from there, he reckoned. Let him keep his eyes open now. He might be there a long time. It would be nice to recollect these scenes and think about them. Perhaps they would let him write home and he could then tell his folks how things looked up in the North, tell them about the crops and such.

He could not write them about the things that happened first just after he was captured. He would be glad to forget them himself; but he never would. The Yankee who had found him had treated him mighty well, had done the best he could. He had said that they would go together to the field hospital where the ankle could be fixed, and with this notion James had been content. With the brandy inside him, he had begun to feel somewhat reconciled to his lot. Had he not done the best he could? He surely had; and now with a clear conscience he could let the Yankees, so plentifully supplied with brandy, food, and doctors, take care of him. He pictured a white cot and ample bowls of soup.

Instead, they had halted outside a circle of torchlight, from whose centre, where two men with saws in naked bloody arms bent over a table, came shrieks and desperate, crazy laughter. In the shadows around he heard gibberings, long trailing moans; he caught the odor of hot flesh. From the table something flew through the air, fell with a soft, wet thud on a heap, cha-

otic, greasy, red. He had clutched at the Yankee by
his side and started hobbling. No field hospital for
him.

He was well content at last to lie down with the herd
of prisoners and sleep surrounded by a ring of fires
and of Yankee guards. Next morning the Yankees
gave them all the biscuits they had, and with awkward
and good-natured words started their long march toward the rear. The deplorable column trailed its length
through the backwash of the battle-field. Abandoned
equipment littered the road, spilled out over the ruined
fences to lie scattered through the trampled fields beyond. Under every tree, in every fence corner, strag-
glers slept, or made small fires to boil coffee. In the
hot, half-clouded sunlight, flies swarmed, lit on the eyes
and guts of dead gun-horses, crawled curiously under
forage caps that covered dead men's faces.

Above a crossroad a corpse hung from a limb, slowly
it turned to show from time to time a placard "Deserter," across its pinched and formless chest. The
head leaned forward as if to read this sign.

And all the while no prisoner spoke. Their feet on the
dusty roadway made no sound. They moved in utter
silence, still ghosts who journey on through hell.

And ghosts they had remained, ghosts who, without
thought or feeling, passed impalpably down endless
roads, through camps, through endless countings and
cross-questionings, on board of flat cars, box cars, fer-
ries.

And now they drifted here against the brown plush
seats, ghosts beyond fear, beyond sense, beyond exist-

ence, grim and ironic mockery of the Yankees who thought they had captured and were guarding something.

The sun touched the sombre hills across the river. They passed through a small, brick town where people merely glanced at them. At the farther edge the brakes ground on; the car lurched to a stop, the sentry opened the door. They filed out on a wooden platform and stood between two lines of soldiers in the chill evening air. Ahead of them, a huge whitewashed fence stretched away on either hand as far as they could see. On top, from little boxes, sentries peered down at them. The endless fence seemed to break open as two tall gates swung backward to receive them.

As the gates bumped shut behind them, they halted. Before them in the shadows stretched a dark, boundless plain. At first it seemed a deserted waste of roughly broken ground. Then slowly James Fraser had a sense that everywhere something stirred, that every foot of its tormented face was alive and slowly crawling. He narrowed his eyes. Among the mounds, the holes, the mud, crept shapes, dark, silent, moving slowly, ceasely. Prisoners.

While he stood, stupefied, a plate and spoon were thrust into his hand. They faced to the right and moved off. Hobbling unsteadily, he passed through a low, wicket gate into the land of cold and shadows, of myriad holes and caves among the mire. And now from these caves and holes a stale old smell of dissolution seemed to creep like a mist and, reaching out, to steal around him.

Half veiled by this faint and evil mist, gray cadavers, reared up on their haunches, silently watched his coming, with eyes like stones, deep-set, inscrutable as death.

BOOK IV

CHAPTER XXXV

In the chill dusk of an undated autumn day, James Fraser squatted before his prison hovel. The mists and shadows hung over the dark plain. Among them, silent forms were stirring, meagre fires glowed; through them, the last pale yellow shaft of light crept down. It fell upon James Fraser's gray and naked knees, on his gaunt wrist and on his finger, yellow-knuckled, dry, and ancient as a mummy's, which, tracing slow figures in the dust, wavered, halted, hung trembling, moved uncertainly on again. Behind that wavering finger his mind too, stumbled, faltered, wavered, caught now and then a gleam of what it aimed to do, then drifted off again, drifted off among beckoning mocking fancies, among vast repetitions which stretched away like corridors, interminable, maddening. He clenched his bony fist. Some day it would drift away and not come back. But now he must think. That was it. He must think. Think. He dropped his finger to the figures in the dust. It hung there idle. But of what was he to think? What had he set out to do? These figures must mean something; regular figures all in rows.

But even as dazed, uncomprehending, groping, he stared at them, they were veiled by pictures, memories, and hallucinations, each a treacherous vista leading to oblivion, which wheeled processionally before his eyes: —ringed always by the endless prison fence, long lines

of faces, ashen gray, stood in ranks that stretched away
forever, opened starved mouths to answer "here" to a
never-ending roll-call—long lines of sodden figures
waited to draw rations in an eternity of wind and rain,
dissolved, floated, swam together in groups who toiled in
frozen clay, chipping out graves for rows of sheeted
forms. Firelight touched the cheek bones of card-play-
ers and the yellow, hairy ankles of a man who clogged on
a prison hovel floor, clogged with mournful and de-
mented changelessness to the patting of skinny hands.
It came to James that this prisoner who used to dance
had died a year or more ago; and still the man's yellow
legs shook lugubriously before his eyes. Though now
that he looked at them attentively they faded. Their
rhythm turned into the squeaking of a fiddle in some
long-distant, incredible life when he was young. He saw
the flippant coat-tails of Uncle Dunc, he saw his father
and mother's glance of disapproval, he saw the little boy
who hollered out, "Hurrah, here's Jim!" He looked at
the doorway in the log wall of the schoolhouse, waiting.
Waiting the coming of the figure in the purple gown.
The veins on his forehead fluttered. The door swung
open—a file of prisoners lurched and shuffled in, filled
the schoolhouse, burst it to fragments, spread out
flowingly over the dark plain, crept and crawled slowly,
unceasingly among the tents, the shacks, the holes, the
little fires. He heard unnumbered dragging feet around
him, and looking up saw that the scene to which once
more as always he had drifted back remained the
same. Silent, sombre, the dense swarm still moved,
swayed together. At hand they brushed past the narrow

opening before the hovel, brushed past by ones and
twos, never hastening, never halting, never speaking.
He did not wish to look at them. Besides, there was
something he had set out to do. His gaze, swinging help-
lessly, fell again on the figures scratched in the dust. At
the sight of them, uneasy fears assailed him. His heart
quailed. Those figures; he had made them just now.
Already they were inscrutable. And when he tried to
solve them his mind fled from him to wander among an
ancient, endless maze of floating fantasies. A spark of
rage flared up; it was enough to make a man beat his
fist against his brow, gnaw his own knuckles!

As if that petty, impotent burst had aroused him, a
thought, clear, swift and perfect, crossed his mind.

He raised his hand and pressed it to his breast. Inside his jacket paper rustled. It was there! With sly
and secret triumph he made it rustle once again. That
was the letter! Always there, to guard him from the
corridors, to draw him back from them. Across his
blurred mind, soft, yet sharp and clear, rang the words,
"Stewart Prevost." He raised his head. His dry lips
formed her name.

Now he could think. He looked at the figures on the
ground. At the top, scratched in the dirt, stood the
numerals "365." Now he knew. He had started to
figure how many days he had been in prison. Some time
next month it would be two years. Two years. And
how many days was that? There was the first year,
three hundred and sixty-five, and for the second year,
more numerals, thirty days from September twenty-
ninth to October twenty-ninth. Then came a trailing

line across the dust. He frowned. That was where his
mind had begun to drift away. As soon as he touched
the letter, thought of her, it came back. Uneasily he
withdrew his eyes from the figures and stared into space.
All around silent, slowly moving forms haunted the
tiny fires. Winter was coming on. He would be wet
and cold, his mind would wander away from his starved
body, wander more often, wander on further through
the labyrinthine halls. Now he could call it back by
rustling the paper folded against his breast. But one
day he would not think to touch the letter. He had
better let the figures alone. A moment ago his mud-
dled brain had fancied that to know the number of his
days in prison was of vast importance. Now he saw
that it was not so. It made no difference.

Pushing a filthy carpet to one side, he crawled on
hands and knees into the hovel. The carpet swung
back behind him but still allowed a slit of light to enter,
showing the damp earth walls, the two heaps of rags
and bedding, the ashes underneath the smoke-hole in
the roof.

Though the cave was empty, James Fraser first
looked around suspiciously before he drew the letter,
wrapped in a piece of old, brown buckram, from the
breast of his jacket. Under the slit of light he spread
out the small black-bordered sheets, blurred with the
damp and worn with handling. Other letters had come
since. He kept them buried in a package underneath his
bed. He read them over, too, and lived in expectation
of the next. But none of them held the potency of this,
the earliest, unexpected and incredible, which had finally found him here in the first dark winter of his

imprisonment, to warm him, cheer him, lift up his head
and make him live again. Even now, the words had all
the power to move and comfort him as on that day
when first they had shone before his dim and unbe-
lieving eyes. He moved a little closer to the light and
read:

Beaumont, September 2nd, 1862.

DEAR JAMES:

("September second, eighteen sixty-two," he muttered. And now it was sixty-three; no, sixty-four.
Then it would be sixty-five. Then—his mind shrank
back from that treacherous corridor. But he could
think of sixty-two. That was a good number because it
came before he had been captured. In sixty-two he was
still free. But even then there had been troubles. There
had been the marching. And worse, there had been the
tormenting thoughts of her. Her brother had been killed
with him. No answer had come to the letter he had
written her. He had given up. And at that very time,
she—he could see her, slim and graceful, thoughtful,
earnest, bending over the desk—was writing this very
letter which he held in his hand, which he carried in his
breast. The letter had followed the army in its march-
ings, had missed him here and there. And then, months
afterward, when he had given himself up for dead or
buried alive in prison, it had found him here. He always
liked to pause and think about these things before he
read. But now he would go on. He looked down at the
folded sheet.)

Your letter telling of Charles' death came three days
ago and I wished to write immediately but I have been

with my father every moment until now. He did not eat or speak, only sometimes he patted my hand and tried to smile. At night he walked among the live-oaks. I feared that the blow would be too much for him, but to-night he asked me to read to him from the Book of St. John, and now he has gone to sleep, so I can write.

And yet, though I have a hundred things to say to you, somehow I cannot begin. I am overwhelmed by our loss, although, as I told you once, I knew in my heart that it would come. I should be better prepared to meet it if only I had known how. Perhaps I shall do better later on. Will you write me if you care to, from time to time? I hope you will do so, because your letter troubles me very much, indeed. You seem to blame yourself on account of Charles, or to think that I may blame you. Let us not have any more misunderstanding, James. I think you are as brave and as devoted as Charles himself. I know there is nothing you would not have done or suffered to have saved him, and far from thinking of you with any slightest hint of blame, I shall always be comforted by the thought that you were with him at the end, because I know that, with you there, nothing could have been otherwise. Had it been some one else, I might sometimes have thought rebelliously and bitterly, "If only Charles had been with James Fraser."

Listless footsteps sounded. Hastily he thrust the letter in his coat.

The carpet swung slowly aside. A soft, white beard, two wild, shy, wandering eyes appeared.

The eyes blinked uncertainly and with an air of deprecation. The beard was stroked by a fumbling hand.

"Mo' prisoners come in." The voice was soft, high-pitched, and sing-song, like a child's. "Considerable info'mation."

The old man crawled down into the hovel and crouched on the other pallet, an ancient, sad, and apprehensive ape. That pallet was his, had been since time began. But always on entering the cave, he hesitated, ventured a tentative remark, to make sure of his reception.

It had been this old man, Jeff, who, when James first arrived, so long ago, had taken him in, had with nervous eagerness fixed him up a bed, and ever since had dogged him faithfully. And all because he fancied James held some resemblance to the son that he was always seeking. James felt mighty sorry for the old man, but the way he stopped and hesitated every time he came in was getting on his nerves. Some day he'd grab old Jeff and pull him through that curtain.

The old man fixed his sorrowful, brown eyes on James and nodded sagely.

"Yes, seh, considerable info'mation!" He paused. "But no'hing about the boy."

"Too bad," said James mechanically.

"Too bad. Too bad," Jeff agreed. "He was a mighty good boy, just about your height, he was, with gre't big han's. He was——"

"Yes, I know," James cut in hastily. Jeff subsided. Lost in thought, he rubbed his blue knuckles together slowly. Behind his shadowy, downcast eyes his mind groped for something to cling to.

"It looks to me," he murmured, "like the mo' prisoners come in, the mo' chance they is to get news of him." He raised inquiring, diffident eyes to James. "Wouldn't that seem like good sense?"

"Yes," said James. "It would."

"And they's mo' prisoners comin' all the time. Many mo'."

"That's a fact," James answered gloomily. "They're catching whole regiments of our boys now."

Old Jeff brightened. "Maybe they will catch the boy and bring him in here."

"I tell you what we could do," he went on, "we could dig out a little piece beyond the smoke-hole. Then there would be room for another pallet across the end." He nodded. "I reckon that would be the warmest bed of all."

"He could have my bed," said James.

The old man shook his head. "That would not be right. No, seh. And he wouldn't take it. Because you are a friend of mine."

"Well, then," said James, "we will dig him out a place."

"I wish I hadn't lent my knife," the old man said with resigned regret, "to those boys who were tunnelling out. It was a good knife to dig with."

"Yes," said James, "it was."

"If it had done them good I wouldn't complain. But they was all caught and shot."

"We can sharpen a spoon," said James.

"The clay is stiff," Jeff said, "a spoon will bend. That's how come them to borrow my knife. Their spoons were bent."

"That was a good tunnel," James observed.

"Tunnels are no good," said Jeff, "they's been seven since I come hyer. They was the one down by the creek and one out toward the railroad and—and many others." His voice trailed off.

"They catch them—every time," he remarked and fell silent. He shook his head. "A tunnel takes too many men. The news leaks out."

James' heart stirred. "We're not far from the fence. We could start and tunnel right under my pallet, and dig and dig—" his voice sank to a whisper. "Just you and me. Then one night we would burst out the end of the tunnel——"

Again Jeff shook his head. "It would take years, and when you're out, eve'y one hunts you. They chase you and shoot at you. You can't rest." He looked around at the slimy walls with foolish pleasure. "Here we have a tolerable good little place. And besides," he turned grave, "if my boy was to come and find me gone, he'd feel mighty bad——"

Unpremeditated, fantastic, dangerously intoxicating, a wave of desperate, crazy rage swept James Fraser to his feet. Stooping under the roof he crouched over Jeff, shook a fist in his face.

"I've got to get out of here!" he shouted. His voice cracked, he trembled, he wanted to dance, to shriek, to butt his head against the wall. The notion held wild and terrible fascination. He wanted to act the zany till the old man jumped out of his skin. But already Jeff had shrunk back, speechless. At the sight, some sense came back to him. His voice sank to a biting whisper. "You hyear me, old man!" Then uncontrollably he shouted again, "I've got to get out!"

Jeff's hand flew up in warning, his thick, white beard stirred as his lips formed the whisper "hush!"

A formless, despairing sound tore James' throat. He dropped, face down, on his pallet.

He heard the old man rustle on the straw, he felt his trembling arm around his shoulder. The gentle, toneless voice was in his ear.

"Now then, James, you be a good boy." For a long time the arm rested on him. He heard the voice again. "And don't you holler so. Some Yankee prison spy might hear."

He thrust the arm aside, sat up on an elbow.

"If I could catch a prison spy, you know what I'd do?" He crooked a bony hand before Jeff's eyes. "I'd hook my fingers in his mouth and tear his face in two."

"They are bad men," Jeff answered. "Yes, I would call them bad men. But you ought to take things easy, James. We are better fixed in this cave than most."

"I know. . . . I know," James muttered. "And you've been good to me and all. But I can't make out to stand it. My mind—" he checked himself; he looked at Jeff uneasily. "Sometimes," he murmured, "it looks like I didn't know what I was about."

"Why don't you get them to put you on a burial party?" said Jeff. "That way you could go outside and look around. It is a mighty nice change—and something to do."

"No!" his voice was strangled, he shut his eyes. "Their feet stick up."

Jeff nodded. His patriarchal beard and eyebrows gave him an air of sagacity, but his eyes were mild and witless.

"We might be exchanged," he ventured.

"Exchanged? They's been no exchanges for a year." What ailed this old fool? Did he think to comfort him with pap? In a last futile spurt of passion he seized Jeff's wrist.

"You listen. One of these days I expect I'll walk across the dead-line to the fence and let the sentries blaze away."

He gave a short and disconcerting laugh. Puzzled, grieved, the old man studied him. "You lay here a while," he said. "I will go out and borrow some good smoking-tobacco for you." But he seemed reluctant to leave. "Don't let your courage run out, James. When my boy comes," he smiled serenely, "You will have good company."

"He is just about your height," his nod was serious, "and he favors you mightily. Mightily. He—" The old man recalled himself. "I will get the tobacco." His pinched and meagre quarters climbed up through the hole.

CHAPTER XXXVI

MONTH by month fresh prisoners came in, more than enough to take the place of the sheeted forms which the Yankees hauled out in their army wagons every morning. The first snow fell; by twos and threes rough wooden barracks, first skeletons of framing, then sheds of yellow pine, sprang up down the hill. At night prisoners stole through the guards around these buildings, delved for chips and shavings in the snow, silently wrangled and fought over splinters for their puny fires.

The barracks were done. The snow lay thick. Still the old-timers clung to their fox-holes in the ground. They were too wise in misery to be trapped into a frame shack for the northern winter. Down by the gate through which the prisoners entered old Jeff kept watch, his rag-wrapped feet stamping patiently on the trodden snow, his dim, uncertain eyes searching the faces of the mournful lines that filed in past the sentinel.

They listened with patience to old Jeff's long tales of his boy, missing since Shiloh years before. No one had heard of him, but next day some one might come who knew. Or in the very next batch which trailed in through the gate Old Jeff might see the boy himself.

He was a mighty good old man. But now and again, and oftener of late, James felt blind flashes of fury against him, the way he talked without looking at a man, his eyes fixed on the gate, the way he told over and over his maddeningly tedious tale of sorrow. Above

all, James began to wonder uneasily whether old Jeff
were not a little touched in his head.

But in between times he clung to the old man. He
was a good old man to talk to; he nodded wisely and put
in with a grave, "Yes, that is so," whenever James'
voice trailed off and left a gap. In that way the gap was
not noticed. It was a good thing to have some one to
talk to. It made him put his mind on what he was saying. He didn't feel like talking to any one but Jeff, because one time when his voice had trailed off the man
he was with had looked at him. So he didn't talk to
folks if he could help it. Only old Jeff. Because old
Jeff always nodded his head and said, "Yes, that is so."

Old Jeff talked to everybody, though. But he always
said the same thing. That was no way to talk. Right
now as James, his big hands hanging, listless, over his
knees, sat in the hovel and stared at the blotched and
dripping wall of earth, he could hear Jeff running on outside. The same old talk— "A good boy—about six
foot——"

The old man's familiar shuffle sounded at the door.
His bearded face came through the carpet. "Hyer's one
of the boys that come in to-day," he announced. "I
found him a bed down at the Big Shack. A lot of fellows
died there last week," he explained. "They was room a-
plenty." Behind Jeff a stubby hand pushed the carpet
aside. A pair of large, dark, mournful eyes peered at
them over a large, soft nose. "This boy," said Jeff,
with the air of a showman, "was captured in the fo'ts
in front of Richmond not three days ago."

"Howdy," said James. "Wher' you from?"

A dark, little man whose figure still showed signs of plumpness stood before them, crouching under the low roof, uncertain and ill at ease. "Savennah. I have a business there."

"He means what regiment?" said Jeff.

"Ninety-second Georgia," said the little man, squatting on James' pallet. He took off his forage cap and placed it carefully on his knee.

"Well, what's the news?" said James.

The little man raised his mournful eyes. "Bad, all bad! At Richmond we are back in the forts. The Yankees shoot into the town. There is little for the soldiers to eat."

"You look good."

"Me, I am lucky. In Richmond I have a friend."

"Don't it look like they ought not to stay in them fo'ts?" said Jeff. "They ought to get out in the country where they can maneuver."

"In the country, too," said the little man, "things are bad. The food is gone. The money is no good for anything."

"Money . . . no good," said James.

The little man looked startled but he nodded, then pursed his lips. "When the soldiers hear that the pay they send home will not buy food for their families then they will not fight." He hesitated. "Many are going home to see what is wrong; some they catch and shoot, but many get away. If they can get home they will be safe because the people hide them."

"When I was in the army with that boy of mine," said Jeff, "some, especially mountaineers, used to sneak off. But whenever there was a battle to be fowt they came flocking back. Yes, seh."

"Now," said the little man, "they go home to stay." He started. "Hach! What was that?"

"Rat," said James.

"Yes," said old Jeff, "now that our rations have been raised they are getting right plentiful."

The stranger looked uncomfortable. "So!" he tried to speak politely. "They get more to eat now, eh?"

Jeff looked at him with patient surprise. "They don't get eaten."

The little man's dark eyes widened in shocked incredulity. "Get eaten?"

"Many's the time last winter," Jeff remarked in his gentle, careful tone, "when a rat, a good, fair-sized one, would bring two dollars gold. There was a fellow down in the tin-roofed hut that made a pile of money. He had him a little whistle made from a turkey bone and he used to whistle to the rats. He gave the money to a guard to let him escape, but that very night they sent another regiment to guard us and he got shot."

"Niggers," said James.

"So it was," said Jeff. "A nigger regiment." He nodded into his beard. "Those niggers was mighty rough at first, "he observed to the new arrival. "They used to shoot into the camp at night and holler things, but then the boys got a couple of niggers that was sent into the camp with orders and after that none of the other niggers would come in. So when the Colonel found the niggers wouldn't carry orders into camp he got white troops again."

"Heh!" His voice was charged with placid melan-choly. "Those was bad times sure enough. Rats and niggers and everything to fret us."

"A rat, though, would not be bad," he mused, "if a man could have him a little mustard."

The little man from Savannah was not reassured. He looked toward the carpet-covered tunnel which ran up to the surface of the ground outside. But Jeff had no notion of letting him go.

"So the news is bad?" he clicked his tongue the way Sam Scroggs' mindless boy had used to do. "I reckoned it might be. We could hear the Yankees cheering and firing salutes. That means bad news. They cheered after Gettysburg last year and after Mobile."

"They cheered after. . . ." James could not think of the word. "Chandlerville," he said with an effort.

"After Chancellorsville," said old Jeff quickly. "Yes, that is so. But that was because General Jackson was killed. And then last week," he went on, "they were cheering again."

"Last week," said the little man, "Hood's Army was wiped out in Tennessee. We heard that in Richmond. And Sherman goes through Georgia. They cannot stop him."

Old Jeff clicked his tongue. "Bad news," he ob-served calmly.

"Yes, it is bad," the stranger hesitated. "Do you think maybe the secession concern is going to smash?"

Encouraged by Jeff's mournful but resigned nod, he exclaimed, "Me, I do, as well. And what I say is—if she is going, I hope she goes quick," he snapped his stubby fingers, "Like that! Otherwise we will all be ruined. My business——"

James began to giggle. The little man, so plump and serious, and his business—talking about ruin—he could not stop giggling—he rocked like a man in agony —he gave a long whoop of tortured mirth. Ruined— My Lord! Ruined!

Through his half-closed eyes he saw the little man spring up in alarm. He was making for the tunnel.

"I think I better go look about my bed," he muttered. "Good evening, gentlemens."

"Hold on," said Jeff, "I'll go with you." He stopped beside the carpet and looked back benignly. "It's good to hyear you laugh so, James. But not too loud," he said uneasily. "Not too loud. . . . Prison spies."

James fell silent, stared at the ground, while old Jeff crawled up out of sight. Good to hear, eh? One more such laugh would finish him. Still shaking from his spasm, he reached a hand up to his breast. The letter rustled. He drew a steady breath.

Bitter mirth, rage, even despair ebbed away. He felt only puzzled, softly confused, passive, and detached. He drifted in speculation, his mind blurred, fumbling without rebelliousness, content merely to wonder—dimly, patiently to wonder at the strangeness of his world. For was it not strange that the letter in his pocket had been written by her hand? That her hand had formed the faded letters, touched the paper, that her face had bent above it? And was it not strange that this charm which brought her close to him—so close that she could lead his stumbling mind back from the pit—could not bring him to her? It was incredible that the tall, white fence should hedge him in forever, should hedge him in pitilessly until his heart and mind went whirling down to nothing. What good was served by this? He shook a puzzled head. It seemed like a grotesque and monumental blunder. It would be such a little thing to turn a man loose. What difference could it make to any one? He pondered laboriously. There must be some sense to it, some sense so profound, mysterious, that he could not fathom it.

Outside the hovel, a shout, taken up, repeated in long-drawn sing-song tones, drew nearer. Now James could make it out. They were calling "Fraser, Seven, Nine, Two, Six!" A clutch of terror seized him. When the men called out a prisoner's number like that it meant that he was wanted at Headquarters. He had never been there, but it was bound to mean a punishment. Some other prisoner caught stealing or trying to escape had made false charges against him, maybe, or—his heart died out—some prison spy had heard his talk of tunnelling or something else he might have said when he was not just himself.

The shout was at the door. Rifle butts were pounding the ground. It trembled. He trembled, too.

"Fraser, Seven, Nine, Two, Six!"

Like a cornered fox he looked around the damp and narrow walls.

"Fraser!"

Through the cold mist, which seemed to hang before his eyes, he started crawling toward the door.

By the light of a lantern two soldiers with fixed bayonets stood above him. He stood up and turned his weak eyes aside from the glare.

"You Fraser, Nine, Seven, Two, Six?" James Fraser slowly moved his lips, formed the word, "Yes."

Then the man said something. He did not understand it. He could not understand it. And yet it must be something immeasurably portentous, for his heart was leaping against his ear-drums and the lights on the watch-towers trembled before his eyes.

The man was speaking again. "Say, your name's Fraser, ain't it?" Again James moved his lips.

"Well, I said you're exchanged." He went on talking. There were broken phrases. "Report Headquarters at midnight . . . parole. . . . You ought to be in Richmond Thursday. . . . Home? Well, I couldn't say just when." There were more details and orders. But try as he might James Fraser could not make them out. His mind was breaking up. He stood, his hands clutched tight together, shaking like a wraith, while slow, hot tears ran down his twisted face and down his breast.

CHAPTER XXXVII

BENEATH his feet and in his ears the car-wheels mumbled, "lunka-tunka-tunka—lunka-tunka-tunka." And now and again, briefly, sharply, a trestle rattled past. His dim and weary eyes half saw, half guessed that outside in the morning light the tops of twisted pines and of cypresses wheeled by.

A gentle hand fell on his shoulder. The voice of Captain Joe, the old conductor, murmured in his ear.

"I reckon you'll have to rouse up, son. We're coming into Wilmington."

He looked up at the old face so mild and friendly beneath its cap of office—"All right, Cap'n."

He tried to sit up straight, but failed. The conductor's quick, sure hand was under his arm. Now he could make it. But the movement brought back the raw pain in his belly. His mouth filled with evil-tasting water. He was going to be sick again. He had eaten too much of that good food the ladies gave him in Richmond. Sweat broke out on his forehead, he swallowed, held on until the spasm passed.

The conductor patted him. "That's better, son. When we get in we'll fix you up with some eggs and coffee."

James nodded dumbly. The conductor moved a step away, then looked back at him. "When the train stops," he said, "you just set right wher' you are until I come."

He was able to take a look around the car. It was

littered with sprawling and unsavory forms, fat, dark, and greasy, pimpled and shifty-eyed, weak-jawed, and sallow, dirty and down at heel or bedizened with flashy rings and jewels. The backwash of the war, sutlers and speculators, contractors, smugglers, substitute brokers.

Across the way the gold braid of a Major's sleeve stood out from the rabble. Above it a shaggy, gray head nodded in sleep. A big, sharp nose jutted between bushy eyebrows and under a beard a big mouth smiled, content and placid. James Fraser's mind struggled to remember. Where had he seen this Major before? A scene came back to him. It had been right here in the car. Maybe the night before, or some other night. Whenever it was, he now remembered it. There had been some trouble about his pass. He should have had a pass; maybe he had had one, he couldn't remember. Anyhow, once when the train stopped a provost guard had come aboard and said to him, "Where's your pass?" He could only fumble and shake his head.

"You're one of them damn deserters!" the soldier had shouted so loud that every one could hear. "You come along." The man had seized him by the arm. His heart had died within him. He had no strength to fight, no strength even to think, to speak. It was all up with him now. At that moment the Major's face, not peacefully dozing as now, but blazing, bristling, had come in view. "Take your hand off that boy!"— the lamps in the ceiling had jumped in their sockets— "You stinking little Provost Marshal's puke! You —!" Here had followed language. James wished he could remember it all. A good many words were new to him and curious. "Why, damn your louse-bit hide," the Major had concluded. "This man's my orderly!"

"What's your name, son?" the Major had asked him when the provost guard had gone. James told him. "If anybody comes, just say you're my orderly." The Major had gone to sleep again.

The train was passing rows of slattern negro cabins. The freight-yard, grass-grown, littered with broken cars, came into view. He saw the shops, the roundhouse and the station-shed. The Major woke.

"Well, orderly," he said with a paternal grin. "How you?"

James Fraser started to rise; the Major pushed him back.

"You need some help, I reckon."

Now he must speak. He put his mind on forming the words. "Major—I'm all right— The conductor—a friend——"

"Well, good luck to you then!" The Major wrapped a hairy fist around James' hand.

With the conductor taking slow, short steps beside him, he walked into the waiting-room. At the farther end were stools and an oil-cloth-covered table from behind which a little old lady looked up at him with sweet, tired eyes.

"Miss Sarah," the conductor said, "this boy is bound for home. I reckon he'd like some eggs and coffee."

The little old lady nodded with emphasis. "Home ought to be the place for him." She lighted a spirit lamp, poured a cup of coffee. "Where is your home, my son?"

He leaned hard on the table and moistened his lips. "I want—" he spoke most carefully—"to go to Beaumont."

Down by the docks, piles of goods covered with tarpaulins were guarded by a soldier. At the sight of him, James' heart wavered. Would the man ask him for a pass? But with the little lady and a stout gentleman on either side he passed safely by. The stout gentleman— at least he had once been stout—had come up on the street, had said "good evening, Miss Sarah—allow me, sir," and slipped an arm around him.

The sentry was left behind, the roof of the steamboat wharf was over him. He stumbled up a gang-plank into the hands of the furry-faced captain who used to peer down at him from the wheel-house. There were steps, brass-edged and slippery. He was on a red plush couch in a long saloon.

"Well, sir," the gentleman said, "you'll soon be home."

"You'll soon be home," the lady said. She turned and whispered to the Captain, shook her little bonnet at his beard.

"Yes, Ma'm, Miss Sarah," the Captain said, "I surely will."

James understood that the little lady was about to leave him. "I certainly am obliged, ma'm," he said. "I certainly——"

"Hush, hush," she answered, "you go to sleep

now." She rested a hand on his an instant and was
gone.

They swung down the stream. Curious ships were
tied up at the docks, lean, knife-like ships, their funnels
raking aft, their low hulls painted white or silver-gray.
From the wheel-house forward the Captain called to
him out the open door. "Reckon you ain't seen any
of them before. Blockade runners." He pointed. "This
is the only port still open. They're waiting for a moonlight night." He turned back to the wheel. He touched
a signal-bell. The vessel shuddered and swung toward
the wide reach lined with cypress swamps.

Abruptly it came back to James' mind where he was
bound. He was bound for Beaumont, for the tall house
in the grove, for the myrtle-trees, the shaded gallery,
for the slim and slightly swaying figure in a white
sprigged muslin dress. Could that be so? It seemed
unlikely. And yet it must be; for within him he felt
his tired heart spring to life again, leap up, and shout
wild incoherencies above the drumming in his ears.
The moment passed; he rested numb and weary.

As they drifted through the vast and mournful country of his birth, like the steamer's wake the years since
he had left it seemed to fall astern and fade. The broad,
smooth, shining floor of water closed over them, over
his days in the railroad shops, over his days of marching, fighting, over death and burial in prison. Even
the memory of Wilmington, as he had seen it just now,
began to dim. It was only at most a dream; the feel
of weeds brushing against his feet as, trying not to lean
on the little old lady, he had stumbled toward the

docks down empty streets; shutters nailed up, tattered yellow fever placards hanging beside cobwebbed doors. On a once-familiar porch lounged swarthy foreigners, on another, Englishmen with a glass stuck in one eye.

Along the market street shop windows were empty or boarded shut. Where Mr. Cassidy had kept his store a sign read, "Joel Katzenbach." No carriages, no carts nor drays. The town was silent save for the shuffle of his steps beside the little lady's and the clank of a distant windlass by the waterside. That was this morning. He could still remember it, but already his wandering journey through that solitude seemed long ago.

The vessel crept on, the cypress swamps of home, the silver gables of the tall, unpainted house were ever nearer, past days ever more strange, incredible, remote.

And now the picture of the silvery gables among the live-oaks, forming again as it had formed so often in his mind, did not fade—it drew nearer and, against all incredulity, gained substance, delicate reality.

The Captain raised his hand to the whistle cord and blew a shivering blast. The boat stood in till the dry, abandoned rice fields could be seen; it crept up to the flimsy dock, grunted and groaned against the piles. The Captain leaned above him.

"I'll tote you to the dock," he said, "you'll be all right. I see the Colonel's nigger coming now."

In the clear December sun he leaned against a pile. Orlando, the fat, severe, old negro, stared at him, while in the distance the paddle of the steamboat swished away. By shot, James Fraser thought, I must look pretty bad, I can see it in that nigger's eyes.

Orlando broke the silence. "I hyeared de Captain blow."

James fixed his eyes, his mind on him. "I want," he said slowly, "to go to Beaumont. . . . You take hold of me."

Together they crept along the causeway between the rice fields. The negro was not as fat as he used to be. His stiff, old, broadcloth coat hung loose about him. It was hard to hold on to his shoulder.

"You better stop and rest, boss," he said. "Dey's all 'em steps ahead."

James Fraser gripped him, "Go on!"

Here were the steps, rising into space. He eyed them narrowly. They swayed from side to side, slipped down on one another, flowed away.

Now they were tilting under foot perversely, trying to trip his wandering feet. Orlando's voice came to him.

"Boss, you ought to stop."

Sweat in his eyes, his mouth; his belly, turned to water, seeping away.

"Boss, you ought——"

"Go on," he said.

His lips were stiff and bitter. His face was numb. Mist, foul and whirling dizzily, veiled his eyes, clutched at his throat, his heart. By God, he would not fall! He gripped the negro, raised a leaden foot, and climbed.

Myrtle branches brushed against him. Infinitely distant boards sounded beneath his feet. A dark, stern

portrait looked at him. Orlando's labored breathing
was in his ear. He sank down to a seat and felt smooth
satin underneath his hands.

His mind came back to him a little. He must think
of what he should say. He had thought it out before.
Let him remember. He must do nothing queer. Now
what was he to say? . . . What was he to say? . . .
He must think . . . Nothing queer. . . .

In a doorway, shadowy, silvery-white, she stood, the
white sprigged muslin swaying slightly in the river
breeze, her lips half parted in pitying tenderness, her
dark eyes on his. She was pale.

He gripped the satin arm; he struggled to his feet;
but he had no strength to speak, no words to say. He
simply stood there, shaking, his eyes fixed on her face.

She was coming toward him, her hands were out to
him. No, no, that was not right.

"Don't come nigh me." He moved his head from
side to side. "I'm not clean."

Around him soft, slender arms—they were strong—
his head rested on softness, on strength. And still for a
desperate instant, his stumbling, harried brain was
racked as never before, was racked beyond all bearing
by the tension of long years, of ancient suffering, vain
desire. Tighter it twisted—tighter !—then snapped in
a great, dry sob which tore his breast, and like a demon
fled away, leaving him rent but quiet, wonderfully
quiet, his spirit stilled, bathed and sustained by tides
of peace.

CHAPTER XXXVIII

On the box, the narrow, humped back of Thad, the carriage driver, swung slowly to and fro; below him, facing James Fraser, Orlando sat immobile, dignified, his light-palmed hand curved around a napkin-covered basket from which a sherry bottle raised its slender amber neck. Overhead, pine branches whispered, stirred, threw light fleeting shadows on the green cushions of the carriage and on James Fraser's upraised face. The sky beyond their tracery was a soft and mellow blue, fading mistily to a thin gray vapor along the far horizon, where it bent down to the blue-green silhouette of trees.

Three streams had been crossed and now they dropped down to the last. The breech straps of the horses creaked; the toggle chains of the loose traces clinked; the carriage wheels sank deep in sandy, washed-out ruts, cut into the wet sand of the stream with a sucking, mushy sound, churned water, sent bright crops curving overhead. The horses' feet chugged in the channel, smacked in shoal water. With a heave the carriage came out on the other side, the narrow iron tires clicked on stones.

He would soon be home. Home, after years of marching, of blood and fire, of entombment. But somehow he was not as stirred as he had expected, or as, perhaps, he ought to be. Maybe he was too worn-out; maybe, after

the meeting with Stewart, nothing else could seem like
a very big event. He ought to be ashamed though.
Why Stewart, herself, had shown more concern about
his people than he had.

It was she who had said, "If there were just the two
of us it would be so simple." She had bent her head,
earnest and distressed. "But your people will want to
see you, they will think that I have come between you
and them. That would not be right."

Though he felt better already, better beyond belief;
his mind sluggish and idle maybe, but steady, at peace,
and clear; his body grotesquely thin, but washed,
shaved, and wholesome in the Colonel's borrowed linen,
it was not his feeling better that had prompted him to
leave. It had been the Colonel. Not that the Colonel
had said a word amiss. But he had managed with easy
mastery to keep James Fraser at arm's length. The
Colonel had said, "You must not leave until your
strength is recruited." But he had seen to it that the
carriage was at the door on time.

At the last she had leaned across the side of the
carriage to snatch a moment while Orlando went for
the hamper.

"You have been kind to my father, James. I reckon
it's not easy, but it's a kindness to me, too."

"It's easy to be kind to you," he had said.

"He is slow to change," she went on earnestly.
"Especially if he thinks he has been wrong. But afterward he will think how fine you are. Then he will try
to change so slowly that no one will notice." She gave
a short, light laugh, then turned sober. "Be patient

with him. Remember what the last three years have
been for him."

Before he could answer, Orlando appeared with the
hamper and beside him the Colonel, who was saying,
"Make sure the sun does not fall on that bottle of
Sherry." Orlando placed the hamper in the carriage,
climbed in after it.

"I thank you, Colonel," James said slowly, "for your
kindness. I have maybe imposed on your hospitality."

"It is a privilege, sir," the Colonel's bow was fault-
lessly correct, "to assist a defender of our Country."

"I'm not much of a defender," he muttered, awkwardly. Perhaps if he talked more naturally the Colonel
would do so too. But the Colonel's manner was unchanged.

"You undervalue your services, sir. My son—" In
the brief pause which followed, the Colonel's eyes left
his, left the grove, the fields, the river, and sought, it
seemed, to penetrate the distant blue horizon. He
glanced quickly back to James. "My son's opinion of
you was most favorable."

"He was the finest man I ever knew," said James.

"I believe, sir," the Colonel's voice was steady,
"that he was a credit to our name."

To this there was nothing to reply. The carriage
moved off, he raised his hat, he turned and looked back
at the Colonel's figure, old now and worn, but stiff and
trim, and at Stewart Prevost, white, slender, waving,
waving until the tall unpainted house was lost from
sight among the live-oaks and shadowy Spanish moss.

His home would soon be near. Here was the slope

of scattered pine and wire grass along the cypress swamp; here were the three small gravestones underneath the cedar-trees. The towering well-sweep cut the sky, he saw the weathered siding.

Orlando, looking over his shoulder, surveyed the scene with non-committal eye. "Is dis de place, Misteh?"

"Yes," James answered shortly. The old ape was trying to make out he didn't know where the Frasers lived. The carriage passed the gray, top-heavy corncrib, standing crooked on its stilts, stopped before the door. Over the porch-rail a familiar blue-checked quilt was hung out to air between two slender posts. The door was open. He could see the rose-patterned linoleum within.

Smoke came from the chimney, but no one appeared. "Well," he said, half to himself, "I reckon I'll get out." He would get fixed up inside the house and surprise his mother when she came in. Orlando dismounted, looked dubiously at James' big frame towering above him.

"Thad," he said. "Those hosses stand?"

Thad turned a dried-up, melancholy face. "Dey won't run on de rations dey gets now."

"You get down and catch hol' de other side," said Orlando. Thad gathered the skirts of his coachman's coat into a bundle, pressed it against his breast, and lowered himself carefully over the wheel.

"In de old days," he muttered, "you couldn't look up to tell de time of day without dey take 'vantage of you to juk de ca'iage right out f'om under you." He shook his coat-tails out. But now co'n mighty

sca'ce. Dey don' act so gaily. Now den," he held out
his hand toward James. James slid to the ground between them, together they started for the steps.

As they mounted carefully, slowly, a door slammed in
the house. His mother's gaunt, spare silhouette was in
the doorway. Her peaked shoulders, her head, with its
sparse knot of hair, drooped low. For an instant her
ironic and humorous face, her sharp, squirrel eyes were
turned on him without recognition. Her glance travelled swiftly over the group. "Who is this sick young
man," she was asking herself, "in a planter's carriage
and in planter's clothes, supported on either hand by a
negro servant?" Her eyes swept back to him, her face
went pale, her head and her hands came up sharply.
She strode down the steps, put her strong, crooked
hands beneath his armpits, steadied him. Her black
eyes, travelling over his face, were firm and searching.
Her wrinkled, leathery face was set except for a tiny
quiver underneath her mouth.

"Howdy, Ma," he tried to be cheerful and at ease.
"I'm home." Still she did not answer, just stood there
gripping him and searched his face. He raised his bony
hand and laid it on her shoulder.

Her mouth came open, slowly. "Let go of him, you
two negroes." She spoke with her eyes still fixed on
his. "I'll tote him myself."

Disgruntled, the servants fell away. Still holding
him with one hand, she bent down to lift him. Her
hair was gray, her spine stood out along her back. A
thrust of pity smote him. "You mustn't," he took her
arm and pulled her back. "I can walk. You go ahead.

Lay a quilt down on my pallet," he suggested. He nodded to the negroes.

She tramped up the steps ahead of them, looking back at the negroes to see that they performed their duty. She pulled the blue-checked quilt down from the line and spread it deftly on his bed. He sank down on the pallet. Thad lifted up his legs.

"I'll fetch in de hamper," said Orlando. James roused himself.

"Fetch in the wine," he said. "You and Thad can keep the rations for yourselves." He would show these niggers that folks knew how to do things right. "Ma," he said, "we've got plenty of corn, I reckon."

"Some," she answered, guardedly.

"Let Thad have two ears apiece for the horses." His mother turned to Thad.

"You can take them from the crib as you go by," she said in a tone of dismissal. Murmuring their thanks, the negroes shuffled out.

"Tell the Colonel thanks," James raised his weak voice to call after them. "And say I had a good journey."

"Yasso," they answered, with some respect. "Yasso, we will." His mother closed the bedroom door.

"Well," he said, "this is nice. Mighty nice. How are you?" She simply stood there looking at him.

"How is Pa?" She came up to the bed. "I reckon you've had some mighty hard scraping," he went on. Her old face crinkled into a twisted, tortured smile. Between her shut lids two great tears squeezed out. "Now, Ma," he said. "Why, Ma!" She was falling.

He threw up his hands. Her sharp knees thumped against the floor. Her old head fell across his breast.

"Ma!" he cried out frightened. "Are you all right?" His heart stopped beating. "Ma!"

For answer, her knotty hand stole up his arm, his shoulder, around his neck, hung there an instant, then softly, delicately, began to stroke him on the cheek.

CHAPTER XXXIX

HE lay one morning between sleep and waking, watching through drowsy eyes a thousand shining motes climb up the shaft of light which lay across his counterpane. He was roused by a voice outside.

"Heyo, folks! How you come on? They tell me James is home."

He heard his mother answer, "Hush your fuss, Dunc, he's asleep."

He heard his father's grave salutation. "Won't you come in and rest awhile?"

"Howdy, Uncle Dunc," he called out, and raised up on an elbow. Outside the window, a small ox, elaborately draped in a patched rope harness, slumbered between the shafts. In a high-wheeled cart Uncle Dunc held an umbrella over himself and over Ance, the mail orderly, whose empty sleeve was tucked in the pocket of his jacket.

Uncle Dunc caught sight of him and raised a long "Hey-o!" He waved the umbrella around his head. The ox awoke and made a brief stumbling effort to run. Uncle Dunc clutched at the rope reins, at the umbrella, at the seat.

"I'm awake," said James. "Come on in." His mother opened the door.

"You've not had breakfast, son," she said, reproachfully.

"Well, I can eat while I talk."

Uncle Dunc, Ance, and James' father, each carrying

a split-bottomed chair, filed into the room. Uncle Dunc
reached down, gave him a swift, limp shake of the hand,
blew out his mustache, stared at him quizzically.
"Dod burn my shirt-tails, James," he observed with
gusto, "if them Yankees hain't near about wore you
down."

The three men sat down. "I bet you give 'em hell,
though," Uncle Dunc continued, "befo' they cotched
you."

"I don't know," James muttered, feeling foolish.
"They gave us considerable hell, themselves."

"Sho," said Uncle Dunc, impatiently. "What makes
you talk so, James? Why one of our boys can whip ten
of them damn fellows."

At this remark, Ance, who had not yet spoken, withdrew his eyes from Uncle Dunc, scratched his stubble
chin, spat decorously out the door, and fixed on James a
look, veiled, yet intimate and charged with inexpressible, ironic mirth. James gave Ance a hard-bitten grin
and a wink to show that he too shared the vast, sardonic joke on Uncle Dunc.

"We ought to have more of them old-time Mexican
War officers," observed Mr. Fraser, dropping an em-
phatic hand on one knee. "They was trained just
naturally to go right through the enemy and bust 'em
open." James started to speak. They themselves had
had officers trained like that; and most of them were
dead; but why argue? His father would not understand.
No one understood. He lay silent, frowning at the
counterpane.

Clumping in her wood-soled, home-made shoes, his

mother came in with a bowl of soup. As a matter of etiquette he offered it to the visitors, then drank it while they talked. Uncle Dunc retailed the neighborhood news. Now that Confederate money was worthless the Sheriff was taking a third of every man's crop as a tax in kind. And old man Roon, with a bundle of paper money under his arm, was hunting up reluctant creditors and paying them. Sam Scroggs had joined a gang of bushwhackers who, under the pretense of being Union sympathizers, were harrying the neighborhood, and the Home Guards had burned his house and accidentally killed his mindless boy.

"But what I don't like about the Gov'ment," said Uncle Dunc, "is the way it lets this yer Sherman walk through South Carolina. They ought to send some of our boys down ther' to whip him."

"They ought to send you and me, Ance," said James.

Ance reddened with suppressed mirth, drew back his turkey-buzzard neck. His Adam's apple shot up in a gulp of ecstasy.

"They're closin' in some down at the mouth of the river," said Mr. Fraser. "A fisherman told me they had near about a hundred ships. Fort Fisher is the only thing that keeps them off."

"Yes, sir," Uncle Dunc cut in, "the Yankees have run a heap of them blockaders ashore of late. I don't know wher' our shoes and clothing is to come from."

"It won't make a bit of difference," said Mr. Fraser. "The blockaders don't bring in necessities any more. They bring in French hats and champagne for the rich folks."

"Well," said Uncle Dunc, pleasantly acquiescent, "I reckon they bring in what pays them best."

James' mother returned for the empty bowl. "I reckon you all better set on the porch awhile," she said, "I'm goin' to fetch him a basin to wash himself." They filed out of the room but Ance lingered.

"How you, James?" he murmured.

"Fine. Where'd you lose your arm?"

"Three months ago, in front of Richmond."

"How are all the boys?" said James.

"All right," said Ance, "what they is left."

"How's Dougald?"

"He's a Major. I reckon he's the only one left of your old gang."

"How about Tom MacGruder?"

"He was killed at Cold Harbor," said Ance, simply. "He got to be a mighty good Sergeant before he died." For a time James did not speak.

"Ance," he said at length, "it looks like we were being shot up mighty bad."

"The army's been shot up about all it can stand," said Ance, "but that ain't all," he added, "a good many soldiers are quitting 'most every day. The Racker twins ran away. I heard they caught Whitey and shot him, but I don't know."

"The Rackers never amounted to shucks," observed James.

"I know," said Ance, "but a lot of pretty good men are quitting. They's a lot of talk against the war amongst the folks at home and it's got into the army some." He sank his voice. "They say it's the rich man's war and the poor man's fight," he whispered

dubiously. "They say we all are fighting for the Planters' niggers. Of course," he added hastily, "everybody
ain't that way. The most part of the soldiers is gwine
to stick it out till the day of Judgment. But," he
added, "they talk mighty severe against the Gov'ment.
I know toward the latter end," he said slowly, "I
seemed like I didn't give a damn about the Confederacy or Jeff Davis, or anything in the whole concern.
I was fightin'," he added solemnly, "for Robert E.
Lee. Just like we used to fight fo' Old Jack while he
lasted, maybe mo' so. Yes, seh," he lifted up his small
round head, the cords on his neck stood out. "Fo'
Robert E. Lee."

"I never saw him," said James. "The boys in prison
used to talk about him."

"I saw him once." Ance wiped the corners of his
mouth with his hand and swallowed. "At Gettysburg.
We was in Pickett's Division then." We was lyin' down
behind a long woods waitin' the order to charge. I
reckon it was the most troops they ever was in one
charge."

"All of a sudden I saw him comin' along. I knew it
was him but I didn't know what to do because our
orders was not to make any noise or show ourselves,
nor not even to stand up. Then about the time he
reached our flank company I saw a man raise up on his
knees and take his hat off. The other boys did likewise
and you bet when he come to me I knelt and took my
hat off, too. And so it went all down the line. The men
just kneelin' ther' in ranks and takin' off their hats and
never any sound." He paused, at a loss.

"He wasn't a extra-big man or anything; just what

you would call a medium-sized old gentleman and
eve'ything about him mighty neat, just so. He was
polite and grave the way he took off his hat to
us."

"I don't know," he muttered, impotent and half
angry. "I don't know,—" he struggled for words.
"But when I saw him I just naturally knew that whatever he said to do, I would do it. And that it would
be the right thing to do, too, yes, seh."

"That's the only time ever I did see him," he added,
"but after that I was fightin' fo' him." His small
fierce eyes kindled. "Yes, seh, I was fightin' fo' Robert
E. Lee." He raised his flapping sleeve with a grotesque
jerk. "And by God, I'd fight fo' him now until every
bone in my whole damn carcass went wher' this has
gone."

The three of them were talking the evening through
around the kitchen stove. In the week which had
passed James Fraser had begun to stir about. He sat
now in his old brown kersey suit, the blue-checked
quilt wrapped around his knees. His mother bit the
thread of the quilting on her lap. "Well, she's none
too good for you," she said.

At his mother's words swift anger welled up in him.
He had told her that Stewart was coming. Each day
he had expected her. He must not resent the delay.
Let him show good sense. Something had detained
her. But his mother must not resent it, nor speak
slightingly of her. He did not answer.

"None too good," his mother repeated. She crinkled

up her bright black eyes and smiled at him. "But she's mighty nigh good enough, I reckon." She looked away again. "And, Lord, what a pretty thing," she murmured almost against her will.

His father, having sharpened his jack-knife on an oil-stone, was making a coat button out of a hickory-nut shell. His face as he raised it showed naïve concern at the prospect of a planter's daughter in the family.

"Ann," he said, "how do you reckon she will do about the housework? She's not used to that."

"She will manage. She will get used to it," Mrs. Fraser answered. "And the way the country's going," she added, "she'll have to get used to it if she stays at home."

"Times is hard," his father assented with gloomy relish, "I never saw them worse." He nodded at James with immense foreboding. "You'll be hard put to it to provide for her. A farmer can hardly make a living nowadays."

"I aim to go back to railroading," James answered. "I believe I can make good money there." Encouraged by a glance from his mother, he went on. "Before I left the shops at Wilmington I got a new idea for an engine." His face lit up, he leaned forward. "It would give more power."

"More power!" his father's voice was charged with alarm and heavy disapproval. "The more power those things has got the sooner they'll hop off the track and kill all the folks." He shook his head from side to side and voiced his ultimate conviction. "I never took any stock in railroads."

James grinned. "Didn't I send home three dollars a week when I was in the shops in Wilmington?"

"That may be," his father admitted grudgingly, "but I hold it's against nature for folks to go flying through the air behind a snorting machine. It looks to me," his pale blue eyes lighted up in satisfaction at the thrust he was about to deliver," that if the Lord had intended us to do so he would have given us steam somewheres inside us to do it with."

That night as he slept his dreams were shattered by the sound of distant thunder. The corn-shuck mattress rustled as he sat up with a start. Thunder in January! It could not be. He rubbed his eyes and stared out the window. Above him the sky still showed the deep and dusky gray of night, but eastward, where the thunder sounded, it melted into the faint sea-green of early dawn. And still the thunder grew and steadied to a long, unbroken roar. His feet were on the cold planks of the floor; he fumbled for his shoes. He knew now that he heard the firing of innumerable guns.

Clutching a gray gingham wrapper to her breast, his mother stood in the kitchen. "That's shooting, ain't it, son?"

"Yes," he said. "The Yankees must be trying to take Fort Fisher. I reckon I better go."

"Don't you get in that fight." Her voice was sharp. "You've done your share and you've signed your parole not to fight again."

"I'm going to Beaumont," he answered. "If the Yankees take Fisher they'll come straight up the river."

"Well," she said slowly, "there's some sense to

that." She put her hand on his arm. "You'd best carry the young lady back here to stay with us. We're off the main route."

"Yes," he answered, "that's the best plan." He broke away impatiently and hurried to the barn.

As he fumbled with the throat-latch of the bridle, his mother's voice sounded again behind him. "More haste, less speed." Still in her wrapper she reached out her hand. "Whoa, mule," she buckled the strap in one swift motion. "Here's some pone." She dropped a square of corn bread into the pocket of his old, brown coat. He led the mule out into the pallid, gray-green light and mounted. His mother gripped his ankle, looked up at him. "You carry that child back here to me," she said with passion.

"Yes, ma'am," he said, "I will," and kicked the mule.

"And don't you get in any fight," she added. The mule was trotting down the sandy track. "You hear what I say?" she shouted angrily.

CHAPTER LX

In her purple gown with the wristlets of fur, she met him at the door. For an instant she clung to him in silence. She leaned back, looked up at him and smiled. "How well you look, James, already. Already," she repeated. "But it seems years." She was sober and he saw that her eyes were tired, her face was pale. "I should have come, but I dared not leave Father. He is beginning—" she paused, "he is beginning to despair. And now, those guns."

"Honey," he said gravely, "I'll take care of you, and the Colonel, too, if he will let me."

Footsteps sounded in the hallway. In his old, blue broadcloth coat, Colonel Prevost stepped through the doorway, turned toward them, and paused. Looking at him now without hostility, James noticed in him the change begun no doubt long since but now, it seemed, progressing swiftly. He was indeed an old man. He held himself erect, but with an effort. The silver buttons on his breast rose and fell with his heavy breathing. His fine-cut face, always pale enough, had taken on a pearly hue. The lines about the mouth were deeply cut, the neck, rising from the black stock, was thin and creased; beneath the chin, the white skin sagged a little. Only the eyes retained their old proud strength and fire.

"Here is James, Father," she said. "Will you take this chair?"

"Oh, no, my dear," his gesture of refusal was swift

and perfect though the raised hand trembled slightly. "I will not deprive you."

"But I am going in to see about some breakfast for James," she said, and stepping forward took his arm and pressed it gently to her. He inclined his head and tried to smile. But the smile, meant to be tender and humorous, wavered; his eyes, meant to be bright and lively, could not quite veil in their blue depths a look, yearning and forlorn.

The instant passed. A touch on the straight blue shoulder, a swift fleeting smile, and she was gone. The Colonel sat beside him on the chair. For a time neither spoke. James Fraser felt all pride, all envy, all resentment fade away. The Colonel was no longer a powerful and haughty dignitary. However much he might maintain his lofty bearing, he was a desolate old man.

Yet not so desolate that he could forget himself and the proprieties. Looking at James with an effort, he inclined his head.

"I am glad I see you so improved in health, sir."

"I'm glad I'm enough better not to be a trouble," James replied. "I came when I heard the firing."

"Your promptness will be much appreciated by my daughter."

"I don't reckon they is anything I can do for her," James answered modestly, "or for you either, seh," he paused. "I just came."

The Colonel did not seem to hear him. "I have sent Thad across the river in a boat. Our troops from Wilmington went down the other side last night. Till he comes back we can only wait." He turned his keen blue

eyes on James and inclined his head again. "In the
meantime you have done the proper thing in coming."
There was some kindness in his glance. "I trust it has
not been too much for you."

"Too much?" James' laugh was short. "By shot,
I wish they was something too much for me that I
could do."

The Colonel nodded grave assent. "Castles and
dragons. That is what young men in love demand."
He reflected, looked about the room. "This has been
a castle for you. And the dragon—" He started to
raise a hand to his breast.

"That's over," James' words were quick but quiet.
"I hope you will never speak of it again."

"You have a right, seh," the Colonel said gravely,
"to make that request."

At one o'clock they dined off silver plates with the
picture of a wild boar in the middle, but the food was
pork chops, rice cakes, and corn bread, just like anybody else's. At the end the Colonel said to him: "The
most of my wine has gone to the Army Hospitals, but
I have saved a few bottles for special occasions. I can
offer you Sherry or Madeira."

"I thank you, seh. That wine you gave me to carry
home did me the most good in the world." James hesitated. "But I'm about well, now. I'd be pleased not
to take any to-day. It would save it for somebody else
that needs it sure enough." He looked at the Colonel
anxiously, then looked away, fearing that he had committed a breach of etiquette.

"I am more honored, sir," the Colonel's voice had

some slight ring of cordiality, "by your refusal than I should have been by your acceptance."

In the drawing-room a fire of pine logs threw faint mellow shadows on the fluted mantelpiece. Its light fell on an eagle-crested mirror, on a maplewood piano, and on the sofa, pink and satin covered, where James Fraser had sunk down the day that he got home from prison. Beside the fireplace, Colonel Prevost sat in a mahogany armchair, his small gray head somewhat bent forward and drooping as he stared at the blaze. On the other side, in a low chair, skirted with a ruffle and puffily unholstered, Stewart Prevost knitted steadily. Her hands flew back and forth below the fur wristlets of her lavender cloth gown. Her feet were tucked from sight beneath the flowing skirts. She might even, James surmised acutely, be sitting on them to warm them from the draft which swept across the floor from an east window, left open in order that they might hear. But though they seldom spoke and always listened they heard no further sound of firing, no sound except the rustle of the rose-colored satin window curtains swaying in the breeze.

The firing had ceased at noon, abruptly. It had not been renewed. James Fraser, with some satisfaction in his powers as a military expert, had figured out that Fort Fisher must have fallen to the Yankees. The firing had ceased when the troops made their attack. If the attack had failed the gunboats would have opened fire again to cover their retreat. He would have liked to explain this to the Colonel but an hour ago the Colonel had broken the silence to remark: "The at-

tack has been repelled, I have no doubt. Our Government," he continued, judicially, "knows, of cou'se, that
Wilmington is the last open port in the Confederacy
and will defend the fort accordingly." Swiftly he smote
a hand on the arm of his chair. "It must be defended.
The enemy is trying to throttle us." He stared into
the embers. "The last open port," he muttered. He
leaned back, his head sunk on his breast, his slim delicate fingers gripped the arms of his chair, relaxed,
gripped them again.

The guns they had been hearing might mean the end
of everything. James Fraser felt mighty badly. But
not as badly as he ought; not as badly as the Colonel.
Had he not been a soldier? And ought not a soldier
to feel that he would rather die than accept defeat?
And now that he was to marry Stewart, he ought to
feel the way her father did. It was the Colonel's in-
fluence with men high in the Confederate Government
that had obtained his release from prison. True, when
he had tried to mumble out his thanks, the Colonel
had said: "You owe no debt to me, sir. I will not dis-
guise my reason. I found that my daughter had given
her heart to you. That left me no alternative. In our
family, we give our hearts but once. Never again."

As if she guessed his thoughts had turned to her,
she rose, whispered to her father, left the room. James
heard her light, swift footfall overhead.

It was the Colonel who had set him free, had saved
him from death or from a broken mind. Yes, he should
be standing, in spirit, with the Southern garrison at
Fisher. But should he? Could anything further be
demanded even of his spirit? He and all of them had

fought while they were able, had fought the Yankees time and again and beaten them; their dead would make a bigger army than their living. Still the Yankees closed around them, and though many of them still fought on, and still would fight until the last, he knew that many more, reading the truth in letters of fire, were through; and he could understand. He knew that he himself was through, that he only wanted the war to end. Let preachers, old women, and politicians holler as they liked. By God, he was through! He took no stock in them any longer. He had had enough. Enough! A sight too much, and the most of the army had had more than he.

But that was not all. He felt that he had been fooled about the business, or perhaps that he had fooled himself, though that thought made him no better satisfied. At first it had seemed a fine idea to chase the Yankees in a brief campaign. Then it had turned out not to be so easy, and the longer the business went on, the more he had stopped to ponder. The Yankees were fighting to maintain the Union about which he cared nothing one way or the other. They were fighting also to free the negroes. That was a fool thing to fight for but, on the other hand, why should he fight to keep them slaves? Not one of them was his.

He heard her light tread on the stairs and listened eagerly, watched the doorway for the slender, lovely figure in the purple gown. All that wealth of gracious tenderness, of humorous fine-tempered courage, was his. She, for some unfathomable reason, by some preposterous and incredible twist of fortune, was destined to stand beside him, to believe in him. What he wanted was an end of the war, so that he could make her happy, and, to be fair, make himself happy, too.

She stood before him holding an oval, silver frame against her breast.

"This," she said, "was my mother." She turned the frame.

He was on his feet. He saw a slender lady, dark-eyed and wistful, chapleted with roses.

"I would like," his voice was low, "to hold it."

Around the bottom of the frame an engraved inscription ran: "1823—Carey Stewart Prevost—1853." And at the top between two maltese crosses the words: "In Deo Pax." He looked at the face again. Gazing at that long-vanished loveliness, so fragile yet so vivid, so mute yet so speaking, he felt himself bereft.

"That is surely a beautiful lady," he murmured sadly.

"Yes, she was beautiful." She took the softly colored miniature to carry it away. "I will put it back beside my father's bed."

The Colonel raised his head.

"You may leave it here, my dear. James—" he had never used the name before—"may wish to look at it again." His voice held faint and tragic echoes of his desolation.

James Fraser turned and made a small, shy bow. "Thank you, seh. I would have liked to ask that favor."

In the hallway, a tall clock began its premonitory whirr with a violence out of all proportion to the flat, tinkling sound which followed; it struck four. In his old green coat Orlando came through the doorway, stopped, placed a hand over his twitching mouth, and bowed.

"Colonel," he said in a low, sad voice, "Thad come

back." The Colonel started forward. Immediately he relaxed the grip of his hands on the chair and leaning back crossed them quietly on his knee.

"Show him in, Orlando," he said.

Thad came to a halt just inside the door, and bowing to each of them in turn stood nervously plucking at a big bone button on his coachman's overcoat. With his other hand he clasped his beaver to his narrow chest. His sorrowful, uneasy, bloodshot eyes looked just beyond the Colonel into space.

"Well, Thad," said the Colonel, "have you news?"

"That I has, Colonel." Thad's high voice was portentous and suffocated. "Too much news!" He paused for his effect. "De Yankees comin'."

"What makes you say that, Thad?" The Colonel's voice was sharp.

Thad fixed his eyes on the bright, brass handle of the fire-tongs and composed himself for speech. "When I git to de other side of de river, I set down by de road. Long about two 'clock, hyer come a young nigger gal with a pullet on a string. I holler out, 'Sis, wher' you gwine?' And de gal and pullet dey fetch two squawks and flewed off th'ough de woods. I reckon," Thad observed reflectively, "de big shootin' dis mo'nin' make dat wench uneasy in her mind."

"Well, 'en," he resumed, "about a hour ago I hyear a tromp, trompin' in de sand. I knew it was folks a-marchin' and I git out in de bushes because maybe it was de Yankees. Down by de water," he went on, indignantly, "I hear dem two black boys jump in my boat and put off in de stream. Yes, suh," he repeated, "dey put off an' left me alone wid de whole Yankee Army."

"Only," he added, after his effect had been achieved, "dey weren't de Yankees, dey was our own soldiers comin' back. Dey look mighty nigh played out, and when I come out de bushes dey holler, 'Shake your brogans, nigger, de Yankees gwine to catch you and boil you in tar.' I ax 'em what de news, but dey just cuss me and 'en dey comes a officer on a ho'se and when I tell him dat I'se de Colonel's carriage driver he stop and write out dis paper." Thad produced a crumpled slip from the pocket of his overcoat and advanced toward the Colonel.

The Colonel read the note. Not a muscle moved. With a slight bow, he handed it to Stewart. He motioned James to read it. James stood behind her chair and glanced at the hasty scrawl:

DEAR COLONEL:
I can't give military information but I suggest you prepare to leave Beaumont at once.   BURGWYN.

The fort has fallen, thought James. He should feel the shock. But standing behind her chair he was conscious only of the long, slim curve of her neck, of her slim yet softly rounded shoulder. The Yankees were coming, he would have to take care of her now.

The Colonel was speaking quietly.

"You have done very well, Thad. Tell Orlando to give you some tea and rations in the kitchen and wait there."

In the dark and windy grove of live-oaks, James and the two old negroes worked. They lugged out heavy canvas sacks of plate and buried them deep among the gnarled roots. They did not dare to show a light for fear the other negroes would discover them. Already at the Quarters they had learned the news. James Fraser saw their blazing bonfires and heard, borne on the fitful wind, snatches of their unending song:

> "When de Lincoln gunboats come,
> We shall be free!
>
> . . . .
>
> Lord Jesus, he done hear us pray,
> We shall be free!
>
> . . . .
>
> We shall be free!
>
> . . . . . .
>
> We shall be free,
> We shall be free!"

At the door the carriage loomed dimly in the light of its own lamps. Old Thad, shrivelled and bowed with labor and calamity, held, with one hand, James Fraser's mule, and with the other, the carriage horses, who laid back their ears and snorted at the companionship. The carriage itself was piled high with trunks; on top of which, inappropriately jaunty, sat a flowered hat-box of Stewart Prevost's. Wrapped in a dark green, hooded cape, she climbed into the small space left for her on the seat behind. She turned and seized the Colonel's hand.

"You will follow right away. Your riding horse is saddled and there is a mule and sulky for Orlando."

Looking more than ever old and fragile in the feeble light, the Colonel straightened up and gave her his gallant smile.

"I must first," he said, "arrange protection for our people." He turned to James, abruptly, reached in the pocket of his blue, broadcloth coat and drew out a long, slim duelling pistol. With a bow he presented the butt.

"At such a time," he said, "it may be well to carry this. It has never been in the hands of any one outside my family. I hope," he added gravely, "that you will regard my parting with it, not merely as an act of necessity but as evidence, perhaps belated, of my personal esteem."

James Fraser balanced the beautiful weapon in his hand and looked at it. "Colonel," he said, "I may not add anything to this pistol's reputation, but I won't take anything away."

He mounted the mule. The carriage started. Standing erect and slim before the lighted windows, the Colonel raised his black felt hat.

"Stop, Thad!" Stewart cried. "Turn back! Father!" she called out, desperately, "I will not go without you."

He took a firm step forward and raised his hand.

"My dear, you will obey me." His face relaxed. He smiled again. "It is the one thing left which you can do. Thad!" His voice was kind but strong as iron. "Go on!"

CHAPTER LXI

JAMES sat beside Stewart Prevost on the narrow porch, listening for the sound of the Colonel's horse. He should have come by now.

A lantern at the barn showed where his father helped Thad with the carriage horses. Inside, his mother tramped about, fixing a bed up for the Colonel.

"He should be here," Stewart said.

"If he don't come I'll go and fetch him."

"I hate to have you, James. You're not strong, and you never spare yourself."

"I can take care of myself."

"You! Look what you did when you came to Beaumont." She voiced reproach. "That was a crazy thing to do, James, to walk up all those steps."

He did not answer, but he was not abashed. By shot! he reflected with some pride, it was a pretty good piece for him to have travelled considering how he had felt and how many steps there were and how the nigger's coat kept slipping.

Her voice, gently insistent, came to him.

"Why didn't you stop or send for help?"

"I'd waited a long time to climb those steps." He looked at her. "I was through with waiting."

She reached out to him, laid a firm, slim hand on his. "You were foolish."

She was speaking again. "If only I had gone to meet the boat!"

"It would have been nice," he agreed, absently, then paused. "In a way though," he went on, "I'm glad things turned out as they did. It was the way I always used to think they would. I used to think about it all the time up there." He nodded to the North. "I would see the wharf and the rice fields and the house up above, and then I would be walking along the causeway and up the steps and into the house." "I used to think about you, James." Her voice was low. "Whether you would come. I knew you would. Because often I could see you coming." He closed his hand on hers. "I always tried to see you that way when I could," she paused, "because then I would forget other ways I used to see you." Her voice turned sad, sank lower, "walking away, so angry, on the hill; running away through the grove that night——"

"Be quiet," he said gently, then added, "I didn't know you thought of me."

"Yes, from the first. From the time you drove up with the load of rails to Beaumont."

"Did you, sure enough?" he murmured incredulous, then turned sombre. "Why did we have so many troubles then, I wonder?"

"I was proud," she answered. "And so were you."

He nodded soberly. "I was humble at the end, though. I only wanted to climb up those steps. I could see them, and 'way above, at the top of them, the myrtles and the house. And I would climb them and go in." Again he closed his hand on hers. "Then you would come through the doorway." For a moment he was still. "I'm glad it happened so."

She put her other hand on his and looked down at it, shaking her head slowly.

"Those steps were too much for you, James; you were so weak." He seized her wrist strongly.

"They were not too much!" he said in a loud voice. He relaxed his grip. "Do you know," he whispered, "what I kept thinking when I climbed those stairs? I was saying, 'You stood beside her once and went away from her. Now you must climb back.'"

Again she shook her head, this time most earnestly. She looked at him most earnestly. "I want you to do one thing. Never speak again of our old troubles. When you blame yourself you remind me of what I should be blamed for, too. Let us be happy." She bent down, brushed his great, gaunt knuckles with her lips. "I am very happy," she said in a quiet voice.

He raised a hand and touched her shining hair. "I will do as you say," he muttered. His voice was laboring against the pounding of his heart. "I'll try to do the best I can for you in everything."

Her hand, firm and quiet, warm and strong, rested in his. Yet in the touch, for all its power, was some suggestion of dependence, of realization that all was now risked with him. He felt within him the stirring of warmth, of reassurance, which welled up slowly and flowed out to meet her need. He wondered if she felt it too. Perhaps she did, for now her face, turned once again on him, seemed shadowed by a thought which troubled her.

"What is it?" he said. For a time she did not answer

and he did not speak again, merely sat there, her hand in his, and waited.

"Be friendly—" she said at last, then hesitated. "Be friendly with my father, James, if you can. He is worn out," she went on, "with grieving over Charles and now over the terrible battles which seem to have no ending. If only we could win right soon," she murmured, "it would mean so much to him." She turned. "Do you think we'll win, James?"

Win? He almost burst out in a mirthless laugh. Could she not read the signs?

"I don't know," he answered uncomfortably. "We couldn't find out much in prison." He hoped she would not press him further. She did not, nor did she speak again of the Colonel. He made a wondering note of that. All women he had known before were great ones for sticking to a point until they got a promise.

"I will try to please him," he said.

"Then, you *will* please him." She rose. "You should lie down and rest. I'll call you if—" she stopped. She motioned to the door of his lean-to room. "You go to bed. I will help your mother."

He took her hands. "It don't seem natural to have you here in this house of ours. I used to make pictures of myself going to Beaumont. But I never figured about you coming here."

She gave his hands a little shake. "Now you'll have to think about my being where you are."

Almost immediately it seemed that a candle was shining in his eyes. She stood beside him in a white, ruffled dressing-gown, her hair about her shoulders, her eyes dark-ringed with sleeplessness. "It's morning," she whispered, "and he has not come."

"All right," he said, "I'll go. Ask my mother to get me something to carry along to eat."

"I've got it," she answered with a touch of pride and held out a bulging napkin.

.   .   .   .

The sun was well up in the mackerel-clouded sky when he rode his mule through the gates at Beaumont. At first sight all seemed peaceful. But the lodge-keeper was gone, the rail fences were gone, too. Then in the stubble fields on either hand, evenly spaced, lay the charred logs of abandoned fires. Troops had camped there the night before.

The quarters were deserted. Not even a lanky hog or draggle-feathered chicken moved among the trash piles by the doors. The Yankees had been there sure enough. He kicked the mule.

The tall house of Beaumont seemed abandoned. No smoke came from the broad brick chimneys; no songs or ring of pots from the low log kitchen at the rear. And though every door and window stood open wide, James had a swift, infallible sense that no life stirred within. It was as if death had overtaken the house itself and transfixed it in its attitude of open-handed hospitality.

In haste he tied the mule to the horse-block. He walked to the double gallery at the front. There he stopped. His hand flew to the pistol in his pocket.

A figure in Yankee blue hung suspended from the

upper railing of the gallery. Incredulous, he stared. It must be an effigy, some unfathomable and ghastly prank. The figure still was turning slowly below the rope around its neck. Slowly its face, a human face, the stupid eyes protruding, the mouth half open like a fish's in stupefied surprise, swung into view, swung away again.

With his pistol in his hand, he ran beneath its dangling feet. A swift glimpse of wreckage smote him as he passed along the porch, down the dark hall— a litter of myrtle branches—smashed lamps and chairs —a cut-glass chandelier pulled down—the dark, stern portrait slashed from side to side. He sprang up the stairs over splintered spindles, broken dishes, ladies' gowns. He turned the glass knob of the Colonel's slatted door. The door flew open, banged lightly against the wall, swung slowly to and fro.

Inside the high, white chamber all was peace and order. Three walnut chairs stood neatly against the wall; a tall, steel-mounted mirror hung above the dressing-table's glittering array. In the mirror James Fraser saw reflected a great, four-posted, walnut bed and on it, in the blue, broadcloth coat and light-gray trousers, the figure of Colonel Prevost.

Steadying himself, with a hand against the wall, he stepped into the room. The Colonel lay on his back, his steel-blue eyes wide open, his face, a fine-cut mask of ivory, raised to the lace-fringed canopy above.

"Colonel!" James whispered. The name stuck in his throat. He saw the blue hole below the fine-spun, silver hair along the temple. A black mist dropped before his eyes. He stumbled forward and gripped the bedpost with his hands.

His vision cleared. He nerved himself to look again. All was in order. The Colonel's coat was brushed; the silver buttons shone; the light-gray cashmere trousers strapped tightly beneath the pumps were pressed as for a ceremonial. The very pumps themselves, lying so pitiful and helpless, were varnished to perfection. On the marble-topped stand beside the bed, in its frame of silver stood the miniature of the lady, dark-eyed and chapleted with roses.

All was indeed perfection, neatness, elegance, except for the great pool on the floor. At the sight of that pool, James Fraser's hackles rose. His lips drew back; his eyes turned dry and hot; he thought of the wreckage down below, he felt in his hand the weight of the duelling pistol.

Outside on the sand he heard a dragging step. Low, inarticulate sounds of grief drew nearer. He stepped to the window. A negro's face, yellow-green in the thin winter sunlight, a negro's eyes, furtive and despairing, looked up at him. It was Orlando. Shorn of pride, of dignity and glory, wrapped grotesquely in a tattered counterpane, he hobbled forward on feet bound with rags.

James turned, closed the door softly behind him and hurried down the stairs.

"Orlando," his voice was tight and small, "what happened?"

Orlando raised deep-set, tragic eyes which seemed for the first time to recognize him. He hugged the counterpane around his wrinkled, quivering throat.

"Misteh James! Misteh James!" he cried out brokenly.

"What happened?"

"I lay in de bushes wher' dey lef' me; with my feet all burnt. I hyear dem go up to de big house. Den in de house I hyear 'smash . . . bang . . . smash!' I creep up an' look in th'oo de window. In de drawin' room a Yankee act like a crazy man; drink f'um a bottle; th'ow de bottle at de mirror. An' all downstairs I hyear 'smash . . . bang!'"

Orlando wiped his eyes on the corner of the counterpane.

"An' den de Yankee dat I can see cock a gre't big pistol an' point it. He point it right at de picture of Miss Carey in de silver frame. An' in dat minute de Colonel step th'oo de do'." Orlando's head came up, his eye caught fire. "I never see him look so proud and high. He reach fo' de picture in front dat pistol des like it had been Miss Carey herse'f. An' den de pistol go off 'bang!' an' de Colonel he stan' dere in de smoke an' hug dat picture to hisself. An' den he crumple down."

Orlando clapped a hand to his mouth; tears fell.

James gripped the butt of the pistol. "Go on." Orlando swallowed.

"Right den a Yankee officer come up on a ho'se when he hyear de shot. He see de man wid de pistol an' he don't waste no time." The old man cast one swift, oblique glance at the blue figure swinging from the railing.

"What else?"

"Das all, Misteh James. When de Yankees leave I carry de Colonel up to his bed." He clutched his mouth and shivered. "An' I set de picture back wher' it belong. Ev'ything des so." He sought James' face for approval. James nodded. "But I don't go back no mo'."

"No mo'!" he echoed. "No mo'!"

At the tragic cry James Fraser's thoughts turned to the negro.

"You look mighty bad."

"Befo' dey come to de big house," said Orlando sadly, "dey taken all my clothes away, an' dey put fire to my feet to make me tell wher' de plate is hid." He looked at James with quiet dignity. "But I don' tell."

"Which way did they go?"

"Up de road to Wilmington. Thousands an' thousands."

James' foot was in the stirrup.

"Misteh James!" Orlando said, "don't you fight dem Yankees. Dey's thousands." He shook his head entreatingly. "Too many troubles now." Without an answer James rode down the lane between the live-oaks.

As the mule, now tired and reluctant, stumbled along the road to Wilmington, James Fraser figured what he ought to do. His heart cried out to find the Yankees, take a shot at them, and trust the rest to chance. He might not find the men who had wrecked the Colonel's house, but no matter, any Yankee would do. He paused. Could he ride in and shoot any Yankee—it might be the one who had helped to hang the Colonel's murderer? Then he thought of the wreckage, of the tortured negro, of the neat, still figure on the walnut

bed. To hell with rights and wrongs, he had started
and would not turn back!

At a turn in the road, an old, white-bearded negro
sat on a stump and anxiously watched his coming. He
rose and pulled off his old, straw hat.

"Boss," he whispered cautiously, "is you got a pistol?"

James stopped the mule. "Why?" The negro
shielded his mouth with his hand.

"Dey's three Yankees down in de swamp, yonder. I
hyeard 'em talkin'!"

James pulled the pistol from his pocket. Camp fol-
lowers and deserters, without a doubt. Here was a
chance for an accounting.

"Show me the way," he said, "and don't you cut
any shines." He tapped the barrel.

The negro hobbled before him through the pines.
At the edge of a cypress swamp he stopped and pointed
to a thicket-covered island. Tying the mule, James
stepped cautiously from cypress root to tussock across
the stream. Now he could hear their voices. He parted
a mat of wild grape-vine and peered.

Three pallid, gaunt-eyed figures were crouched in the
grass. Their matted hair hung down to their yellow
cheek-bones; their naked arms were caked with slime.
They had no weapons, no shoes, no hats, no clothing
save a bunch of flapping rags.

With a stride, James stepped on the island. They
scuttled feebly into the bushes, crouched, and stared at
him. In the damp, still air of the swamp he caught
the sweetish, sickening taint of gangrene.

"Who are you men?" he demanded, holding his pistol ready. One rose up, lifted his claws unsteadily above his head. But he did not speak.

"Are you Yankees?" said James. The man shook his head. But at the question a yellow-haired man, who was still squatting, raised a cracked voice in song:

> "The Union forever!
> Hurrah, boys, hur——"

His companion clapped a hand across his mouth.

"I reckoned that was it," James said. "What prison are you from?" The man who stood up looked at him with the eyes of a cornered rat.

"What do you calculate to do with us?" he countered. James paused. These men were prisoners, sure enough. Their faces bore the deathly prison gray. Their eyes held dark reflections of the tomb.

His mind filled with memories, filled with pity, undesired and hateful. These men had lived with rats and filth and the stench of bodies, starved and stale and wasting. Their hopes had beat in vain and endlessly against the gates that opened only in. They had felt their minds like run-down tops wobble ever further and further from the pole, their spirits, struggling ever more feebly, sink ever deeper in the slime. Try as he might he could only feel toward them the profound, secretive, and mysterious fellowship of misery and dread. These were his companions in slow-creeping bestiality and degradation. Between them and himself lay bonds stronger than friendship, stronger than comradeship in arms, strong as the death itself which forged them. Pity and shame and terror tugged at him. He put the pistol in his pocket. These were his brothers of despair.

"I spent two years in a Yankee prison," his voice was grave.

The standing man lowered his hands.

"We're looking for the Union lines," he said, in a toneless voice.

"I'll put you on the road," James said. He remembered the corn bread in his pocket and held it out to the man who stood. The man snatched it, paused, weakly took James Fraser's hand in his.

"Colby's my name," he said, "Eighth Ioway. You won't remember that, I guess." His eyes, deep-set and luminous, fixed on James. "But, stranger, I'll remember you."

"I've done nothing," James muttered. "You'd have found the Yankees anyway."

He watched the ghastly scarecrows gulp the bread with crunchings and low whining sounds. He wanted to fall down on his face and cry, cry till the load of wretchedness and horror which weighed him down was somehow washed away. Instead, he stiffened his lips and turned aside.

Beyond the darkness of the swamp, the sunlight slanted through the green of pines; tawny and ruddy, the feathered broom-straw glowed. The mule, his patient muzzle against a trunk, was waiting for him. He would go back to Stewart Prevost.